JENS LAPIDUS

STOCKHOLM DELETE

Jens Lapidus is a criminal defense lawyer who represents some of Sweden's most notorious underworld criminals. He is the author of the Stockholm Noir trilogy, three of the bestselling Swedish novels of this past decade: *Easy Money*, *Never Fuck Up*, and *Life Deluxe*. He lives in Stockholm with his wife.

STOCKHOLM DELETE

STOCKHOLM DELETE

JENS LAPIDUS

Translated from the Swedish by Alice Menzies

Vintage Crime/Black Lizard
VINTAGE BOOKS
A Division of Penguin Random House LLC | New York

A VINTAGE CRIME/BLACK LIZARD ORIGINAL, APRIL 2017

Library of Congress Cataloging-in-Publication Data
Names: Lapidus, Jens, 1974– | Menzies, Alice, translator.
Title: Stockholm delete / by Jens Lapidus ; translated from the Swedish
by Alice Menzies.
Other titles: STHLM delete. English
Description: First American edition. | New York : Vintage Crime/
Black Lizard, 2017.
Identifiers: LCCN 2016031546 (print) | LCCN 2016040887 (ebook) |
ISBN 9780525431718 (paperback) | ISBN 9780525431725 (ebook)
Subjects: LCSH: Women lawyers—Sweden—Fiction. |
Murder—Investigation—Sweden—Fiction. | Psychological fiction. |
GSAFD: Suspense fiction. | Mystery fiction.
Classification: LCC PT9877.22.A65 S7413 2017 (print) |
LCC PT9877.22.A65 (ebook) | DDC 839.73/8—dc23
LC record available at https://lccn.loc.gov/2016031546

Vintage Books Trade Paperback ISBN: 978-0-525-43171-8
eBook ISBN: 978-0-525-43172-5

Book design by Joy O'Meara

www.blacklizardcrime.com

Printed in the United States of America
10 9 8 7 6 5 4 3 2 1

STOCKHOLM DELETE

Värmdö

Tony Catalhöyük didn't love his job. His real dream was to be a policeman. But he'd failed to get into the training course twice. He had perfect vision and hearing, and he'd passed the physical tests with ease. He didn't have any of the inadmissible health problems, either, and his grades were good enough.

It was the psychological tests where it had all gone wrong. They'd said that he didn't see himself as a part of the wider group. That he tested as a lone wolf. When he called the recruitment people, they just parroted more of the same story. They repeated the same words as the report, over and over again.

The sky had started to lighten, but the forest around him was still dark. He was driving quite a bit above the speed limit, but his bosses normally encouraged that, at least during night shifts. Not that they would ever officially admit it. "We can't just take our time out there," they said. "We should either be at the monitoring center or with our customers, where we can put ourselves to some use. People appreciate us getting to them quickly, even if we are just caretakers in uniform."

Tony hated that: caretakers in uniform. He was no caretaker. He was there to fight the bad guys, just like the police officer he planned on becoming someday.

The alarm had come in about fifteen minutes earlier, from a

house in the woods on Värmdö island, to the east of Stockholm. It was a power outage, though the electricity had come on again after a few minutes.

Without slowing down, he turned onto a smaller road to the right. He hadn't been along this road before, but the risk of meeting another car was virtually zero. There were hardly any houses around.

He was only about a quarter mile from the house when he spotted something behind a big bush on the verge up ahead. It looked like a car in the ditch on the right. Maybe he should stop to see if something had happened? No, the alarm had to be checked within twenty-five minutes. That's what their customer guarantee said, anyway.

The gravel in the courtyard crunched as he pulled up.

There was a garage beyond the house, but he couldn't see any cars in it.

It was quiet. The alarm was no longer sounding. Tony assumed the owner must've turned it off. That wasn't so unusual, either. It was the middle of the night, and their customers usually just went back to sleep after turning off a false alarm.

But it was too quiet here somehow, too still. Like everything was holding its breath. He took out his cell phone and tried calling the customer again. No one answered.

The front door was painted yellow, with a little window set into it. The place looked dark inside. Tony held down the bell, heard it ring faintly.

No one came to the door, so he rang the bell again. This time, he pressed it down for even longer.

He knew what to do in this kind of situation. SP: standard procedure. Visual inspection of the exterior, check the area. Make notes. Report back to HQ.

Any discarded tools in the damp grass, broken electricity enclosures. Forced doors, muddy footprints on the porch, broken windows.

That was the kind of thing he was meant to look out for.

Then his eyes fell on one of the typical causes of false alarms—

an open window on the ground floor. Normally, it was down to nothing more than the customer forgetting to close it. In this instance, though, the alarm had gone off because of a power outage, not because someone had opened a window.

Tony went over to it. The grass was long and made his combat boots damp. The room inside was dark.

When he stood on his tiptoes to look in, he realized that a circular hole had been cut into both panes of glass. It was a classic, albeit advanced, burglary technique, and one that he'd seen only twice before.

This was no false alarm. Someone had tried to cut the power. His pulse picked up.

He took a few steps away from the house, called the monitoring center again, and told them what he'd found—that it was definitely a break-in.

"Ongoing or finished?"

"I don't know. There could still be someone inside, cleaning up."

Tony shoved his phone back into its holder and walked around the edge of the house, toward the front door.

He made up his mind that if anything shady was still going on, he'd put a stop to it.

He looked at the front door again. This time, he tried the handle and realized it was unlocked.

He stepped into the house.

The coats and jackets hanging on hooks in the narrow hallway fluttered as he opened the door. The place smelled of old wood and open fires.

He felt for his flashlight.

To the right, a staircase led upstairs. Straight ahead, he could see the kitchen.

Tony took out his collapsible baton and grasped it in his hand. Black hardened steel, the longest model—twenty-six inches. In training, they often used them to practice attack and defense. He'd never needed to use it in service. There was a first time for everything, he thought.

He took a step forward. Heard the crunch of broken glass. He bent down with the flashlight. The hallway floor was covered in tiny shards of glass.

The kitchen seemed clean and tidy. He saw the wide-open window again, this time from the eating area. A big, round clock hung on the wall. It showed quarter past four in the morning.

The room was open plan, the living room on his right.

There really wasn't much furniture.

An armchair. A coffee table.

Something on the floor behind the coffee table.

He moved closer.

It was a body.

He felt the nausea rise up in him like a jolt through his body.

The head. There was no face left; someone had blown their head to pieces.

Tony's vomit hit the rug.

He looked down at the floor.

Blood everywhere.

He was shouting and crying into the phone.

"Calm down. I can't hear what you're saying."

"It's a fucking murder, a bloodbath. I'm telling you, he wasn't breathing. Send the police, an ambulance, this is the most messed-up thing I've ever seen."

"Is anyone else there?"

Tony looked around. He hadn't even thought of that.

"I can't see anyone. Should I search the house?"

"That's up to you. Did you see anything strange outside?"

"No, not really."

"Did you see anything strange on the way to the house?"

He ran out onto the porch again. He'd almost forgotten.

"What're you doing, Tony? What's going on?"

Back along the road he'd driven in on.

"Fuck, there was a car in the ditch. I saw it when I drove past."

He started to run.

"I'm calling the police, but keep your phone on you. Follow standard procedure."

He felt better now, out in the fresh air. He tried to forget what he'd just seen; the real police could take care of that. Right now, he was just glad he wasn't one of them.

A caretaker in uniform.

In the faint light of morning, the dark blue car almost seemed to be burrowing its way into the earth next to the bush. When he pushed the foliage to one side, he saw that the front half was completely crumpled. The car must have gone at least fifty feet into the ditch.

Tony saw the torn earth in its tracks. In the background, the spruce trees were still dark. The bushes had hidden how smashed-up the car was when he drove past earlier.

He moved forward. The baton was back in his hand.

It looked like there was smoke rising from under the hood, or maybe it was just dust swirling in the glare of the headlights.

The mud squelched beneath his feet, and he had to hold on to the thin grass to keep his balance.

It was a Volvo, a V60.

He tried to see whether there was anyone inside, but it was hard to make out.

He clambered alongside the car and peered in from one side.

Then he saw. There was someone slumped forward in the driver's seat.

"Hello?"

The person didn't move.

The windshield had been forced inward, and the thousands of cracks in the glass reminded him of ice. It hadn't shattered.

Tony bent down and opened the driver's door. The air bag had discharged.

The driver seemed to be a youngish man, probably in his twenties, blond hair.

The limp air bag looked like a white plastic bag spread over the wheel.

Unconscious, maybe dead.

Tony prodded the man's arm with the tip of his baton.

No reaction.

PART I

MAY

1

Eat shit.

Nikola had been forced to take shit for so long now.

One whole year he'd been here.

But it was almost over. Tomorrow: the last day. Thank God. He was almost ready to start going to church with Grandpa Bojan.

He was nineteen. Sweden was messed up like that—they could lock you up somewhere like this even though you weren't a minor. Though that was his *majka's* fault. Linda, his *always-fucking-nagging* mom. She'd threatened to throw him out, cut all ties with him. And worse: she'd used Teddy as a threat. Honestly, that was what got to Nikola—the risk that Teddy would be disappointed. He loved him more than the freshest snus in the shop, more than all the ganja in the world, sometimes even more than the crew. The guys he'd grown up with, his brothers.

Teddy: his uncle.

Teddy: his idol. An icon. A role model. He only knew one person you could even compare him with. Isak.

That hadn't been enough, though. The amount of community service, all that crap, it got too high. The fines too big. The whining from social services too loud. Linda had wanted him to go into custody. She *wanted* her own son to be put into a drug-free, fun-free, completely pussy-free care home.

So that's where he'd been the past year. Spillersboda Young Offenders' Institute.

Care shall be decreed if, through the abuse of addictive substances, criminal activity, or any other socially destructive behavior, the individual subjects his/her health or development to a significant risk of damage.

Fuck the place: he'd heard that paragraph fourteen million times by now.

It was still worthless.

Every other minute, the same thought going through his head. Like a broken record by some tired old house DJ. The chorus on rewind: fucking Mom, fucking Mom, fucking Mom.

"I've tried to do everything for you, Nikola." That was what she usually said when he went home on release. "Maybe things would've been different if your dad had been around."

"But I've had Teddy."

Linda would shake her head. "You think? Your uncle's been inside eight of the past nine years. Is that what you call being around?"

Nikola was sitting at the back of the classroom. Like usual. Eating s-h-i-t. They really were trying to keep him down.

Every now and then, a few new words would appear in the chorus: fucking Sandra, fucking Sandra, fucking cunting Sandra. . . .

She was his so-called course support officer here. She talked about job applications. *You need to be able to present yourself well, write a personal statement, know how to kiss ass.* Nikola had trouble working out the point of all her talk: he'd chosen a vocational program just so he didn't have to sit around talking crap endlessly. And besides, he had no plans for a regular nine-to-five life, or even cash-in-hand manual work somewhere. There were much quicker ways to make some dough. He knew that from experience. The stuff they did for Yusuf paid off straight away.

Mini conversation group. Just Nikola and five other guys, once every week. The rest of the time, they expected him to turn up at the work experience place they'd organized in Åkersberga: George Samuel Electrical. There was nothing wrong with George, but Nikola just couldn't be bothered.

According to the head of Spillersboda, and according to his mom, it was good for him to have group hours on top of the work experience. "It increases your ability to concentrate. You might not pass Swedish, but it's still good to be able to read properly." They went on and on worse than the drunks on the park benches in Ronna. 'Course he could read. His grandpa was the biggest book lover ever, for God's sake: the reading genius from Belgrade. He'd been teaching Nikola literary magic since he was six, sat by his bed and plowed through the good old stuff. *Treasure Island, Twenty Thousand Leagues Under the Sea, The Mysterious Island.*

Nikola wanted to fly under the radar, float like oil on water. He wanted to be a shadow, live life the way he wanted. Not be caged up in a classroom. Not controlled by any stupid abbreviations or acronyms.

Anyway: it was almost time. His twelve months in the ass end of boredom would soon be over.

Life would have some meaning again.

Life would be *Life* again. Things had already started to happen. They knew he was on the way out. Yusuf had been in touch to ask if Nikola would give them a hand with a thing in a couple of days.

Some kind of guard duty. Not just any old small job: this was a negotiation. Their own law court. A trial between two warring clans in Södertälje.

And Isak would be the judge. He'd decide the matter—a replacement for the system that had decided to lock up Nicko here.

Man, Isak. It was a step up.

But Nikola hadn't said yes yet.

Stockholm County Police Authority

Interview with Mats Emanuelsson, 10 December 2010

Interview leader: Joakim Sundén

Location: Kronoberg Remand Prison

Time: 14:05–14:11

INTERVIEW

Transcript of interview dialogue

JS: Just so you know, I'm going to be recording everything we say here today.

M: Okay.

JS: We're in the interview room, Kronoberg Remand Prison, and it's the tenth of December, 2010. With me here, I have the suspect, Mats Emanuelsson, forty-four years of age. Correct?

M: Yes.

JS: And you agree for this interview to go ahead without a lawyer?

M: Uh, what does that mean?

JS: It's not unusual. You'll be out of here much quicker if we forget about contacting the courts; they have to get in touch with a lawyer, who then needs to have the time to come over. Look, I'll put it like this: if you want a lawyer, I can't promise we'll manage this interview today or tomorrow. And that means you'll go back to your cell to wait.

M: But . . . I panic when I'm locked up. I got kidnapped once, did you know that?

JS: No, I didn't. What happened?

M: They abducted me, nailed me into a box. It was about five years ago now. I can't cope with stuff like this. . . . I've seen a psychologist about the claustrophobia. I need to get out of here as quickly as possible.

JS: Well, okay, then I suggest we get started without a lawyer, and if you feel like you want to stop, just let me know.

M: Yeah, let's do that, then. I need to get out of here.

JS: In that case, I'd like to start by talking about why you were arrested. You're suspected of aiding in a drug offense in Gamla stan the day before yesterday. It's suspected that, in agreement and partnership with Sebastian Petrovic, or Sebbe as he seems to be known, you helped in the handover of an unknown quantity of narcotics. Do you understand?

M: A drug offense?

JS: Yes, that's the claim.

M: Are you sure?

JS: Completely sure. Shouldn't I be?

M: Is there anything else?

JS: I can't go into that right now. But I'd like to know your thoughts on this.

M: I've got nothing to do with that.

JS: So you deny any crime?

M: Yes, of course.

JS: In that case, there are a few more questions I'd like to ask.

M: Okay.

JS: What exactly were you doing in Gamla stan?

M: Nothing much, I was just there.

JS: Do you know Sebastian Petrovic?

M: No comment.

JS: Do you know who he is?

M: No comment. Is he being held?

JS: You don't want to say whether you know him, but you want to know if he's being held?

M: Yes.

JS: Well, since it would be public knowledge if he was being remanded in custody, I can tell you that he's not being held. He's a free man. I'd like to ask you a few more questions.

M: Right.

JS: Does the Range Rover, registration number MGF 445, belong to you?

M: No comment.

JS: Do you know who Sebbe was meeting in Gamla stan?

M: No comment.

JS: Do you know what he was doing there?

M: No comment.

JS: You have no comment about anything?

M: No, I really don't. I told you already, it's got nothing to do with me. I don't know why I'm here. I just need to get out. My head's going to burst in here. . . .

JS: You were involved in the incident the day before yesterday.

M: I don't know anything. That's not my world, drugs . . .

JS: No, I see that. I'm surprised, if I'm completely honest. Okay, we might have to do things another way. Wait here, I'll switch off the tape recorder, and we can take a little break.

Interview terminated, 14:11.

MEMORANDUM 1
Transcript of dialogue

JS: The tape recorder's off, so this isn't a formal interview anymore. Think of it as a conversation. Just between me and you.

M: What does that mean?

JS: It means we can be freer in what we say. I won't report any of this to anyone, not if you don't want me to. And I'll be straight with you, Mats, I've done a bit of research on you. You've got two kids, you had an ordinary job, and it's true: you were kidnapped a few years ago. That must've been awful. You shouldn't be locked up somewhere like this.

M: Can't you just let me go, then? I've been here almost two days. I'm still traumatized from before. I've been through too much crap. Please, I'm begging you. I feel really bad in here.

JS: The thing is, we're talking about a drug offense here. We've been using covert measures against certain people in this investigation—not you, but others.

M: What does that mean?

JS: Covert wiretapping of rooms, phone tapping, surveillance. We've got strong evidence. You'll be convicted, I can say that with certainty. You'll get at least ten years. And I don't really think prison's the right place for you, either.

M: But . . . (sound of crying) . . . I can't be here . . . it's been going on for years now.

JS: You'll be sent to Kumla for a couple of years first, that's the toughest jail in the country, and I'm sure you know what happens to people like you there. It's not a fun place for softies. . . .

M: But . . . but . . . (inaudible)

JS: I know. None of this can be easy. Wait a second, I'll get some tissues.

M: (Inaudible)

JS: There you go.

M: Thanks . . . (sniffing sound)

JS: Look, I know this is awful, but I'm a straight talker. It's like this: I have a proposal for you. It's a bit outside the box, but like I said, I don't think you fit in here.

M: Please, tell me. I'll do anything.

JS: It's pretty simple. We understand you've had extensive contact with certain people who are of interest to us—we've seen and heard this, if you see what I mean. So, I want to know everything about them. I want to know what you've been working on. And if you can help me with that, then I promise we'll keep things like this. No interviews, no recordings, no judges or lawyers. Your name won't appear anywhere. And then I can help you in return.

M: You'll let me go?

JS: If you help with this, I'll let you go and we won't take things any further. We'll do a deal, you and I, do you understand what I mean?

M: I don't know. . . .

JS: Think about it. Weigh up your different options. Eight, maybe ten years in Kumla versus a few hours talking to me.

M: It could be awkward . . . It's dangerous. I've been through a lot, believe me.

JS: Yeah, that's what I suspected. But you're not one of the lowlifes. You're normal. And if you go along with my suggestion, it has to be your own decision. I can't force you. But what I can do is arrange the guarantees you need.

M: What about my kids?

JS: I'm only going to use what you say as a basis for further investigation. You'll never need to testify or be named in any way. You'll be under an alias, "Marina," and I'll be the only one who knows about it. Complete secrecy. You don't need to worry about yourself or your kids. We can take a break now, if you like. I'm going to go out, so you can have a while to think.

M: Yeah, okay.

JS: Good. Just remember: at least ten years. Kumla. Or a couple of hours of talking.

2

They made small talk as they waited in the velvet-clad armchairs and sofas. Emelie knew a few of the others from before. She'd studied with some of them and met others at Swedish Bar Association training courses—one of them was even her colleague at work.

But beneath all the niceties there was tension. Of course: one by one, they were being called in to see the examiners. They had been asked to put their phones into small plastic pouches on a table at the end of the hall. All they were allowed was paper, a pen, and a folder containing the ethical guidelines and disciplinary committee's questions.

It was time: very soon, she would be called in to her examination. The verbal exam, which would determine whether she would become a lawyer. Everything up to this point had, more or less, been a journey toward this goal. Twelve years of school followed by a year abroad in Paris—though she'd spent most of her time there partying in the Bastille area, she'd also learned fluent French—and then three and a half years as a law student before she gained her bachelor's degree. Finally three years of work as a legal associate with the Leijon law firm.

During that time, she had taken Swedish Bar Association courses on ethics and professional regulations. She'd gathered all the necessary references. It wasn't like applying for a normal job, where you just gave the names and contact details of your two favorite bosses. No, the Swedish Bar Association wanted the names and addresses, plus an account of the context in which you'd met, of all the opposing lawyers and judges you'd ever faced.

For Emelie, that hadn't actually been too extensive. For the most part, the partners had fronted the cases she'd been involved in. But still, that was more than twenty people they were talking about. Each of them had to be contacted by the Bar, and all had to give their opinion on whether she was worthy of being allowed entry into their holy chamber.

And now, today, the final exam. If she made it through this, the rest would be pure formality. She would soon be able to give herself the title of lawyer.

"Emelie Jansson," a voice called from the hallway.

It was her turn.

The examiner handed her an 8½" x 11" sheet of paper covered in text. She now had twenty minutes to think through the issue, prepare her presentation, and plan for the cross-examination. She went into a separate room, furnished with nothing but an oak desk and chair. A copper engraving representing some old case was hanging on the wall. She glanced through the first point.

QUESTION A

Discuss the questions of an ethical and professional technical nature arising in the situations apparent in the below account.

Mr. English businessman Mr. Sheffield has made contact with the legal firm Vipps, and asked for help with the acquisition of a property complex in Gothenburg.

Mr. Sheffield tells the lawyer, Mia Martinsson, that roughly ten years ago he worked with the law firm. This was when the previous partner, Sune Storm, helped him with a complex matter. Mr. Sheffield says that he "really feels like a client of the firm, and expects assistance thereafter."

After several weeks of correspondence with Mr. Sheffield, Mia starts to feel slightly hesitant about who Mr. Sheffield really is. He does not require any bank loans, and wants to transfer the entire purchase sum, 220 million kronor, to one of the law firm's client accounts. The transfer will not, however, come from Mr. Sheffield's account in the UK, but from a company based in the British Virgin Islands.

Emelie underlined several words in the question, and picked up the folder of regulations. She quickly put it back down again. Before she started searching for clauses, she needed to think. Identify the actual issues. The ethical pitfalls.

Shouldn't the firm and the lawyer have run some kind of check on the client? Made a copy of his identification documents, run him through the firm's conflict-of-interest database? Should Mr. Sheffield really be regarded as their client, just because he had been ten years earlier? When did a client relationship really become a reality? And what were the Financial Supervisory Authority's rules when it came to checking and preventing money laundering?

She jotted down some notes.

Eventually, she heard a knock at the door: her time was up. The twenty minutes had passed much more quickly than she'd thought. She'd dealt with the questions as best she could, four situations similar to the one about the lawyer, Martinsson, and Mr. Sheffield. Each of them contained different problem areas. The firm community, witness management, committee questions. Conflict of interest.

The examiner was a lawyer in his sixties, a man with an incredibly well-groomed mustache, and the external examiner was a woman, probably about ten years younger than him—though she was trying to look like she was twenty. Both were formally dressed: the man in a dark blue suit and tie, and the woman in a burgundy dress.

"So, let's start with the lawyer, Mia Martinsson? How should she act?" the examiner asked.

That had been three weeks ago.

Today, Emelie was in the office. She needed to work, but her mind was elsewhere. They might get in touch at any moment.

The phone rang.

"Hi, it's Mom."

"Hi."

"How are you?"

"I thought you were someone else. I find out today."

"Find out what? Something at work?"

"Kinda. If I passed the exam and my application went through. Whether I become a lawyer or not."

"Oh, that's exciting. Congratulations. Does that mean a pay raise?"

"I haven't even found out yet, but there probably won't be any pay raise. It doesn't mean all that much in this firm. Being a lawyer has the most formal value for people working on criminal cases—you need it to be appointed as a defense lawyer. But for me, it's mostly symbolic. I'm full-fledged, if that makes sense."

"Well, it's still exciting."

Emelie could hear that something wasn't right.

"How are you both?"

"Oh, you know." Her mother started speaking more slowly. "I've barely seen your dad over the last three days."

"Like before?"

"Yeah, like before. He comes crashing in in the middle of the night, but he didn't even come home yesterday. Could you come down to see us this weekend?"

"*Us?*"

"Yes, us."

"So Dad'll be back?"

There was silence on the other end of the line.

This was what Emelie's world had looked like during her entire childhood. Dad's drinking benders. She hadn't really realized it before she left home, got to university, and started thinking everything through. But she knew how he could be. How she *herself* could be.

They could never find out at work.

Emelie ended the call with her mother. She studied herself in the round mirror hanging on the end of the bookcase. Her dark blond hair was parted to one side, tucked behind her ears. She might not have enough makeup on today—she might not have put on any at all, now that she thought about it—but her gray eyes still looked huge. She really should go down to Jönköping on the weekend. Find her dad. Try to make him understand, once and for all.

An hour later. The door opened, and Josephine came tumbling in. They still shared an office despite the fact that Jossan was a senior associate now and should've been given a room of her own long ago. Maybe that was a bad sign for her roommate.

But Emelie liked sharing the office, even if Jossan could be incredibly self-absorbed and spent ten times as long talking about her manicure girl on Sibyllegatan and the sale on Net-a-Porter than about anything important. Anyway, she always practically tripped through the door, like Kramer in *Seinfeld*, and that alone was worth at least one laugh a day.

"Pippa," Josephine roared once she'd closed the door. "I can see it on your face: something good's happened. You've got dimples, even though you're not laughing. Did they just call?"

Emelie nodded. Five minutes earlier, someone from the Bar had finally called to let her know that she had been accepted as a member of Sweden's Bar Association.

She had the title now. The journey was over.

"Congratulations, Pippa. You're a lawyer. That calls for celebrating with a glass of Bollinger at dinner."

Josephine always called Emelie Pippa. For some reason, she thought Emelie was the spitting image of Pippa Middleton.

"You know what my favorite author always says. *Happiness is something that multiplies when it's divided*."

"So cheesy. Who said that?"

"It's not cheesy. It's from the world's most insightful man: Paulo Coelho." Jossan blinked. Then she started talking about all the books by him she'd read, how they had changed her life. They'd helped her find herself, she could be happy even during difficult times, she'd become much more aware of her spiritual self, and she could do without her materialistic lifestyle.

Emelie pointed to the three handbags hanging on a hook on the wall behind Josephine. Céline, Chanel, Fendi. "What about those?"

Josephine ran her hand over the Céline bag. It looked as though she was caressing it tenderly. "That doesn't count as materialistic," she said. "A woman's got to have something to carry her stuff in."

At seven thirty, Emelie lit a cigarette on the way to Riche. Jossan and a few of the other girls from the office were already inside the restaurant, eating *moules frites* and waiting to celebrate with her.

She paused. Hesitated. Maybe she didn't have time for this. She'd been working like a madwoman. The breakup of Husgrens AB— in which the profitable parts were being sold to a Chinese industry conglomerate, and the unprofitable sections were being taken over by one of EQT's opportunity funds—had meant fourteen-hour negotiation sessions with the Chinese for three weeks in a row. The sale of Airborne Logistics to an American industry giant meant eighteen-hour stretches in the due-diligence room, with no breaks, even on Sundays. Emelie was in charge of the other legal associates. The air in the room was always so heavy when they left that she handed out painkillers to the team every evening.

Her phone rang. Unknown number.

She answered with her first name.

"Hello, this is Detective Inspector Johan Kullman. Is this Emelie Jansson, the lawyer?"

Emelie Jansson, the *lawyer*. That sounded good. All the same, she wondered why a detective inspector was calling her.

"It is. What's this about?"

"I'm calling from the custodial wing of Kronoberg Prison. We've got a suspect who's requested you as his lawyer."

"Sorry, what did you just say? A suspect has requested me as his lawyer?"

"Answer: yup."

"At this time?"

"It's his right to request a lawyer. And as we understand it, he's requested you. That means it's our responsibility to check whether you accept the task."

"But I don't work on criminal cases."

"I have no idea. All I know is the suspect requested you."

"What's he suspected of?"

"Murder. We think he killed a man out on Värmdö last night."

"And why does he want me?"

"That's a little tricky to answer, I'm afraid. He's actually more or less unconscious. He was in a car accident."

Emelie took a final puff on her cigarette.

She'd made it to the entrance of the restaurant.

Everyone seemed to be having such a good time inside.

3

He'd been sitting in the car since five that morning. Shoving snus tobacco under his lip and chewing xylitol gum. Waiting for Fredric McLoud.

The man he was tailing hadn't followed his usual pattern today. It was past ten now.

Teddy wondered what was going to happen, what he would have to do to finish this job—finding something big on McLoud—without getting himself into trouble. Whatever happened, he'd made up his mind: he was going to live a different life. He wasn't going back to the slammer.

He pushed a new piece of snus under his lip. Snus and chewing gum: his new favorite combination. The snus almost too earthy otherwise. Like it needed balancing out somehow, pushing back.

Banérgatan wasn't the world's most interesting place on an ordinary morning in May. From five till seven, it had been deserted, like no one even lived in the grand old apartments in this part of town. Just over a year ago, he'd walked this street on another job. A dark, unpleasant start to his new life as a free man. But that felt distant somehow. Teddy had been out for almost a year and a half now.

The first people out on the street were the dog owners. Older men in hats and green wax jackets, waiting patiently as their dachshunds pissed on the nearest lamppost. Younger women in sneakers and lightweight down-filled body warmers, quickly bending down to scoop up the dog shit in their plastic bags before heading off toward Djurgården with their golden retrievers.

By quarter to eight, the men in suits and women dressed for business started to appear. They moved quickly toward their luxury cars, or else they headed off toward the city on foot.

Fifteen minutes later, it was schoolkids streaming along the pavements, aside from those who were picked up by taxi directly outside their front doors. The cars waiting for these seven-year-olds weren't exactly Taxi Stockholm's climate-neutral Volvos or Kurir's environmentally certified Toyota Priuses, either. They were different cars, different companies. Teddy didn't know their names, but he'd heard of them. These cars were booked in advance, paid for using credit cards, and ordered using the relevant app.

The family lived on the very top floor, in a pristinely renovated attic apartment more than thirty-two hundred square feet in size. Things had moved quickly for Fredric McLoud these past few years. But now, perhaps, they were on the way back down. All depending on how Teddy did his job.

At nine thirty, he finally came out. Fredric McLoud. Not wearing the suit and tie you might expect of the millionaire business leader. Instead, he was dressed in what looked like sweatpants and a polo shirt with a huge sailing brand logo on it.

Teddy noticed it immediately: Fredric's behavior was different today. He stood still for a few seconds, just looking about, before he crossed the road and started off down Riddargatan. Every three hundred feet or so, he stopped, turned, and glanced all around him.

Teddy stepped out of the car as his surveillance object passed. He went up to the parking meter and started fiddling with his payment card as McLoud continued down the street.

Pay with your phone, EasyPark, he read on the machine. Next time, I'll bring the fucking bike, he thought.

After a few seconds, Teddy slowly started off after him. As soon as Fredric dropped the pace, Teddy took out his phone and stopped to write a pretend text message.

This was his life now. He'd been offered the job with the Leijon law firm by one of the partners he knew from before, Magnus Hassel. The firm didn't employ him directly—Hassel had thought that would be too much—but they had some kind of company they used for the so-called freelance jobs, Leijon Legal Services AB. The deal was actually pretty generous. They paid for a hire car and even helped him get a Visa card, despite the fact that the credit checks the bank had run must've shown his declared income over the past twenty years wasn't even close to subsistence level.

His work for the company mainly consisted of so-called personal due diligences.

Fredric McLoud was one of the two founders of Superia, an online-payment service that had grown enormously over the past few years. The company had been valued at more than "a yard," as Magnus Hassel put it, "and that's in euros."

Leijon's client wanted to buy a 20 percent stake in the company. The only problem? There was talk about young Fredric McLoud being a bit of a coke fiend. And according to those same rumors, it wasn't just a little partying here and there, no. He was snorting on a daily basis; the guy couldn't even make it through a morning meeting without doing a couple of lines in the bathroom first.

Teddy had been tailing him for three weeks now and hadn't seen anything odd. Either McLoud had a huge stash at home or else he got the stuff delivered to him some other way, Teddy had no idea how. The alternative was that his habit wasn't nearly as bad as people said. Rumors were just rumors, after all, and they were often spread deliberately to ruin someone's career.

But today he'd caught a whiff of something. He just hoped it wouldn't all go to shit.

His surveillance target continued across Nybrogatan and on toward Birger Jarlsgatan. If McLoud had been even slightly more cautious, it might've been tricky for Teddy to follow him today. But as things stood, his gestures and movements were all exaggerated. He would slow down noticeably a few seconds before he stopped completely, stood stock-still, and glanced all around. As long as Teddy moved slowly, he wouldn't bother McLoud.

There was a beggar on the corner of Nybrogatan and Riddargatan. Colorful headscarf contrasting with her dark, furrowed
skin. Pieces of cardboard on the ground beneath her flowing black
skirt. The woman was humming a melody: a dirge from another
world. There hadn't been as many beggars in Stockholm before
Teddy was sent down; that was something new. He watched people's eyes as they passed. They looked down, turned away. Pretended she wasn't there.

The Leijon office was only a few blocks away. Not that Teddy
needed to go in today. He didn't have an office there, and he was
happy about that. He ran these investigations more or less on his
own, and it was often enough just to report to the lawyer involved
by email or phone. Besides, he didn't want to bump into Emelie
Jansson.

They'd made plans to get dinner together a year or so ago, her
idea. But she'd called to reschedule it, and he'd had to put their next
date back, which she'd then canceled at the last minute. Their dinner plans had slipped away like shampoo down the drain.

Since it was only quarter to ten, most of the open-air cafés were
empty, but there was a surprising number of people out on the
street. Teddy couldn't help but think that those who earned the
most—the people who worked in this part of town—seemed to
take life the easiest. The working day didn't start before now for
some of them.

Many of the people were extremely well-dressed; the men rushing past wore slim-fitting suits with slacks that looked too short,
though that was probably intentional. The women were in high
heels, with fluffy, well-washed hair and rose-gold Rolex watches.

He thought of his sister, Linda, and his nephew, Nikola. Teddy
had gone over to her house for dinner yesterday. She'd had her
hair in a bun; she'd looked tanned. Teddy wondered whether she'd
started going back to the tanning beds again.

"Nikola gets out the day after tomorrow," she'd said, "and I
don't know what I should do."

Teddy had cut a potato he'd just peeled, added some butter. "He's a man now. It's not your responsibility. But he's gonna be fine."

"How do you know?"

"I don't know anything. But we've got to believe in him. He needs our support."

Linda had carefully cut her meat into five equal pieces. Her hands didn't look young anymore. "He looks up to you, he wants to be like you. But the one thing I hope is that he *doesn't* end up like you."

"Like I *was*, you mean?"

Linda had looked down at her plate. "I don't know what I mean," she'd said.

Fredric McLoud stopped and went into an Espresso House.

Teddy paused. Should he follow him in and risk making him suspicious? Fredric must've noticed the huge man walking behind him all the way here. So far, there hadn't been anything strange about it, but if Teddy turned up in the same café, there was no way it could be a coincidence.

He followed him in anyway. McLoud's routine was off today. That had to mean something.

Plus, honestly, Fredric McLoud seemed so far gone that he could've had half of Stockholm's plainclothes policemen creeping after him and he wouldn't have even noticed there was anyone else on the street.

Teddy got in line by the counter. He saw Fredric sit down at a table opposite a young man with a bottle of Coca-Cola.

There was a plastic bag under the table.

Fredric shook hands with the kid. He looked young, dark hair, dark eyes. Dressed in a Windbreaker and Adidas sweatpants.

Sweatpants: Teddy remembered wearing them himself at that age. Once, Dejan had been in court for assaulting someone in a metro station. A shitty thing, but Teddy and some of the other guys had decided to go watch the trial. To support Dejan, but also for fun; they'd had nothing better to do that day. During the break, Dejan's lawyer had come up to Teddy and said: "Get out of here, I don't want a load of people wearing trousers like that in the public seats."

"What d'you mean, trousers like this?" Teddy asked.

"You know, you all look alike, and the judge knows exactly what kind of guys you are. So get out of here. It won't do your friend any good to be associated with *sweatpants*. Believe me."

The ironic thing today: Fredric McLoud looked just as much a thug as the kid did.

Teddy already had his phone in his hand, the camera rolling. He pretended to be busy doing something on it, but he was really just making sure it had a clear shot of the table where Fredric and the kid were sitting. These new phones, they were pretty much magic.

Document everything: that was one of the golden rules he'd been given by Leijon. His job was all about collecting evidence. Collecting evidence without fucking things up for himself.

It only took a couple of seconds. Fredric said something. The kid nodded. Fredric took the bag from under the table, stood up, and left.

Teddy watched him through the big windows out onto the street—it was an unnatural sight, one of Stockholm's richest thirty-seven-year-olds with a battered old supermarket bag in his hand. But he'd caught it all on film.

Teddy was still standing by the counter. It was his turn now. Macadamia nuts, raw food balls, green juices. In the past, *pre-jail*, the baked goods had all contained flour and sugar.

"What'll it be?" the girl behind the counter asked.

"You have any normal buns?"

"Yeah, we've got sourdough."

"Sounds too healthy."

The girl's eyes flashed.

Teddy turned and left.

Fredric "coke fiend" McLoud was thirty feet ahead of him, heading along Riddargatan again.

Teddy wondered why it was so important to Magnus that he

do this, but the partner had been explicit. He wanted irrefutable evidence, even if it gave away that they'd been following him.

It was a bright, clear day. The sun glared in the windows. Teddy could feel his stress levels rising. He went up to a middle-aged woman who was busy jabbing at the buttons on a parking meter.

"Hi, sorry to bother you. Could you do me a favor?"

The woman turned around. Now she was holding her phone. She looked stressed—maybe she was trying to work out which app she needed to solve her problems—but she answered softly, "Of course."

"Great, thanks. Do you see that man there?"

Teddy pointed to Fredric.

"Yes, why?"

"Just watch."

He took out his phone again, but this time he switched on the sound recorder. Leijon had given it to him, it was a smartphone, and he'd learned how to use it much more quickly than he'd thought he would. All the same, he sometimes felt like throwing it into the water or dropping it from a balcony somewhere. Teddy refused to use the calendar function on it, but he'd given in to some of its applications: in this line of work, it was a fantastic tool.

He caught up with Fredric McLoud. Tapped him on the shoulder.

"Sorry, but I think you took my bag?"

Fredric clutched the plastic bag to his chest.

"Who are you? What're you talking about?"

"Yeah, I lost my bag. This one's not mine, is it?"

Fredric stared at him. His eyebrow twitched.

"Are you crazy? It's definitely not yours."

"Can I just have a quick look in it?"

"No way."

Teddy moved quickly. He grabbed Fredric's arm and reached for the plastic bag with his free hand.

Fredric raised his voice. "What the hell are you doing? Get off my bag."

"I just want to have a look in it. There's no problem is there?"

"Like hell there's not. It's *my bag*."

Teddy couldn't give up now. He needed to be in the moment—act, not analyze. JDI—just do it, like Dejan used to say.

He snatched at the bag again and pulled Fredric's other arm to try to knock him off balance. They stumbled.

Teddy was bigger, beefier, but McLoud wasn't some stick. And he was fighting for his career, his business, his family. His life.

Their fumbling continued.

Suddenly Teddy felt a searing pain in the hand holding the bag. He looked down. Fredric had bitten his thumb.

No. No, he couldn't yell. Couldn't shout. This had to work. He'd promised himself.

He could have stuck a finger into Fredric's eye. Hit him square in the nose. Grabbed his Adam's apple and just ripped it out. But instead, he pushed Fredric's head, pressed his hand against his cheek, tried to *force* him into submission.

Eventually, Fredric let go of his thumb. Teddy saw blood on the man's teeth.

He needed to take control now. Calm the situation. He was standing close to McLoud.

The woman was shouting something in the background. "Stop this now. I've called the police."

Teddy was panting. "You heard her. I'm pretty sure you don't want the police to come snooping around that bag of yours. Just let me have a look."

Dilation. Panic in McLoud's eyes. The guy understood.

Too late for Teddy. McLoud had started to run.

Teddy had thought it would all be over by now. He rushed after him.

Along Riddargatan. To the left, onto Artillerigatan.

Uphill. McLoud had long legs. And Teddy knew he saw his personal trainer in the fancy Grand Hôtel gym three times a week.

Teddy could feel how heavy he was.

Up the hill. Army museum to the left. A home electronics shop to the right.

On to Storgatan. He wouldn't be able to make it much farther. People were staring at them. Some of them were shouting.

Then, all of a sudden, Teddy couldn't see him anymore.

Where the fuck had Fredric McLoud gone?

He saw a police car farther down the street.

Shit, shit, shit. It couldn't end this way.

He slowed down. Swedish Enterprise's offices to his left. A men's clothing shop to the right. The first thing the cops would home in on was anyone running. He tried to catch his breath. Analyze the situation.

Where had Fredric McLoud gone? He had to be here somewhere, just a few feet away. He couldn't just disappear.

The police car was only a hundred or so feet behind Teddy now. It was crawling forward.

He had to do something.

Fifty feet.

Teddy looked both ways. People had seen him running; they could point him out. He had no other choice. So, calmly and quietly, he made a decision: he entered the clothing shop.

Tweed jackets, corduroy trousers, hunting caps. The place didn't exactly radiate a spring feeling. He moved deeper into the shop—still completely focused on what was going on behind him.

The police car: he hoped it had rolled on by.

And then he almost burst out laughing. In front of him, by the suits, Fredric McLoud was standing with his back to him. He was still clutching his plastic bag. He'd clearly had the same idea as Teddy.

Teddy tapped him on the shoulder and said: "I think it's gone. If you and I can stay calm, anyway."

McLoud's face was no longer panic-stricken. He seemed to be close to tears.

"Who are you? Why are you doing this?"

Teddy said: "Bound by professional secrecy, I'm afraid."

4

When the day's conversation group ended, Nikola was already out-side the classroom. That was him in a nutshell. Always first out. One image in his mind from all the classes of his youth: the empty hallway, the graffiti-covered lockers, the silence before the rest of the class came storming out seconds later. Nikola: always too much energy to calmly pack up his things, chitchat with his friends for a few minutes. Always stressed out by some invisible force, desperate for a nanosecond of quiet hallway. A slice of tranquillity.

But that was long gone. He hadn't spent much time at school these past few years.

Linda and the director called his behavior mild ADHD. Not that Nikola took Ritalin or self-medicated with junk like some of the other guys did. They just wanted to stick a label on the energy that burned beneath the gold cross on his chest. The gold cross he'd gotten from Teddy, before he'd gone in to do his eight years.

But all that dick sucking faded into the background today. Life: *fucking sweeeet*. Today was the day. The *last* day.

Chamon was coming to pick him up and take him away from this shit hole.

One last little piece of crap: before Nicko could leave, he had to have a final chat with the director.

Somehow, Anders Sanchez Salazar managed to get his room to look *exactly* the same every time Nikola was forced to go there.

It wasn't just that the two visitors' chairs were pushed in under the front of the desk in the same way, or that the curtains were half drawn like they had been the last time. Everything was an *exact* copy. The papers on the desk, the pencil case behind the computer screen, the pictures of his kids. Everything was in the same place. Even the coffee cup with the Hammarby logo on it was on the same corner of the desk as the last time he was there.

The only thing that had changed was the color of Anders's cardigan. Bright red today. It had been burgundy last time.

"So, Nikola. How's it feel?"

Nikola tried to stop himself from smiling too widely.

"Really good, actually."

"I know it can be a bit daunting to leave Spillersboda when you've been here as long as you have. What do you think?"

Nicko had to try even harder to stop himself from laughing.

"Yeah," he said. "A bit."

"But I'm sure everything's going to be fine. You're going to be living with your mother, aren't you?"

"Yeah, she said she'd let me in. I promised her I'll get my act together."

"Are things better between you now?"

"Yeah, definitely. She's the best."

Years of contact with nags from social services, with head teachers, welfare officers, and cops—Nicko: the expert of all experts. It wasn't hard to work out what they wanted to hear. The tricky thing was making it sound trustworthy. The only true part was that he really did think Linda was the best.

"One piece of advice, Nikola," said Anders. "Stay away from your old pals. I'm sure they're good guys, it's not that, but it'll just end in trouble. A load of grief, like you all say."

Chamon fiddled with his rosary. It was less than three months since he'd passed his driving test, but the Audi he was driving looked newer than that. The twenty-inch rims were as shiny as Nicko's gold cross had been when it was new. He knew the A7 belonged to his friend's cousin, but when you came somewhere like Spillers-boda, you wanted to show you lived a *different* life.

"*Meksthina?*"

Nikola grinned and pushed a piece of snus under his lip. He answered in the same language. "*Abri*, let's go, man. Do a Zlatan."

To most of them, he was just Nicko, but the brothers some-times called him Bible Man, because they thought he spoke Syr-iac like people did in the old days. They were impressed all the same. Nikola was the only non-Syrian or Assyrian guy they knew who spoke their language. But was it really so surprising? He'd grown up with them. And like his granddad always said, when in Rome . . .

"What d'you mean, do a Zlatan?"

"Hat trick, man. I scored three joints from a guy in here. He owed me. We'll smoke 'em all when we get home."

"Too funny, bro. You gonna get in on the thing soon?"

Nikola knew what he was talking about. Yusuf's question. *The thing.*

Directly for Isak. Real shit.

They started heading for the gates.

The guys in the yard moved aside as Nikola and Chamon passed.

"So, you been getting any? I didn't even see you last time you were out."

"Hell yeah, been getting more ass than the toilet seats in the ladies' room at the Strip."

Chamon roared with laughter. "*Walla.*"

They opened the gates and stepped out. The spring sunshine was strong today. The leaves on the trees outside were pale green. They looked a bit like marijuana leaves, only bigger. Sandra had said they were chestnuts.

"Shit, I should probably be Instagramming those leaves to cel-ebrate. Last time I'm gonna set foot here, and I've been staring at those trees from my window for a year."

"*You've* got Instagram?" Chamon asked.

Before he had time to answer, they heard a voice behind them. "Nikola, could you come back a minute?"

They turned around. It was Sandra. She was standing by the gates, her face beaming. Weird: she was actually pretty cute.

"What for?" asked Nikola.

"I just need to talk to you about one last thing. It'd be great if you had time."

"I'm done here, Anders signed me out fifteen minutes ago. I'm in charge of myself now."

"I know, you're right. But this is important."

Nikola glanced at Chamon. "She's such a fucking pain, man."

"She been cool or was she a bitch?"

"Today?"

"No, while you were inside."

"She's all right, really. She wants the best for you, you know what they're like . . ."

"I get it, so you can show her some respect. You're a free man. Just go see what she wants, then we'll get outta here."

Sandra walked ahead of him toward the main building. Nikola followed her.

The moment he stepped inside, he knew something wasn't right. He couldn't say what, it was just a strong feeling that came over him. He followed Sandra into one of the so-called supervisor rooms anyway.

It was calmer and cleaner inside than it was in the inmates' rooms. Some kind of informative poster pinned up on the wall: *Student integrity online. Sign up for our Internet Days now!*

"Are you going to continue with your work experience place now, do you think?" Sandra asked.

"Dunno."

"It was electricity and telecommunications you were working with, right?"

"Yeah."

"And it's almost summer. Good, isn't it?"

"Yes."

"How does it feel?"

"What?"

What the hell was this? Sandra trying to make small talk like they were friends or something—he was done with this place, for God's sake. He turned to leave.

Then he understood. A side door opened, and Simon *cunting* Murray came in.

Sandra must've known. Simon Murray was a cop. The plain-clothes one who'd always been after Nikola and the boys. Who stopped their cars and paid visits to their parents. Who always turned up like some kind of genie outside Chamon's house, at the club, at O'Learys. He was a part of Project Hippogriff—the joint action force in the southern suburbs, aimed at creating a safer city—as they called that shit.

Simon gave him a wave.

"How're things with Nikola, then?"

Sandra showed them into a separate room. There were a couple of coffee cups on the table.

Simon closed the door and sat down. Nikola was still on his feet. He could turn and leave whenever he wanted. Simon had no right to keep him locked up or to interrogate him. He had nothing to say to the pig.

Simon: cropped blond hair. Black boots. A rubber pulse meter on his arm. Slim blue jeans and a gray sweatshirt with *G-Star* on it. He looked like he always had: cop from birth. There had to be something in his blood, in his DNA. Nikola didn't get how the man could work as a plainclothes officer when it was so obvious to everyone what he was.

"I just want to ask you a few questions, Nikola. Is that okay?"

"No, it's not okay. I just got out of here."

"Sandra told me. Maybe I should say congratulations?"

"Say what you want."

"Nicko, it's nothing weird. Five minutes, tops. Can you just lis-ten to me?"

"You all are snakes."

"You hate the police?"

"Never met a good one."

"It makes me sad to hear you say that. I don't want to do you any harm. Honest."

"Stop talking. You gonna arrest me for something?"

Nikola thought back to the hot computers he'd helped move right before he got sent here, and to the guy in the next room he'd demanded ten grand from—the guy who'd been about to piss himself, he was so scared—a few months earlier for trying to play boss. Then he thought about the thing in the forest when Chamon had almost lost his shit. They'd shot a man then. But for fuck's sake— that was more than a year ago. It couldn't be about that.

"I'm not here to bring you in," Simon said. "I just have *one* question."

Nikola was still on his feet. Yusuf used to say that sometimes it was smart to listen to what the cops had to say, to work out what they knew.

"I'm wondering about this trial I've been hearing about," Simon said. "Have they asked you to take part?"

His head was burning. His stomach was rumbling. How the hell did Simon Murray know about *the thing*? It was internal. Top priority. Isak level and everything.

"I don't have a fucking clue what you're talking about. Is it some court case or something?"

"No, I think you know. You're still in touch with Yusuf and Chamon. The problems between Metim Tasdemir and the Bar-Sawme family. I'm sure you know them?"

"No idea what you're talking about."

"You don't know anything about it?"

"I just said I don't have a clue. What's wrong with you?"

"Calm down, I'm not here to put anything on you. I just wanted to say this—and feel free to pass it on to Chamon, as well, though it's harder to get him to listen. . . ."

Simon got up from the chair: face-to-face with Nikola. His eyes were small and grayish.

"You two don't belong there. You're too young. The whole thing could end really badly. I don't know where you're planning on having it, or exactly who's going to be involved, but stay away, Nikola. Promise me that. Please. Don't go."

Nikola took hold of the door handle to leave. He didn't want to listen to any more of this bullshit.

Simon said: "One more thing, Nikola. Take it easy tonight—I guess you're planning to celebrate being out. Don't do anything stupid. You don't want to end up back inside, do you?"

Kendrick Lamar's nasal tones, full volume. Chamon was in the driver's seat, his hands drumming the wheel. Nikola climbed into the passenger seat. Audi S embossed into the leather.

"Shit, man, that took ages."

"Fucking hell."

"Everything okay, bro?"

"Yeah, no problem."

Chamon grinned. "I've got big plans for you tonight. Best party ever, man; sickest release fest. Special effects and everything."

"Sounds sweet."

"You'll see, man. I've organized everything."

Stockholm County Police Authority

Interview with informant "Marina," 11 December 2010

Interview leader: Joakim Sundén

Location: Älvsjö centrum

MEMORANDUM 2 (Part 1)

Transcript of dialogue

JS: Are you feeling better?

M: Yeah, a lot. Thanks for letting me go. Those few days were some of the worst in my life. So many memories came back.

JS: Did anyone ask where you were?

M: No.

JS: Not even Sebbe?

M: We haven't spoken. I think he's gone underground.

JS: I see. Well, I promised you immunity, and you promised to talk. So before you start, I just want to say that I need all the details, all your thoughts. Your impressions and ideas, too. Is that okay?

M: I think so. I've been thinking about what to say.

JS: Sounds great. Maybe you could start with an overview of the background, and then move on to everything else, in detail.

M: Okay, that's roughly what I was thinking anyway.

So, it was like this: I've always loved games, and in high school I started playing backgammon with a few friends. At first, we were just playing for fun in cafés after school, messing about with the pieces and trying to figure out how the game really worked. We were all pretty interested in math—I was tak- ing the science route in school, probability theory and differential equations and stuff like that, so I picked it all up pretty quickly. Then after a while, a load of Iranians, Turks, and other people from the Middle East, guys who were older than us, started coming to the café to see who these Swedish kids were, kids who thought they knew how to play *their* game. *Shesh besh,* they called it. We used to wipe the floor with them whenever we played.

JS: When was this?

M: The mideighties. I was at Brännkyrka school then. Anyway, I finished high school, did my military service in Berga, and then worked for my dad for a couple of years. He had a little printing company. I started at Stockholm University when I was twenty-three, the same year I met Cecilia, my wife. That was 1990. Three years later, we had our first child. I'd just turned twenty- seven, the same year I finished university. I kept it in check all those years, the gaming, but we would see each other from time to time, me and the guys.

Then I started at KPMG, the audit company. I think it must've been 1995. That's where I met another guy who was into backgammon—poker, too. He invited me to a club by St. Eriksplan, the kind of place you could play pretty much all day long. I started going there sometimes, after the kids were in bed, or on the weekends. In a way, it was a really dynamic and creative environ- ment. Or it would've been, if it hadn't been for the hunger. The bug, we call it. I mean, most people there were absolutely crazy for it.

JS: What did Cecilia say about the club?

M: I told her that I went there every now and then, maybe not *every* time I went, but usually. She just accepted it as an odd hobby of mine, but she never came with me.

I went to other places, too: Carlo's Poker in Sundbyberg, Pot Raiser on Folkungagatan. I made quite a bit sometimes, even though I didn't really play all that many money games. I went home with more than ten thousand kronor once. I remember I just put the money in a nice little heap on the kitchen counter so it would be the first thing she saw in the morning.

JS: Didn't she think it was strange?

M: Maybe the first time, but then she thought it was pretty cool. Plus, it was hardly ever that kind of money. So in the beginning, there was no problem. But later, well . . . it was different later . . . though I'll get to that.

Anyway, at some point in early 2002, I played my first poker game online. It was a revelation. Now I could play whenever I wanted. This was when broadband was just starting to develop, and I'd bought a better computer, so that meant I could play multiple games at once. I often had four or five going at the same time. On my work computer, too. Cecilia was happy I wasn't going to the "game hole" as much anymore, that's what she called the club, her joke. But she had no idea how much I was playing at work. Online poker's different from the real thing. It's more aggressive, and it's usually quicker. Above all, it's less psychological and more mathematical. I mean, you never see your opponents when you play online, so your game is all that matters, no stupid poker faces or psyching people out. That was an advantage for me. I learned a lot about the game, stuff I could use when I played real games in the club.

I sometimes call the years that came next the golden era. Tons of players, but not many good ones. There was so much hype around poker. In the Stockholm clubs, you could bring in plenty of dough playing Texas Hold'em and PLO—that's Pot Limit Omaha. Just to give you an example, at one point in 2004, I made fifteen thousand euros in *one night*. The levels I was playing at, you had to have a proper bankroll, because even though I had a certain amount of credit with the clubs, I would sometimes lose thousands of euros in a single week, and you didn't get any credit online. It wasn't good for the nerves, the wallet, or your relationship with the clubs. So I started asking around. I needed a backer, a sponsor. Eventually, I got a tip about someone who could help.

JS: Who?

M: Sebbe.

JS: From Gamla stan?

M: Yeah. Sebbe offered to be my staker. That's what it's called. My financier. The deal was that he'd pay all my tournament and cash game stakes, and he'd bankroll me, give me credit of up to two million kronor. For that, he took 60 percent of my winnings. The club raised my credit up to one mil, too, but whenever I needed more, I just went to Sebbe's guy, Maxim, and got more cash. They trusted me completely, that I accounted for it all.

JS: What did you do with the money you won?

M: I paid off a bit of the mortgage, stuff like that. But then in early 2005, it all went to hell. I started playing really badly. I'm not too sure why—I think it's because some new guys started to turn up, people who'd learned to play online, who used programs.

I had to start going to the club almost every night to counter the losses, or else stay late at work and play online there. Cecilia started asking questions, of course. And I was having trouble getting up in the morning: used to stay in bed while she took care of dropping the kids off and things like that.

I remember one morning she came in and sat down on the edge of the bed while the kids were eating their breakfast. She shook me.

"What's going on, Mats? Talk to me."

I mumbled something in response. I'd only been asleep for a few hours.

"Mats, you need to answer me. I need to know what you do all night."

I turned over, tried to wake myself up. "I told you, work's been crazy. Sorry, darling. I'll try to wind things down."

She stroked my cheek. And in my sleep-deprived, fuzzy brain, I actually promised myself to try to sort the situation out.

I might've been able to do it, if I'd just stopped there and then. Sure, I had losses to pay off, but I could've lived with it. Instead, I started playing on tick.

JS: What does that mean?

M: It means I went over the limit. In the end, I owed different players and online companies so much money that I didn't have any kind of coverage. In theory I was bankrupt.

But then in early April, I knew Sebbe would be in Macau for a few weeks. So I went to Maxim and took out a million. Do you follow?

JS: No, not really. Explain.

M: I had no credit left with him. But I told Maxim that I'd spoken to Sebbe and he was okay to increase it. I got the money in a bag and went straight to the club. Maxim trusted me. I screwed Sebbe over. And I lost the entire million, of course.

I was an idiot. And that's where it all started.

JS: Okay, keep going.

M: How detailed do you want me to be?

JS: How well do you remember it?

M: I've got a memory like a book. I could tell you every single word.

JS: That sounds great. I'd like you to be as accurate and detailed as you can. Give me everything.

M: Okay, then. Two weeks later, I got a call from Sebbe. He was back and wanted to meet, he said. I was busy tidying up after dinner, but five minutes later he called again and said he was waiting outside in his car. He wanted me to go down.

He drove a Porsche 911. At first I thought I'd get to sit in the passenger seat, but when I went round, I saw Maxim was already sitting there. I remember that Sebbe rolled down the window and said, "Get in the back, there's plenty of the room if you squash up a bit."

We drove through the tunnels under Södermalm. I tried to make conversation, ask how Macau had been, tell him a bit about the next poker tournament, and so on, but neither of them said much. We came out by Gullmarsplan, and then drove down to Södra Hammarbyhamnen. There were a load of cranes, huge cement blocks waiting to become the foundations of the new part of town they've built there now. We pulled up behind a couple of construction warehouses.

The light in the roof automatically came on when Sebbe killed the engine.

I looked at Sebbe and realized I'd made a huge mess of things.

"You son of a bitch," he hissed.

I didn't know what to say. I was living a completely normal life back then, even if I burned thousands, hundreds of thousands on the poker sites and at the club. I saw myself as someone who could keep his head, keep his cool, someone who could roll with the big losses and then go back home to the family as though nothing had happened. But that was the first time I realized I'd gone too far. That I was like a tiny insect, balancing on the edge of the world.

Sebbe grabbed hold of my neck and pulled my face close to his.

"Look me in the eyes, you pathetic bastard."

And then I caught a flash of metal. Suddenly he was holding it against my face: a knife. I squeezed one eye shut as tight as I could, and I remember I could only think one thing: that my son had a football tournament that weekend. That I couldn't miss driving him to the first match on Saturday morning.

"Who the fuck d'you think you are?" Sebbe asked.

The cold tip of the knife was on my eyelid. It felt like it was scraping my brain.

"I know, I'm sorry, I can explain . . . ," I stammered.

"You went behind my back, you little whore. Did you think Maxim and I wouldn't talk?"

I could feel pain in my eye by that point.

Sebbe turned to Maxim.

"We'll take it straight to the garage after this. Get this thing properly cleaned."

My eye was burning.

My whole head was screaming.

Then Sebbe turned back to me, his face even closer to mine. I could smell him—L&M cigarettes and aftershave.

"Okay, I'll give you another chance. I'm a kindhearted man. You get me my money back in two weeks, I don't give a shit how you do it. Win it, rob a bank, sell your wife on the street. I want my money. Three mil."

"But . . . but . . . it's impossible."

"Don't start that crap now. Two weeks, Mats."

(Inaudible)

I, I mean, it was so fucking . . . (inaudible) I don't know if I can . . . (inaudible)

Memo continued on separate sheet.

5

The conversation with the detective inspector had ruined her chances of a good night's sleep more than she'd thought it would. Though if she was honest, it wasn't just that. It was *the idiot*, too.

She hadn't been able to enjoy herself with the girls at Riche, celebrate her new title with a glass of bubbly and some fun. Instead, she'd taken two sips of her champagne, thanked them for being so brilliant, and told them she had a super intensive case and needed to get back to Leijon.

In actual fact, she'd sat down at her desk and thought about nothing other than what the policeman had said. At ten thirty, she went home.

A young man, suspected of murder. In some kind of coma. Requesting *her*. She'd never worked on a criminal case in her life.

She'd asked the policeman if she could get back to him. Kullman wanted her answer by eight the next morning. He explained: "The suspect isn't on a respirator or anything like that, and he managed to talk for a few minutes yesterday. He was very clear, he wants you to represent him. I've talked to the public prosecutor, Rölén, and we feel we have to honor his request, despite his situation. That's it, really."

They wanted to interview the suspect, and that meant a lawyer had to be present. Emelie would have to make up her mind.

So what was the problem? It was a clear no-go. There was zero chance Leijon would let her take it on. Why didn't she just tell it like it was: "I'm not interested in taking on any defense work"?

But for some reason, she couldn't get it out of her mind.

And now: the night had been one long, drawn-out frustration. Crumpled sheets. Irritation at the light creeping in under the roller blind. Aching muscles from yesterday's sparring class.

But no: it wasn't just the detective inspector's question on her mind. There was also another insanely annoying issue: her neighbor. The idiot.

It was three in the morning, and it wasn't the first time he'd done it. William was twenty-three, worked as a salesman somewhere, and seemed to have a soft spot for Avicii and Calvin Harris. At full volume. In the middle of the night.

His stereo had thundered away two nights every week, on average, since he'd moved in six months earlier. It made no difference what day it was. Night or early morning. The idiot seemed to lack any understanding of the fact that ordinary people had to get up in the morning. Emelie had gone over and knocked on his door four times already. She'd talked to him during the day, too. He'd promised to keep the volume down.

She was trying to fall asleep. She thought about her years at university. It had been there when she first started studying law: the thought of a job involving people. But as her years in education went by, the idea had gradually been eroded. Her classmates seemed to have gone through the exact same process—the defense firms never turned up at open days, and people were constantly talking about how much more you could earn in business law. The human aspect, and the practicalities of defending someone, they just weren't something people spoke about. And with that came the insight of how difficult it was to get a job with one of the defense firms. When they finally graduated, it had been obvious to Emelie and the majority of her peers: they applied either to the law courts or to the big legal firms.

She hauled herself up out of bed. Pulled on a pair of tracksuit bottoms under her nightdress and went out into the hallway.

The sound of the idiot's music was lower here.

She pressed his buzzer.

No answer.

It was three thirty in the morning.

She pressed again.

After a moment, she heard the lock turn.

William opened the door: hair on end, eyes red; clearly drunk or high on something. She could see two others behind him, looking at a laptop. Probably a Spotify playlist full of even more bass lines, she thought.

He grinned at her.

Honestly, what a fucking i-d-i-o-t. This couldn't go on.

She said, "I've asked you so many times now. You know your speakers are right against the wall in my bedroom. Could you please just turn the music down?"

He continued to smile. "Don't be such a miserable bitch."

Enough. Emelie needed her sleep, especially tonight.

Her right hook caught him in the face.

"What the fuck!" he shouted. Blood was streaming from his nose.

"Just turn it down. Or do you want another one?"

His friends seemed to have noticed that something had happened. They got up, grabbed William, and pulled him inside.

Emelie went back to her apartment. She locked the door.

At six thirty, the alarm on her phone burst into life. She immediately called Magnus Hassel.

Less than three hours' sleep. She couldn't bear to think about what she'd done last night. She'd gone far beyond what was normal. And the thing that surprised her most was that she'd actually dared; that she'd completely lost control like that and hit him. Maybe she should go over with a bottle of wine later, grovel.

"Hello?" Magnus sounded groggy.

"Hi, it's Emelie Jansson. I'm so sorry to call you so early, but I got a really strange request for representation."

"Can't we talk about this at the office in a few hours?"

"No, they need a reply before eight."

"Okay, and they didn't request one of the partners?"

"No, I don't think so. It's a criminal case. A murder suspect. He requested me as his defense."

Emelie could hear her own breathing down the line, or maybe it was just Magnus's sighs. She was standing by her bed, looking out the window. There was a blackbird on the roof opposite, watching her.

"Well, let's put it like this," Magnus said. "A firm like Leijon can't get involved with that type of case. It's outside our area of expertise, for one, and even worse, it could give us bad will. Dirty our brand. Make our clients think we associate with riffraff. You understand that, don't you?"

"I thought as much, but I wanted to ask anyway. I don't know, for some reason, it seemed like an important case to take. It seems really peculiar."

It almost sounded like he groaned. Either he was tired or he wanted to indicate that enough was enough.

"Emelie, what you think is peculiar or important is irrelevant here. You work as a lawyer for Leijon. You're not some fucking human rights activist."

The metal door might have been in the middle of the enormous police station complex on Bergsgatan in central Stockholm, but it was actually quite modest. The only thing indicating that Sweden's biggest remand prison lay behind it was the little white sign on the stone wall by the entrance: *Kronoberg Remand Prison*.

Emelie had never even thought about there being any kind of prison here. Right in the middle of town: a building full of suspected murderers, robbers, rapists, and drug dealers.

After her conversation with Magnus, she had remained on her feet by the bed, staring at the bird on the roof opposite. For some reason, she didn't feel like she had a choice, no matter what he said.

A booth made from bulletproof glass. Four metal doors, heaviest weight category. More than ten surveillance cameras. Emelie was standing in the little reception-like room known as central guard.

The man on the other side had close-set eyes and squinted at her so intensely that, to begin with, she thought he had such bad vision, he couldn't actually see her through the reinforced glass.

He pressed a button, and a speaker crackled to life.

"And you are?"

"We spoke on the intercom just now. I'm a lawyer. Emelie Jansson. I'm here to meet a client."

"Do you have any ID?"

Emelie fished her driving license from her bag.

"Have you been appointed?"

"No, I'll be registered as private defense."

"Private?"

"Yes, Detective Inspector Johan Kullman should've passed the message on."

"Right . . . ," the guard mumbled as he started tapping away at the computer behind the thick glass. "There we are . . . private defense . . ."

Emelie could see black-and-white surveillance images on some of the other screens. Lifts, entrances, booths. Soon, she would be face-to-face with a suspected murderer.

The rooms reminded her of a hospital, the main difference being that it smelled different and all the doors were closed. She'd handed her visitor's permit to yet another guard, and after that they'd buzzed her through three more nine-hundred-pound doors. She thought about what would happen to all these electronic-locking mechanisms and those shut up behind them if there was ever a fire.

Section six: the hospital wing. On the wall, there was an old poster with information about CRISIS—Criminal Rehabilitation

Into Society In Stages. A woman who, judging by her name badge, was named Jeanette Nicorescu came to meet her by the entrance. Emelie couldn't tell if she was a prison warden, a nurse, or a doctor.

The room he was in had no windows. The floor and walls were covered in plasticky material, painted pale green and white. It was hard to imagine it had ever felt fresh. There was a hospital bed in the middle, two cushioned seats next to it. The light was flush against the ceiling. Emelie could guess why: no one would be able to hang themselves from it, or use the cable to injure any of the guards. Or their lawyer. Though today, the thought was slightly absurd—the young man in the bed was hardly in any state to hurt anyone.

Aside from a big red mark on his forehead, she couldn't see any visible injuries. He looked peaceful, his eyes closed, like he was sleeping. His hand was on top of the covers, and one of his fingers was connected, by wire, to a machine by the bed. It was probably measuring his heart rate. Another machine seemed to be doing an EKG.

Emelie sat down in one of the chairs.

"Is he completely in a coma?" she asked.

"No, not entirely. We measure it on a scale—the Glasgow Coma Scale—and that goes from three to fifteen. At three, there's no verbal or motor response; below eight often means the patient is on a respirator. At fourteen, patients can walk, stand, and talk, but they're still extremely confused. We think he's somewhere between eleven and twelve."

"That sounds pretty good, then?"

"Yes, but only time will tell whether he'll get any better."

"Can I talk to him?"

"Maybe. It depends how he's feeling. He has spoken, but he was obviously confused and disoriented. He has a head injury, and that led to a number of smaller cranial bleeds, but the doctors don't believe they're so bad that he needs to be operated on at present. That's why he's here, in section six."

When Jeanette Nicorescu left and closed the door behind her, the room was quiet. Every now and then, Emelie heard the sound of footsteps in the corridor outside.

Nothing happened. She thought about her dad. Then she went through the night's events again: how could she have been so stupid that she'd punched her own neighbor? Imagine if he reported her to the police? Or kicked up a fuss with the housing board? She *had* to calm down, control herself. Maybe she was working too much, or just needed help destressing. She knew what she'd tried in the past.

For some reason, her thoughts drifted to Teddy. She wondered if he knew she'd just become a lawyer. And if he knew—why hadn't he been in touch to congratulate her? He worked for the firm from time to time, after all.

She leaned forward over the bed. "Hi, I'm Emelie Jansson. Your lawyer."

The young man didn't move.

"Can you hear me?"

She watched him. He was slim, and his blond hair seemed unwashed. He had thin lips that looked like they'd been drawn in with a pen and a ruler. Kullman had told her his name was Benjamin.

There was a rushing sound from somewhere in the ceiling, maybe a waste pipe from one of the toilets on the floor above.

"Please, Benjamin. Give me a sign if you can hear me."

She got no reaction.

The digital graph on the machine was calm and steady.

Emelie stood up to leave. She wondered how you went about defending someone you couldn't even communicate with.

Then she heard a faint voice from behind her. "Teddy," it said.

She turned around. Benjamin's eyes were still closed.

"What did you say?"

His voice was weak, but she had no trouble understanding him. "Get Teddy to understand."

6

A morning walk. Gainomax and a coffee from 7-Eleven. Fifteen-minute phone call about Nikola with Linda: he was out of the young offenders' institute now. She was already worrying herself to death, had no idea how to deal with him.

Teddy went over to see his nephew and congratulate him on being out. Nikola had locked himself in his room. Teddy knocked. "Can't an uncle give his nephew a hug?" But Nikola just mumbled something about being too hungover right now.

Linda suggested they go for a walk instead so that Nikola had a chance to rest. They walked along the water's edge on Linavägen, up toward the little harbor. The garbage cans were overflowing with the detritus of student parties.

"I wanted to apologize for what I said last time, Teddy. That the only thing I wanted was for Nikola *not* to be like you."

"It's okay, don't worry."

"I'm worried about him, though. I wouldn't be able to cope if he went back in."

"Hopefully he's learned something this past year."

"I don't know. Can't you talk to him? You're the only one he listens to."

Maybe she was right. But at the same time—they needed to have a functioning relationship even when he wasn't around, otherwise it would never work. Still: he had to help out. See Nikola, spend some time with him, maybe even find him an apartment, a job. But his nephew was nineteen now. He and he alone could live his life.

Teddy took a shower. When he came out, he saw he had a missed call. Emelie had called. It was the first time in more than a year he'd seen her name on his phone.

He listened to the message. Her clear voice. "Call me back as soon as you can. It's important."

Of course he'd get back to her. He just couldn't figure out what she wanted.

Last time he bumped into her, it had been in the elevator in the Leijon office. She'd been carrying a laptop case in one hand, and she'd tried to ignore him at first—looked the other way, pretended he didn't exist. But that was pretty hard when one person was waiting in an open elevator, and the other was just outside.

"Hi, Emelie. It's been a while."

She'd stepped out of the elevator and twisted to avoid brushing up against him.

"How are you?" she had asked as Teddy stepped into it.

"Fine. You? Working hard?"

"Like always."

Teddy had said: "Take it easy, you look a bit pale."

"*Transparent lawyer*, not exactly unusual in these parts. I promise not to haunt you down the hallways."

Teddy had pressed a button. The doors had closed between them. He'd been able to smell her in the elevator. Her scent reminded him of lemons.

He'd asked for sixty thousand kronor for the Fredric McLoud case. After payroll and tax, that left just under half of it to be paid out by Leijon Legal Services. Still, it was enough to live on for a few months; he didn't have an extravagant lifestyle. Magnus Hassel was happy with the "operation," as he called it.

Teddy had reported back to him yesterday.

The chain of evidence was the most important thing. Teddy

had a video recording of the bag being handed over on his phone. The woman had stated that McLoud had been carrying the bag. And finally, in the clothing shop, while they'd both been hiding out, Teddy had checked the contents of the bag and transferred some of it to his own. For analysis.

"I guess there won't be a deal now? Your client is hardly going to want to buy McLoud's company?"

Magnus laughed. His fondness for art seemed to have gone crazy lately. On a shelf behind him, Teddy could see something that looked like a greenish vagina made from plastic and marble.

"Teddy, Teddy, Teddy, you're new to this world. Of course there'll be a deal. The chances increased dramatically thanks to your work."

Teddy didn't understand. He'd just collected enough material to land the CEO at least two years behind the same bars that had locked him up.

"Fredric McLoud is an extraordinarily good CEO," said Magnus. "The only difference now, with the information you've given us, is that our client's going to pay two hundred million less for his company."

"What, some kind of blackmail?"

"Here at Leijon, we never let a client down. Remember that, Teddy. If we see an opportunity to do a better deal, it's our responsibility to take it. I call it haggling. It's just what happens in business. The more you know, the better the deal's going to go. Would you listen to that, I just rhymed."

"I've been appointed private defense counsel for a young man accused of murder," Emelie said when he finally called her back. Her voice sounded tense.

"I didn't think you worked in that field. Is this through Magnus?"

"No, and it's not from anyone else at the office, either. The suspect requested me, but the whole thing seems really important."

"And you said yes?"

"Oh, yeah, didn't I say? But as *private* defense."

Teddy himself had never had a private defense counsel. Usually the only people who did were those with plenty of money.

"Who's paying?"

"No one. I decided to do it pro bono. There are two alternatives in Sweden. Private or public defense."

"I know, but why . . . ?" And suddenly, he understood. "Leijon doesn't know you've taken it on, do they? It hasn't been made public."

Breathing pause.

"Right," said Emelie. "And no one can find out, in case it's dropped. The suspect's name is Benjamin Emanuelsson, by the way. Do you know who that is?"

Emanuelsson.

He said: "Can I call you back in a few minutes?"

Harenpark. Saturday. Teddy had gone there four months ago, on the anniversary of Mats Emanuelsson's death.

They always took this route to the metro station, the Emanuelsson kids. The snow was already lying thick and white on the ground between the swings and the sandbox, but the gravel path had been sanded.

The kiddie pool was full of frozen leaves. Teddy didn't know much about Mats's suicide, but he'd wanted to wait there today. See whether anyone walked that way.

The snow was swirling in the air. It almost seemed to be rolling forward, an impenetrable mist rising from the ground, about to swallow up him and his memories.

Teddy had kidnapped Mats Emanuelsson. He'd also been convicted and spent eight years in prison for doing it. And then, in the middle of his sentence, Sara had told him that Mats had killed himself.

Sara. He tried not to think about her. He still didn't know why things had ended the way they had, other than that something didn't make sense. She'd suddenly just cut off all contact with him.

Teddy had a rough idea of what Mats had been subjected to during the kidnapping; he'd seen certain things, and above all he'd heard Mats himself talk about it during the trial. Teddy wasn't surprised it had swallowed him up. And the fact he'd committed suicide hadn't so much shocked Teddy as grabbed hold of his heart. Until Loke Odensson, his old friend from the slammer, some kind of computer genius these days, called him to say that the real reason he'd been hired to kidnap Mats Emanuelsson was because a couple of kiddie fuckers wanted to shut him up. Because they were afraid that some information Mats had somehow come into possession of was on a hard drive. Teddy had done it for the money, hadn't had a clue about the other stuff. But it made no difference. Not now. He, Teddy, had helped the predators.

He'd waited in the snow for four hours.

Eventually, they appeared, both of them. Maybe they were on the way to see their friends. He'd watched them walk along the path. A young man, a teenage girl. It had to be Benjamin and Lillan. Mats's kids. Teddy was standing some distance from them. They didn't care he was there. They probably didn't recognize him, weren't expecting to see the man who'd done eight years for kidnapping their father there, of all places.

He caught up with them.

"Wait."

They turned around at the same time.

"My name's Teddy Maksumic. Don't be scared."

Lillan's eyes looked like they were about to pop out of her head, and she started to reach for her cell phone. Maybe she wanted to call the police. Benjamin took a step forward, as though to protect her. But they didn't leave.

"I just wanted to say that I'm sorry for what I did to Mats. If I could turn back time, I'd do anything to stop it from happening," Teddy said.

He tried to see if they were listening, if they understood what he was saying.

"I didn't know what they wanted from him, and I didn't hurt

him. That was the others. Not that it's an excuse. I kidnapped your dad. For that, I'll always be guilty."

He'd thought only about what he wanted to say, nothing else. He hadn't thought about what he'd do next. The three of them were unmoving, like shy children waiting to be told they could leave.

After a minute or so, Benjamin had said: "Why did you find us?"

"Because I was tricked."

Teddy hadn't had anything else to say after that. He bowed slightly, and turned to leave.

And now, four months later: Benjamin, accused of murder. The kid had been twelve when Teddy kidnapped his father. He was twenty-one now. And he'd asked Emelie to be his lawyer.

The whole thing was so strange, it almost couldn't be true. But Emelie wouldn't make something like that up.

What the hell had happened?

7

Nikola was in bed. Not like when he'd been on leave before. Then: at Chamon's or one of the other guys' places. No, this time he was at his mom's. Maybe it was home now.

He was lying in the fetal position, curled up under the covers.

He should be ecstatic. No doors being locked at nine in the evening. No room searches. No checking for booze, pot, porn. No Sandra, Anders, or any of those other idiots constantly nagging at him.

But still, he felt fucking awful. Threw up three times in a row. There was nothing but bile left in his stomach now. That, and a bad feeling. He hadn't even felt up to opening the door when Teddy dropped in to say hello.

It wasn't just some winter sickness bug, either. It wasn't too many smokes. Not some bad food—however much he wished it was. It wasn't even last night's partying—he hadn't been that wasted. He knew what it was.

He was Nikola Maksumic—the nephew of Najdan, aka Björne, aka Teddy. He was a free man.

But he was sick with worry.

Last night Chamon had been serious. Gone all out, generous, invited the guys. Booked a table at Yama's Bar on Saltsjögatan. Chamon, Yusuf, Bello, and four other guys.

Chamon: on form. "You pay for the food yourselves, but the

drinks are on me. Our man's out!" Nikola wondered where he'd gotten the cash from.

They eyed up girls, flirted with the waitress, talked to familiar faces who came over to the table. Södertälje wasn't exactly a metropolis—honestly, it was just a big suburb of Stockholm—and they were Yusuf's guys, the whole group of them. If you were in Yusuf's gang, you were in Isak's. An air of respect around the table.

They ate steak, drank beer.

Chamon brought over the shots after the food.

Chamon waved a rolled-up five-hundred-krona note in the air and hissed that he had enough Charlie for everyone.

He ordered a bottle of champagne—shouted, "Moët and Chandon's my middle name."

Chamon: didn't care about anything but having a good time. Climbed up on the chair. Yelled so loudly you could probably hear him out on the street: "*Kas b'houbouk* to the Bible Man! Welcome out."

Thoughts from last night spun through his mind.

Nikola: a fraud, a wannabe tough guy fooling them all; a weak, dickless kid.

What the hell was wrong with him? Why couldn't he just be like the other guys? So confident. Act chilled. Act crazy. Head high, oozing authority.

He should be the happiest man in northern Europe. Instead: just an overanxious loser.

He didn't get why it wouldn't pass; he was almost twenty, for God's sake. But somehow, he knew it never would. The same thing had happened plenty of times the past few years. He hung out with the boys. He did jobs. He talked about wanting to move up, do more, be part of the big jobs.

But at the same time, he was so fucking scared.

He could never tell anyone. How he felt. That he didn't want to be part of Isak's trial.

That he was a weak fucker who dreamed of wimping out.

The others had been busy doing lines in the toilets. Nikola had done one himself about half an hour earlier, the rush starting to subside. Now he was standing by the bar. Alone.

A girl pushed her way in next to him and tried to order. The bartender ignored her.

"Lemme help," said Nikola. He leaned over the bar.

"*Hey*, man. This girl here wants a drink."

The bartender cocked his head: gave him a who-the-fuck-d'you-think-you-are look. Then the idiot's eyes widened. He came over and took the girl's order like a nice little lamb. Nikola turned around: Yusuf was behind him.

The girl's name was Paulina, and she was only seventeen. Technically, she wasn't allowed in the bar, but she was clearly using an older friend's ID. She told him how she and her friends had been having a night picnic down by the marina on Viksängsvägen, and that they'd been drinking "space boxes."

"What's that?" Nikola asked.

"A boxie," Paulina replied, giggling.

"What's a boxie?" Nikola asked.

"You don't know what a boxie is?"

"No."

"Box wine, y'know?"

They laughed. Paulina had brown eyes.

She said: "Is it true you speak Syriac?"

In Södertälje, lots of people his age knew him for that reason alone. He nodded, used to the question. "I grew up with these guys."

"Impressive. I can't even speak Polish, and both my 'rents are from there. Is it true your grandpa read you the Russian classics when you were a kid?"

Nikola nodded to that, too, but more cautiously. He wondered how she could know. He changed the subject. Started talking about who she was there with.

He looked around. Now Chamon and the others were circling them like hyenas. All waiting for him to pounce on his prey: he deserved a fuck tonight. He hoped they hadn't heard Paulina's last question.

He'd really rather just stay there *talking* to her the rest of the evening.

That was his other big lie: he wasn't just a scared motherfucker. He'd never had sex, either.

The bed felt uncomfortable. His mom had gone out with Teddy.

Tomorrow was the day. Isak's trial would take place. He didn't know exactly where or when it was going to happen. Chamon didn't, either. That was how it always was—no one knew anything before the last minute. But tonight, Nikola needed to sort something out; he knew that much: it was part of the job.

He really should've been working at George Samuel's today, but honestly: the way he felt, it had to count as being ill. Plus, George Samuel Electrical was in Åkersberga, that was more than a fucking hour away. How exactly did they think he could keep working there?

He looked at one of the framed photos on the bookcase. Linda when she was younger, wearing her student cap and a bright blue summer dress. She looked happy, and Grandpa was clearly proud. Nikola had been born a year later. Once, when Nikola was eleven, she'd blurted out that Grandpa hadn't been as happy after that.

"Why?" Nikola had asked. "Grandpa loves me, doesn't he?"

"Of course he loves you, more than anything else on earth. But he wanted me to go to university, and he didn't think I'd make anything of myself once I had a kid so young."

Nikola remembered how he'd replied: "Twenty isn't young, Mom. You'll see when I'm twenty. Maybe I'll own the whole of Södertälje by then."

He was even a fake in front of his mom.

At three in the morning, Chamon had staggered over to him. The place was closing. The girl, Paulina, had left more than an hour earlier.

"She was totally hot for you, man. Why didn't you take her home?"

"I don't know."

"No biggie. Time to go. The party continues."

Nikola didn't know what he meant. The only places in Södertälje still open after three were the underground clubs—but you didn't go there to party, just to play cards or dice.

"What are you talking about? Back to yours, or . . . ?"

"Nah, like hell. I said I'd organized some special effects for you, didn't I? We're off."

Almost all the others had left. Some too wasted, others too high. Some with a bit of tail. Yusuf had gone to Bårsta to play cards. But Bello was waiting outside.

People were pouring out of the place. Nikola really wanted to just go home. He was tired, wasted enough, and didn't know what Chamon meant by special effects.

Bello made a couple of calls. Five minutes later, a battered old Ford Focus pulled up. Chamon opened the door. "Our own taxi service."

They left Södertälje. Nikola had never seen the driver before, but Chamon seemed to know him. Up onto the highway. Ten minutes. Then they turned off at Norsborg. Shit—Nikola was usually the driver. But not tonight.

"What're we doing?"

Chamon grinned. "Something tasty. Just for you."

The air was cool.

Chamon took out his phone: made a call in English. "We are here now. What is the code?"

Nikola looked at his boys: they looked like they'd just won the jackpot.

The elevator didn't work. The stairwell stunk of piss. Chamon's laugh sounded like a badly tuned moped. They rang the bell.

The woman who opened the door was wearing some kind of dressing gown. "Welcome," she said, hugging Chamon.

The apartment: a studio with a kitchen. The walls were bare, and there was a single bulb hanging from the ceiling. On the floor, a double bed. The sheets were crumpled. The place smelled of perfume and jacked-off dick.

Chamon led them into the kitchen and closed the door. His eyes glittered. There was a stack of unwashed plates in the sink.

"Okay, we all get a go, but you're up first, Nicko. However long you want. I did a sweet deal with Darina."

He opened the door and pushed Nikola out. "Congrats, man." They closed the door behind him.

The woman was sitting on the edge of the bed. When he looked closer, he realized she wasn't a day older than he was. Pinkish lipstick and high-heeled shoes. Dark eyes and dyed-blond hair, at least two inches of growth at the roots. It looked weird: her heels and dressing gown combo.

"So, you are Nikola?" she asked in English.

"Yes."

"What do you like?"

His face burned. He was standing about three feet away from the hooker. It felt like she could read his mind.

"It is first time?"

Nikola nodded.

"Sit down."

He sat on the other side of the bed. Darina moved over to him. He felt a hand on his shoulder. She started massaging his back.

He wanted to get up and leave, but he had no idea what he would say. For some reason, he thought of his uncle: an image of a visiting room in a prison somewhere. Nikola and Linda on a two-hour visit. He was maybe fourteen. Teddy's voice: "You take a bit of me away with you every time you come to visit. I love you for that." His uncle had been locked up for eight years. Nikola wondered what he'd done about women?

After a few minutes, Darina took a firmer grip on his shoulders and turned him toward her. She took off her dressing gown. The light was lousy. Her body looked gray. Her breasts were small, almost triangular.

She lay down on the bed in front of him and held out a tub of lube.

"I help you," she said.

Nikola took the tub. He was on his knees on the bed. Unbuttoned his jeans. Closed his eyes for a second.

Right then, the door flew open. Chamon came in.

"*Abri*, sorry 'bout barging, but we got a problem."

Nikola did up his pants.

Chamon: "We gotta go. Yusuf's got trouble in Bårsta. Some motherfucker banging on about him cheating. We've gotta go help."

Nikola climbed down from the bed.

It felt as though he was swaying.

Stockholm County Police Authority

Interview with informant "Marina," 11 December 2010

Interview leader: Joakim Sundén

Location: Älvsjö Centrum

MEMORANDUM 2 (PART 2)

Transcript of dialogue (continuation)

JS: You said that during 2005, you had gambling problems and that Sebbe threatened you, that he wanted three million kronor back in two weeks.

M: This is still totally off the record, right?

JS: Absolutely. It's just for me, so I can build on it. You're giving me information, that's all. I'm the only one who knows about you, and you have immunity. I'd like you to keep going through everything.

M: Okay, okay. I'll try.

I had no idea how I would get the money for Sebbe together. Even if I was having one of the best weeks at the club and online, it'd be virtually impossible. I'd never even won a tenth as much money in such a short space of time. But I had no choice.

So I phoned in sick and stayed home playing all day—for some reason, I didn't want to spend too much time in the club. It felt embarrassing in front of my friends there. And so no one I knew in that world would realize I was spending so much time on those sites, I registered new usernames.

The days passed. I was hoping Sebbe would change his mind, give me more time, but I couldn't even get ahold of him.

I've played lots of games in my life, but the ones I played in those two weeks were the craziest. I took risks I'd never taken before, at levels I'd never even dreamed about, and just in Pot Limit Omaha rooms, mostly against Chinese and American players. The wins weren't steady, though. One day I brought in sixty thousand euros. The next, I lost thirty thousand.

I forget games quickly, but there's one I'll never forget. I'd managed to get about a million kronor, and I was in a no-limit room on a site called Poker Kings.

It was a hell of a hand, and we were playing stupidly huge stakes. When the hand started, we each had fifty thousand euros in chips. I placed big blind, a thousand euros. Everyone folded, apart from small blind, who hung in. I checked, a queen and seven, both diamonds. The flop was ace, queen, four—two of which were diamonds. The other player, Balrog666, checked, and then I raised like a fool—ten thousand euros. For some reason, I was sure my queen was good enough, since Balrog666 should've raised if he had an ace pre-flop, but if he'd found something, a pair of fours, for example, I knew he'd keep going to the end—he, or she, I don't know, did it all the time: overestimated the value of their hand. That's why I raised like I did—worst case, I'd still take the fifteen hundred euros already in the pot. But that bastard went *all in,* completely unexpectedly. He could've just as easily had as great a hand as the pair of fours. Like I said, I'd played Balrog666 a few times before, and he or she was normally cocky at first and then careful toward the end, but they did some crazy bluffing sometimes—it was impossible to tell right then, because they seemed to be going for it with all their chips. I just thought: Okay, let's do this, I've only got one chance. So I called it, forty thousand euros. Balrog666 had a double ace. Insane. Do you know poker?

JS: Only vaguely.

M: The chances of that bastard sitting on double aces were tiny, especially since he hadn't raised before the flop. But he'd tricked me. I was in serious trouble. I was about to flake out. I didn't know what to do. I'd probably just lost more than I'd managed to bring in over the past few days.

I held my breath, closed my eyes.

Then it was the turn. It was a diamond. Do you understand?

JS: No.

M: The cards I'd been dealt in my hand, they were both diamonds. At the flop, two more diamonds came out. And then another one. I had a flush. As long as it didn't all go wrong on the last card, I'd take the whole pot.

JS: What happened?

M: It was a glorious six. I took the money. A million kronor.

JS: Wow.

M: Yeah, it was fantastic. I almost started believing I'd manage what Sebbe wanted.

But I didn't have much time left, and I couldn't bank on always being that lucky. So I started resorting to different methods. First, I tried to sell our car online, a Renault. A few buyers came to look at it, but they thought a hundred thousand kronor was too much. So I lowered it to ninety, and then some other people turned up, wanting to buy it for eighty.

I sold my stereo and the boat from our place in the country. I even sold the sofas and chairs from out there, too. I couldn't touch the house and the property itself, because they were in Cecilia's name. I sold my shares in Nordea. I increased the mortgage on our apartment by three hundred thousand. I couldn't get any more than that because we already had a big mortgage. Then BlueStep loaned a further two hundred thousand, at nine percent interest. They took the last of the apartment as security.

I took out ordinary loans with Konsument Kredit and Collector. I thought that if I filled out the forms and sent them off on the same day, they might not see the other's decision and be willing to give me more. I even begged two of my best gaming friends, Bosse and Boguslaw, to loan me some money. They realized I was serious, but I never told them what it was about.

With two days left, I'd managed to win close to a million and a half, and I'd pulled together more than eight hundred and fifty thousand by selling my life and mortgaging my family. But I still wasn't quite there. Sebbe wanted his three million on a plate.

So that's when my forty-eight-hour race started. I planned to join the real high-stakes rooms online, not take any breaks. I told Cecilia I had some really important work thing and that I'd need to stay in the office for the next few days. She didn't really understand that kind of effort at work. She worked as an administrator for the county board.

"But you've been ill," she said, putting her hand on my forehead. "Has your fever gone?"

I didn't like lying to her, but at the same time, I could hardly tell her the truth. I pushed her hand away.

"I still don't feel great, but there are a few things I need to take care of. It's nearly summer, and I'll be finished with this, so I promise not to put off taking a vacation because of work this year. Maybe you should just go out to the country now?"

Cecilia smiled her crooked smile, the one she normally used when she didn't quite trust me but wanted to show she'd understood anyway.

"Okay," she said, "but do you promise? Four completely free weeks with us this summer?"

I kissed her on the forehead. "Absolutely," I said, trying to sound calm.

I had four different sites open, two games on each. I'd never tried to play that many at once before, but I wouldn't make it otherwise. So I loaded up with coffee, PowerBars, and energy drinks. I slept three hours in the middle of the day and two in the early morning, all to maximize the amount of time I had with the big guns in the U.S. I used eyedrops once an hour and drank a huge amount of water. I put five spoonfuls of sugar in every cup of coffee, played Beethoven's sonatas on the stereo, and set an alarm on the computer to remind me to get up and stretch once an hour. It would've been a catastrophe if I got a cramp in my arm or back just then.

I'd never played better or more intensely ever before. It was like all my experience and mathematical ability fell into place. I started to see patterns in the very basis of the game. I could see structures in my opponents' games that I hadn't even thought to look for before. I understood the very essence of Omaha, the heart of the game. I outclassed them all.

But time ran away like the energy drinks I was downing. I'd stopped getting up every hour. There wasn't time. Sebbe would be back that evening.

Forty thousand euros left, roughly four hundred thousand kronor.

Then he turned up in one of the rooms, or maybe it was a she. Balrog666.

I realized it was my chance. Balrog666 wanted to win back what he'd lost a week earlier. He'd play high, and that was exactly what I needed.

It was insane. We were both taking risks like newbies, but the whole time I was playing with my new understanding of the game. The feeling of being on a higher level than the others.

After two hours, I'd managed to bring in another hundred thousand or so. It was great, but I wasn't there yet.

I was running on caffeine and sugar and sheer determination. My eyes were watering, my head was pounding. I didn't bother going to pee even though it hurt. You can't underestimate the power of the adrenaline that starts pumping in a good game.

I noticed how Balrog666 was getting more and more careless. With half an hour to go, it was just the two of us left.

I had the chance to win the rest of the cash I needed. It would all be over.

I could shut down the computer, wait for Sebbe's call, and then just lie down and sleep.

I had my moment. A chance I had to take, I went all in. I could just see it, how there might be a couple of hundred thousand left over once I'd paid Sebbe. How I'd be able to repay the debts to my friends and maybe buy back the furniture for the place in the country.

But instead, I lost more than forty thousand euros.

I died.

Sebbe called an hour later.

"You got my money?"

"Absolutely. Nearly. I've practically got three million. Just give me another day, I'll fix it."

"Mats, what exactly is it you don't get? I want all my money, and I want it tonight. Now."

The click on the other end of the line was like a gunshot.

Ten minutes later, there was a knock at the door.

I was so relieved Cecilia and the kids had gone away. I peered through the peephole. It was him—Sebbe. Maxim was next to him.

"How're we gonna fix this, then?" was all he said when he stepped into the hallway.

His eyes were like a shark's. I remember that one of my legs started to shake uncontrollably. But then I took a deep breath.

I did actually have an idea.

It was ten in the evening, the start of my new life—the reason I'm sitting here with you now, more than five years later.

Memo continued on separate sheet.

8

The gym. The rhythm. Left hand first.

Clean shot. Always draw back the fist the same way it had come. Power from the hips. Strength in the stomach.

Boom, boom, boom.

Like a cobra.

Left-right-left. Always keep your guard up. Always twist your foot with the punch, stay steady.

Focus on your target. Feel your range. Ignore the other girls' determined faces. Everyone was landing punches like machines around her.

Forget everything else.

She just didn't know how well it was working today.

Jossan was always going on about CrossFit and HIT—high-intensity training. She said that in twenty minutes flat she could burn calories and increase her strength more quickly than in any other exercise she'd tried. And she'd probably tried every kind of yoga going in this city, every kind of group training class at SATS and Balance, plus the firm's own running club, led by Jacob Lapin, the former marathon runner.

But in Emelie's world, nothing came close to tae kwon do.

Right-left. Hook-uppercut-elbow.

Her fists hit the pads Leo was holding up. *Mata, mata, mata.* He was holding them at head height, shifting around the blue rubber floor, and Emelie followed his movements. Chin against chest.

Eyes on the pads. Breathing through her nose. Back leg moving first with each step. *Million Dollar Baby*.

When Leo asked them to wind down and stretch on the mats, her arms were shaking.

Emelie's luck: the Husgrens negotiations with the Chinese had broken down that morning. Disappointed, Magnus had declared: "You can all put down your pens. We can't charge any time from now on. If anything happens tonight, I'll let you know. Keep your phones on."

She should prepare for the court proceedings that would probably take place tomorrow. But she couldn't concentrate. Why hadn't Teddy been in touch?

At first, when Benjamin mentioned him, she hadn't understood.

"I only know one Teddy. Do you mean Teddy Maksumic?"

Benjamin had nodded once.

And then he had disappeared again.

"Everything okay?"

Leo tapped her on the shoulder as she was about to go into the changing room to shower.

Emelie had been training at Östermalm's Martial Arts Center for two years now. It was a genuine basement club, nothing fancy, just white-painted walls, the usual blue flooring, and sandbags hanging from huge hooks on the ceiling. There were photographs from Leo's golden years in reception, back when he'd won gold in tae kwon do at the Swedish championships and taken bronze at the European games.

"Yeah, think so. Why?"

"Just now, at the end, when you were going for me, I don't know . . . it was like you disappeared a little. Like your killer instinct was gone."

Emelie wiped a drop of sweat from her forehead with the back of her hand. She hoped he wasn't right.

She was last into the showers. Most of the other girls just went home in their workout clothes; they lived nearby. It was ten in the evening.

She grabbed the showerhead and directed the jet of warm water at her legs. She needed to shave them, but she hadn't had time these past few weeks. Jossan would laugh if she could see them, start calling her the gorilla or the fur coat or something like that. Not that it mattered at all. Emelie had no plans to show her legs to anyone in the near future, and besides: if that anyone couldn't handle a few hairs, that was their problem.

She dried herself slowly with the hand towel. Suddenly she heard the muffled sound of her phone in her bag. She saw Teddy's number.

"Tell me what this is about," he said bluntly.

"You know Benjamin Emanuelsson?"

"Maybe."

She explained. About Benjamin's condition, about the very little else she knew. She told him what he'd said to her. The *only* thing he'd said to her: "Make Teddy understand."

It was weird, everything about it.

9

It was time for him to do his thing. He'd been in bed all day.

In the end, Yusuf had called. "Thanks for yesterday, man—what a fucking mess. Great you came and told those sons of bitches where to go. Ha-ha. Gonna need you to go get the stuff now."

"Where?"

"Gabbe's."

Nikola's stomach turned. Hot weapons. He'd been asked to go to Gabbe's and pick something up before, but back then, it hadn't been *him* the piece was for.

He didn't know what Gabbe was called, aside from Gabbe, but it had to be a short form of Gabriel. The guy lived alone in a terraced house on Gårdsvägen in Enhörna.

And you only went to Gabbe's at night.

He looked up and down the street. It was dark, but he could see the lights from a bar in the distance. Only two of the streetlights were working. Dumb kids must've been dicking around with rocks or something. There were low wooden fences and hedges in front of the houses, and behind them was a line of enormous BBQs. Nikola could respect people who blew money on their cars. But BBQs—what was that all about?

He peered over the fence outside Gabbe's part of the street: a wooden deck, two plastic cane chairs in place of a grill.

The house looked dark inside. He rang the bell.

"What fucking *kelb* rings the bell this time of day?" came a voice inside.

Gabbe opened the door. He looked exactly the same as last time Nikola was there. Messy, gray-flecked hair; unshaven. He rubbed his eyes. He was wearing shorts and an untied dressing gown, but his stomach and chest were so hairy, you could've mistaken it for a wool vest.

"Who're you?"

Nikola said: "You don't remember me?"

Gabbe grinned. "Yeah, now you mention it. Little man who speaks our language. Come in."

The living room had a high ceiling. Gabbe had switched on only one light in the hallway, so the rest of the house was dark. The walls were covered with Syriac saints and church fathers.

"The TV's been giving me grief. Can you help me tune the channels?"

Nikola just wanted to get what he needed and run.

"Yeah, later."

Gabbe stopped. "I've reached a point in my life where I don't need any more technology. I'm happy with what I've got. But then Yusuf and all those other guys turn up, and they bring me a load of TV equipment, phones, those tablets for surfing the web, stuff like that. Tell them I don't want any of this crap."

"You wanna give it away, I'll take it for you." Nikola smiled.

"Give away, no, no. I sell it to the guys at Vincent's. All I want's a good signal on the sports channel, and something I can listen to music on, you know, a bit of Walter Aziz and Noman Hanna."

"Okay, but where's the stuff?"

Gabbe didn't move. "You know, I don't need to be able to record films on my phone or play all those complicated games on it. I'm fine, y'know, it's enough. You understand?"

"Yeah, yeah, you don't have to get a new phone, you know. Just keep the old one?"

"Mmm . . . but my grandkids send so fucking many pictures all the time. I want to see photos of them while they're still cute, but they just take pictures of what they're eating, their nails, clothes, the coffee they're drinking."

Gabbe kept the door to one of the bedrooms locked. He opened it with a key he fished up out of the earth in a flowerpot.

They went in. There was a bed in the middle of the room. Other than that, it was empty. Gabbe went over to the wardrobe and opened the door. There were six boxes inside, stacked in two neat piles.

Nikola helped him lift them out onto the floor. Behind them, there was some kind of handle. Nikola hadn't noticed it until Gabbe started pulling on it. The wardrobe clearly had a false back.

"I'll show you, my little friend," Gabbe said, and he pulled the fake door to one side.

This hadn't happened when Nikola was here before, last year. Back then, he'd just been handed a bag with something heavy in it.

The sickest thing he'd seen. If he got arrested now: so many years in the slammer, he'd probably be as old as Gabbe when he got out.

There was stuff hanging up on the back wall of the wardrobe. He could see what it was. Two Glock 17s, three AK-5s, a Kalashnikov, a couple of Sig Sauer pistols, a Mini Uzi. On the floor, a box of what was either dynamite or explosive putty. But craziest of all: a massive thing, a greenish beast. It looked like a drain pipe with handles.

"What the hell's that?"

Gabbe grinned. "Carl Gustaf—pride and joy of the Swedish army. It's what Isak used when those fucking idiots from Stockholm tried to take over here."

Nikola knew what he was talking about. Two dead, four cars blown to pieces.

Gabbe said: "I thought you'd like seeing what we've got."

Nikola could feel the nausea rising again. He needed two pistols, that was all.

10

He'd been to Emelie's place once before, but that had been in the middle of the day. Tonight, her apartment seemed messier. There were clothes draped over the chairs in the kitchen. He recognized the design of the seats, but couldn't remember the name, kryp something. Tights strewn across the floor in the hallway; newspapers, magazines and bread crumbs covering the kitchen table; and unwashed coffee cups sitting proudly on the counter. Teddy was surprised: hadn't thought she would be able to cope with this much disorder. He could still clearly smell her perfume, just like he had the last time they met. The scent of a person: to Teddy, it was more unique than DNA. She seemed to be freshly showered; her hair still looked damp.

"Sorry about the mess. I'm having some work done," she said, folding up a couple of newspapers.

"Yeah? Where?"

"Just kidding. It's been crazy at work lately. Hence the mess."

Emelie wrung out a cloth in the sink and wiped the round kitchen table. "Want a drink?"

"You got any whiskey?" For some reason, he felt nervous.

"No, but I've got port, cognac, and gin."

"I'll have a cognac, then."

Emelie pulled out a chair, climbed up onto it so she could reach the cabinet above the fridge, and took down a bottle. She was barefoot, and he noticed that her toenails weren't painted. It wasn't an especially good cognac, and she didn't seem to have the right glasses. But it had a rounded taste, and Teddy could feel himself relaxing.

It had been her idea for him to come over. He realized that if they were going to meet to talk about the case, it couldn't be at Leijon. But still, he didn't understand. Why would Mats Emanuelsson's son want anything from him? What was he meant to understand?

"You could come over to my place, we can talk?" she'd said.

"You didn't seem so keen to talk last time I saw you."

"What do you mean?"

"I mean in the elevator in the office, a few weeks ago."

"You weren't, either. But things are different now. We're both stuck in the middle of this."

Somewhere, deep down, he knew she was right: they were in it together—thanks to Benjamin's request. He had a debt to repay to the Emanuelsson family. An eternal bad conscience.

Teddy leaned gently against the rounded back rest—it creaked, like it was about to collapse under his weight. "Where do we start?"

"I guess you can tell me what this is all about, and then you could help me ahead of the hearing tomorrow, if you have time?"

He leaned forward again and tried to find the right words. "I'm not sure I know. But I probably know more than you."

And so he told her about the kidnapping nine years earlier, and about how Sara, a guard he'd met in prison, had started to root around in the case. Later, Mats Emanuelsson had committed suicide. Teddy told her how he'd asked a friend, Loke Odensson, to look into what, exactly, had happened, and how Loke had eventually managed to hack his way to finding out that Mats had somehow come into possession of a computer or hard drive containing information that someone absolutely didn't want to get out. Something to do with men sexually abusing small girls.

Emelie listened in silence as he talked, but he couldn't work out whether what he was saying surprised or scared her. Or both. It was almost one in the morning. He caught sight of his reflection in the kitchen window. His dark blond hair was getting long now. He'd only cut it twice since he got out. Snub nose, big eyes—they looked even bigger in the window, like dark spots into which his reflection had vanished. The tooth he'd had pulled out when he was inside, replaced by an implant that would've taken him four months at Leijon to pay for—but which had been covered by the insurance he'd been given in return for working for the firm.

Teddy took a sip of his cognac. "I don't really know what Benjamin wants, but I know I regret the shit I did to his dad nine years ago. I told him that. And now he's accused of murder? There has to be a connection to what happened to Mats, otherwise he wouldn't be asking *me* to understand anything."

Emelie shook her head. "What kind of connection?"

"No damn idea. I know zero about Mats's life until he killed himself. All I know about is the kidnapping."

Five minutes later, the two of them were hunched over the few documents Emelie had been given. The prosecutor's application for a remand order was very brief. Right now, Benjamin was just being held, but in order to keep him any longer than four days, the court would have to rule on whether he could be remanded.

A completed form.

APPLICATION

Crime and grounds for remand

* Benjamin Emanuelsson's continued detention is sought on suspicion of murder, or accessory to murder, 15/16 August, Värmdö.
* There is a risk that the suspect, whether by removing evidence or through some other means, may hamper the investigation.
* For the specified crime, imprisonment of no less than two years is stipulated, and there are no clear grounds to oppose custody.
* It is of particular importance that the accused is taken into custody pending further investigation of the crime.

Notification has been given to the accused by Detective Inspector Johan Kullman in accordance with Code of Procedure 24:11.

Emelie hadn't been given the actual memorandum containing
the investigation that the prosecutor wanted to submit in support
of her claim.

"It's completely ridiculous. How am I supposed to defend my
client when I'm not even allowed to see the material?"

"Welcome to Sweden," Teddy calmly replied. "You'll get the
remand memo tomorrow, right before the hearing. That's how it
always is."

"Why do they want to keep someone unconscious in custody?
That's even weirder."

That, Teddy agreed, was unusual. He'd never heard of anything
like it. But he knew what they were thinking. "He's been talking a
bit, and they know that. So from the prosecutor's point of view, he
could get in touch with someone and try to influence the investigation. We're talking about a murder here."

They were fumbling around in the dark—Emelie hadn't even
been given information about what evidence there might be
against Benjamin. They talked about whether someone else could
be involved, and what that might mean for Benjamin. They read
legal commentaries on the presumption rule. Because of the serious nature of the crime—the lowest sentence was definitely higher
than two years in prison—it was up to Emelie to show that there
was no clear basis for keeping Benjamin in custody, not the other
way around.

She moaned about the reversed burden of proof: the prosecutor asserted something—she had to prove *the opposite*. But Teddy
simply shook his head.

"Like I said, welcome to Sweden. If the prosecutor says you've
kidnapped the king in a spaceship, they'll remand you for it, and
that's that. End of story."

They talked about why the identity of the deceased hadn't been released and what the police technicians would be looking for at the crime scene out on Värmdö.

"Your only chance of getting him out is the rule of proportionality," said Teddy.

"You mean the whole thing of him being unconscious?"

"Exactly. It's hardly proportionate to keep someone who can't even piss by himself in custody."

They moved on: to whether Emelie could request more of the meager material, to the order of the hearing, whether members of the public would be permitted. How the case should be presented. How Benjamin's position should be clarified.

"Do you actually know what he'd plead?" Teddy wondered as he refilled their glasses. "They must've tried to interview him?"

"Yeah, the policeman and I sat on either side of his bed, and Kullman asked him some questions. Benjamin didn't reply to a single one. I don't think he could. So honestly, I don't even know if he admits or denies it."

They were sitting close together, looking at Emelie's laptop.

Teddy was helping her write some kind of script. How she should express herself. Which questions she needed the prosecutor to answer.

The glowing numbers on the microwave read three in the morning.

She closed the lid of her laptop and got up.

"I feel like I'm as ready as I'll ever be. Thanks for helping. You've really picked up a thing or two during your err . . . career in the court world."

They went out into the hallway.

"It's good if any use comes of it," Teddy said as he put on his shoes. Emelie was watching him with a strange look in her eyes. Like he was funny somehow.

He opened the door.

"What?"

She leaned against the doorframe.

"I've got a question," she said. The hallway outside was dark.

The light from the apartment was like a halo behind her head. "You don't want to stay over, do you?"

Stockholm County Police Authority

Interview with informant "Marina," 11 December 2010

Interview leader: Joakim Sundén

Location: Älvsjö Centrum

MEMORANDUM 2 (PART 3)

Transcript of dialogue (continuation)

M: We drove through town in Sebbe's Porsche, just like we'd done two weeks earlier. Sebbe and Maxim were talking like nothing had happened, completely normal. About football, mostly.

"What a fucking hero, man. First, those two saves after Andriy Shevchenko's chance at the end of added time, then the penalties. Did you see the game? The Liverpool fans never stopped singing 'You'll Never Walk Alone,' even though they were three-nil down at the end of the first half."

"Does Pamela Anderson sleep on her back, or what? 'Course I saw it. Y'know, Jerzy Dudek, he didn't realize Liverpool'd won, even when he saved that penalty. I saw an interview with the guy afterward."

"I know, what a player. Slavic king. Stood up to shot after shot, didn't care about anything else, just saving them. Did that whole spaghetti legs thing."

But there's no doubt about it—something would've happened to me if I hadn't gone with them. I thought of Benjamin, my son. He was about to turn eleven, 2005. I didn't want to miss a single early-morning car ride across the county to stand on the sidelines in the freezing rain, cheering him on as his team lost yet another match. I thought about Lillan, too. She was six and liked bead necklaces and paper planes more than anything. She could sit for hours with her pearls, making patterns with the beads, different color combinations. But if she made a mistake, she might cry for ten minutes, throw them all over the room. I longed for those tantrums, for being on my knees, clearing up the aftermath.

I saw Cecilia's abandoned coffee cups on the kitchen table, too, and her makeup in the bathroom. Right then, I missed those cups and powder brushes so damn much.

Sebbe and Maxim didn't seem to care that they'd parked the Porsche in a handicapped space. But when we got out of the car, I saw they had a permit on the window. Sebbe grinned. "No point taking any risks. You sort this out for us, I'll get you one, too—you can have a discount."

My job at KPMG was in the bookkeeping department, on the seventh floor. I worked on the accounts for small- and medium-size businesses. Our tax and financial consultants worked late, sometimes 24/7, but the pace was slower in my department, less pressure. At eleven at night, the only person you risked bumping into in the absurdly open-plan office was the cleaner.

Sebbe snorted and groaned. He fit in about as well among all the screens, computers, and desk chairs as a lion in a swimming pool.

"You work here?"

"Yup, every day. But I took some vacation and called in sick to try to get your money together."

"How tragic. What the hell is this place?"

"It's an ordinary office."

"But what do you do here?"

Maxim yawned. "Dream about life and jerk each other off because they're never gonna live it."

I took them to my desk and tried to keep an eye on the elevator doors at the other side of the room. No one could come in now. There'd be too many questions.

"That true?" Sebbe asked. "You jerk each other off?"

"Most people here are married with kids."

"Keep up. You know what I mean. You want what we've got."

I didn't want to joke around with him. I just wanted to get out of there as quickly as possible.

Sebbe paused. "What the fuck's your problem? You pissed off or something?"

"No, no. But I need to concentrate to sort this out for you."

"Fine, but you can still answer. You want what I've got, don't you? Right? You wanna live like me and Maxim. Not spend all day trapped in this fucking cage, talking about the finale of *Survivor,* your shitty flexi-fuel cars, and your boring kids' school reports. You want to fucking live, don't you? Get plenty of pussy. Like free men."

He was breathing more quickly, but I still didn't know how to reply.

"You pretend you're happy, but you're really just pathetic losers. Other people control your lives. Shit, I feel so sorry for you all."

Eventually, I said: "But I'm a gambler. That's a little bit of your life."

Sebbe turned to me. His eyes were red, like he was the one who'd spent most of the past few days awake.

No, I thought. No more now.

But he said: "You're fucking right."

My plan was to borrow money from a couple of clients I was doing the bookkeeping and invoicing for. We called it the Plus Package. I had access to bank fobs and account details. But first, I printed out . . . By the way . . . we're clear I'm telling you this freely, and there won't be any legal repercussions, right? And my name won't ever come out? Right?

JS: Yes, that's the agreement. I never hang my informants out to dry.

M: Good. Okay, well, I printed out a few invoices I'd created. Processed them properly and then transferred about a hundred thousand kronor from each of the different companies. It was simple. And no one would ask any questions until *maybe* when they did the end-of-year accounts, but that was at least six months away. I was planning to pay the money back by then—I could do it by sending credit notes from the made-up suppliers.

Sebbe was pacing behind me. Maxim was next to the computer, watching everything I was doing. All I could think was that I didn't have a choice.

The whole thing took less than half an hour.

On the way out, when we were in the elevator, Sebbe smiled. His fillings didn't look Swedish—they were all gold.

"You should be proud of yourself, pal."

The weeks after that were like normal, but I had loads to do at work. I was relieved, though. Back from hell. I'd made it, paid off my debt. I wouldn't have to deal with Sebbe or his henchman again. All I needed to do was to win a bit more money so I could at least pay back my friends.

Cecilia and I went out to eat one night. Her parents had come down from Umeå to see the kids, so we were covered for a babysitter. I remember we went to King of India on Pontonjärgatan.

It was close to our place, and Cecilia loved Indian food. I had nothing against it, but the air conditioning in that place was lousy. Last time I'd been there, I'd had to send my jacket to the dry cleaner to get the smoke from their sizzling plates out of it. This was back when the smoking ban had just come into force in restaurants and pubs, but it didn't seem to have made any difference in that place.

"It's so good to finally get out," Cecilia said when we sat down. I really agreed with her.

She ordered some vegetarian dish I can't remember the name of, and I had a chicken tikka masala. We talked about the kids, like usual. Now that life felt better, I wasn't longing for them the same way I had been. I felt more like just getting away somewhere with Cecilia, experiencing something different for a week—you know, just walking around, going to museums, whatever.

I looked out the window, toward the park on the other side of the street.

Spring, five years ago. I don't know if you remember it? It snowed like hell in February, and then the bad weather dragged on for ages. But then the sun arrived, boom, just like that, and everything turned green, and quickly, too. I remember thinking that it matched my life well.

"I had a call from the bank yesterday," Cecilia said. "They were asking me questions."

"About what?"

"Loans on the property, savings, stuff like that."

I immediately felt sick. The panic welled up. I just said: "Do we have to talk about that tonight?"

And then it was summer. A few weeks into our vacation, my phone rang while we were down at the beach. I'd just been windsurfing, and all my equipment was lying on the sand.

I recognized the number.

I didn't pick up.

It rang again a few hours later, from a blocked number this time. I went up toward the trees and answered.

"It's me, pal."

"What do *you* want?"

I looked over at the kids. Lillan was sitting at the edge of the beach, playing in the sand. There's something magic about the combination of water and sand, it never gets old. Benjamin had a friend with him, out on the jetty. They were diving into the water and then bobbing back up with smiles on their faces. Then they climbed out and jumped back in. Ordinarily, I would've enjoyed watching them.

"I need you to help me with something," Sebbe said.

"I've already done more than I should've. I'm not playing poker anymore."

"I doubt that. The bug always comes back, you know what they say."

"There's no reason for us to talk."

"Of course there is. I need your help. I just told you."

"With what?"

"Bit of this, bit of that. I want you to come to Clara's tomorrow. Know where that is?"

"Yeah, but it's the middle of summer. I'm on vacation, in the country. And I don't want to see you. You can understand that, right?"

"Come on, Mats. Why so boring? Someone fucking with you at your place in the country, or what? We used to work so well together, until you tried to screw me over. And if you're going to be such a pain about it, I might just have to let your lovely employer know what you got up to when Maxim and I were with you a couple of weeks ago. It's a rule of mine. You gotta keep a hold on people in this world. And I happen to have a pretty fucking tight grip on your balls."

I looked over to Cecilia and the kids again. A few other families had spread out blankets on the grass and the sand. I wondered what they would think of me if they knew.

That was just the start. Jesus . . .

Clara's wasn't my kind of place. I didn't go out for beers with my coworkers or my best friend, Viktor, very often, but when we did, we chose sports bars. O'Learys, Ballbreaker . . . Stockholm's got plenty of places with that British kind of feeling, TVs on the walls. I just think it's all so much easier if you can talk about what's going on on the TV every now and then.

Clara's had screens, too, in the entrance, showing close-ups of different drinks—the drops of condensation on the outside of a glass, mint leaves, ice cubes, straws.

We walked through the place. The black floor looked dusty with the lights on full. The red seats, they were probably faux leather, seemed to be flaking. The only impressive thing was the bar, it must've been at least forty feet long, with bright shelves along the walls and bottles of spirits being lit up from behind. It was like there was some kind of competition to come up with different flavors of Absolut Vodka: blackcurrant, peach, mandarin, vanilla.

Sebbe punched some numbers into a keypad by a black door at the back of the bar. We went in.

It was an office. There was a huge desk, room for two people on either side. It was covered in papers, folders, laptops, plastic pouches, hole punches, pens, and mini calculators. Empty beer glasses too. Water bottles, lighters, and I saw at least two knuckle-dusters.

There were framed photographs and diplomas all over the walls. Pictures of a man and woman on vacation in various places. Pictures of a kid. Pictures of more and less luxurious cars. The diplomas were even more varied: second dan in karate, Pub of the Year as nominated by stureplan.se, AAA credit rating, Best Restaurant from *Dagens Nyheter*.

There were pictures of the man from the family photographs hugging different celebrities: Joe Labero, Mikael Persbrandt, Princess Madeleine, Madonna.

A young woman was sitting by the desk. She didn't look much older than twenty-five, and she had long, dyed-blond hair, dark brown eyes, and unnaturally big breasts.

Sebbe kissed her on the cheek. "This is Michaela. She'll be helping you with whatever you need."

The girl lit a cigarette and slowly blew out smoke through her nose.

"What exactly do you want from me?" I turned to him.

Sebbe moved a pile of papers from an armchair and sat down.

"You didn't bring your phone, did you?"

"Of course I did."

"Aha, because that's my second rule: no private phones in here. At all."

"Why not?"

"You'll see soon enough. They're listening everywhere these days."

Sebbe held out his hand, and I gave him my phone. He pulled off the back cover and took out the battery.

"It's all very simple, Matte. You're a smart guy. You might not like me right now, but I've actually always been pretty cool with you. You're gonna help us fix something."

"Fix?"

"Exactly."

"Meaning?"

Michaela took over. "It's nothing to worry about. You're going to help me. I've been doing this for a couple of years now, ever since I left school. We're handling money. That's what you work with anyway, isn't it?"

"This is just too much, Sebbe," I said. "I paid back every single krona I owed you. You can't ask for more."

Sebbe lit a cigarette. He took a deep drag on it. "You know the score," he said.

The smoke made my eyes water.

11

The club on Storgatan wasn't normally open this time of day. It was only four in the afternoon. But this was a special occasion: they were using it for *the thing*.

Nikola and Chamon, on the door. Chamon with the list of names, and Nikola with the metal detector in his hand. Each with a piece hidden inside their jacket. The list: pretty much pointless— only eight people other than Isak would be coming. Nikola and Chamon knew exactly who they were. But Isak wanted things done professionally. He and Chamon should be polite, in shirts and jackets. Go by the list, just like the real thing.

Metim Tasdemir arrived first, with his number two, Christian Tasdemir, also known as Lil-Crille, even though he was as big as a Range Rover. Two of Metim's gorillas were waiting outside. They went in a few minutes later. Isak wanted it that way: for one side to arrive fifteen minutes after the other, so they could avoid any trouble out on the street.

"Could you stand with your feet apart, and hold out your arms?" Nikola asked as clearly and calmly as he could.

They must've felt like they were in the slammer: he moved the detector over their arms and legs, backs and stomachs, shoulders and dicks. Degraded, humiliated. But on the other hand, Metim and his guys were probably more used to being searched before they got into places than they were being let straight in. Still: it felt risky—these guys weren't the kind of men you messed with.

But Isak had told them in advance. They knew the score.

The detector started to beep over one of Metim's pockets. Nikola saw Chamon straighten up, saw Metim's gorillas freeze. But again: Yusuf had told them Isak's rules about how things would go. "Arrive at four sharp, no metal objects, not even phones. I don't want any crap here. You come as you are, like men."

Isak didn't compromise: that's why he deserved the respect he got.

But now: bleeping like crazy over Metim's pocket. He had something metal on him. It could be anything. *What the fu—*, man.

Metim moved slowly, but he didn't take out whatever had set off the detector. He smiled, but his eyes were dead.

Nikola felt for the weapon in the holster under his jacket. He and Chamon had tested the Glocks that morning. He remembered the recoil, how he'd gripped the butt with both hands, how Chamon'd told him to keep his left thumb behind the right one so he didn't get it caught.

Metim stood still.

Breathing through his nose.

Lil-Crille moved toward Nikola.

This wasn't normal.

They were preparing for something.

But Nikola couldn't see himself using his damn pistol on anyone. What would happen if Metim pulled one on him?

He felt the cold metal against his fingers. His hand was practically cramping. Chamon's forehead was covered in sweat.

Nikola thought back to what Simon cunting Murray had said.

Chamon took a step back and shoved his hand under his jacket.

Eyes fixed.

The stink of sweat.

The tension in the room: a thousand megawatts.

Images flashed before Nikola's eyes: scenes from Hollywood shootouts, from *real* shootouts, when Chamon shot that guy in the woods.

Fuck—he blinked. Had to hold back now.

Metim grinned. "You gotta keep your cash somewhere." He took out a silver-colored money clip with at least twenty five-hundred bills in it.

Nikola breathed out. Relaxed.

"Leave that here, and take the coins out of your pocket," said Chamon. "Isak wants the detector as quiet as a busted phone."

Metim grinned again. "This is worse than a trip to the Kumla fucking bunker."

"Yeah, exactly, just like in the slammer, so now I want you to drop your pants and bend over."

Metim jerked back.

Chamon said: "I'm kidding, man."

Nikola tried to turn away. How could Chamon be so ballsy?

Twenty minutes later, everyone in place.

Danny, the other one involved in this conflict, had arrived with his boys at the right time.

The two card tables were pushed up against one wall, and the office chairs that normally stood around them had been pulled forward into a U. Nikola thought back to a group conversation he'd had at Spillersboda. The obligatory how-can-I-change conversation. *"I overreact sometimes, but I feel like I'm getting better at controlling myself." "I've started to understand myself, I've had a pretty tough time. But that doesn't give me the right to attack others."* The guys all suddenly had something angelic about them. They spoke softly. They all knew how to deliver the bullshit.

Isak greeted them all. They quickly got down to business. Nikola couldn't follow everything: tons of talk about people he didn't know, business deals he had no idea about. But on the other hand: he was just the helper's helper. In truth: pretty incredible he'd even been allowed in—he had less Syrian blood in him than, like, the king. And he'd been out of the game for over a year. But Yusuf was Isak's man, and Yusuf trusted Chamon, who trusted Nikola. They'd grown up together. One man's friend was the next man's friend. One man's enemy the next man's enemy. They were soldiers in the same army.

They were blood brothers.

The trial was important: they had to sort out the conflict with a capital "C." Two months earlier, one of Metim's cousins had been eating at the Kebab Palace. Danny's cousin had been there, too. There was some pushing and shoving in the line: one of them had said all the usual crap about the other one's mom. Then one of them had grabbed a Heineken bottle and smashed it into the other's forehead. Two days later, someone had driven past Metim's uncle's dry cleaner's and unloaded more than twenty shots into the place with an automatic weapon. Some of the bullets even got stuck in the extractor fan in the restaurant *on the other side* of the building. People said it was a miracle no one had died. And then a week after that, a masked man had gone into a restaurant where Danny's cousin was eating lunch and taken four shots. He'd been hit in the groin, the knee, and the thigh. The guy would be in a wheelchair the rest of his life.

The police had just stood by, no idea what to do; they'd been watching from the sidelines for ages, it made no difference what happened—this city had its own rules. You didn't talk to the pigs, because pigs are disgusting. Everyone was shitting themselves that things might escalate, full-blown war. If pistols and AK-47s weren't already war.

So they'd turned to the church. The Syrians did that sometimes—the Orthodox Church was strong in Stockholm, and the priests could mediate. They had power. But things were inflamed, and Danny's family were Assyrians; they weren't religious the same way. So when the priest suggested reconciliation, Danny and his boys had just gotten up and left. It was an insult to the community. Metim swore at the God-defying cunts who didn't even respect Jesus.

Talk in town got worse than after the triple murder a few years earlier. People in the neighborhood stopped going out at night, mothers half ran their kids home from day care, and the dry cleaner had to fight back—no one wanted to run the risk of having Kalashnikov bullets tear up their cashmere sweaters.

This shit had to stop, and there was only one way to do it if they wanted to avoid a mass tragedy—they had to get Mr. One to solve the problem, the guy who actually ran this town.

That was what *real* men did. This was their trial. Isak's trial.

Metim's voice was dark, gruff. He had authority, too, no doubt about that. But he knew the score. He had things to explain; it was his cousin who'd called the other guy's mother a *sharmuta*.

"He was wrong. I talked to him, serious, no worries about that. He shoulda sorted it out through me. Instead, he got a concussion, in the hospital for two weeks, he's got a two-inch scar down the back of his head and can't even tie his shoes himself, his balance is so fucked up."

Patches of sunlight darted in through the high windows. The men had ten minutes to give their side of things. Isak looked like a wax figure, the way he was sitting there listening to them.

These were guys who wouldn't hesitate for a moment before smashing someone's head in just for *breathing* disrespect, but now they were here, like dogs on leashes. Under Isak, everything was civilized. He was this city's only real bigwig.

They went through it all again. Talked about the injuries. About the different debts. Metim wanted to be paid. Danny did, too.

Chamon winked at Nikola and whispered: "Bet they all want Hook to pay 'em, too."

Hook: the man with a nose so bent, it looked like a hook. A real player—professional poker star, gambler, betting specialist. Always at the bookies on Hornsgatan. The thing was, his game had been seriously off lately, so now he owed millions left, right, and center. Nikola knew of at least eight people who wanted their money back from him. And for that reason, he was probably the safest man in town—no one had the balls to clip him, because then someone else would automatically be angry that they'd lost their money. "Safe as

Hook—no one safer," that was what Nikola and the guys usually said about people with protection.

An hour later, they were done talking. All eight left the room. Metim and his guys went down to the entrance, Danny and the others into the kitchen.

Isak was left alone. Chamon and Nikola were still leaning against the wall.

"Come here," Isak said.

The dark patches beneath his eyes looked like bruises. The only hint of life in his face came from the reflection of the bright patches of sunlight on the floor.

"You guys listen, understand everything?"

Chamon slowly opened his mouth. His lips looked dry. "I tried," he said in Swedish. "I reckon he was wrong."

"Who?"

"The one who smashed Metim's cousin's head with the bottle. It was too much."

"Maybe, but did that give them the right—in your opinion—to almost slaughter his father, brother, aunt, two of their kids, and three customers at the dry cleaner's?"

"No, guess not, but the guy could've cracked Metim's cousin's skull with that bottle."

"What about you, Nikola? You're a Slav—what do you say?"

Nikola had hoped Isak wouldn't turn to him.

He tried to clear his throat, but it sounded more like he was about to have a coughing fit. All that came out was a gurgling sound.

"I think . . ." He coughed again. "They were both wrong. Maybe they canceled each other out?"

"Is that what you think?"

Nikola's hands were behind his back. His fingers were twitching like a speed freak on a grand's worth of junk.

"Think so."

"Don't *think*, Nikola. You gotta have an opinion. And never back down from it." Isak nodded but said nothing more.

He called the men back in. They sat in silence. It was like

everyone was making a special effort not to interrupt. Isak stared down at the floor. His fat gold watch glittered: number one topic among Nikola's friends. Audemars Piguet, Royal Oak Offshore. The rumor? It'd cost more than two mil. He was wearing a dark blue Nike sweater and Adidas pants, three white stripes down the side. The comfier the clothes, the harder the guy.

He looked up. "I've made my decision."

Nikola noticed that Danny's eyes were locked on Isak's.

"We're already under pressure in this city. You know what I'm talking about—this Hippogriff project of theirs—his pigs are stopping our cars several times a week just to fuck with us, they're running extra tax checks on every company we set up, sending the bailiffs and the migration authorities after our families, inspectors to our relatives' restaurants. That's their plan: *follow the money*. That's how they got Al Capone, you know that. Tax offenses, bookkeeping offenses, fraud, fucking about with informants, what a load of shit. When they can't pin anything concrete on us, they start acting like bitches. But whatever I think about that, we don't need any conflicts like you started. We don't wanna be another Malmö up here. You acted like idiots."

Isak turned his chair slightly, toward Metim.

"I'm saying that to both of you, 'cause that's how it is. We've got a rule that's worth more than fighting all the pigs in Sweden. Your cousin knows that rule, and he knew it three weeks ago, too. Everyone here knows how they're meant to behave."

Nikola felt like he was starting to understand.

"And *you* and your men know the rule, too. We haven't moved on that far. The politicians and journalists can talk all they want, but we never forget our principles. You know that. It's because of our principles that we've survived for thousands of years. We're the ones who built civilization as Europe knows it. And I don't give a shit if we call ourselves Syrians or Assyrians, Armenians or Chaldeans. When the others were running around, hitting each other on the heads with wooden clubs, we were inventing mathematics. While the others were busy raping women and children, we were developing astronomy. And because we've got our systems and our rules, we're still here. Those principles are our religion."

Isak turned so he was addressing both sides again.

"We respect women and children. That's the most basic rule. Someone who says something about someone's wife, daughter, sister, or mother hasn't shown respect. What's that mean? In this case, that it wasn't wrong to attack your cousin, Metim. It was their duty, actually, since he said what he did about another man's mother. Everything that came later was because he crossed the line. You understand?"

Nikola understood.

Isak continued: "So, my judgment is that your cousin should pay three hundred thousand to Danny's family in damages."

Everyone was openmouthed. The patches of sunlight had disappeared now. Their faces looked gray.

Deep down, they knew Isak was right.

Again: the faint scent of sweat. It was coming from himself. He hoped no one else would notice. The past few hours: super tense. But Isak had tied it all up. A judgment.

Danny's boys were just waiting for the money now. Metim had called for two runners to bring three hundred large. One of them had already arrived. Banged on the door, used the code. One normal knock, four quick.

Isak had the bag of dough in his hand. Ready to hand it over to Danny.

It would all be over in a few minutes.

Another knock at the door.

Isak gestured to Nikola, who went over.

One normal knock, four quick—the same code the first runner had used. And both Danny's and Metim's guys had used the same signal when they arrived.

One normal, four quick. Nikola unlocked the heavy metal door.

It flew open.

Two men in balaclavas rushed in. Nikola had no time to stop

them—he couldn't have stopped them. Balaclavas, automatic weapons in their hands, he couldn't see what type.

He dropped to the floor.

Isak yelled something from farther inside the club.

The two men ran in.

Their weapons spluttered. Nikola heard someone shout.

The sound echoed in his ears. He looked up. Had to do something.

He reached for his pistol, pulled it from the holster.

Got up.

Shit, he was shaking.

The place smelled of gunpowder.

He held the piece out in front of him. Arms tensed.

Some kind of fucking mass murder was going on in there. He had to help Chamon and Isak. Had to help the others.

He was so fucking scared.

Peered into the main room.

Two loud bangs. One of Metim's gorillas yelled. They'd shot him in the thigh—he dropped to the floor, groaning.

The robbers shouted for everyone to put their hands on their heads. One of them jammed his Kalashnikov into Isak's face. Told him to hand over the dough.

Isak answered calmly: "First of all, this isn't for you. Secondly, your mothers are whores."

You could've cut the silence in the room with a knife.

Nikola stepped in. He pointed the Glock at the man threatening Isak—his back: a nice big target. He'd caught the other guy off guard, too—even his piece was pointing away from Nikola.

Just a gentle squeeze of the trigger. One shot. He'd been practicing in the woods with Chamon just a few hours earlier.

It was self-defense, for fuck's sake. The men in the balaclavas had already shot one guy in the leg. They were threatening Isak. Threatening them all.

Shooting wouldn't be wrong. It was legal.

It was a must. But still, he couldn't.

For some strange reason, he thought of his grandpa, a picture in his head. A candle being lit for his grandmother.

"Nicko, man, blow him away," Chamon was whispering.

Slowly Nikola squeezed the trigger.

It felt weird.

"Shoot, for fuck's sake." Chamon again.

Nikola took a step toward the guy in the balaclava. Gun still raised.

The other man tried to turn around. Nikola: "Move an inch and I'll shoot your friend in the fucking head."

He pressed the Glock against the robber's back, between his shoulder blades.

"Drop it."

Nothing happened.

Deadlock. Nikola could feel the nausea rising. His body putting up a fight.

He pressed the gun harder into the man's back.

Then: a clatter. The guy dropped his Kalashnikov to the floor.

Nikola immediately turned to the second one.

But it was too late.

The two robbers moved fast, past him.

He should shoot. Take them out, one by one. *Bam, bam.*

He lowered his weapon.

The men sneaked out onto the street.

Nikola looked down. One of his legs was wet. Piss.

PART II

MAY–JUNE

12

The stairwell in Cecilia Emanuelsson's building had a certain smell to it. Like the fifties, maybe. Or something to do with dust. The wooden handrail wound upward. The tiles on the floor looked like granite. The waste disposal chute was taped shut. Before Teddy was sent down, people in this town had still used them. He wondered what Stockholmers did now. He threw his own trash into a container, which, for some reason, was always outside his door in Alby.

Cecilia Emanuelsson. He and Emelie were there to visit her. Emelie to talk about her stuff, Teddy to talk about what Benjamin wanted.

After what happened at Emelie's place yesterday, all he could think was that she hadn't acted like he'd expected—that somewhere, deep down, someone other than the rigid career girl was hiding.

"I need to go home," he'd replied to her proposal.

Emelie's eye had twitched. "Yeah—it's late, and yeah—we have the remand hearing tomorrow, but I think it would've been nice."

Teddy had shifted his weight from one leg to the other. He didn't know what to say.

Emelie had smiled.

Eventually he'd said: "Nah, I really do need to get home."

Cecilia Emanuelsson's apartment was in a building on Bränn-kyrkagatan in Södermalm. Emelie had called and briefly told her about Benjamin's situation, explained that he'd expressed an interest in Najdan "Teddy" Maksumic being involved. All the same, they'd agreed that only Emelie should be in the doorway when Cecilia opened the door. That seemed the politest, and safest, thing to do. Teddy would wait in the stairwell. She would be able to see him from the doorway, but he wouldn't be too close.

"Him over there, he can come in, too," Cecilia said when she opened the door.

She had good posture, was very thin. Her movements reminded them of a robot's, jerky somehow.

Emelie kept her shoes on, and Teddy decided to do the same—it was dry outside.

"I'm sorry, I know this must be really tough for you," Emelie said, and she took Cecilia's hand.

For a few seconds, Cecilia's face was calm, then she started to cry. Silent, stifled sobs. She lowered her head.

"I don't understand any of it, not a thing," was all she said.

Emelie laid a hand on her arm. "Let's sit down."

They went into the kitchen.

In contrast to Emelie's apartment, the place was clinically clean. The countertop and the blender were gleaming as though they'd just been polished. The wooden kitchen table looked newly sanded; the plants in the window were placed at precise intervals. Next to them, a number of brochures, neatly stacked. Aside from that, the place was completely devoid of things. No empty food packaging, no bread crumbs, no cutlery. Teddy couldn't even make out any specks of dust in the sunshine coming through the windows. The only thing giving the room any kind of character was a small, black cross hanging on the wall above the table.

They sat down. After a couple of minutes, Cecilia's tears stopped, and she sniffed: "Would you like anything to drink?"

Emelie asked for a coffee. Teddy was too tense for anything right now.

"Did Benjamin specifically request you as his lawyer?" Cecilia asked.

"He's only said a few words, and I think he has only a vague idea of who he is and exactly what's going on," Emelie replied. "But yes, he asked for me. My guess is that it's because he knows I've worked with Teddy."

Cecilia turned around and fiddled with the coffee machine. Teddy noticed that she was wearing slippers, the kind you normally got free from hotels.

Emelie continued: "And I'd like to add, I have permission from Rölén, the prosecutor, to come here and talk to you about how Benjamin is doing, but not about anything to do with the investigation itself."

"How is he, then?"

Emelie repeated the information she'd been given by the prison staff. She explained that Benjamin had specifically asked for Teddy. "Do you have any idea what he might mean by that?"

"No, I'm sorry."

The machine bubbled in the background, and the smell of coffee spread across the kitchen. Cecilia poured two cups. "We really fought, you know. And then this happens."

She was still standing at the counter. Teddy didn't know if she meant that she and the kids had fought to keep it together after Mats's suicide, that she and Mats had fought to make things work after the kidnapping, or if they'd fought within their relationship.

"Ehh . . . could I have milk, please," Emelie said when Cecilia showed no sign of being about to bring the cups to the table.

Cecilia opened the fridge: inside, the food was organized in poker-straight rows.

"Tell me. Why did they arrest him? What's all this about?"

"Like I said, I can't go into any details, the investigation is confidential at this stage. All I can say is that he's being held on suspicion of murder."

Cecilia put her hands to her face. Teddy couldn't tell whether she was crying again. He couldn't hear anything.

The coffee machine continued to bubble.

"My son's not a murderer. I don't understand. Who is the dead person?"

"We don't know, unfortunately."

"So what evidence does the prosecutor have?"

Emelie spent the next fifteen minutes trying to explain the process to Cecilia. That Benjamin might be held in custody for some time. She talked about the restrictions on him, about being kept in isolation. About how, since he'd just turned twenty-one, he might be facing a life sentence, but since he'd been seriously injured in the car crash, she thought he'd probably avoid that. She carefully avoided touching upon the prosecutor's so-called evidence, or whatever their suspicions were based on.

Teddy glanced at the brochure on the top of the pile in the window. He could see a picture of a mountain landscape. The colors were exaggerated, probably altered in some computer program. Over the picture, the words: *There is a before and an after pilgrimage / The Church of Sweden.*

Cecilia was sitting completely still now. Teddy wondered what she was thinking. What she knew.

Emelie asked if there was anything else she wanted to know. Cecilia got up from her chair and took the coffee cups over to the dishwasher. "No, not really. But call me as soon as anything important happens."

Emelie got up, too. Teddy's mouth felt dry. He'd been wondering how he should start. He thought about how he and Dejan had kidnapped Mats Emanuelsson nine years earlier. How heavy his body had been, how he'd struggled and tried to put up a fight.

"Teddy," Emelie said, "you wanted to ask some questions?"

He cleared his throat. "Yeah, Benjamin wanted me to look into all of this."

Cecilia didn't seem angry or reproachful. Her face was just full of sorrow, and she said: "But he's got a lawyer. Isn't that enough?"

"Maybe, but it's not enough for me. Benjamin wants to know something, he wants my help understanding whatever it is. And I plan on helping him."

Cecilia sat back down.

Teddy said: "What exactly happened when they called you to say they had Mats, that he'd been kidnapped?"

"What does that have to do with Benjamin being accused of murder?"

"I don't know, but I'd still like to hear."

"Right, but if there's anyone who should know anything about that, it's you."

"Maybe I do, but now I'm asking you."

"Money," she said with a sigh. "You wanted money in exchange for him."

Teddy wondered whether she was consciously lying, or whether Loke had been mistaken. Maybe Cecilia didn't know about the things Loke had found out. For the whole of Teddy's trial, she and Mats had insisted in interview after interview that the kidnappers wanted money. For normal people, avoiding the truth so consistently was no easy task.

"I found out that it wasn't about money, Cecilia. And I think you know what we really wanted in exchange for Mats."

She turned to the window and seemed to be staring at the building across the road. They could hear birds outside. A bus drove by down on the street.

"Cecilia?"

She turned to him. "It's nice, with the birds, isn't it?"

"Cecilia, what do you know about the kidnapping?"

She laid her hands on the table. "It's right, what you said. You wanted Mats's computer. But I still don't see what that has to do with Benjamin's situation."

"Why did you never mention the computer during the trial?"

"This is all I can say: all I know about that computer is that my ex-husband paid a terrible price for it. He had nothing to do with what was on it."

"How do you know that?"

"I just do. And I've got nothing else to say about it."

She got up, a sign that she wanted them to leave. It was clear that his questions made her uncomfortable. But Teddy had to try to understand. He owed Benjamin that much.

"When did you get divorced?" he asked.

"A few years after the kidnapping."

"Why?"

"Living together got too hard. Why?"

"That's part of all this, too."

"Of what?"

"Of whatever Benjamin wants me to understand."

"You'll have to explain the connection to me."

"I don't know what the connection is. Yet. Why did you get divorced?"

"If you really want to know . . . he changed, he became a different man than the one I married. And . . ."

"And . . . ?"

"I think he'd been having an affair."

"Do you know who with?"

"No, I don't, I was never sure. But I had my suspicions."

"He never told you? Didn't you bring it up?"

"Talking to Mats wasn't exactly easy. But I don't blame him."

"For what?"

"He was who he was, and I loved him until I stopped loving him. I was naive for such a long time, but lately I think I've started to understand what it was all about."

"What do you mean?"

"Well, this probably isn't something you know, but Mats was addicted to gambling. You often hear people talking about the spouses and kids of alcoholics or drug addicts, that they get addicted, too. But I was addicted to a *gambling addict*, someone who couldn't deal with his need to play. And everything that led to. All the self-deception."

This was news to Teddy. Sara had never mentioned that; neither had Loke.

"What kind of gambling?"

"He loved all kinds of games, but mainly poker, I think. He'd always been that way."

"Did he play for money?"

Cecilia turned to the window again. "For money? Oh yes, very often. The gambling was at the root of it all. I've realized he must've been living a double life, but now he's dead, and at some point, you have to forgive people. And there's one more thing I'd say about Mats: there was something in his relationship with the kids, there was a certain comfort there, he was the best father I could've wished for."

Cecilia closed her mouth. Maybe she'd said all she had to say.

But Teddy wasn't done, not yet.

"How did he kill himself?"

Cecilia went over to the kitchen counter and started to wipe the already-gleaming surface. "He jumped from a ferry, one of the ones to Finland. It was so awful. But I don't really know why. We weren't living together then. All I know is that he hadn't been well during certain periods. That was obvious."

"Hadn't been well how?"

"He wasn't always very stable, which is understandable given what you did to him. He got depressed. He was even hospitalized at one stage."

Cecilia's words cut deep—maybe Mats had never recovered from what Teddy had been a part of. Teddy almost regretted coming here. But he needed more. He said: "Do you, Benjamin, or Lillan still have any of Mats's things?"

Cecilia left and came back after five minutes. She was carrying a bag.

"Benjamin had this in his room for years. The police didn't take it when they searched the house."

Emelie bent down to look at the things Teddy was carefully lifting from the bag. A watch, a few small photographs, a key, an A5 sheet of paper, two ties, a pair of cuff links, a pack of cards.

They laid the objects out on the kitchen table. Cecilia moved away again, let them look for themselves.

The first photograph was of Cecilia, Mats, Benjamin, and his little sister, Lillan. It must've been taken some time ago, more than a decade; Benjamin looked about eleven or twelve. They were all wearing swimsuits—Mats was tanned. He was smiling, but there was still something drawn about his face.

"He's smiling with his mouth, but not his eyes—don't you think?" Emelie said quietly.

"I don't know," Teddy replied. "You can't tell who someone is from a picture. It's close contact that counts."

The sheet of A5 seemed to have been torn from a notepad. The handwriting was ornate, careful. Teddy read.

Don't blame me for everything that happened. Be stronger than I ever was. This has nothing to do with the divorce or with Mom. I love you all.

Dad

Simple words of farewell—Teddy tried to make out what they meant. It was clear enough what it was.

"This?" Emelie said, taking out another photograph.

Like the earlier one, it also showed the family, and must have been taken even longer ago. Benjamin looked about seven. Mats, Cecilia, Lillan in a baby carrier, and then Benjamin. They were standing on a moss-covered stone, trees in the background. Mats was holding up a box full of mushrooms.

Teddy picked up the picture. Someone had poked two holes where Mats's eyes should have been.

Later, outside, they stood opposite one another on the street. Teddy took a step forward.

Emelie took one back.

He said: "Want to meet up tonight?"

She took out her phone and started scrolling through it. "I've got tons of work to do. Plus I've got to go down to see my parents in Jönköping."

"How often do you see them?"

"Normally just at Christmas and over the summer."

"Is it a birthday or something now?"

Emelie's mouth looked taut. "No, I just feel like I need to see them."

"Okay, but we've got to talk things over sometime."

"Yeah, we should go out to the house in Värmdö and take a look there, too."

"Definitely."

"What are you going to do now?" Emelie asked.

"I'm gonna call Tagg, my old pal from the slammer. I'm going to ask him about Topstar."

"What's that?"

"The pack of cards in Benjamin's bag. Did you get a good look at it?"

"No, not really. I thought the farewell note and the holes poked through that photo were more interesting."

"There was a name on the back of the cards. it's a promotional pack. Topstar—I think it must be a club."

"Okay, but maybe they're Benjamin's?"

"Maybe, but everything else in that bag seemed to be linked to Mats."

Zinkensdamm Station. Farther up the hill, over toward Skinnar-viksberget, he could see the small, picturesque cottages still standing from years ago. He wondered who lived in them, these tiny houses in the very heart of Stockholm—his instincts told him it wasn't the wealthy. This wasn't their part of town; a different hierarchy ruled here, a different class system.

A man in ripped jeans and a Windbreaker was standing nearby, talking loudly on his phone.

Teddy thought to himself that he would have to help Nikola find a place of his own. And a job. He should visit his father, Bojan. He needed to call Tagg. Look into Mats's gambling. Get to the bottom of who'd been killed out on Värmdö. And above all, call Loke, double-check everything he'd told him about Mats's kidnapping.

The entrance to the metro station was gray, with huge fans in the ceiling. He turned around. The man in the Windbreaker was walking toward the station behind him.

Teddy stopped by the barriers, pretended to search for his metro card.

He didn't know what to think. Windbreaker man stopped, too. Peering over, almost. Like he was waiting.

Teddy took the escalator down.

He felt the back of his neck prickle.

The walls were filthy.

Step after step after step—the escalator was swallowed up by the ground.

He walked toward the platform. There were people everywhere. But the man was still there. Thirty feet behind him.

The train pulled in. Norsborg. Teddy didn't get on.

Guess what: the guy in the Windbreaker didn't, either.

Three minutes later, the next train rolled in.

They got into the same car.

Teddy stood up. Thought: What the hell's going on?

13

The area around the house almost looked abandoned. Not what Emelie had expected. The branches of the apple tree were sprawling, clearly hadn't been pruned for years, and there was already so much grass growing through the gravel that unless someone did something about it, the yard would be one big lawn before summer was over.

The house itself looked fresh, though. Painted red. Lots of intricate woodwork. She could see water in the distance.

Värmdö, Ängsvik: the house where the dead man had been found.

She'd tried to find out who owned it—it was registered in the name of a Spanish citizen, Juan Arravena Huerta, but she couldn't find any information about him, not on the Internet and not even when she called the Spanish authorities. She promised herself to keep searching: check the deeds. Look into who had owned the place before the Spaniard.

They pulled up on the gravel and climbed out of the car: Emelie, Teddy, and Jan from Redwood Security—the ex-cop who'd retrained as a private security consultant, who'd helped her with investigations in the past. Jan was dressed like he always was: blue shirt and jacket, both too crumpled to belong to an office monkey, but smart enough to give the right impression. His old pulse meter was gone, replaced by a smartwatch that looked like a mini version of a phone.

"Means my hands are free more often. Plus, it's pretty snazzy, too, right? You can change the strap. And it even keeps track of my health."

"Snazzy"? Come on, Emelie hadn't heard that word since she was about seven.

For the most part, Jan looked grumpy. Narrow lips and small, pointed creases at either side of his mouth. But he really wasn't the sullen type. Emelie liked him a lot.

She'd called him straight after the remand hearing and told it like it was: "I've kind of changed tack, taken on a criminal case. Would you do some work for me?"

What she didn't tell him was that she had no idea how she would pay.

In a few weeks, Sweden would fall into its annual summer coma. She and Jan had joked in the car on the way there: talking about new DNA techniques; Elias Ymer, the hope of Swedish tennis; and the latest epic Volvo ad. But not Teddy. He'd kept quiet.

Emelie thought about her proposition to him a few days earlier. She couldn't believe it had slipped out. It was just so obvious: Teddy wasn't her type. A former super-gangster. Jailbird. Loser. Maybe it was just the booze; she couldn't handle it very well when she was tired. Or maybe it was the stress, the fact she'd been flung into something unfamiliar, her first remand hearing the very next day. That had gone to shit, too. She was a newbie, completely green.

She'd talked to her client in private once the video-streamed hearing was over. He'd nodded when she asked whether he knew what had just happened, but exactly how much he'd really understood was another matter. He'd been lying quietly in bed, unmoving.

She'd sat down next to the bed anyway. "You know I haven't worked on this kind of case before, don't you? And that I've only been a lawyer a few days?"

Benjamin hadn't said a word.

"So honestly, I'm far from an expert in any of this. You should have someone with a few years' experience defending you."

His eyes had remained closed.

It wasn't just in relation to Leijon that what she was doing was risky. Benjamin Emanuelsson had been given full restrictions. That meant he wasn't allowed any contact with the outside world, and this also applied to Emelie. She couldn't just break the restrictions. But Benjamin had asked her to make Teddy understand. She wondered what that meant. Did involving Teddy break the restrictions? What if Benjamin was actually manipulating her to get rid of, or maybe even introduce, information that might influence the police investigation?

To put it bluntly: it wasn't just her job at Leijon on the line. It was her entire fucking career—her newly earned title, who she was. She wondered whether she was going mad: why she'd even agreed to take it on.

Was it worth it?

That depended on what Benjamin Emanuelsson wanted.

Who he was. What this was really all about. Who the *dead person* was. What had happened on Värmdö.

She'd tried again: "Benjamin, can you hear me?"

This time: a faint nod.

"Did you understand what I just said, about having me as your lawyer? Do you still want me?"

Again, he'd nodded.

The police tape was still stretched across the entrance. The 27:15 notice was taped to the door: *ACCESS PROHIBITED pursuant to ch. 27, § 15 of the Code of Judicial Procedure. Trespassers will be prosecuted.* But Emelie had permission from Rölén, the prosecutor, to take a look around. And Jan—her CSI guru, crime scene genius, her very own forensic super-consultant—maybe he would manage to find something the police had missed.

She thought about the remand memo she'd been given before the hearing. The police had found blood-spattered clothing in the woods. Clothing that might belong to Benjamin—and that might have the victim's blood on it. That didn't sound good at all. With any luck, the National Forensics Centre wouldn't take too long to analyze them.

Benjamin had been in custody for almost a week now, but she hadn't been given any new information about the case. That was just how things were in Swedish criminal proceedings, or so she'd been told. The prosecutor and the police conducted the initial investigation under so-called preliminary inquiry secrecy. Neither the suspect nor their defense counsel was allowed to know a thing before they felt they were done—until the prosecutor felt ready to present their preliminary findings. Most lawyers just waited patiently for their opponents to finish, but Emelie had other plans. She would try to get somewhere on her own.

Jan stooped carefully beneath the police tape. He was wearing latex gloves.

"Please don't touch anything."

He tried the handle on the outer door. It was unlocked.

They entered the house.

The place smelled musty.

A small hallway, no coats on the hooks. Maybe there hadn't been any to begin with, but in all likelihood, the police technicians had emptied the place.

They continued, deeper into the house. The kitchen was on the ground floor. It seemed pretty deserted. Jan opened cupboards and drawers. They were virtually empty. He found some cutlery and a couple of plates in the cupboards. The pantry was empty. The fridge, too. One of the windowpanes had been replaced with plastic.

Jan said: "The police probably took the window, and they'd definitely empty the fridge. But the rest seems odd."

"Why?"

"Let's move on."

The living room contained an armchair, a sofa, and a small wooden coffee table. An old TV on a bench. A lamp on the floor, and a bare bulb hanging from the ceiling. But there were no rugs, no pictures on the walls, no curtains, and no other lighting.

They stopped by the table.

Emelie pointed. "Well, we know one thing for sure: the victim was in here somewhere."

"Do you know who they were?"

"No, the prosecutor hasn't released that information, but it was a man. They probably haven't identified him yet."

Jan bent down and poked at some dark patches on the floorboards with a cotton swab.

"The body was down here somewhere," he said. "There's been a lot of blood on these boards, let me tell you. And here, too."

He pointed to the wall behind them. Then he got up, pulled out a camera, and took a few photos.

The stairs creaked alarmingly, particularly when Teddy went up them.

Upstairs, the house was even sparser. The three small rooms were virtually empty other than a bed and a small nightstand in each of them. The sheets were gone from the beds, but the blinds were still down. Again: no pictures, no curtains, no other furniture.

"It's *too* empty here," said Jan.

"What's that mean?" Teddy asked. It was the first thing he'd said since leaving the car.

"The police don't normally empty a place to this extent. They don't take the furniture, the pictures, and crockery."

"I think I can guess what that means."

"Me too," said Jan.

Emelie looked at the floral wallpaper. It looked like it had been there since the house was built, at least a hundred years earlier.

"Doesn't seem like this place was being used as a normal house," said Teddy. "There's not even a vacuum cleaner in the closet downstairs."

"Wait," said Jan. He bent down. They were in the narrow hallway again. Emelie stepped into the kitchen to avoid brushing up against Teddy.

This time, Jan didn't take out a cotton swab. He pulled out a flashlight instead.

They squatted down. Teddy's and Emelie's heads only a few inches apart. Jan took out a magnifying glass with his free hand, the flashlight still shining in the other.

Near the base of the wall, around eight inches from the floor, they could see four small, dark flecks.

"What do you think that is?" asked Jan.

"Dirt? Blood? Food?"

Jan asked Emelie to hold the flashlight as he took out a cotton swab and poked at one of the spots. Then he got up and fetched something that looked like a vial. He dropped liquid onto the cotton swab.

"I just added something called leucomalachite green—watch this."

The soft tip of the cotton swab looked brown.

"Then I add a little hydrogen peroxide." Jan dropped a different liquid onto the cotton swab using a pipette.

"*Et voilà.*"

Suddenly the cotton swab was blue.

"Those flecks on the wall are blood. And this chemical reaction only occurs with *human* blood."

Emelie bent down and studied the four small flecks again.

Jan pointed. "And they're not just any old shape, either. See that? They're smaller at the top, bigger and rounder toward the bottom."

He got up.

"Conclusions, anyone?"

Teddy cleared his throat. "The shape means they hit the wall from above. Meaning something violent happened in the hallway, too—not just in the living room. Someone injured a person who *wasn't* lying down or sitting. In other words: someone got injured here, while they were on their feet. But there's not a lot of blood, so it probably wasn't fatal."

Stockholm County Police Authority

Interview with informant "Marina," 15 December 2010

Joakim Sundén

Location: Haninge Centrum

MEMORANDUM 3 (PART 1)

Transcript of dialogue

JS: How are you today?

M: Still not great, actually. You know, if you go through what I went through, the old memories can come flooding back sometimes. Those days . . . I'm still not sleeping well . . .

JS: I know, but it's good you came today anyway. No one knows you're here, do they?

M: God no, definitely not.

JS: Good. Let's continue from where we left off?

M: Sure, fine, I was telling you about how I met Michaela for the first time in Clara's office, right?

JS: Right.

M: Okay, well, I started helping them toward the end of summer, 2005. Mostly in the evenings. Cecilia and the kids were going to be out in the country for a few more weeks before school started.

Michaela did her best to teach me, though I already knew most of it from my regular job. We started and registered businesses, came up with company descriptions and HQs. I sorted out addresses, churned out those OTPs people used back then, fobs and authorizations, did the accounting and looked after the formalities. It didn't take long to work out that Sebbe wasn't the end man, we were doing it for someone else.

After a few weeks, Sebbe decided I should go along to a meeting with a bank manager at Handelsbanken. It was the first time I'd be . . . fronting what I was doing.

But the minute I saw Michaela, I was worried. Maxim was waiting for us in the car outside. You can't just go into a meeting with a serious bank manager looking like she did—in super tight jeans and a pale top that was so low-cut that her fake boobs looked like they'd pop out at any moment, plus such high heels that even she—and I'm assuming she was used to wearing them—couldn't walk properly without something to lean on.

JS: Who exactly is Michaela?

M: Uhh, I don't want to get into that right now.

JS: Is she in a relationship with Sebbe?

M: Definitely not. A guy like Sebbe is hardly someone the women flock to.

JS: What about you, then, you and Michaela?

M: What does that have to do with anything?

JS: Just curious.

M: I promised you I'd be thorough, tell you everything. And I will.

JS: So you don't like women in that way?

M: I didn't say that. But I always planned to be faithful to my then wife. I don't really want to talk about this thing with Michaela anymore. That's just how it is. What I will say is that when I saw her on the street that day, I said: "It'd probably be best if we got you a different top or some kind of scarf."

She just looked at me like I'd suggested she have a sex change.

Fifteen minutes later, we were in the bank manager's office. Michaela had made an irritated-sounding call in Yugoslavian or whatever it was, and then run off to a fancy department store. She'd come back ten minutes later wearing a round-necked blouse. There were small jewels around the collar, shining like crystals. To be honest, I wasn't sure it was much better than what she'd already been wearing.

Anyway, the room wasn't exactly fancy. Just glass dividers separating us from everything going on at the counters a few feet away.

The bank manager introduced himself as Stig Erhardsson. He seemed nervous, and when he hung up his jacket, I saw he had big damp patches under his arms.

After some pleasantries, I took over.

"I'm here on behalf of Power Work Pool and Power Kitchen Pool, and our business is run by people who've been in the staffing industry for ten years now. Our goal at PWP, that's what we call ourselves, is to lease out a workforce to building firms and construction bosses across the whole southeast of Sweden. PKP is active within the catering industry. Our parent company in Sweden is called Power All Pool. We have other businesses, too, but we want to see how things go with you here before we move on to the others."

Stig played with his pen.

I had no trouble reading him—years of trying to interpret people's expressions around poker tables had certain benefits. The man just wanted to get out of there.

"Very good, and now you'd like to use us, if I understand you correctly?" he said quickly.

"Exactly. We have three companies that need transaction accounts, business accounts, and wage accounts."

"Okay, fine, we can arrange that right away. I'll introduce you to Gabriella Hernandez. She can help with all of the paperwork, and she'll be your personal contact here at the bank."

"Great. There's just one thing I wanted to bring up. It's sort of particular for us."

I explained to Stig Erhardsson that our principal owner and some of the businesses were based in the Baltic states. I told him that we were busy with some internal restructuring and had strategies for reducing our tax liabilities.

He nodded.

I thought: He's not even asking who the main owner is, hasn't asked to see any share registers, no information about our past business. He's happy with what I'm telling him. He didn't even ask for copies of our IDs.

Before we ended the meeting, he opened the door and called for Gabriella, our new contact person.

In the car with Maxim later, Michaela grinned.

"Did you see the sweat stains under his arms?"

"Yeah, he was stressed."

"Drove a nice car, too."

Maxim laughed.

"A nice car?" I asked.

"You have to get to them when there's something else on their minds," Michaela said. "We smashed up his Mercedes-Benz CLS 350 AMG an hour ago. It was in the parking garage under the shopping center. Then we called the cops. They should've called with the bad news just before he spoke to us."

"What the hell are you saying?"

"You like cars? It was a really nice one: metallic paint, eighteen-inch wheels, hardwood interior, two hundred and seventy horsepower. He bought it the day before yesterday. Right, Maxim?"

Maxim drummed at the wheel.

"Vrlo fino," he said.

On the way back to our place in the country, it started—if you'll excuse the language—absolutely pissing down, and I was stuck in traffic. We were planning on going back to Stockholm the next Monday. Everything would go back to normal—at least for Cecilia, Benjamin, and Lillan. I remember I called Viktor from the car, I wanted to tell him about the mess I'd gotten myself into. He'd just moved to Skåne, but maybe he could help me find a way out. The rain was pounding down like machine-gun fire outside.

"Heeeeeey, Matty boy." He sounded happy.

"You seem well."

"Yup, we get some sun down here. It's different from up there."

"It's pissing down. What're you up to?"

"Picking blueberries. We've got some friends coming over later." The traffic finally started to move. The rain didn't let up.

"Aha, listen, there was something I wanted to talk to you about."

I heard another voice in the background.

"Sure," he said. "But Fia is right here with me."

The congestion eased. I stepped on the accelerator and followed the car ahead.

"I'll call you later," I said. Viktor sounded relieved. I could just see him shaking his head at his wife, letting her know the conversation wouldn't last much longer. He had no idea what I was heading toward right then.

For a split second, a helplessly bleak thought raced through my head.

In the rain: I should undo my seat belt, turn sharply on the wheel, slam into the rock wall at the side of the road.

In the rain: how the slippery surface would explain my death.

In the rain: how it would wash away the blood from a tragic individual.

Memo continued on separate sheet.

14

Isak had headphones on. They were black, with a red "b" on the ear cups: Beats by Dre. Nikola wanted a pair of his own, but they were too expensive for a guy who'd just spent a year in a young offenders' institute.

Mr. One was eating.

Mr. One was eating with headphones on.

The only sound he could hear: his boss's chomping.

Nikola was still standing. He didn't know if he could sit down. Waiting for Isak to look up. Or at least show he knew Nikola was in the room.

Isak: shaved head, stomach squeezed in against the edge of the table, even though he'd pushed the chair back. Syriac eagle tattooed on his forearm. Though it wasn't really an eagle. Chamon had told him that: it was a flashlight, or maybe a sun, with wings. "The eagle should be red, for all the blood that's been spilled. We've been persecuted for centuries." Chamon's voice had been serious. His friend's words reminded Nikola of when his grandfather got going, started talking about the war down there, in the homeland. But it wasn't Nikola's war. And it wasn't his homeland, either, no matter what the Sweden Democrats said.

A few days had passed since the events in the club: the masked men who'd forced their way in and taken the cash, who'd shot Metim's guy in the leg.

Yusuf had asked Nikola to come to the Steakhouse Bar alone. Everyone knew that it was in this room, in this restaurant, that Isak had a table. That this was where he ate his meals. That this was where he held his meetings.

The feeling in his stomach: shitty.

The vibes in the room: really, really crappy.

Nikola had stayed at home, in bed, since it happened. Hadn't dared go out. Hadn't even dared call anyone, afraid of what Yusuf or Chamon would say. Worried about police wire taps.

But then Isak called. When that happened, you came. Even if it might be the end.

The Steakhouse Bar was dark inside. The walls and floors were black, covered in fake Tex-Mex stuff: buffalo skulls, plastic cacti, sombreros, and stupid white guitars that looked more like drums with strings. There were usually more people here on the weekend.

In the first room, the one closest to the street, there were eight dark gray tables. Next to the windows, there were six booths, two sofas opposite one another. And above all: a purple bar, model XXL.

The next room was nicer. Seven round tables with white table-cloths. Chairs with burgundy-colored leather seats, wooden floor-ing that creaked as Nikola slowly made his way over to Isak.

They were alone. Yusuf had met Nikola in the entrance, taken his phone, and then pushed him inside. The door closed.

Was it all over now? Would Isak say a few well-chosen words and then ask him to get into Yusuf's car? Drive over the Brooklyn Bridge in the pouring rain. Sleep with the fishes. Spend two hours digging in the gravel pit at Tuvängen, and then stand on the edge of the hole, eyes closed. Waiting for the bullet.

Those idiots must've thought there'd be at least three hun-dred thousand in cash. Honestly, though: you needed your head checked if you thought three hundred big was worth the risk. Maybe they'd thought there was more. That Isak would demand a higher amount. They must've followed one of the runners—hoped he had all the money—and then just knocked on the door.

So the big question was: Who'd given them the code? Who was the traitor among them?

One normal knock. Four quick.

Isak took off his headphones and pushed the plate away.

"You tried the entrecôte here, the rib-eye steak?"

"No."

"Come here."

The boss cut off a chunk of meat. He clearly wanted Nikola to stay standing.

"They call you the Bible Man, yeah?"

"Sometimes."

"You need dough?"

He didn't even ask how Nikola was.

"No, not really."

"You need attention?"

"No, what d'you mean?"

"You've been away a while."

"I was in Spillersboda."

"I heard the guys celebrated with you."

"Yeah, it was pretty sweet."

Isak scratched his ear.

"How's Teddy—Björne?"

Isak and Teddy. Friends from *waaaay back*. Nikola didn't think they'd seen each other for the past ten years, not while Teddy was inside or after. But still.

"He's good, got his own place. Works for a law firm." It was nice to talk about Teddy, or Björne, as Isak clearly called him.

He said: "Makes no sense to me. Björne working like every other Svensson. Paying tax. Grinding away for someone else. My old friend, the guy who never backed down, always had a piece hidden in the toilet, just in case, always beat millions out of the state—has a job?"

"Yeah, I dunno . . ."

"You have the same genes as him?"

Nikola could hear the music from the next room.

"If you weren't Teddy's nephew, I'd bitch-slap you, kick you out of here, and tell Yusuf to take you out to the woods. Grab a baseball bat, beat your knees to kebab meat. Understand?"

Isak drank the last of the Coke in his glass. "You stupid little son of a bitch. You fucked up. How the hell could you just let him run off? Why didn't you blow that motherfucker away—he had his fucking piece right in my mug?"

Nikola's mouth: dry, like he'd just smoked a mammoth blunt. Couldn't utter a sound.

"I swear, I'd fuck their mothers in the eye . . . ," Isak continued.

Nikola felt relieved: at least the boss didn't think he was involved.

". . . so now, you little shit, you've gotta fix Danny's money. The damages. Those bastards ran off with the bag with one hundred and fifty in it. Understand?"

Nikola couldn't do anything but answer: "Yeah."

"And they shot Metim's man in the leg, eight inches from his dick. He's gotta be paid for that, too. So there's another hundred thousand. That means you've gotta get me two hundred and fifty grand. Understand?"

Nikola croaked something in reply.

"And one more thing," said Isak. "You need to find out who those bastards were. I thought it was Metim at first—but then his guy got shot. Then I thought, it's gotta be Danny—but he would've got the cash anyway. So now I think I don't have a clue. You do what you want, however you want. I just want the names. Get it? Then I can forget you acted like a dickless wonder."

Outside, on the street, his head spun worse than after his first joint as a free man.

The money was hard enough.

But finding out who'd been crazy enough to attack Mr. One: how would Nikola even stand a chance? He was done for. Still, somehow, he had to regain his position. If he ended up with a bad rep, he might as well leave the country.

He had no idea what to do.

"Nicko."

Someone said his name. He scanned the street. The square was almost deserted. The courthouse in the distance looked like it was swaying.

"Nicko, here."

It was a girl, wearing sunglasses, though the sun was going down.

"Don't you remember me?"

And then he understood: Paulina. The girl who'd been drinking wine with her friends in the park. The girl he'd met at the party his first night out. Who'd asked whether his grandfather read him the classics. "Yeah, hey. *Cześć!*"

"You learned Polish? That was quick."

Nikola: head a total mess. First the stress of standing in front of Isak. The ultimatum. The terms. And now Paulina. He didn't know how to handle this. He just wanted to go home and get into bed. But at the same time: he wanted to stay here, talk to her.

He said: "It sounds like Serbian."

"Want to hang out? We could go to Stanleys?"

AC/DC crash. He was about to short-circuit.

Wanted to. Couldn't.

Wished. Couldn't manage.

He tried to smile. "Another time. Be great another time."

"Okay, then I'm gonna take your number so we can talk sometime."

At home, later that evening.

In the tub.

In the kitchen.

In bed.

His pulse thumping in a vein on his temple. Two hundred and fifty grand. *Bom.* Find two insane hitmen. *Bom.* Two hundred and fifty grand. *Bom.* Two insane hitmen. *Bom.*

He couldn't let Linda see him cry.

How the fuck was he going to fix this?

She came back at eight. He recognized the sound in the hall-way, the thud when she put down her bag. The squeak of the ward-robe door when she hung up her thin jacket.

He'd locked his door—couldn't talk right now.

Hours passed.

He tried to play something on his phone. Tried to sleep.

Nothing worked.

He called Chamon.

"Hey, man."

"Hey."

"What's up?"

"Nothing."

"Haven't spoken in a while."

"Nope."

"We okay?"

"No."

"Why?"

"Yusuf said Isak wanted to talk to you. That I should keep away."

"I talked to Isak today."

Nikola could hear video games in the background. Chamon was probably home. Gaming like usual.

"So you talked? What'd he say?"

"He said I messed up when I let 'em go, and 'cause I didn't shoot that guy in the back. But I'm still in. He's not gonna throw me out. Not gonna hurt me. Not yet, anyway."

"Shit, man, that's great. Nicko, I'm happy."

Good vibes. Warmth in his heart.

"But there's a catch. I've gotta find two hundred and fifty grand in a month."

"Oh shit."

"Wait, that's not all. I've gotta find out who those idiots were, too, who took the money."

"How're you meant to do that?"

"No idea. But I've gotta do it. I'm gonna find them, and I've got an idea."

Nikola was lying. He had no idea how he was going to do it, but what else could he say?

Chamon said: "Listen, Nicko, you're not on your own."

Silence in the background. He must've paused the game.

"I'll help you. You're my *aho*."

Nikola felt even more warmth.

Chamon: a real friend.

A brother.

15

The sun was shining. The sky was blue. Every single Stockholmer seemed to want to sit outside the cafés and restaurants, wrapped up in blankets but still shivering, and pretend summer had already arrived.

Teddy had read through the declaration of legal presumption of death from the Tax Agency. To sum up: Mats had been caught on CCTV as he jumped from the sun deck at the stern of the boat—level eight on the M/S *Viking Mariella*, one of the smaller Viking Line ferries. Forty feet above the water, rough seas, half-storm (47 mph), a farewell note, the lifeboats' fruitless search over the following day. A cautious diagnosis, in conjunction with the declaration: Mats Emanuelsson had shown signs of deep depression. The rest of the documents were variations on the same theme. The Tax Agency's officials considered it appropriate to make an immediate decision based primarily on the weather: *In light of the circumstances, it is to be assumed that Mats Emanuelsson is deceased.*

He, Emelie, and Jan had talked in the car on the way back from Värmdö the day before.

Could they test the blood they'd found? That was *the big question*, after all: Who was the dead man?

"How are you meant to defend yourself against a murder charge when you don't even know who the dead person is?" Teddy asked.

Jan grinned. "Which of you is the lawyer, exactly? That's a very good question, though. I'll test the blood. See if I get any matches."

"Is there anything else we can do?" Emelie asked.

Teddy thought: She knows so little. He said: "We'll just have to wait and see. The preliminary report'll turn up sooner or later. But there's still plenty we can do now."

Teddy got in touch with Dejan and asked if he had time to meet. Dejan's voice practically reached falsetto. It always did when he was happy about something. He immediately suggested a dive bar in Flemingsberg.

They met there a few hours later. Greeted one another: arm swing, *hand slap*—firm grip. Not like the Swedes: a limp handshake and a shy look in the eye. Teddy got straight down to business: "Look, Dejan, I know you don't like going on about the old days, but you know what I got sent down for."

"Sure, man."

"I've never asked before, but what did you know about that guy we grabbed?"

"Nothing. Honest. No more than you."

"They told us he was flush, that we'd get a share of the three mil. They said that was why he was living in a hotel, d'you remember, when we were watching him, he was living in a hotel?"

"Shit, Teddy, 'course I remember. I thought about it the whole time you were inside. And I get it if you're bitter, but you should forget it now, man. What's done's done."

"But what did you know about him, can you just tell me that?"

"I told you, not much."

"Did you know he was a gambler?"

"Ivan mighta mentioned it. Probably why he had loads of cash. But y'know, it all went to shit. Shame you can't ask Ivan, if you really want to know."

Teddy took a swig of his beer. Ivan was the one who'd told them what to do. He was the one who'd told them to grab Mats. But he'd died six years ago. Lung cancer, apparently.

"Was it just the ransom Ivan wanted?"

Dejan hooked the lump of snus tobacco from his mouth and stuck it under the bar.

"Yeah, Jesus, you hear something else? I mean, me and you, we never did stuff for anything but the dough."

After he left, Teddy called Loke.

Loke: first-rate hacker, but they'd gotten to know each other in Hall Prison. Loke was doing two years for file sharing—*information wants to be free*, and all that crap. The strange thing was that they'd locked up a twenty-seven-year-old nerd with pale, skinny arms and a slight lisp with drug dealers, gang members, and all-around criminals, but that was just how things were.

Anyway: Teddy liked the guy. Loke'd called a new inmate—Ibbe Salah—a "gassy nobody." The problem was that Salah—other than being inside for GBH and serious weapons offenses—was sergeant at arms in Scorpions Sweden.

They'd forced their way into Loke's room and said it like it was: "You hand over a hundred big, we forget about it." But Loke had refused, thought he could talk his way out of it the same way he'd almost managed to turn Swedish public opinion on its head during his trial.

The next day, someone had shat in his food.

A day later: someone had stamped on his foot so hard, they crushed his toes.

By day three, he'd started to get it: someone sneaked into his room and put a nail, on end, in his mattress.

Eventually they'd all gotten together in Teddy's room. Salah, Loke, Teddy, and two of Salah's guys. Teddy was a veteran on his wing. Everyone knew he was a man of honor. In the end, he fixed it so Loke paid five thousand to the Scorpion members' account, and like that, the problem was gone.

Teddy had thought that Loke would be bitter and angry—but the opposite was true. Since that day, Loke Odensson had been unerringly loyal to him.

"All right, darling," Loke shouted down the line when he realized it was Teddy.

"Hey, man," said Teddy. "I need to ask you something. You remember when you checked out Mats Emanuelsson for me?"

"Yep."

"I've been thinking about it. Can you check again? Was he really part of some sick network, all that stuff?"

Loke sounded happy, like always. "I'll see what I can find out."

Teddy went back to Cecilia's apartment. Asked if he could take a look in Benjamin's room. Asked if she knew anything about Topstar.

"I wish I could help you, but I have no idea. Mats had a separate life as a gambler, and I didn't know anything about it."

He asked anyway. Names of Mats's friends, bosses, colleagues. Cecilia answered as best she could. Teddy asked her to go back over everything she knew about the kidnapping.

She stood by the sink and started pouring coffee, just like last time he'd been there. Turned her back to him. Demonstratively.

"I don't want to talk about what happened to Mats anymore."

Before Teddy left, he asked to take a look in their basement.

"Why?"

"I'm just trying to help, you know that. We found some interesting things in that bag of Benjamin's. So I just thought that maybe in the basement . . ."

"Okay, fine. We've got the biggest basement space in the building, and my kids refuse to let me clear it out, so you've only got yourself to blame. They're nostalgic."

She was right. Their space was unexpectedly large for an apartment. And it was one big mess, all kinds of things filling the space right up to the mesh walls. Teddy riffled through old winter clothes, karate outfits, skis, sacks of earth, and lampshades. It was insane, the amount of stuff these ordinary Swedes kept in their storage spaces—they were like squirrels: they hoarded stuff for no real reason. He found an old helmet that looked like it was from World War II, a wet suit, and a collection of bowie knives. He opened football kit bags, baskets of swimming things, and old toy boxes. In one of them, he found an air gun.

He asked Cecilia about the knives, the gun, the helmet.

"That's Benjamin's stuff," she quickly said. "He collected things like that when he was about fourteen."

Teddy tried to see the pattern. The kidnapping—the predator who'd wanted the computer—the gambling—the suicide—the suspicions against Benjamin today. But his mind was still as blank as a cloudless sky.

He thanked Cecilia and headed home.

Loke called back that evening.

"Sweetie, it's me."

"Have you found anything?"

"Not exactly, but I'm not as certain as I was before."

"Why?"

"I mean, I'm not a hundred percent sure Mats himself was part of the network. But there were files linked to disgusting kiddie fuckers on his computer, that's one hundred percent. So honestly, I should probably take back some of what I told you before. I can't be sure some network was behind you kidnapping him."

"Okay, thanks. Is there some way you can find out more about them?"

"I'd need access to the computer or a copy of the hard drive."

"Right, okay. I've had confirmation from others that it was a computer that we, if you know what I mean, seemed to want."

"Maybe, but still, I probably went a bit far before."

"Okay. One more thing. Topstar: can you check if there's any club with that name in Stockholm? Or that used to have it?"

Loke smacked his lips. "Cutie pie, this is right up my street, and sounds much less grim than that computer. I'll trawl the net for the club. See what I can find."

16

Riche: classy, stylish, great people watching. *The* place for lunch in Stockholm for generations, and at night: timeless bar *numero uno*.

"You look like a fucking Moomin," Jossan said as she hugged Emelie when they met there for lunch.

"What d'you mean?"

"White as a sheet, white as milk, whatever you want. Is everything okay? Doesn't look that way."

She hadn't seen Josephine for a few days. Emelie: drowning in work at the office again. A new case had started. She had to set up a number of SLAs for a telecoms operator.

Jossan: busy in the marathon negotiations between Cross Port Dynamics Ltd. and the serious venture capitalists who wanted to buy their way in. She'd been in Luxembourg since a week back, battling eighteen hours a day for a bad-tempered client younger than she was.

Emelie never really felt all that comfortable at Riche, but Jossan kissed the head waiter on the cheek, adjusted her Chloé bag on her shoulder, and swept in like she owned the place.

The glasses were hanging in a circle above the bar—promising success in the so-called divorce bar. Anders Timell, the restaurateur, was running about with his hair a mess, kissing people on the cheek like a madman. It was pretty bright inside, but the noise and the buzz were already at midnight levels.

Riche: Emelie only recognized the most well-known faces from the financial elite, but there were sure to be many more there. Hedge fund managers, analysts, venture capitalists. And then the usual celebrities: Viggo Cavling, Sven Hagströmer, Tintin von Thulin, Jonny Johansson, and Magnus Uggle, of course. Plus Douglas Kreuger. The latter was one of the youngest partners Leijon had ever had.

Emelie put down her menu. "How are you? How was Luxembourg?"

"I mean, it's impossible to find quark there."

"Right, because you need your quark and sugar-free juice for breakfast every day?"

"Every day. I'm not a woman who likes to compromise. Avoid all kinds of calories, that's the trick. Plus, the hotel gym was really depressing, so I came up with my own Tabata workout. Burpees first, then push-ups, then sit ups, then squats, then—"

"The plank, then the side plank—on both sides—then knee raises with rotation, and last of all, back lifts."

Josephine put down her menu, too. "You know me, girl." She smiled. "But I feel like I don't know you anymore. You never tell me when something's wrong. Because I can tell, you know, something's not right."

There were plenty of things you could say Jossan wasn't. Intellectual, environmentally aware, interested in gender power structures—just a few examples. But there were three things she knew more about than anyone Emelie had ever met: asset-transfer agreements, Hermès bags, and people.

Just to be on the safe side, Emelie had disconnected her cell from the office telephone system. It was a pure precaution: if she got a call about Benjamin from prison or the courtroom, she didn't want it going through to the main switchboard. Someone from Kronoberg Remand Prison looking for Emelie Jansson. That kind of call would definitely raise eyebrows. She'd given her home address to the court, too, and given them her own email address—one she'd created for free on Gmail.

The only thing she couldn't shield herself from was the press. After the custody hearing, there'd been a few articles about the murder in both *Expressen* and *Aftonbladet*.

Unconscious man held on suspicion of murder.

Unidentified victim brutally murdered.

They'd even interviewed her old professor in penal law, asked him why someone unconscious was being kept in custody. As luck would have it, her name hadn't been mentioned anywhere.

She couldn't bring herself to think about what the hell she was really doing.

"Hello, *ground control to Major Tom*. Anyone home?" Jossan set the cutlery down on her plate. She'd barely touched her food.

"Other than having loads of work and something being wrong, not that you want to talk about it, how's life?"

Emelie had no answers to Jossan's questions. Her head was spinning.

No, it wasn't spinning. It was burning.

They got up from the table. She hadn't even noticed that Jossan had paid the bill.

Outside, in the fresh air.

"Let's do something another time, since you couldn't be here today," Jossan said.

It was only once Emelie walked away that she realized what she'd said. She really hadn't been a good friend. Completely absent. The one small consolation was that Jossan could clearly joke about it.

"Welcome to passengers traveling with us on this service to Copenhagen today. My name is Marcus, and I'm your conductor for this part of the train. Smoking is not permitted anywhere on this train, and I would like to remind you that nor is the consumption of alcohol not bought on board. I hope you enjoy your journey with SJ today."

No cigarettes, Emelie thought. Not even in the bathroom. Even though I'm traveling first-class.

She really just wanted to sleep. Use the gentle rocking of the train to relax. She would be meeting her mother in a few hours. Maybe her father, too.

He worked as an official with the Swedish Board of Agriculture, though Emelie had never quite understood exactly what he did there. All she knew was that they were much too forgiving when it came to signing him off in his bad periods. Still, he'd mostly been fine during her childhood, when he hadn't been going through a rough patch. Always encouraged her to do well in school without putting pressure on her, supported her in the choices she made. Both he and her mom had been active in the Isolate South Africa movement and other idealistic groups, but their political engagement had long since dropped off, and these days, they seemed to be most interested in different types of self-realization. Big ideas about the world around her had, for her mother, been reduced to thoughts of healthy food, mindfulness, and home interiors. For her dad, there seemed to be nothing left, other than the odd bit of woodwork and his bad red wine habits.

Emelie wondered what the next few days would be like.

Norrköping. Linköping. Mjölby.

She would be arriving soon.

The prosecutor, Annika Rölén, had requested an extension. In other words, she wanted to keep Benjamin in custody for a few more weeks while the police continued their investigation. They would analyze DNA, continue the search for footprints, check fingerprints, look for traces of gunpowder and fibers from clothing. They would probably be performing an autopsy on the body, getting Forensics to analyze the results, and looking into Benjamin's activities in the days leading up to the murder. They would empty his phone, check which cell towers it had pinged from, look into his bank cards.

The most important point was who the clothing in the woods belonged to, and whose blood it was covered in.

Detective Inspector Kullman had tried to conduct another

interview with Benjamin—the only words they'd managed to get out of him were: "I don't understand." For the rest of the interview, he'd just lain there like he was dead.

But Emelie had continued with her own parallel investigation.

The Land Registry records showed that the house in Värmdö had been sold to the illusive Spaniard by Dag and Linnea Rosling about five years earlier. Emelie had contacted them and spoke to Linnea first. She was elderly, that was clear from her voice, and she'd handed the phone over to her husband.

Dag Rosling knew little more.

"We sold the old summer place through an agent. It'd been in the family since 1894. Can you believe that? But our kids weren't interested, even though it's a lakeside plot. They just want to go to Gümüslük every summer."

"Did you meet the buyer?"

"No, never. You'll have to talk to the agent."

The agency that took care of the sale was called Fastighets-partner. She'd tried to get in touch with the agent, but apparently he'd left the company. They passed her on, and she got hold of his telephone number, but not him. She left a message, told him what was what. "My name is Emelie Jansson, I'm a lawyer, and I'm calling you in regard to a very sensitive issue linked to a house you sold near Ängsvik, on Värmdö, around five years ago. I need to know who bought the house."

She hoped he would get back to her ASAP.

She'd checked elsewhere, too. She'd gone out to Ängsvik and knocked on the door of the closest house. A yellow-painted villa about a quarter of a mile away, at the turnoff from the main road. A woman with a slightly off posture and a pair of toddlers who seemed to be doing Brazilian jujitsu in the hallway behind her had opened the door.

Emelie introduced herself. The neighbor's name was Helena.

"I was just wondering if you knew who lived in the house back there?"

The woman shouted at the wild animals in the background: "If you don't calm down, there'll be no bedtime story." The two small boys didn't seem to hear her.

She turned to Emelie. "I don't, actually. We hardly ever see anyone there. We used to see the Roslings a lot. They were so nice."

"So is anyone even living there, since the Roslings left?"

"We think so. But it's pretty well shielded by the woods, you know, so even when you walk along the road, you can't really see in. The lilacs and privet hedges are pretty thick."

"But you're saying you think there's usually someone there, that someone lives there?"

The kids in the hallway seemed to be committing serious violence against one another. Emelie didn't know how anyone could think with all the noise, but it was probably normal for this house.

"Probably not," Helena had said after a moment. "But we've seen cars driving that way. And I saw some people on the jetty below the house when we were out on the boat last autumn. My guess is it's just someone's under-loved summer place."

"How often have you seen cars there?"

"Honestly, not that often. I can't remember seeing anyone drive by more than three or four times since the Roslings sold it."

"And only during summer?"

"Actually, no, now that I think about it. I know it was definitely winter once."

"Do you know what kind of cars you saw there, the model, that kind of thing?"

"No idea, but I can ask my husband when he gets home. He's better at that stuff."

"And the people on the jetty, what did they look like?"

Helena turned to her children. "Please could you just be fucking quiet!" They looked at her like she was mad, then got up and loped off. It worked, though: they stopped screeching.

She continued: "It was two men I saw. And now that you ask . . .

there was something about them, even though I was so far away, I just got a feeling of . . . that they were really different."

"Different how?"

"I don't know. I just had the feeling they were from different planets, if you get what I mean."

"Not really."

"I mean, as far as I remember, they were dressed differently, their hair, builds—all different. Everything. Their style, you know, they had completely different styles. That's what I mean."

Again, Emelie had no idea whether she'd just moved even an inch closer to something. All the same, she'd confirmed Jan's theory. No one lived in the house, at least not permanently. But someone, maybe several people, visited every now and then. People who were very different, whatever that meant.

Emelie had also asked to see all the papers Cecilia had left from her time as Mats's wife. She wanted to try to understand him. Deeds, documents—her specialty. Cecilia didn't have all that much left. Emelie called banks, the Tax Agency, other authorities: with power of attorney from Benjamin, she could get access to all kinds of additional documents.

She studied declarations, tax statements, loan agreements, and fund reports. The Emanuelssons had lived in Kungsholmen and then bought a house in Älvsjö. They'd borrowed money like everyone else. She checked the land registry records again, looked into pension statements, insurance letters. She didn't find anything strange, so she checked everything through again. The second time around, she started to see things.

Roughly a year before the kidnapping, Mats had taken out new mortgages on the family properties, and he'd taken out huge personal loans, too. Then, a few years before he killed himself, he'd started earning less money; his declared income had sunk to practically nothing. She called to ask Cecilia.

"I have no idea," she said, "but all that stuff with the loans, our bank manager told me about that much later, once we were already divorced and Mats had paid them back. And his job, I mean, I thought he was working full-time, but what do I know. I realize now how trusting I was. Poker was his second life."

Emelie thought: declaring almost nothing and simultaneously paying off massive loans. Just how good had Mats been at poker, exactly?

17

Teddy wanted quick answers. He called Nikola. They'd seen each other properly only once since Spillersboda.

Nikola and a friend. Teddy had met the guy before. Chamon. That time, things had gone a bit crazy, but today the kid was cool. They met in the Espresso House on Hamngatan. Teddy thought back to Fredric McLoud: that a place like this had been his downfall.

Inside, it was like they'd put a library in a jungle, though everything just screamed fake. Wooden tiles on the floor, a load of plastic plants everywhere, pretend books on pretend bookcases. The leather armchairs were nice, though. Teddy thought about how places like this had invaded Stockholm. Again, there'd been cafés before he was sent down, of course there had, but they'd all been independent, unique. Now there was hardly a single one that wasn't part of a chain. It was like people were too insecure to drink any other coffee or eat any other brownies than the exact same kind they could get three blocks down the street in the next branch.

Chamon and Nikola were talking about things close to home. Linda's nagging. Bojan's talk about going to church with him.

Teddy said: "Nikola, you've gotta understand how Linda feels. Right? You're a grown man now—behave like one."

It was a shame his nephew had brought Chamon along—he talked with so much more attitude when he was there. Plus: there was something else going on with Nikola; Teddy could see it in his face. But since his friend had come along, it never came up.

Chamon and Nikola wanted to talk about the olden days.
Hear stories from back then. When Teddy and Dejan grabbed
five hundred bottles of luxury bubbly from a conference center in
Vallentuna. When Teddy more or less singlehandedly chased the
Screwbacks out of Södertälje.

After a while, Teddy brought up the pack of cards they'd found
under Benjamin's bed. "Any ideas? Topstar. Gambling club, I think.
Five to nine years ago. You know if it's still around today? Maybe
under a different name?"

They stared at him. "You serious? We were eleven then," said
Nikola. "I can check with Yusuf, though, he might know something. He goes in for a bit of that, like, every night. We had to rescue him the other day—some small fry went apeshit."

They came out into the fresh air.

Chamon and Nikola were heading into town.

"He's gonna look at a watch," Nikola said with a wink. "Bling
bling."

Teddy thought back. The car. The chain. The watch. What
the hell was the point of having a place of your own and getting
sick pay if you didn't have a proper ride? And a fat watch on your
wrist.

He hugged Nikola. His nephew smelled like he always did.
Flashback: the first time he'd babysat. Nikola must've been three.
In bed: Nikola had wanted Teddy to lie next to him until he fell
asleep. So Teddy lay down, squashed up next to him so he didn't
fall out. Bent his neck as best he could—breathed gently, calmly—
afraid he'd take all the air Nikola needed otherwise.

He turned around. The guy in the Windbreaker was there
again. Teddy was sure—the exact same dude who'd tried to shadow
him by Zinkensdamm.

Teddy said: "By the way, Nikola, I need your help with
something."

He saw Nikola stand up straight. Chamon, too. Finally: an
opportunity for them to step up for the guy who'd once been one
of Isak's closest.

"I've got a pig tailing me, or whoever the fuck he is. See that guy over there?"

They started to walk toward Norrmalmstorg. Reverse game: Teddy was normally the one tailing and watching out for people.

They passed Kungsträdgården. The cherry blossoms around the fountains were in bloom. Still: Stockholm's shabbiest park, which was dumb because it really could've been the city's crowning glory. For some reason, whoever was in charge chose to fill it with temporary tents full of candy canes and beer in plastic cups. As though Stockholmers needed any more unoriginal places to eat.

The man kept his distance: he was good—but not *that* good. Gallerian, the classic shopping center, was a little farther up the street on the left.

Teddy turned off onto Regeringsgatan. Nikola and Chamon looked at him. "What you gonna do?"

"Just have a chat," Teddy replied.

The Parkaden parking garage was a block away. When they reached it, he stopped at the elevator doors. Turned to his nephew and his friend. Gave them instructions.

Then took the elevator up.

He heard the man's footsteps in the stairwell. The guy was probably trying to listen for which floor Teddy got out on.

The doors of the elevator squeaked. The place was full of cars.

He stopped by the side of the stairwell.

Six seconds later, Mr. Windbreaker opened the door—what an idiot.

He jumped when he saw Teddy so close to him, their faces only about a foot apart. The guy had long eyelashes, cropped hair, and a crooked nose.

There was no one else in the garage. Teddy: "What the fuck do you want?"

The man's eyes were wide. The material on his jacket rustled. "Ehh . . ."

And then he turned on his heel. Opened the door, started to run back down the stairs.

Shit, now Teddy was the idiot.

He rushed after him.

The guy was clearly in good shape. Teddy was taking four steps at a time and still didn't catch up to him. He was already out of breath. Saw the guy a few feet ahead of him in the stairwell. Concrete gray walls.

He picked up the pace. Still wasn't enough. The man kept his distance. Teddy was worried about falling. Rolling down the stairs. Breaking his neck.

He was taking five steps at a time now.

They would be out on the street soon.

Then: Teddy changed tack. Stopped. Panting as loud as a hundred-meter runner.

Heard the guy's footsteps disappearing.

Maybe it would work anyway. He'd given clear instructions to Nikola and Chamon. "Wait down here. If he comes out and goes back to his post, office, or wherever the hell he's come from, you guys follow him, okay?"

"Got it."

"You'll have to take turns tailing him. So he doesn't spot you. Right?"

Nikola's smile had practically reached his ears. So happy.

The guy in the Windbreaker should be opening the door down there in exactly seven seconds.

18

She'd made it to Jönköping. Emelie and her mom ate dinner in silence. Strange: her mother was usually full of questions, loved to talk. Emelie normally made conversation, too. If for no other reason than to keep her parents happy.

But not today. His absence reminded them of before.

Her mom served cod with boiled potatoes, horseradish, and melted butter. It was delicious. The kitchen looked like it always had. If the average Stockholmer renovated their kitchen every third year, her mother and father were the exact opposite: "No point changing a winning design," her father normally said with a chuckle. "I built this kitchen with my bare hands."

Wooden panels and stainless steel work surfaces. Terracotta tiles behind the stove and the sink. Kitchen anno 1995. Emelie had been nine then.

Dessert: chocolate fondant with raspberry coulis. Her mom really had made an effort. Emelie couldn't bear any more of it: "Okay, enough, tell me what's going on."

Her mother put down her spoon.

"You've hardly shown much interest this past week."

"I've been snowed under at work. You know what it's like there sometimes."

"A phone call takes five minutes. You could do that when you go to the bathroom. Or don't they let you pee there?"

"I don't, anyway. It takes too long." Emelie hoped her mom

would laugh. Instead, she picked up the plates and started loading them into the dishwasher, her face stony.

"I'm going to go and look for him," Emelie said, getting up.

Jönköping by night.

It was late May. The sky was still light.

She cycled along Huskvarnavägen toward the center. The huge windows in Kinnarps Arena looked like they'd just been polished. She thought back to all the ice hockey games she'd watched there with her dad. They'd had season tickets: standing in the cheapest area, the blue section. When he'd been in a good mood.

The bike was hers, a relic from her school days. It rattled and clanked, but after she pumped up the tires, it went like a racer.

The waterslide outside the swimming pool was deserted. One spring night in high school: they'd climbed over the fence and swum in the outdoor pool. Drunk. Ecstatic. Enthusiastic about the future that awaited them. Though Emelie had known even then that she wanted to get away.

Lake Vättern lay like a gray blanket to one side of Strandgatan. On the other side, the waters of Munksjön bobbed in the evening breeze. It was mysterious: why was the huge lake still, while the little pond glittered?

She started at the Bishop's Arms. Hundreds of different beers, Irish-themed interior, checked tablecloths. The place was half-empty. Still, she went from table to table just to be on the safe side. He wasn't there.

She cycled to Juneporten and Murphy's. People seemed to be having a good time. She saw an old classmate, but turned away. Her dad wasn't there, either.

She checked a few more places. Dive bars, pubs, licensed pizzerias. Sports bars, Thai restaurants, lunch places that were still open. Most were virtually empty. And he wasn't in any of them. She knew he sometimes went to his friends' places, but she didn't know where they lived.

Finally: One Thousand and One Nights. The place inside the

market hall. She hadn't thought of it at first, assumed it would be closed. She stepped inside. Brown interiors, small black tables. A bar that looked like it was covered in tiles.

There he was. By the far wall. With two other men she didn't recognize.

Though in a way, she did: their scruffy clothes, unshaven cheeks, lumpy red noses. They seemed calm, not rough, but the volume of their conversation showed just how drunk they were.

It was eleven o'clock. Her father had been home only sporadically the past ten days.

She moved slowly.

Thought about her movements. Tried to stay calm.

The pub was half-full. Low music coming from the speakers, considerably higher average age than the places she usually went when she came back home.

She stopped at their table. The coasters were advertising Mariestads Beer. Hands in pockets. She was steady.

"Dad," she said with a clear voice.

No reaction.

Again: "Dad."

One of the men looked up. Red eyes. Rotten teeth. He elbowed her father.

Emelie's dad leaned back and met her eye. She'd seen it so many times before: the bad conscience, the self-pity, the shame. The glassy eyes. And also: the anger. That someone was interrupting him. That they couldn't just accept his weakness.

"It's time to come home now," Emelie said.

All she could think: I never want to be like you.

The two other men started to mumble: "She's right, Lars." They knew who she was, though she hadn't introduced herself. The similarities in their appearance were striking, as Dad himself often pointed out, but maybe they remembered her from when she was young.

He started looking for something in his pants pockets. He still hadn't said a word to her.

Eventually he took out a wad of bills with an elastic band wrapped around them.

She wasn't used to seeing money like that: it was so unsophisticated. Old-fashioned. She'd read somewhere that Swedes used bank cards more than any other country on earth.

He peeled off a couple of hundred-krona bills. Emelie realized that he must keep his money like that to hide just how much he spent in places like this from her mother.

He got up. "Okay, then. Taxi?"

He held out the wad of bills to her.

"No, I biked. But I'll push it. We can walk."

Two thoughts ran through her mind: Mom'll be happy. Also: they'll fight.

And a third: the wad of bills.

More common in the past.

Mats Emanuelsson: a gambler, Cecilia had said.

Maybe his accounts and fund reports were the wrong place to look? Maybe Mats had been more of a cash man?

19

Star Gamers. The logo: glamour, a sense of luxury. The "a" in the word "Star" swapped for a spade. The edges of the letters: golden. And underneath, in glittering text, *The club where anything is possible.* Sitting outside the place, a beggar missing a leg. And when Teddy went down the stairs and into the club, the feeling was anything but luxurious. He'd already been there once before, the same day he'd received the text from Loke—just to make his face known, otherwise keeping a low profile. Tonight: the second time—he'd need to stay on the ball.

Even more snus and chewing gum than normal. He had to keep his focus. Things should be at their peak down there now.

Star Gamers was one big basement room. The walls were covered with posters advertising different gaming sites and web casinos, and there was a bar at one side of the room. Four big tables covered in green felt dotted the place, and some booths along the other wall: probably meant for drinking beer or playing smaller games, one-on-one. They also had a few slot machines here and there.

Ninety percent male. Teddy had clocked the atmosphere last time. Gambling-mad Swedes, occupational criminals, Asians. They were making bets at the bar: the club staff acting as bookmakers. The odds of AIK winning the league were four to five. And the tables were all full: focused, silent men, cards facedown on the table in front of them—this was the kind of place you just lifted one corner to check what was what. Teddy thought back to the games they'd played in the slammer.

Star Gamers did everything it could to keep people there, get them to play for hours, and at high stakes. Lots of the people there seemed to be able to get credit at the bar. There was beer, cola, Red Bull, speed . . . coke for those who really needed to keep going. Teddy could see people handing out toothbrushes and cold hand towels for putting on your head. There was a room where you could sleep and another with two of those massage chairs you always saw in airports. A woman was walking around, giving people neck massages for a hundred kronor. For five times that, you could get a little extra in a back room.

Teddy thought about Nikola. He and Chamon had tailed the man in the Windbreaker. Just like Teddy had hoped, the man had rushed out of the car park, stopped to look around like a crazy person, and then jogged quickly along the street and down the escalator to the subway.

He'd gotten off at Fridhemsplan: Nikola and Chamon watched him go into a house on Sankt Eriksgatan. That was enough for Teddy—he'd checked the address. On the third floor: Swedish Premium Security, a private security firm, something like Redwood, where Jan worked.

He tried to find out who worked for the company, but that wasn't exactly something they shouted about. So he'd asked Loke to help again: "I'll find out somehow. I promise, snuggle muffin."

Otherwise, no news. Teddy had called Mats's old boss; Niklas was his name. Niklas remembered Mats, but he didn't have much to say.

"It's a shame," he'd said. "Mats was ill a lot. He wasn't well, especially after what happened."

Teddy was sitting at the bar. He'd asked to talk to whoever ran the place. Given them a rough indication of what it was about.

After a couple of hours of boredom, his body was itching. All around him, people were staring down at their cards.

He thought of Sara. It had been more than a year since he'd stood outside her house in the dark. Sara, with a baby in her arms. A man in the house. Maybe it was understandable that she didn't want to talk to him.

Then: a chubby guy in dark sunglasses appeared next to him at the bar.

"Hey," he said. He put something into Teddy's hand. His fingers were callused. "Call me."

Teddy opened his hand. In it: a slip of paper with a phone number on it.

The next day, Teddy got up at five. That's when he woke up anyway. He wandered around the older part of Solna. The clean streets, the absence of any strong smells. Kingdom of the birds and the homeless for a little while longer.

Sara dropped off her son at the nursery early.

The little boy had to be about eighteen months old by now. Teddy felt like a stalker: waited in his car outside her house. Followed her when she walked the quarter mile to the nursery with the stroller. Stood on the other side of the street when she opened the gates and disappeared into the green wooden building.

But on the other hand: following people was what he'd made his living doing this past year—he should be used to it by now. And he was sure no one had followed *him* here today. He'd changed cars on the metro several times, stopped, taken elaborate detours.

———

The years hadn't been the least bit unkind to Sara's appearance, he saw when she came back out. Her face had the same glow as before, her eyes the same intensity. Standing in her kitchen with the boy in her arms. Or before that: in the visitation room in prison—it was more than four years since he'd seen her close up.

She'd been a warden; he was doing a long stretch. She'd slowly fallen in love with him; he'd been crazy about her. Their relationship had started tentatively, but once they both realized what they wanted, she'd decided to hand in her notice, said she couldn't do her job properly if she was in a relationship with an inmate. Teddy had understood the logic behind it, but it had hurt all the same.

They'd continued to see each other after that. She visited him regularly, they talked on the phone every day, wrote long letters about life and the future.

Sara had started asking questions about what Teddy was serving time for—she'd started looking into the kidnapping, but then everything collapsed, and she cut off all ties to him.

He'd tried to call her when he got out a few years later, they'd even talked—but she'd been clear: they couldn't meet. Ever again.

Teddy walked over to her. Probably the only woman he'd ever loved.

"Hi, Sara."

She was wearing blue jeans and a black leather jacket. It struck him that he had no idea whether she was still working as a warden.

"Teddy, what're *you* doing here?"

Neither of them moved. No hugs. No handshakes.

"I need to talk to you."

"Have you been following me?"

"No, no, well yes, I was waiting for you here."

She took a few steps back, toward the low fence surrounding the nursery.

He said: "I just need to talk to you, please."

Her shoulders dropped, she relaxed. "It's good to see you. You look really well."

"Better than in a long time. I'm working now, I've got my own place, everything's moving forward. How are you?"

"Great. I'm a researcher these days, at the university."

"Still in criminology?"

"Exactly." She smiled.

"Sounds like a good match for you." There was so much he wanted to say. But he'd come here for a reason.

"Look, something's come up, and I don't think you're going to want to talk about it, but I need to ask anyway."

She glanced around. Women and children had started streaming out of the building behind her. "What?"

"Mats Emanuelsson's son is being held on suspicion of murder."

"What? Mats's son? The guy you kidnapped's son?"

"Yeah, and he's asked for my help."

"Oh Jesus, so something's going on again?"

"Yeah, something to do with what happened back then, that's what I thought, too. I just don't know what. But I remembered you'd been looking into what really happened when I did what I did nine years ago. You don't have to tell me anything, but I know someone got to you. I know someone made you stop snooping around and cut off all contact with me."

Sara's face looked different now: no longer her strong, mature self. Teddy could see something else now—and clearly. Fear. He could see fear in her eyes.

"I hear what you're saying," she said. "But you've got to realize, I can't talk about it. I'm not on my own anymore. I've got a son. I've got a partner."

"I know. I don't want to pressure you."

Sara scratched her head, put a hand to her brow.

"Maybe, Teddy, maybe. I don't know. . . ."

"It's up to you. . . ."

"I'll think about it."

"Okay." He gave her his phone number.

They walked along the edge of the fence. The sound of the kids in the nursery in the distance.

"Your son, how old is he now?" asked Teddy.

"Nineteen months."

"What's his name?"

She slowed down.

"He's named Edward."

"Nice name."

Silence around them now.

She said: "Thanks. I call him Teddy."

Stockholm County Police Authority

Interview with informant "Marina," 15 December 2010

Leader: Joakim Sundén

Location: Haninge Centrum

MEMORANDUM 3 (PART 2)

Transcript of dialogue (continuation)

M: Life was pretty much like normal again. The kids were back at school and nursery. This was autumn 2005. The usual morning stress again—packing gym uniforms and ballet clothes. That's what life was like for me back then. You know what I mean. Have you got kids?

JS: No, unfortunately not.

M: Aha, well, anyway. Hamster wheel. Everyday life, you know, office frenzy. I used to sneak off for long lunches quite often, cycle down to Clara's.

We kept the official accounting for the companies in folders in the office, but the special files, and by that I mean the *real* accounting, we kept that on laptop computers you needed loads of passwords just to get onto.

We looked after our relationship with the bank. We couldn't risk them getting suspicious about the flow of money, the big cash deposits and withdrawals, or about the fact the companies had started renting eighty-foot yachts in Croatia and Marbella, Hummers in Stockholm, paying bills of more than seven thousand euros a table at Zaranda in Palma.

We moved money to accounts in Estonia then shipped the same money back to a currency exchange in Stockholm. Sometimes we'd send money over to banks in Luxembourg, Dubai, Hong Kong, and the Channel Islands. This was back before those countries' banks had to stop being so secretive. Everything went according to my plan. We produced invoices for Swedish building firms and pubs, kept track of the black loans and clean declarations. I arranged authorization for our smurfs to manage new accounts. We created minutes from board and committee meetings. Registered addresses and partners with the authorities. Maxim made sure we always had the personal details of people who were apparently willing to lend us their names. And after a few weeks, my name wasn't linked to a single one of our companies.

I put together loan and leasing documents. I dealt with the owner of a super villa in Palma. One of our companies was going to rent it. Everything ran as smoothly as the ball bearings in Stig Erhardsson's Merc probably did before it was written off.

But there was one more thing I did. For some reason, I couldn't get Sebbe's words of wisdom from a few months earlier out of my mind: "You gotta keep a hold on people in this world."

That was how they got me. Their hold on me's the reason I'm here. So what I did, I started gathering things for myself. I bought a laptop and decided it'd be my life insurance. I transferred, copied, and saved everything that might be of value on it. Names of clients, bank accounts, company names. Businessmen who worked in the gray zone, transaction methods, links to our encrypted accounts. I thought to myself: You can't have too much of a hold on things.

JS: Where's the laptop now?

M: It was my only guarantee, you can understand that, but it's what got me into much worse situations. Unfortunately.

JS: I want to see it.

M: I don't have it anymore. I'll get to what happened, I promise.

A few months after that, Sebbe sent me a message to say he wanted to meet at Clara's. But not for work. "We're just gonna have fun tonight," he said.

I told Cecilia I might be late.

"Work, like usual?"

"No, actually, I'm going to meet a few old poker friends."

She frowned. "Oh, I didn't realize you did things socially."

She turned around and started to wipe the kitchen counter.

"Benjamin has football after school. Can you pack his shoes and shorts and stuff now?"

I started to gather his things.

And then I heard my phone beep on the counter. Cecilia picked it up to pass it to me. But she pulled back her hand and started pressing buttons.

It was like the room went cold. She glared at me.

"What's this?" she asked, holding it up.

I saw the message: "See you tonight, right? Hugs/Michaela"

JS: What did I say . . . (sound of laughter)

M: Mmm . . . it wasn't funny, let me tell you. Cecilia was just holding the phone, staring at me. Different options went through my head. Maybe I should tell her the truth: say I was in a bind, had to meet Stockholm's mafia elite in a club down by Stureplan, that I was helping them launder money on a daily basis—money I could only guess where it came from. But Cecilia never would've believed it—plus, I just couldn't. I knew I had to fix things myself, without dragging her into it.

So I took the phone from her and said: "She's the croupier at the club. She might be coming tonight."

Cecilia's head jerked. "I thought you were all guys."

"No, we're not," I said.

I hoped she'd never ask again.

I was at Clara's pretty much every day, in their office. Always during the day or at night on weekdays. But it was almost eleven on a Saturday night. It felt weird to be meeting Michaela. I knew I hadn't done anything wrong as far as she was concerned, but still—we'd never met in that kind of context before.

There was already a huge line outside the place. It actually looked more like an angry crowd. People were shouting and pushing, and the bouncers were pacing back and forth with their earpieces in, refusing to look anyone in the eye. It just wasn't my world. I didn't even know how I'd get in.

Then someone tapped me on the shoulder. I turned around. It was Maxim. He winked at me.

He pushed through the crowd like some kind of bodyguard breaking up a group of paparazzi, some Old Testament prophet parting the Red Sea. I followed him in.

There were entrance hosts in dark suits and black gloves standing in the corner, their heads slowly turning this way and that, and they nodded at Maxim. The girls were wearing handbags with different monogram patterns on the leather, and they were taking long strides past the counter, foot after foot, like they were in some kind of fashion show. They didn't look at anyone else.

Stairs, narrow hallways. Red ropes. More bouncers. Even more stairs. I thought I knew my way around the place, but now I was confused.

Crystal chandeliers. Silver buckets full of champagne. People dancing on chairs. The music in the background: someone with a lazy voice saying *drop it like it's hot* over and over again.

Eventually: the VIP room of VIP rooms. The walls were covered in red velvet, and the lights looked like huge spiders. It was a bit calmer inside—people were even eating at some of the tables. I'd had no idea that floor even existed.

A man got up from one of the tables and came over to us. It was Sebbe. He was wearing a black polo shirt and a dark suit. He looked really elegant that night, I have to say.

"My man," he shouted over the noise and the background music.

I sat down in one of the empty chairs. Sebbe aside, there were four other men around the table.

"Where's Michaela?" I asked.

Sebbe grinned. "Boys' night tonight."

Honestly, I can't really remember who all the people were, but there was one guy who had a restaurant somewhere in Södertälje, a place called the Steakhouse Bar, if I remember right.

JS: What else do you know about him?

M: Not much. He had dark hair, Syrian, he said. The others were more like Maxim. Big guys, blunt noses, short hair.

The hours passed. I sat quietly for most of the evening. I even went over to the blackjack table at one point. It wasn't my favorite thing to play, but better than roulette anyway. Us poker players, we like horses and card games, stuff where skill and knowledge mean something.

The others were talking, toasting, and moving about the place, chatting with other people. Women came over, young girls, sat on the men's knees; there was champagne and shots. The music got louder.

At one point, the guy from Södertälje leaned toward me.

"Want one?"

I looked down. He had a white tablet in his hand.

"To stop the hangover?" I asked.

He grinned. "Nah, this is better. Easier to keep when it's like this, less for curious eyes to latch on to."

He crushed the pill in his palm and it turned into a fine powder. Then he got up and disappeared for a while.

I gradually got pretty drunk. There was nothing wrong with Clara's at night. Sebbe's friends were nice. They asked about my son's interest in football and what my wife did. We talked about the Italian penalties in the final against France. They talked about the Mohammed cartoons—I remember those were a pretty hot topic back then. The gang was divided. The guy from Södertälje and Sebbe both thought it was stupid, provocative to draw Mohammed like that. The others saw Muslims as animals who only had themselves to blame.

Sometime after midnight, I noticed that everyone's focus had shifted from whatever they were doing. There was a man standing in front of the empty chair next to me. He was pretty short, with side-combed hair and a white shirt he hadn't tucked into his wide-legged jeans. The biggest gold watch I've ever seen. I recognized him from the photos on the wall in the office.

JS: Who was he?

M: You don't know?

JS: No.

M: Their boss. They called him Kum.

JS: Aha.

M: They went forward, one after another. Kum held out his hand. He had a tiny tattoo of a cross between his thumb and index finger. I'd seen one like that before. Four cyrillic letters, CCCC, one in each quadrant of the cross. But I'd never seen grown men do what happened next: they all kissed him on the hand.

Kum sat down next to me. Asked how I liked the place. If I'd eaten, whether it was good. If the staff were doing their job. If Sebbe was looking after me. We started talking about other stuff after that. How insane it was that some Swedish guy had sold a company called Skype for more than eighteen billion kronor. How sick the bombs on the London tube were.

"What do we learn from that?" he asked.

"No idea," I replied.

"That we should stick to our principles. I haven't been on the metro since 1991. And what happened in England just proves it was the right choice."

I couldn't tell if he was joking.

"A man should only travel in his own or another reliable driver's car. That's my rule."

"So you don't take taxis?"

Kum raised his glass to me, almost like he wanted to toast.

He seemed to be drinking water. "No, never. When I go somewhere, I want to know who's behind the wheel. See what I mean?" he said. "By the way, I have to say hi from Michaela, too. Things're going well, I understand—she likes you."

Then Sebbe bent down and said something into his ear. Kum got to his feet, and Sebbe led him away.

20

Emelie and Teddy were in a taxi, en route to somewhere in Öster-malm. The address: super flashy. Narvavägen 4.

The man who'd given Teddy his card in Star Gamers had been brief when Teddy called him up. "My friend and I would like to meet you. I heard you were asking around. We knew Mats from the club. Come to my friend's place. We can talk."

"Have you managed to get anywhere?" she asked when she sat down next to him in the backseat.

"Not really." Teddy spoke quietly so the driver wouldn't hear. "But I've been thinking about the background to all this. I think we can be pretty sure that someone, maybe even a group of peo-ple, were behind the scenes when we kidnapped Mats, that it had something to do with whatever was on that computer. I'm not a hundred percent sure Mats himself was a member of any network anymore, but *they*'re out there, whoever wants to stop the informa-tion on that computer from getting out. I'm a hundred percent on *that*. And even if it was nine years ago, I'm sure Benjamin's situa-tion has something to do with it, otherwise he wouldn't have got-ten me involved."

"So what does that mean?"

"Benjamin wants me to understand, so I think he wants us to figure out the link between whatever happened to his dad and the murder on Värmdö. I don't know if it's got something to do with this network, or with the guys I used to work for, or with anyone else, but we need to find out who Mats used to hang out with. What he really lived for in the years before he died. Who he was. We need to map him out to find the link."

"Yeah, that's what I thought, too."

"Did I tell you stuff is still happening? I was being followed."

Teddy continued in a low voice. He told her about the man from Swedish Premium Security.

Emelie felt like she needed something to calm her nerves.

It wasn't an apartment, it was an entire *floor*. Mental calculation: at least thirty-six hundred square feet, nearly thirteen-foot-high ceilings.

A young woman met them in the hallway. She looked a few years older than Emelie. Long black hair extensions, shapeless silk trousers, a beige cable-knit cashmere sweater, and black ballerinas with the Chanel logo on the toes—the ultimate Stureplan outfit.

"Your little guests are here now," she shouted into the apartment when Teddy introduced Emelie and himself.

A man came out. He had to be the girl's father. He was wearing something incredibly odd: Emelie had never seen anything like it—it looked like a cross between a dressing gown and a tuxedo, burgundy colored, with an intricately patterned scarf around his neck. Then she realized what it was: a smoking jacket. The man shook their hands and introduced himself as Bosse. He showed them in. An oddball, clearly.

They passed a billiards room, a library, and something that looked like a parlor. Specially lit art was everywhere on the walls, surpassing even Magnus Hassel's collection in the office, though these paintings were older—she was almost certain that a huge canvas in the hallway was a Miró and that another was a Rothko. The walls were painted varying shades of pale green and gray. On the floor, genuine Persian rugs. She'd probably never been to a more luxurious home.

Finally a room that matched the smoking jacket style.

"Please, sit down," Bosse said. "This is what I call the men's room. Either of you like Cubans?"

Neither Emelie nor Teddy were willing. She could see an oak

bookcase full of books, plus two built-in cabinets with dark glass doors. She guessed they were humidors.

Teddy greeted the man who was already sitting in one of the armchairs.

He held out his hand to Emelie, a loose, unfocused hand-shake, and introduced himself as Boguslaw. "But you can call me Boggan. I'm the one who asked Teddy to call, in case you were wondering."

Teddy nodded. "Right. And I'd like to get straight to the point. Did you know Mats Emanuelsson?"

"Hold on a minute," said Bosse. "I haven't even offered you anything to drink. What'll it be? Whiskey soda? Maybe I can ask Ayleen to mix some cocktails? She's a genius with a straw, if you know what I mean."

Emelie didn't know whether she should get up and leave, pay no attention to what he'd just said, or laugh along. Was that his own daughter he was talking about? Or was the girl who'd shown them in his partner? Either way, there had to be at least thirty years between them. She wondered what kind of reaction he'd wanted.

"Okay, so it's like this," Bosse said after a moment. "We were both friends with Mats. He was a nice guy, with a great mind for probability theory and a bit too much of a gambling habit. Though we probably all have that. Why do you want to know?"

Teddy looked at Emelie. This was her call—she was the one bound by confidentiality. She decided to waive it.

She briefly explained who she was, and then said: "Mats's son is being held on suspicion of murder. So without going into any more detail, we'd like to know a bit more about Mats."

Bosse took a sip from his tall glass. He'd made himself a Bloody Mary, and spent at least five minutes talking about how important it was for the component parts to be cold enough.

"Oh God, that's not good. I met Mats's son once, on the street, must be ten years ago. Cute kid. What happened?"

"I can't say any more than that, I'm afraid. But we'd like to know as much as possible about his father."

Boggan started to talk. "I mean, Mats, he was a real kosher guy. Always cool. Played real first-rate games sometimes. He brought in fifteen thousand euros one night, but he screwed up a lot, too. A *lot*. We used to play in Topstar, Oxen, and at Sumpen, too, but so did everyone else. He came with us to Vegas once, looking for nice big fish. I mean, you know, *fish*—every guy's dream, loose players—idiots with too much dough who don't know when they should stop playing. He had a sponsor for a couple of years, too. Then that bad stuff happened. He got kidnapped. And after that, he wasn't the same."

"A sponsor?" Emelie leaned forward on the sofa.

Boggan downed his drink: a martini—these were guys with some kind of shady elegance. Clearly gamblers, too. Clearly living in a financial gray area. Worn-out. But still with plenty of energy and humor.

"Right," said Boggan. "Those of us that don't have loads of dough or who didn't inherit big bucks and properties like Bosse here, sometimes we need one. To be able to play the big games, you know. But Mats would never tell us who his staker was."

Bosse didn't know, either. "You never saw the guy, he never came to the actual club—it was like Mats didn't want us to know who he was."

Boggan butted in: "But he wasn't just any old guy; once, a few years after the kidnapping . . . a real bloody mess, fighting and everything. Then you could see what he'd got himself into . . ."

Bosse wanted to finish Boggan's sentences—these two reminded Emelie of a couple of girls from her class in high school: like two peas in a pod, Tweedledum and Tweedledee. They'd always been together. Liked the same music, had the same thoughts: that was what they'd said. They dressed alike, talked alike. They acted like *one* person.

Boggan said: "So that's why we wanted to talk to you. Because it seemed like the guy had something to hide. We think Mats had more to do with him than just playing for his money."

"Like what?"

"We don't really know, but after the kidnapping, Mats was spending more and more time with him. And by then, he'd really cut back on the poker, so it couldn't just be about financing some game, or not just that anyway."

Bosse filled in: "And this staker of his, what I remember about him, he had a tattoo of a tiger on his arm, he was like *you*."

He pointed at Teddy.

Emelie was working sixteen hours a day. Sleeping like crap at night. The stress was gnawing at her. The sleeping pills she was popping were about as strong as gummi bears. During the day, her exhaustion made her see double. She was worried about making mistakes. Exactitude was valued even more highly than legal shrewdness in this job. She recognized the warning signs, but right now, she didn't have time *not* to take any shortcuts. She needed to do something.

After the meeting with Bosse, she took a quick walk into town. Not to go shopping or for a coffee. She needed something to help her. Maybe she was weak, but she had no alternative.

The doctor's office was on Norrlandsgatan. She'd been there a few times before. A year or so ago, she'd had tonsillitis and needed penicillin. The insurance plan she had from Leijon had actually directed her to a big private hospital, but it was farther away, and she'd gotten a different vibe from this place.

Third floor: Direct Health. As far as Emelie knew, there was only one doctor working there, and it was Dr. Gunnarsson she wanted to see. After she visited last time, she'd looked him up—it should work.

She didn't have to wait long. It was nice to be able to avoid the usual women's magazines and the beady-eyed fish in the waiting room aquarium.

Gunnarsson checked her blood pressure and made some notes on his computer. Emelie explained: "I'm stressed. I've got so much to do. I'm not sleeping, my shoulders and back are so tense. I get anxious and can't concentrate."

Gunnarsson asked a few questions. If she'd experienced these feelings before. If they were worse in some situations than others. She answered yes to both.

"I think you should start taking better care of your over-all health," Dr. Gunnarsson said. "Do some more exercise, eat properly—no more fast food. You should try some form of relaxation, yoga, meditation, mindfulness maybe."

Emelie didn't have time. She said what she knew he needed to hear. "I've already tried all that. It doesn't help. I need something else. I'm one hundred percent sure."

She pushed an envelope over the table. Gunnarsson's fingers looked well-groomed. He opened the envelope. Emelie had put three thousand in five-hundred kronor bills inside.

His voice was suddenly completely toneless. "I see. Well, let's write you a prescription, then."

Stesolid, 5 mg.

When Emelie got up to leave, he said: "Just be careful with these. Under no circumstances take more than the dose I prescribed. Stesolid can be addictive, it sometimes causes drowsiness. In the worst cases, it can cause depersonalization."

"What's that?"

Gunnarsson leaned forward over his desk. "Well, how to describe it? A feeling of unreality, uncertainty about your identity."

There was a pharmacy nearby. Emelie got into the line. She really needed something right away, her hands were shaking, her mouth as dry as a DD report, she was seeing triple.

Apotek pharmacies these days—after the privatization drive: they spent more time trying to sell moisturizer and hair conditioner than they did medicine.

It was her turn. The prescription should already be in their system. She gave her ID number to the pharmacist, who disappeared behind the counter to get what she needed.

"Hi there."

Emelie turned around.

No. *No.*

Magnus Hassel.

From the corner of her eye, she saw the pharmacist heading back toward the counter with the tablets.

"Hey."

She didn't know what to say.

"Buying toothpaste?" she eventually asked, apropos of nothing at all.

"Why, you think I have bad breath?" He smiled.

She needed to get out of there. Run. Flee. But that would look even weirder. Plus, she still had to pay.

"No, no, just that's what this place seems to be for these days."

Emelie held out both hands, quickly cupping the bottle. Hoped Magnus hadn't had time to read the label.

The pharmacist smiled. "Paying by card?"

Magnus was still next to her. Emelie clutched the bottle tight, hoped the pharmacist wouldn't say anything about what she'd just been given. But how would she manage to get her card holder out of her bag with just one hand?

Magnus said: "No, just picking up some allergy tablets. Pollen season's almost here."

Emelie did it all in one movement: pushed her bag toward her left hand, dropped the bottle, grabbed her card holder.

She was out on the street two minutes later. This was all just too much.

She opened the bottle immediately and swallowed a pill. Hoped it would kick in soon.

21

Pirate Bay, swefilmer.se, megadownloader.com.

Linda didn't have subscriptions to Netflix or HBO like any normal parent—she didn't even have the cable channels C More or Viaplay.

Either it was because she was short of dough or because he'd been away from home too long, hadn't been nagging her.

Nikola hated the pirate sites: everything looked so cheap. Homemade, poor. But that's where he got all his vids from now. *The Avengers, The Hobbit, The Fast and the Furious* films: several times over.

At home: on his bed, in front of the TV, by the microwave—he'd lived on microwave pizzas these past few days. He felt so sluggish. Couldn't even be bothered to jerk off.

Linda was constantly on him. "You need to call George Samuel again. He's been so good to you, let you leave on time when you were there. I'm sure he'll take you back."

But it was already too late. George had called to say it wouldn't work out: "Sorry, man, but it's probably best if you look for a job somewhere else."

Mom said: "I'll talk to him, then, maybe he'll change his mind. He doesn't want to lose you."

Nikola twisted on the sofa. "You know something, Mom?"

"What?"

"You're actually pretty fucking fantastic."

She looked up, probably thought he was just messing with her.

"You never give up when it comes to me, do you?"

She ran a hand through his hair like she used to do when he was little. "A Maksumic never gives up, Nicko. You know that, don't you?"

Two hundred and fifty grand: what he needed to get hold of. Plus the other thing: find the guys.

The money: impossible. He'd thought about talking to Teddy—but it hadn't been the right time when they met, when he'd asked Nikola and Chamon to shadow that guy.

Finding the robbers: dangerous shit—they'd had enough balls to go for Isak when he was surrounded by his people. They had to be insanely insane. Enough now. That was enough.

He had to take charge of the situation.

The robbers: one of them had dropped his piece on the floor when Nikola pressed the pistol into his back. That was all he had to go on: a Kalashnikov. An AK-47, which, right that moment, was hidden in a box of his old winter clothes in the basement.

Just having it down there: too much heat to live with—serious weapons offense. Ten months minimum if the cops caught wind of it.

His idea: take the weapon to Gabbe so he could have a look at it. The guy might be able to tell him where it was from.

The cash. Planning under way. He and Chamon had gotten some dark Everest jackets from a couple of friends, same with the pants. And their own shoes: dark as the night.

They lifted the balaclavas from Mickes MC on the edge of town—the biker guys called them bike hoods. Whatever: the point was to hide their faces from any CCTV cameras.

They'd been buzzing about the idea before. Ica Kvantum, Willys, Lidl, the huge food shops. There were loads of them. All over the Stockholm area. From nowhere: Swedes becoming Americans. Only shopped in massive out-of-town shopping centers. Crazy depressing parking garages. Shopping carts, model: supersize. Screaming kids and shelves of bread stretching half a mile into the distance. Nikola wondered what people used to do before these places turned up. Maybe the Svenssons had grown their own crap back then. Like weed these days. Every motherfucker had a mini greenhouse in their wardrobe at home, complete with sunlamps, fans, and nutritional additives in the pot.

Nikola had first come up with the idea on one of his periods of leave from Spillersboda. "One of those giant shops, could do a hit on one of those. They've gotta have so much dough in the safe after closing on Sundays."

Chamon had grinned. "Get with the times, bro. They have those cash guards these days. All the cash from the checkouts gets guarded and picked up before the day's out. But you're right, though. They've got bills, shitloads of cash. Just not from the regular checkouts."

It had to happen. He refused to be an outcast, relegated to the subs' bench—playing in the lower leagues. He wanted to count.

If only he wasn't so scared.

He needed to change now. Big-time.

He went over to Chamon. Sitting on the sofa like usual: *GTA V* on the screen, Red Bull cans everywhere, crazy pile of weed on a plate on the table. His friend had started to grow a little goatee—he looked like a cross between Jack Sparrow and some hard rocker: like the guys in Slayer.

Nikola tried to set the scene. "We go in, take what they've got, and then get outta there. Like, how hard can it be?"

Chamon laid it out for him: the shops had money from the other areas. BBQs and charcoal, compost and plants, fresh potatoes, strawberries, cinnamon rolls and bread: everything they sold from the stalls outside. Plus the lottery, the scratch cards, and the newspapers they sold from a special counter by the entrance.

Chamon paused the game. "There's one thing we can't forget, bro. We need an insider, someone who can tell us where to go, where they keep the cash."

Paulina had sent him a message a few days earlier. Nikola's mind in chaos. But still, he was happy.

They met one night at O'Learys: same place they'd met the first time. She came alone: only the brave—seventeen years old and going to meet the mysterious Slav who talked Syriac, the Bible Man. Though maybe he wasn't so mysterious. Off the market for a year. Plus: who exactly had he been before?

He ordered a beer and she had a glass of champagne, and they talked about everything: her school. His time in Spillersboda. And not least: the books they'd read—a weird feeling. He'd never talked about books with anyone but Teddy and his grandpa.

She had her hair up: you could see her entire face. Her straight nose, her eyes full of questions about him. What the hell, he should take her home now and get right on top of her. Then call one of the guys to tell them all about it. What a *fox*. She wanted me, like all the rest of them. Blew my load in her face four times.

The only problem: he didn't know what to do. It was like someone had pinned him to the floor in the bar, his hand in his own pocket.

He should move closer to her, put a hand on her thigh, whisper gentle words. Flirt with her, just play it cool. *We going back to your place or mine?*

But he couldn't. Same thing over and over again.

Him: weak.

Him: an idiot.

Him: so scared.

They went their separate ways at twelve thirty.

They weren't like everyone else.

The next day, he called one of the guys who'd been in Spillersboda at the same time. Vague memory: the dude had talked about his cousin working in one of those massive shops. Saman.

Bingo: Saman'd had a job in the warehouse at the ICA Maxi in Botkyrka for seven years now. An honorable man with a crazy *shurda* for a cousin. But according to his friend: Saman was going through a divorce. He needed dough.

Nikola didn't say what it was about, but they agreed to meet by the pool in Slagsta, probably close to the guy's home turf. Nikola had no idea—all he knew: they had to make it work somehow.

He got out. He'd borrowed the car from Linda.

The beach was to his left—it'd be sweet in a few weeks' time when it got really warm and the chicks started spicing up the beach like jalapeños on a pizza.

The guy's cousin had covered his face with a scarf. Plus: a hat pulled down low, sunglasses. He looked crazy, like some super-heist guru—what the hell, he wasn't even sure it was Saman coming toward him.

Stomachache. Rumbling. Nikola wished Chamon was with him.

Was he a cop? Some filthy grass? He wasn't getting that vibe—but what did he really know about that?

He raised a hand. Greeted him from a distance. The guy took a few steps forward.

They were opposite one another now. The dude was wearing leather gloves: what the fuck, man, it was so over-the-top.

Or? Maybe he should've hidden his face. He wondered what his guy in Spillersboda had actually told this dude.

"Hi, hi."

Nikola said: "Not that I don't trust you, but maybe we can take a walk?"

If this was a police sting, he didn't want to be standing in the trees. If this was for real: he wanted to seem experienced.

"Yeah, no problem. I thought this'd be a good place, but if you want, sure."

They walked along the beach.

Nikola said: "I love your cousin. We got up to tons of stuff together."

The cousin replied: "Don't talk to me about him. He's the black sheep of the family."

Nikola needed to know this really was Saman.

"You been to see him inside?"

They took a few steps on the sand. His shoes sank into it, it didn't feel good.

"In Spillersboda? Nah, I haven't had time."

"But in the place before that, Häggvik?"

"Häggvik? He was never there. He's got a good heart. From a good family. His dad's an imam, you know."

That was enough for Nikola—the guy knew plenty. He was the real deal.

He said: "I've got an offer you can't refuse."

"What?"

"Ten percent of anything we take."

Stockholm County Police Authority

Interview with informant "Marina," 17 December 2010

Handler: Joakim Sundén

Location: Farsta Centrum

MEMORANDUM 4 (PART 1)

Transcript of dialogue

JS: The weather today! Snow, snow, snow.

M: Mmm . . .

JS: Have you had time to do your Christmas shopping yet?

M: No, not really, no.

JS: I see.

M: I can't remember where we left off.

JS: It doesn't matter. You can start where you want. Like we said, Mats, the most important thing is that you're comfortable. I'm here for you. To listen to what you have to say. There's no need to be worried.

M: Thanks.

JS: Maybe I can ask you a question. I'm interested in things with Cecilia. Was the message from Michaela the only thing she ever wondered about? I mean, your extra job was mostly at night, wasn't it?

M: Yeah, she had questions about a lot of things, but I started doing the extra stuff more and more during the day. In late autumn in 2005, I went down to

70 percent at KPMG. I blamed it on stress. They sent me to see the company doctor, and I didn't even have to lie all that much when I told them I wasn't sleeping and had stomachaches every now and then. It was mild gastritis, the doctor decided. I've always weighed about 170. I've been pretty much the same weight all my adult life, but that autumn, I dropped to somewhere around 150.

Cecilia still wanted to know why I had to work so much, but I kept on blaming it on my bosses and on our clients' unpredictability, and on going to the club a bit too much again. That last part was true—I was playing a bit. And I think she probably thought I was having an affair, too. But anyway, I was so worried about Cecilia.

First, I'd gambled away everything we owned, then I'd had to do a ton of stupid stuff. And now I was having to lie about virtually everything I did. I was getting tired of it. I didn't want her to give me the same worried or suspicious looks all the time. I wanted her to look at me the way she used to.

JS: How did that work, financially, if you weren't working at KPMG full-time?

M: Ehhh . . . (inaudible) . . . get a bit of money. The last Monday of every month, there'd be an envelope with twenty thousand kronor in it on the desk. That pretty much made up for what I'd lost from going down to part-time, plus it was uh . . . tax free.

But I had more and more to do, and in early 2006 I asked my boss, Niklas, to cut my hours even more, down to half time.

That January, I bought Cecilia tickets to see *Mamma Mia* in London. She was really into music, she'd even started singing in a choir, which I think was good for her—it meant she had her own things to do in the evenings sometimes.

We went over to London for a long weekend in February, and when we checked in at the hotel, they told us we'd been upgraded to a suite. The view was incredible, and it was a great start to the weekend. I never asked who'd fixed it so we ended up there, but when I came home, Michaela was pretty curious about whether we'd had a Jacuzzi and a terrace, whether we'd been able to see Trafalgar Square from the window.

I started to get other ideas then, too. The economy in Sweden was on the rise, everyone had forgotten the dot-com crash a few years earlier, and the economy was charging ahead like a train with no brakes.

My friend Bosse was the one at the club who was always talking about the stock exchange. He brought it up when we were playing once.

"There are really fat takings for anyone willing to give it a chance. It's just like Hold'em. If you can count, you can beat the system. You know, I bought a little company called SinterCast for forty-nine kronor a share. They make metal for car engines. I went in for two hundred grand. Then the news broke that Ford Motors had bought their technology. Three weeks later, the shares were worth a hundred each. That's two hundred thou without lifting a finger," Bosse said.

His friend Boguslaw picked at his nose. "But that's like a fart in the wind to you. You blew that much at the table last month."

Bosse looked at his cards before he put them down on the table. "I don't think you get it. That's the whole point. Things go up and down here. On the exchange, they just go up, in the long term anyway."

I was listening. Thinking. And trying to understand.

I started reading the financial papers and business magazines. I signed up for newsletters from different analysis companies and stockbrokers. I talked to Bosse at the club and Stig Erhardsson at the bank. I read chat rooms online—everyone was shouting about their stock successes, explaining their thinking. I started paying attention to business valuations, P/E ratios, and technical analysis. I got an account with a cheap online broker, Nordnet, just to study the movements in the market.

I drew my own conclusions. It wasn't quite as easy as Bosse made out, but there were definite similarities with poker—math and psychology in predictable patterns. You could make massive amounts of money if you did everything right. I could feel the bug coming back with a vengeance. Again.

Around the same time, Sweden launched something called the Third Money Laundering Directive. It was an EU thing, led by the Financial Action Task Force, mostly for fighting terrorism and stuff like that, but it had a massive impact on my extra job.

Suddenly every customer would be identifiable through documents, details, or information coming from sources other than us. In the past, the banks'd just had a policy called Know Your Client, but suddenly all kinds of businesses and consultants could do the same thing. Accountants, lawyers, and above all, the currency exchanges, they started wanting to meet personally, hear what kind of business we ran, get information about the purpose of the business relationship, understand why it needed to happen with cash. It was a fucking mess, completely over-the-top—a bit crazy, actually. We were hardly Al-Qaeda.

The worst thing was that even cash-heavy branches like antique dealerships or car dealers, dry cleaners and building firms ended up under the magnifying glass. Any cash payments more than fifteen thousand euros had to be checked and reported.

I spent every night calculating and thinking. The likelihood of a crackdown. The possibilities of the leverage effect. Exchanging investments. I decided we needed to spread our eggs into more baskets, you know. In practice, that meant getting in touch with and building up trust with new banks, finding new ways of doing what we were doing. So I made calls, sent messages, had meetings in different offices all over town. In the end, our companies had accounts with SEB, Handelsbanken, Nordea, Swedbank, and Danske Bank, but also with loads of plastic banks, as I call them, Ikano, Resurs, yeah, you know what I mean.

At the same time, I was always thinking about my own setup. If I could just borrow some money from our cash flows for a couple of weeks, I'd be able to make enough to give Sebbe and the others the finger, take my family and move somewhere else for good.

But one day, I got a call from a lawyer.

"I'm calling from the Leijon law firm. I was wondering if you would be interested in meeting a client of mine."

"I'm not the one in charge of the client accounts. It would be better if you spoke to my manager, Niklas," I said.

"No, my client doesn't want to meet you like that. He wants to meet you in relation to your *other* work, if you follow."

The law firm's offices weren't far from Clara's. I'd never been there before. The interiors were all natural: hardwood, granite, sandstone. The place oozed competence and trust.

We went up to one of the corner rooms on the top floor. The views over Stockholm were incredible.

On the other side of the table, with a cup of coffee in his hand, the lawyer was sitting next to a man I didn't know then, Peder.

Peder was wearing a tie, and he had round glasses. He got straight to his feet, held out a hand with a smile, and introduced himself, only his forename. His teeth looked unnaturally white. He was probably about my age, maybe a few years older.

"Mats, good to meet you. I've wanted to talk to you for a while," he said. "By the way, do you know my lawyer?"

The other man looked uncomfortable with Peder's forthcoming nature.

"Now that you've been introduced, I think I'll leave you in peace," the lawyer said, and got to his feet.

Once the door closed behind him, Peder clasped his hands together. He had a gold signet ring on his little finger.

"I represent a number of individuals who need your help."

I didn't know why I was the one sitting there, not Sebbe. This was above my head. I'd done a lot over the past six months, but I'd never been in touch with the people who actually used our services.

"We have money in certain places and need it moved to others. It's really quite simple. But the Swedish state, the EU, and that huge Jewish-steered country in the West, they make life difficult for us. As I'm sure you know."

I swallowed, thought that if Sebbe could do it, I could too. I talked as calmly as I could.

"Just tell me what you need, and we'll arrange it."

Peder leaned back in his chair. He reminded me of Sean Penn in *Carlito's Way*. "Excellent."

Memo continued on separate sheet.

22

Dejan had gone crazy for dogs, in the literal sense of the word. He'd bought a bull terrier four months earlier and decided to call it the Mauler, after the Swedish MMA king. He said: "The pooch takes up more time in one day than all the business I do in a week."

"You never thought about doggy day care, or what?" Teddy asked. "Sure they take cash, which is good for you. Maybe they can even adopt it. It looks a bit pale. You sure you're giving it the right meat, yeah?"

The dog was the whitest Teddy had ever seen. Even the inside of its ears were white. But apparently no joking about the Mauler was allowed—Dejan's face went blank. Teddy had seen that look before, and apologized immediately.

They'd met in Flemingsberg again, but in the woods behind the train station this time. Teddy had called and said it was urgent.

Dejan: his old friend from before his eight years in the slammer. His armor-bearer, his crony—his sidekick in so many tight spots, he'd lost count. Above all: Dejan—the guy who'd helped him kidnap Mats Emanuelsson, but whose name Teddy had never mentioned during the trial.

Back then: Teddy in custody, full restrictions, for seven months, interviewed by the police eight times and a number of times in court. They'd offered him a reduction in his sentence, despite the fact that was forbidden in Sweden—plus the witness protection program, "equivalent annuity until you find your feet," they said, and help with his education. They'd threatened to bring his family into it, forcibly remove Nikola, crush his sister, Linda. Unless he told them who else was involved. Unless he gave up his mates. Ratted out Dejan and Ivan. Kum.

And so Teddy had kept quiet. Hadn't said a word. He'd taken his years without complaining.

Dejan should've been the one paying an annuity for the rest of his life. Or Kum.

He let Dejan talk. The Mauler had been on a puppy-training course, plus a course on calls and lead behavior. And one on something called clicker training, teaching the dog to obey him when he used a metal clicker.

"Look, he can nearly do a one-eighty," Dejan said, clicking the metal thing like a madman.

The Mauler looked at him and turned his head.

"Is that what that is?" asked Teddy. A train sped past below them.

"He's getting there, Teddy, getting there. Moving his head to the left's the first step." Dejan bent down and scratched the dog behind the ear. "Isn't that right, little cutie? Yes."

Teddy couldn't believe his ears. The only thing Dejan had ever shown so much affection for in the past was his own dick.

In the distance, he could see the huge library building at Södertorn high school, and to the right, the colorful housing projects. Flemingsberg. This was where the dentistry students, business economists, and gender researchers flocked to. Lawyers, prosecutors, and judges to the courthouse directly behind the station. This was about as far out as they went: they never set foot any farther down the commuter train line.

He needed to get to the point now.

"Dejan, remember I asked what you knew about Mats a few weeks ago?"

"Yeah, but there's no point going on about that. Just forget it."

"Nah, I'm not gonna forget anything. You told me he was a gambler."

"Yeah."

"But you never said he had a backer, one of us?"

"What you on about?"

"Dejan"—Teddy raised his voice—"you know me. You know what I did for you. Eight years. You did zero. So quit lying to me."

His friend's smile faded. Teddy waited for his reaction: this could end any number of ways.

Dejan shoved his hands into his pockets, frowned.

Teddy raised his chin. Never give up.

Dejan: "Okay, Teddy, 'cause of everything you did. I don't know much more than I already said, but that's true. Sebastian Petrovic, remember him?"

"Yeah, a bit, used to hang out at Clara's, right?"

"Exactly. He was Mats's staker. And I think they did business together, too."

"So we *did* kidnap him for money?"

"You asked that last time, and I swear, for me, it was about the cash. But Ivan's dead, and God knows what his plan was with that fucking kidnapping."

"What about Sebbe Petrovic—you know where he's at now?"

"I haven't seen that guy in three, maybe four years. I think he got out, moved abroad somewhere."

Leijon had agreed to extend the rental-car contract.

Now he and Emelie were on their way to Solna to see Sara. He took all the detours he could, wanted to shake off Swedish Premium Security. He'd given Emelie a rough explanation of who Sara was, just left out certain parts.

"You working a half day?" he asked.

She didn't seem to hear what he'd said, just kept looking out the car window. Out, toward the enormous gray glass walls of the new Karolinska Hospital. It was like someone had lowered a new city down from the sky, landed it next to the E4.

"Are you working part-time now?" he tried again.

"Accessibility's everything in this job. If the client wants an agreement completed by Monday, it's Sunday night that counts."

A dark thought: Teddy would be seeing Sara soon. He hadn't been with a woman for years. The last time had been on a vinyl-clad pallet bed in prison, and it had been with her.

"What was your dad like?" Emelie asked as they turned off toward Solna.

"Why do you want to know?"

"Just wondering, y'know, what he was like. When you were growing up."

"Tough question. You can meet him sometime. He lives in Hägersten."

"Was he a family man, helped your mom out? Or was he always away?"

"He worked for Scania in Södertälje when I was little, screwing together trucks and stuff like that. Mom worked in the same place, but in the finance department. As far as I remember, they used to help each other a lot. But then . . ."

He was talking more quietly than usual.

"Then she died, and Dad opened a lunch restaurant in Solna, and after that he was hardly ever home. You might think we would've spent more time with him now he was all we had, but no, other people took care of us."

"Who?"

"My sister Linda, for example. She took care of me and my brother more than Dad ever did."

"But she's only a year and a half older than you, isn't she?"

"Yeah, but when we were younger, it was like she was twice my age. It still feels that way, actually."

Emelie laughed. "You know, Teddy, I feel like your age is really fluid. In a nice way, I mean."

Teddy wondered what she meant.

Eventually they arrived. Solna. Tottvägen 28. Sara's house.

Painted red plaster. The lights were on on the ground floor, and

Teddy could see potted plants in the windows. Dusk was falling.
The street was quiet: the kids' skateboards and teenagers' mopeds
had all disappeared. The villa idyll was winding down for the day.

Teddy thought: people of the night everywhere.

He parked slightly away from the house, didn't want to block
any entrances or stop other cars from passing.

Emelie had her bag on her arm: her laptop was probably in it,
she always had it on hand.

"Did Sara say what she wanted to tell you when she called?" she
asked as they closed the car doors.

"No, she just said she was ready to talk about what she'd found
out, and about what made her stop."

"Made her stop?"

"That's what I think she meant: what made her stop looking
into what happened."

Emelie's heels clicked against the pavement.

They knocked on Sara's door. She answered after a moment.

"Hi," she said, with a glance at Emelie. She paused in the
doorway.

Teddy said: "You can trust Emelie. She's Benjamin Emanuelsson's lawyer."

A car was approaching along the street behind them.

Something made Teddy turn around.

One of the car's windows was wound down. Bad vibes—it was
driving too slowly.

He caught sight of a man dressed in dark clothing; he leaned
out of the car and raised his arm. An object. Something long. In
his hand.

Teddy had seen enough.

He yelled, "He's got a gun," and threw himself to the ground,
pulling Emelie down after him. He tried to grab Sara, bring her
down, too.

They heard the shots. One, two, three, four.

He saw Sara's wide eyes.

The car picked up speed. The tires screeched.

It couldn't be.

Sara was lying on the doormat.

Teddy was burning. *They*, whoever they were, had crossed the line. He was close to exploding.

No, he couldn't do that: he threw himself over Sara.

Her shirt was dark over her stomach.

In the background, Emelie was shouting.

Sara stared up at him. She tried to say something, but it just came out as a cough.

"Get the car," Teddy shouted to Emelie.

He held the towel in place, not pressing too hard on Sara's stomach. Emelie was driving. He'd lifted Sara into the car as carefully as he could—she only seemed to have been hit once, but he'd heard several shots. If the bullet had hit her spine, moving her in the wrong way would be disastrous.

A minute later. They were driving on Solnavägen, toward Karolinska Hospital. Emelie honked at car after car. They were shaken about in the backseat. Sara was in his lap. Her eyes: fixed on Teddy.

Her breathing was quicker now.

"It's going to be okay, it's going to be okay," he repeated, a kind of mantra.

The towel was soaked through. He had to stop the bleeding somehow. If the bullet had hit her aorta, she wouldn't have long left.

Sara gripped his elbow. "Teddy . . . ," she said. She coughed up blood. Her grip tightened.

He could see she was sweating.

"Teddy . . . ," she said again, ". . . home alone."

And then he understood—Emelie had already called 112 to say they were on the way to the hospital, but she couldn't call again now, not while she was flooring it.

Teddy groped for his phone in his pocket. His eyes didn't leave Sara. Her breathing sounded jerky now. He knew what that meant: she'd lost too much blood.

Eventually he found it: dialed 112. Told the operator what was happening. "Someone's been shot, and we're taking her to the hospital. But her small baby's home alone, Tottvägen 28 in Solna. Edward."

Sara mumbled something in his lap. He didn't hear what. Her face was pale, all the color had left her skin.

She twisted her head from side to side, delirious.

Fuck. He could see it. She was crossing over. Her breathing, the pallor of her skin, the cold sweat: she was going into shock, and then . . . *fuck*—he couldn't think about that now. He pressed harder against the towel.

"Sara, look at me. Don't give up. Stay here with me. It's gonna be okay."

Emelie was driving faster than a car thief. They had to be almost there.

"Please, Sara. Listen, you remember when we first met and you told me you'd just started studying criminology? You remember what I asked?"

Her eyes were still open.

Teddy continued. "Remember? I asked if they had a course about me."

No reaction.

"You laughed."

Sara was hyperventilating.

She was elsewhere.

23

Gabbe seemed happy to see Nikola, waved him in. A dent on the sofa: Nikola sank down into it.

The guy was wearing the same clothes as last time. Syriac saints and church fathers still peering down at them from the walls.

A plate of raw onion and sliced tomato on the coffee table.

"Take some food," said Gabbe.

Nikola couldn't help but think of his grandpa. Gabbe didn't seem to fit the role of weapons dealer.

"Where's your phone?" he asked.

"Home," Nikola replied. He knew the score.

"How did you get here?"

"Chamon gave me a ride."

"And how d'you know you didn't have a cop tail?"

"I got out a quarter mile away. I swear, no one's following me."

"You guys aren't right in the fucking head."

"Why?"

"Starting up a war again."

"It's not us this time."

"And then trying to get me on the phone. You need to be more careful, *habibi*."

The old guy: clearly fifty times street-smarter than he looked.

Nikola put on an old winter glove he'd found at home—didn't want to leave any prints. Then he got it out of his bag.

"Here's the AK they dropped."

Gabbe was also wearing gloves. He picked up the weapon. There was black masking tape on the hand grip.

"This isn't an AK-47."

"Uh, what is it, then?"

"An Rk 62. Assault rifle, they call it. It's the Finns' version of a Kalashnikov, pretty much the same thing, but theirs. *Rynnäk-kökivääri*, that's what they call it."

"You know Finnish?"

"No, but this is a good weapon. I like it. Our friends looked into it when they were developing their Galil."

"Which friends?"

"The Israelis. I'm from Lebanon, you know? I'm Christian."

"Okay, so what do you know about this gun here?" Gabbe: didn't just know everything about guns—king of chatter, too.

"Quite a bit. I had a huge deal on the cards about six months ago, all kinds of stuff, but it all went to hell. They wanted too much money. Two of the weapons I was gonna buy were like this, with the numbers scraped off too, both from 1995. The last year the Finns made their Rk 62s with the collapsible butt. They messed about with the shape for a while, made a test model with the selector on the left so you could control it with your thumb. Smart move, actually, but the Finnish military started to moan. So I mean, these particular prototyves . . . protoyke . . ."

"Prototypes?"

"Exactly. They only made twenty of these prototypes. Someone lifted five of them from a weapons store outside Åbo last year. This one here and the ones I was gonna buy were all that kind."

"Oh shit, so three outta five?"

"Yes."

Nikola picked up the gun again.

"Who was trying to sell them?"

"Abrohom. You know him?"

"Abrohom Michel? Metim Tasdemir's cousin?"

"Exactly."

"So Metim's behind the whole thing?"

"You don't know that, and I don't, either."

His mind was spinning. Metim Tasdemir. Clan leader. Head of the family. Career gangster. Metim: let one of his own guys get shot in the leg. Metim: first, tried to get Isak to rule on damages. Then grabbed the same money from right under their noses.

What a player.

But still: Metim Tasdemir—real prophet of violence, mafia strong man. A guy who clearly didn't even have respect for Mr. One.

Nikola didn't know what to do. These guys were leagues above him. Just the thought of it made him shit himself: if Metim found out he suspected him.

He got up to leave. Gabbe asked: "By the way, can you help me figure out my Internet? It's useless."

Nikola hesitated. Then he changed his mind. "Sure, but can I have something in return? I see you've got some."

Gabbe: might not know anything about installing digital TV channels—but he was a fucking genius when it came to weapons.

24

It was time for the yearly development chat at the office. All employees were supposed to be constantly kept up to date on how they'd been evaluated, where they were on the ladder—even if officially, it was all about professional and personal development.

Emelie really didn't want to be there right now, she'd been off sick since the shooting in Solna, but she had no choice. Not if she wanted to keep her job.

The same two partners as last year. Leijon didn't like to buck tradition.

Anders Henriksson was a forty-nine-year-old mega nerd whose second marriage was to a twenty-seven-year-old secretary; he acted like he was thirty but thought Tiësto was an electric car from California. All the same, he was one of Sweden's foremost experts in Mergers and Acquisitions. In the latest edition of Legal 500, he was listed as a *Leading Individual*, and his description read: *"a brilliant analyst—creative and authoritative."* Emelie was sure he was brilliant, at least from a strictly IQ-related perspective, but when it came to so-called EQ, it was probably better to talk about him being incredibly challenging.

Magnus Hassel needed no further introduction. If you worked within the branch, you knew who he was. His description hadn't been updated for years. It had long read that he was *"the brightest M&A star in Sweden"* and *"incredibly impressive."*

Emelie had been interviewed by the police after what happened in Solna. Even they had wondered: "What do *you* have to do with this?" She didn't know what she could or couldn't say.

Sara had lost consciousness for a few minutes before they got to the hospital—for a second or two, Emelie thought it might all be over. Teddy had been screaming in the backseat: "No, no, no."

But yesterday, he'd called to say she'd made it. Apparently they'd operated on her for more than four hours. The fact that Tottvägen was close to Karolinska Hospital, the fact that Teddy had decided they should drive her themselves rather than wait for an ambulance, and the fact that he'd stemmed the bleeding like he had—that was what had saved her.

"So, Emelie, how do you think it's going?" Anders asked with his squeaky, strained voice. Jossan claimed that last time she'd worked with him, the other party's lawyer had asked whether he could do the moonwalk during the break, he sounded so damn much like Michael Jackson.

Emelie was lost in her thoughts. She needed to get her life together. She hadn't had a boyfriend since Felix, whom she'd dated for a few months last year. She never saw her cousin, even though she also lived in Stockholm. She occasionally spoke to her parents on the phone, but when she saw them in Jönköping two weeks earlier, it had been the first time in a long while. She talked to the girls at training, but she never had time to meet them for lunch or drinks whenever they suggested it.

She'd spent a year studying in Paris between high school and university, but then she'd narrowed her focus: competed the nine terms of her law course in seven. Straight ahead. Fixated on the goal. The office was her life. She had Jossan and a few other friendly legal associates there. She had a future. Above all: she meant something there, she was in her element.

They were sitting, exactly as they had a year earlier, in Anders's office, rather than one of the meeting rooms. He had a cluster of armchairs in one corner. On the floor, a rug made from reddish-brown, glittering threads.

"I've grown, focused on client understanding and not least the business side of things. Plus, now that I have the title of lawyer, I can continue to move forward," she answered.

Magnus said: "We've looked through your cases from the past year. Over the twelve-month period, it all looks good. But . . ."

Emelie thought she knew where this was heading.

Magnus continued. "This past month, you've worked less than forty-seven billable hours. You've just had a few days' sick leave, but it doesn't seem like you're especially ill."

Emelie tried to sit as still as she could, not reveal anything. She could feel the sweat starting to build on her back. Magnus would ask about their meeting in the pharmacy soon, wonder what she'd been picking up.

"What happened, Emelie? Why the drop in work from your side? Why are you out sick?"

Emelie smiled at them. She was trembling inside. Stesolid.

"I've just been unlucky this month: I've had a cold, tonsillitis, the flu, a stomach bug, you name it. I haven't been able to work properly."

"But you seem perfectly fine today, if you ask me. If you feel bad, if you've got a fever or you're sick or anything like that, you need to see our company doctor. We have excellent health insurance for you and the other associates. We take care of our employees here at Leijon."

"I know, I'll think about it. I just wanted to do my best."

She had no idea what to say. All she knew was that they couldn't find out what she was really working on, and how she actually felt right now.

They talked for a while longer. Compared her billable hours with the average figures, talked about renewed responsibilities, discussed the company's new working groups. The whole time, she was waiting for the question about what she'd been collecting from the pharmacy.

It wasn't written in any of the company materials, on their

home page, or in any of the brochures they handed out to hungry final-year law students—but the abiding principle was *up or out*. In short, if you didn't keep moving up the pay scale, if they didn't think you were moving along nicely, *on track*, you'd be expected to look for another job. It would be subtle, but eventually, forwarded "Business lawyer wanted" ads would start to turn up in your inbox, no comments attached.

Up or out. The principle was simple enough. If you weren't cut out to make it to the highest levels, you had to go.

Her mother had been indignant about the system ever since Emelie started there. "But sweetie, they can't just kick people out like that. We have job security in this country. Thankfully those right-wingers never managed to abolish it completely."

"But they don't fire you. They just expect you to hand in your notice yourself."

"So they provoke you into leaving, in other words?"

"Who wants to stay somewhere they don't fit in?"

Emelie broke off from her thoughts and looked up. Magnus had just concluded a monologue about client perceived value. He said: "So, Emelie, I think we're probably done here. But think about what I said, that we take care of you, our employees. You're important to us."

Today was the day that the time to bring charges against Benjamin ran out, though it was already clear that the prosecutor would request an additional two weeks. According to her, the investigation was far from ready—and even that would be tight.

Jossan was working on her computer when Emelie came in after her development chat. Finally home from Luxembourg.

"You feeling better now, Pippa?"

"I don't know," Emelie replied. She'd survived Magnus's questions unexpectedly well, in any case.

Josephine told her that after Luxembourg, she'd slept for twenty hours. Drank two cups of Pukka tea, done four sun salutations, and gone straight to bed without even switching her phone on. "They could live with it. It was a done deal, so I checked out for a day."

She was actually annoyed for a change. "Yesterday, we got called to the partner's room, everyone who'd worked on the project. He said: 'You've been invaluable. You've shown true Leijon spirit. Great work, girls. Really.' And then he gave us each a bottle of Sancerre Gitton as thanks. 'A little bonus,' the idiot said. So I checked the price online, it doesn't even cost two hundred kronor a bottle. And I know that Jonas Bergqvist got dinner at Oaxen when he finished project Bubble. Pretty greedy, if you ask me. Want to drink the wine with me tonight?"

Emelie thought about it. Aside from a few trips into the office to deal with urgent matters, she'd spent most of her time at home lately, horrible thoughts floating through her mind.

Jossan lived on Norr Mälarstrand: a flashy two-bed place with Carrara marble in the bathroom and Gaggenau ovens in the kitchen. That's right: ovens *plural*—"You need a steam oven, too," Josephine claimed. Everything felt brand-new. "International standard," the estate agent had said—Jossan had let them value the place, not that she had any plans to move.

They talked about Magnus Hassel's colorful ties and his collection of art. They talked about how stressed they felt—Emelie was on the verge of telling her about the Benjamin case. The pressure from Leijon. The pressure of defending a murder suspect. The shooting outside Sara's house. She was burning the candle from both ends—being torn in half. She needed her pills.

"I went to a doctor and got something for the stress," she said.

Jossan wanted to know more, but Emelie dodged her questions—it was pointless telling her that strictly, they were narcotics, the crap she was taking. She couldn't talk about it, not even with Josephine, one of the few people she could call a friend.

After the bottle of Sancerre and another of Chablis, Jossan told her what had happened two years ago. "Before we shared a room, this is. I was in the middle of a huge transaction that lasted for three months. I didn't have a *single* weekend off, worked past midnight every day. The partner just said: 'In the British offices, they've got hordes of hungry eastern Europeans and Indians willing to give their all. We've got to compete with that, don't we?' I'd booked a long weekend in Rome with my mom once it was over. I felt like I needed to relax a bit. But instead, I got thrown into project Two Star the very next day, had to cancel the trip. It was insane, seriously insane. I worked day and night for two weeks. I mean, really, *day and night*. I think I slept less than forty hours during that entire period. I didn't know what to do, just called my mom and cried and cried. Eventually a guy friend of mine gave me something to try, in a little plastic bag. Totally *Breaking Bad*."

"I don't get it."

"Amphetamine, Emelie. It got rid of the panic, gave me a boost. But after four days, I was using it morning, afternoon, and night, and the *thought* of going without it made me break out into a sweat. It was crazy."

Emelie didn't know what to say. Amphetamine. This job was a bigger health risk than her mother could ever imagine. But things were different with her, right? She was in control. She wasn't planning on losing it.

Everything looked so nice in Jossan's kitchen. Maybe it was the lighting. The lamp shade was incredibly low, two feet or so above the table, and the spotlights under the cupboards were dimmed. The brass blender was gleaming. The rug on the floor looked soft. Jossan herself looked beautiful in a way Emelie had never really thought about before. Maybe it was just the wine and their conversation. The fact they were really talking.

Still, she needed to change the topic. "I've got a few things I'd really like to go over with you. Work stuff, kind of, but not really. Is that okay?"

"Sure."

Emelie grabbed her bag from the hallway. Tipped Mats Emanu-elsson's documents and the other objects she and Teddy had found in Benjamin's bag onto Jossan's kitchen table.

"I don't get it," she said. "I'm doing a DD on someone's private finances, and can't get it to hang together."

An hour later, they'd gone through it all. Old pay stubs, bank statements, and card specifications.

Jossan said: "There's one thing you can be sure of, this Mats Emanuelsson can't have supported an entire family on his income, not from his job or his capital. At least not if his wife was working as an administrator for the county council. It's impossible."

She was right—once they'd gone through Mats's finances together, it was clear, just as Emelie had suspected.

"And that key," said Jossan, "I'm pretty sure it's for a safe-deposit box. Must be a pretty old-school one, if it has one of those, but you see them sometimes. Have you handled anything like that in a case before?"

She pointed at the key from the bag.

25

The woods outside Bårsta. Dense spruce and pines. The ground: constant shadow. Life in the darkness.

In front of Teddy: a hole.

His hole.

He'd been here plenty of times before in the past. He'd borrowed the spade and the iron bar from Tagg.

His old hideaway: he'd never thought he would be back here. Had promised himself to leave the things stashed away there behind him, rusty memories of a past life.

Bar and spade. Sweat on his forehead. Workman's gloves and mud on his boots. His back was damp. Roots, rocks, earth. He'd be deep enough soon. Down in the hole with *his* weapons.

He was fucked-up with rage.

They had tricked him into kidnapping Mats Emanuelsson nine years ago, probably made Ivan think it was all about money, too. He was the only one who'd served a single minute for it. Then Mats had gone and killed himself four years ago. *They*'d made it happen somehow. And now Benjamin was being held on suspicion of murder—somehow, that was connected to all this, too. Teddy was sure of it. *They* were shadowing and following him. *They*'d tried to clip him, but almost killed Sara instead.

The line had been crossed way, way back. Above all: *he*'d helped the predator without even realizing it. He had a debt to repay. He'd already waited too long.

His thoughts turned to Sara. The first time she came to the prison with that other warden, Emma. When she told him to stop asking Emma to do things she wasn't allowed, he'd listened. And right then, at that moment when he listened to Sara. That was when something had started to change in him. Their moments in the common room, their time in the hallways when no one else was around, the hours in the visiting room. The letters, the phone calls. All with her.

He thought he'd let go of her as a woman, just like she'd let go of him. But he knew he hadn't let go of her as a person.

A journey from the bottom up. With Sara, everything had changed.

And now: Teddy was back to square one again. He knew himself, could feel it. He was his old self, and there was nothing he could do about it.

The digging gave him blisters, even though he was wearing gloves. The metal wire he'd wound around one of the trees years ago was still there. The carving he'd made on the bark, too, though it wasn't very clear. He drove the spade as deep as he could into the ground.

There: something hard—the Samsonite suitcase he'd stashed everything in. His very own treasure chest.

Only a couple of swigs left in the bottle of whiskey.

Two pieces of snus under his lip. No more gum. He didn't give a shit: he just wanted to taste the tobacco today.

He was at home. His apartment stank. Half-eaten kebabs. Pizza boxes and Coke cans. He'd shoved the pistol and the sawn-off Remington shotgun into the wardrobe: being buried for the best part of a decade didn't seem to have affected them.

Five days had passed. He hadn't dared get in touch with Sara—for her sake, more than anything. She'd survived the drive-by shooting, but it was his fault it had even happened. It was him they'd been after. He hoped she'd told the police what had happened. He'd done it, if nothing else, during the short interview they'd had with him in the hospital.

Teddy's place was so small, he could see every wall and every corner from his seat at the dining table. He could see the little pantry area, sadly lacking a dishwasher, the door and the safety chain he carefully put on every time he came home.

In some ways, the apartment reminded him of his cell in Österåker. The plastic floor was the same shade of beige. The walls were covered with a similar dirty-white textured wallpaper. The mattress on his bed felt just as spongy. The view from the kitchen just as depressing: another building ten feet away. He didn't want to admit it, but he'd found it comforting. Though now he wasn't so sure anymore.

Anyway, of course he drank sometimes, but with one of the golden rules from before—control. Situations could get quickly out of hand, someone might need a talking-to. When Ivan or one of the others called, you had to be ready. Lying around or sleeping at three in the afternoon was never the problem. But you had to be able to get up, and fast. His trademark had always been F-E-A-R. And control was the key to that.

But today, he didn't give a damn. He didn't give a shit about his name. Teddy: didn't have a trademark.

Teddy: with the growing feeling he wanted to kill someone.

He had an idea. Step one of it was Swedish Premium Security. Time for full contact now. He didn't know if they were behind the attack at Sara's house—it didn't matter. No more wannabe spy bastards would be following him around from now on.

Loke had helped him get hold of a list of the people who worked for the company. The rest was easy: he'd managed to find pictures of most of its employees online. Teddy recognized the man who'd been following him in town. His name was Anthony Ewing.

He picked up the bottles from the delivery point at the supermarket. Propofol-Lipuro. Loke: impressive knowledge of so-called net pharmacies—no need to waste time at the doctor or picking up prescriptions. They arrived in bubblewrap and cardboard. The postmark showed they'd come from Spain, but the markings on the packaging looked Chinese.

After that, he headed straight out to the suburb of Hässelby.

Out there: so calm. So idyllic. Until today.

He waited in his car outside the entrance to the guy's place. It looked like it was from the eighties, the same as all the other houses along the street. Flat roof. Big windows. A huge trampoline taking up most of the lawn. Plus: the same cars, the same values, the same middle-class everything.

Teddy had taped over the letters and numbers on his registration plates.

Somewhere around four, two teenage boys rolled up on skateboards and went into the house.

At about six, a woman arrived, shopping bags in her hands.

Teddy had started to sober up. But the fire in him was the same: he was burning up from the fucking inside.

At seven, Anthony pulled up in his Audi A4.

Teddy's car was parked in front of his garage doors. Anthony came to a halt, waited for Teddy to move.

But he didn't touch the wheel. Instead, he pulled his balaclava down over his face and stepped out. Tore open the door of the Audi. Pulled out the needle filled with Propofol-Lipuro. Jabbed it into the man's neck. The bastard was wearing the same Windbreaker as the last time he'd followed him.

Teddy had done this kind of thing before.

Anthony yelled. Tried to climb out of the car. Teddy held him down.

After five seconds, he was sleeping like a baby.

Teddy dragged him to his own car, shoved him into the trunk. Tore off.

Maybe one of the guy's kids had seen, or his wife. Maybe a neighbor or two. But what could they do? It wasn't like they had a license plate to go on.

An hour later. Teddy slapped Anthony on the cheek. Pinched his arm.

He'd parked out in the woods, Bårsta again. Put Anthony into the backseat of the car. Arms held behind him with cable ties, feet bound with electrical tape.

"What the fuck . . . ," he managed to blurt in an English-tinged accent before Teddy jammed his old Zastava in his face.

"Shut up and listen."

He pressed the gun against the tip of the guy's nose. It was soft, like it was made of foam.

"I just want to know one thing, then you can go."

Anthony's eyelashes trembled; they were long.

"Who are you working for?"

"What d'you mean . . . ?"

"Answer me." Teddy pressed the gun even harder against his nose.

"Please, don't do anything . . ."

"Who are you working for? Who's paying you to follow me?"

Anthony was cross-eyed, his pupils fixed on the barrel of the gun.

"I don't know."

"So what's your job?"

"Please . . ."

Teddy pressed harder.

"Fine, we had to carry out personal secret surveillance of you. Information gathering. We had to document your activities, contacts, times, places." Anthony's mouth barely opened as he spewed out his words. He probably didn't want to move his face too much.

"Why? What are you trying to find out?"

"I have no idea. I promise. We just pass the information on to our boss, who gives it to the client."

Teddy took off the safety catch. "I'm gonna ask you one last time. Who are you working for?"

He sobbed: "I swear, I swear, I've got no idea. My boss forwarded me an email with the job details. We never meet the clients physically. Just see emails."

"What address?"

"Wait. You can look, if I can get my phone."

Teddy cut the cable ties. On tenterhooks now. His pistol still in the guy's face as he fumbled for his phone. Scrolled through his inbox. Held it up for Teddy to see. An email. The message said roughly what Anthony had just described. And ended with the initials KS. The email address looked like nonsense: 459294@countermail.com.

Shit—Ewing wasn't lying. Teddy would have to get Loke to look into this, too.

It was like being inside a bubble. No matter which way he turned, he came to the same slippery wall. He had to burst it, get out.

He thought: Mats had a backer he did business with. Sebbe Petrovic. Sebbe: part of the same crew Teddy used to be involved with.

That pointed in a clear direction, if nothing else.

One that led him to step two: Kum.

26

Handelsbanken's office in Kungsholmen. After some back-and-forth with the cashier, she opened the door and showed Emelie downstairs. On the walls, advertisements for the bank. *Get more from your money—open a Bonus Account today.* What a joke: interest rates in Sweden were in negative figures right now. Maybe it wasn't so strange that people kept their money under their mattresses.

Bills, coins. Not everyone used credit cards and online banking. And especially not a few years ago, when things had all started for Mats.

The key was slim and rectangular, and on a piece of paper she'd found in Benjamin's bag, there were two words and some numbers. Kungsholmen, 3234. When they first found it, neither Teddy nor Emelie had understood what it meant, but once Jossan mentioned the key, it all made sense.

"Not many people use safe-deposit boxes anymore," the cashier said. "We introduced a ban on keeping cash in them in 2012. Plus, almost all bond transactions are registered electronically nowadays. I sometimes wonder what people still want them for."

Emelie wondered, too.

The cashier showed Emelie how to get back out of the vault, and then closed the wrought iron gate behind her. Emelie was left alone. She went over to box 3234 and put the key into the lock. It fit. She'd never done this before, it felt like she was in some old film from the eighties. She pulled out the box—it was about a foot long, and heavy—took it into the booth and pulled the curtain shut. She put the box on the table.

Other than an envelope with the words "Forum Exchange" printed at the bottom, it was empty. There was something inside the envelope. She opened it.

A piece of paper, also from Forum Exchange. On it, she read: MTCNFE 30230403, and: *Ask for everything in a blue plastic bag.*

When she came back outside, her phone rang. It was the estate agent who'd worked for Fastighetspartner when the house on Värmdö was sold.

"I got your message. You wanted to know about the house in Ängsvik?"

Emelie explained everything again. Did he remember who'd signed the papers when the Roslings sold the house?

The agent cleared his throat. "I remember some stuff, actually, which I don't normally do. But this was a bit unusual. The buyer was Spanish, Juan Arravena Huerta, but he spoke perfect Swedish. Didn't look very Spanish, either."

"No? What did he look like?"

"He was huge, covered in tattoos. I remember he had a tiger on one arm."

Stockholm County Police Authority

Interview with informant "Marina," 17 December 2010

Leader: Joakim Sundén

Location: Farsta Centrum

MEMORANDUM 4 (PART 2)

Transcript of dialogue (continuation)

M: By spring 2006, Maxim and his guys really had to start working. Michaela and I started calling him Smurf Man, it almost made him sound cute.

JS: Smurf Man?

M: Yeah, you know, he was Sebbe's right-hand man, and he was in charge of finding our smurfs—the guys who made all the individual transactions. He had to make sure they behaved. But I'm guessing he didn't act too cute as far as they were concerned.

We spent most of our time on work for Peder's individuals, that's what he called them, but we were still doing stuff for the old clients. I really didn't know much about Peder, whenever he called it was always from a hidden number, and when he emailed me—which he hardly ever did—it was always from different, anonymous addresses. I never saw him in that law firm's offices again, but we met maybe once a week at different places in town, and he'd give me the relevant documents and account numbers, plus contact details for different management companies in the Bahamas and law firms based in Lichtenstein.

One afternoon, I was at work—my normal job—and Niklas came over.

"Mats," he said, "something's been bothering me. Could we have a quick chat tomorrow, after lunch?"

"Sure, what is it?"

"A couple of invoices that don't add up. You need to tell me what you've been doing."

My heart was racing: the money I'd taken from clients to pay Sebbe. I'd been waiting for this, but trying to forget it would come up.

I was flat out with other things right then. And I'd gotten an idea in my head, an idea that might be able to take me and the kids away from all that crap for good. It was based on two key things.

The first was so-called options to purchase. It sounds complicated, but it's actually pretty simple—a financial derivatives instrument. You paid a premium for the right—though there was no obligation—to buy an underlying share at a certain price at some point in the future. The whole thing was based on mathematical models I knew well, Black-Scholes and stuff like that. Bosse had made a load on his SinterCast shares. But with an option to purchase, things would've been different. If, instead of just buying the shares himself, he'd paid thirty thousand kronor for the option to buy forty thousand shares at fifty kronor each, and then the price rose to a hundred, just like it had, he would've made two million instead of two hundred thousand. And the only risk would've been the premium on the thirty thousand. The math was clear: earn an insane amount more with a lower initial stake, and in a shorter time. And the good thing was that the trade in that kind of option had exploded in Sweden over the past few years. It was a perfect fit.

The second thing was information. I needed information. Because I'd realized one thing: the trade in bond papers wasn't anything like a poker table, where you could bluff and play on a hand that was actually worthless. You couldn't fool the market like that, or at least not if you couldn't control the spread of news. But information, that was the equivalent of a great bluff—if you knew things no one else knew, you could act ahead of the rest of the market. Kind of an inverted form of poker psychology. I would know what was missing before I went all in.

For every big acquisition, you need an army of consultants. Corporate firms to give advice to the investment trust, bankers to finance the acquisition, the offeree company's own financial advisers. Not to mention all the law, audit, and IR firms involved. In other words, for every big deal, there's a whole slew of consultants involved, and they have knowledge of what's going to happen before it does. Hundreds of people sitting on information that could give you momentum in relationship to the market. My idea built on the idea that it had to be impossible for *everyone* to keep their mouths shut. I started listening carefully.

But that didn't solve the problem of my boss's questions. I'm not finished telling you about that yet. The invoices I'd fabricated.

My life was like a bomb. Everything could've blown up at any moment.

We were sitting at the kitchen table at home. I wasn't working for once. Lillan was asleep, and Benjamin was in his room, reading or playing computer games or something like that. I turned down the lights, lit a few candles, and took out some brie, goat cheese, and crackers. Cecilia was surprised but happy, I could see it on her face.

"I'm in some trouble," I said, trying to sound calm.

The fine lines around her eyes made her look peaceful. Actually, she probably was pretty happy right then. The trip to London had been great. Our finances were slowly starting to get back on track, thanks to the money I was getting from Sebbe. I'd cash in the jackpot option, too, I thought—no limit. Plus, Cecilia was active in the church. She didn't just sing in the choir anymore, she went to seminars and stuff like that. Her mother had always been religious. I guess that's where it came from—and she found it calming.

"I have a meeting with Niklas at work tomorrow. He's worried about something."

"What could it be?"

I'd known she would ask, but I still didn't have a good answer.

"I'm not sure, but I think it must be about a mistake I made a couple of years ago."

Cecilia's engagement ring glittered faintly like a fading dream.

"What does that mean? Is it serious?"

"I guess I'll find out tomorrow."

"You must know more than that? Sometimes it feels like you're disappearing into your work, Mats. I'm never even awake when you come home at night. Is it really just your job?"

It wasn't a good topic of conversation, especially not since she'd seen that message from Michaela, but I still felt a little relieved that she wasn't asking me any more about the conversation with Niklas.

I said to her: "It's work, I promise. But not just at KPMG. I'm doing some other stuff, too."

"Wait, what kind of stuff?"

"I've got a business idea of my own."

"Okay, that sounds good, and I don't want to accuse you of anything, but when are you and I going to have time to talk?"

"Didn't we have a good time in London?"

"It was great, but I mean here, back home, an everyday thing. We need to be able to talk."

"I don't know what to say, Cecilia. I think we do talk."

"Yeah, but only about who's going to take the kids to school, stuff like that, not *real* talking. Not like the way we talk at St. Görans."

"You mean the seminars?"

"They're called existential conversations. We reflect on all kinds of things. You should come along sometime. I think it'd be good for you."

"Hmm."

"And I also think it'd do you good to take a proper vacation for once. Can you do that?"

I should've made a decision right then. Listened to Cecilia. Stopped for a while. A few weeks' vacation probably would've been enough. Away from KPMG. From Sebbe, Maxim, and Michaela. Maybe I could've even gone along to one of these existential conversations with my wife. But I didn't. I chose another path. Christ. . . .

JS: Do you regret it?

M: Things could've been different. It would've been better for everyone. My family, above all. But there's something in me. I don't know what it is, but it drives me forward, even though I normally end up where I don't want to be.

JS: I see. Keep going.

M: We used to meet once a week. Sebbe would tell me what to do the rest of the time, or sometimes I'd tell him, we'd use encrypted emails. He always wanted to meet when he was at the gym. He'd be on the bench press at Gym-

Max, you know the place on Regeringsgatan, it's always open, and he'd be breathing heavily. "This is a real gym. Free weights, no faggot shit," he said. He always had sunglasses on, even indoors.

They had TV screens screwed to the walls, Eurosport on 24/7, and euro techno pumping from the speakers. Ancient posters of Arnold Schwarzenegger striking a pose and Ove Rytter flexing his muscles at the World Gym Championships. Sometimes it seemed like everyone there was just a variation of Sebbe.

Maxim was standing behind him, ready to grab the bar if Sebbe couldn't manage it.

Sebbe's tattoos moved in time with the weights, flexed.

"I got the first one in Holland when I was sixteen. Shit, man, I love Amsterdam," he said. The sweat was glistening on his forehead.

"Then I got the second one in Goa when I was eighteen." He pointed to a long tattoo that ran up, over his bicep. His veins snaked like worms on top of his pumped-up muscles.

"Three and four are from Christiana in Copenhagen. They've got a sweet tattoo place there."

The common denominator for all the places he'd been to was obvious.

"Have you ever thought about how gross they'll look when your skin's old and wrinkly?" I asked with a grin.

Sebbe got up, quickly. "Come here," he said. Maxim cracked his knuckles.

Sebbe took hold of my wrist.

I bent down toward his sweaty face.

He hissed: "You work for me, you get paid by me. But one thing should be crystal clear: don't ever fuck with me. Ever."

That's just what he was like, Sebbe. He reacted quickly.

JS: I know the type. But you still haven't told me what happened with your boss.

M: Right. We met in Niklas's office. He was actually the only one with a room of his own in that place. I'd always liked him, and I think he liked me, even though I was just working part-time. But I still had a really bad feeling in my stomach when I sat down. It had to be about *those* invoices, it couldn't be anything else.

Niklas was waiting for me with his hands clasped. The company had done an internal audit, a random sample of—among others—the companies I worked with. That's when they'd spotted those payments. They'd checked with three of the companies the invoices seemed to have come from, but they hadn't known anything about them. I'd made the transactions, Niklas explained. But the weirdest thing was that all the invoices had the same account number, for an account they couldn't trace.

I'd known it would be about those invoices. I must've looked like an idiot that day, trying to hide how nervous I was.

Niklas asked me whether I could explain it again, whether I remembered anything. I just shook my head and said I had no idea. My mind was blank. There must've been a mistake. I just didn't remember, plain and simple.

He held my gaze. He said: "I need more from you, Mats. You must remember something."

I had that feeling again: like I was an insect, balancing on the edge of hell, the verge of an inferno. Like I was just another inconsequential object about to be crushed under the weight of reality.

I'd managed to duck so many questions in the months leading up to that point, I'd come up with so many explanations as to why I sneaked off for so long at lunch, told so many stories about how I felt and why I'd cut my hours. People had accepted most of it—my colleagues understood, they said; and my clients didn't notice, because I still did what I had to.

"If you can't give me any straight answers, I've got no choice but to send this to internal affairs and maybe even to the police. You know that, don't you?" Niklas said.

The house of cards I'd built up was about to come crashing down. The bomb I'd been riding was about to explode. I needed my sideline investments then more than ever.

JS: You could've just told him everything, couldn't you? If he was a good boss, he might've been able to help you get out of it?

M: Yeah, maybe you're right. He was a good boss. But that's not what I did. It didn't even cross my mind. I was terrified. I'd used the same account number for a lot more transactions after that.

I didn't even go home to Cecilia that night. I slept in the office at Clara's—or "slept," I should say; I shuffled papers, looked into our secret accounts, tried to work out what links there might be between that account and me. And like I said, I didn't ask Niklas for help. I asked my other boss for help instead, Sebbe. I told him what had happened.

JS: Tough situation.

M: Can I tell you something, Joakim? It feels really good to be able talk about this.

JS: Glad to hear it. So how did it all work out with Niklas?

M: Sebbe dealt with it in his own way. He and Maxim paid a visit to the three customers who the fake invoices had been for. Told them in simple terms that if they didn't explain those invoices as a result of internal errors, they'd break their kneecaps, burn down their houses, shove a pipe up their asses, put a rat in it, and tape over the end.

Memo continued on separate sheet.

27

Lidingö. Not like Solna or Hässelby: middle-class vacation homes and comfortable Fords and Citroëns. Here, several rungs up the ladder. Not quite like Djursholm, and not like Östermalm either—but almost. Lidingö: one of the upper class's favorite haunts. Somewhere they could play undisturbed, socialize with their peers, pair up. A place they could avoid coming into contact with anyone but variations of themselves.

Clear pieces of the puzzle. Sebbe, who'd had dealings with Mats. Sebbe, who'd been one of Kum's men, just like Teddy.

Too many things pointing in the same direction. Toward Kum.

There was just one direction: nowhere else would lead anywhere useful.

It was ten o'clock. Teddy was banking on him coming home at *some* point that evening.

Emilijan Mazer-Pavić, aka Father Em, aka Mazern. To those in the know: just Kum. There had been others who went by the same name in Stockholm. Jokso, Radovan, others too. Mazern wasn't the only one—but he was the only one Teddy had looked up to as *his* godfather.

Back then: the myth. Stockholm wasn't like before, during the '90s and early 2000s, when everyone knew who was in charge. But still: there weren't many people respected in all areas like he was. The myth of Kum: the man who'd spent twenty years dodging the police force's tireless attempts to send him down. The man said to

have earned more from tobacco, coke, booze, and money laundering than anyone in Stockholm before him. The man you couldn't
find a single picture of on Google.

Mazern: the Albanians had tried to fuck him up; the Hells
Angels had tried to take him down; competing syndicates from
Montenegro had sent two death patrols to clip him and rough up
his wife. There was talk that the contract killers' bodies were in the
foundations of the Karolinska Hospital, but that their dicks were at
the bottom of a lake. Kum: more lives than ten cats put together.

The history: *Srpska dobrovoljačka garda*. Teddy had been twelve
then. The discussions, his dad in front of the radio every single day:
spring, 1992—Bijeljina and Zvornik. The snipers who'd cleared the
way for the artillery. Who'd swapped their Yugoslav People's Army
emblems for the Serbian Volunteer Guard's. Emilijan Mazer-Pavić:
one of the leading elite soldiers in Arkan's Tigers. Teddy hadn't
even met him all that many times back then, in his old life. He and
Dejan had mostly done jobs for Ivan and the other bosses under
Kum.

Yesterday, he'd been waiting outside Anthony Ewing's house.
Today, he was here. Six hours so far. In the car, on the street, outside Kum's villa.

Teddy pissed into a plastic bottle with an extra-wide top.
Vitamin-water orange. The standard joke: don't forget—it's not
apple juice. Like in his work for Leijon.

He'd done plenty of waiting in his time. The wait before the
cell door opened at seven thirty every morning, the waiting in the
visitor's room while Sara, Linda, or one of the few friends who
came to see him cleared security. The waiting to get into the work-
shop, where they made nesting boxes, three-legged stools, and park
benches. The waiting for the two-hour window when the library
was open every week. When he'd needed to shower. When he'd
wanted to buy chocolate from the kiosk. When he'd wanted to
talk to his sister, his dad. Waiting for hours, days. Everything he'd
wanted to do had been controlled by someone else. Everything
important was limited by other people's time, their power.

He was sick of waiting.

At half past ten that night, an M-class BMW X5 pulled up in front of the gates. A floodlight came on. The gates swung open, and the car drove through.

Five minutes later, the lights started coming on throughout the house.

Teddy got out of the car, spoke as clearly as he could into the intercom by the gates.

After a while, they swung open for him, too.

The gravel driveway crunched, like he was eating nuts with his mouth closed. The sound echoed in his head.

He rang the bell. The door opened. The godfather himself. Teddy was surprised he dared.

Mazern looked just like he had nine years earlier. The acne scars, the ash-colored hair combed loosely to one side. The same small, dark eyes, piercing like nails.

He was wearing a shirt, unbuttoned at the neck, a pale blue linen jacket, and thin suede loafers: a real summery outfit. Riviera feeling. Båstad feeling. Carefree dinner on a yacht somewhere. Or a balmy evening in Serbia.

Teddy made an effort. Kissed Kum on the hand—acted like he was expected to. He saw the initials on the cuff of the sleeve: EMP. Heard the blood thud in his ears.

They went into the living room.

"Slivovitz or whiskey?" Kum asked.

"Slivovitz," said Teddy. "With ice. Thanks."

Kum sat down in an armchair—bloodred with golden arm-rests. He clicked his fingers. Teddy suddenly realized there was a guy behind them, standing by the bar in one corner of the room.

Through the panoramic window: Värtan bay. Closer: the illu-minated garden. The decoration inside: mishmash to the max. Old-fashioned furniture: classic style, or whatever they called it. Ornate golden table legs, leopard-print cushions on the armchairs, huge golden frames around the paintings. The place looked crazy.

The gorilla behind the bar brought them their drinks.

"Sit, please," said Kum. "It's been a while, Teddy, I hardly recognize you. You look like your dad, just without the red nose."

Teddy sat down on the sofa opposite Kum. He was itching to go: just wanted to launch himself at the man. Attack the asshole in front of him. Throw him through the enormous window. He wished he'd brought the pistol with him. But at the same time: that would've been suicide.

"Dejan tells me you're doing well," Kum continued. "That you got yourself an apartment and a good job. Law branch, he said, but I told him: that can't be true. Right, Teddy? You're not working as a lawyer?"

Teddy took a deep breath through his nose.

"Yeah, I do a bit of work for a law firm every now and then."

"Everything's gone mad. BMW makes environmentally friendly cars and Teddy Maksumic is a lawyer. How is that?"

"I'm not a lawyer, but the job's okay. Brings in the bacon, you know."

"A job shouldn't just be okay. It should be fantastic."

"I'm happy. Now."

"Maybe you'd be interested in working for me again? Is that why you're here?"

"No. I wanted to ask you a question. About something completely different."

"Okay. Why didn't you just call? Dejan's got my number."

"I wanted to look you in the eyes."

"Aha, and what're you hoping to see?"

Again: Teddy wanted to launch himself at the man. Break the motherfucker's nose. Smash his head against the floor. Kick him in the kidneys. But he said: "I want to see your eyes, your soul, if you have one."

Kum breathed out. "Okay, okay, take it easy. Let's be civilized here. What do you want to know?"

"It's about Mats Emanuelsson."

Mazern got to his feet. He went over to the little bar and refilled his glass. His back to Teddy, he looked out the window. Outside, the lake lay dark. Sweden lay dark, though it was a bright summer's night.

"I suspected as much. You took a real hit there."

"I want to know what the kidnapping was about. Because it wasn't just money—they wanted a computer, maybe a hard drive, too."

"You might be right, my friend, and like I've said, I'm sorry how things worked out. But Ivan was in charge of all that. I wasn't involved that way. And he's dead now, you know that. Smoked too many filterless cigs—never managed to shake the homeland. Lung cancer's hell. But I don't even think he knew much about the details."

"But the order came from you."

"I have no idea. We helped loads of people back then."

"Sebbe Petrovic? What did he have to do with Mats?"

"Enough, Teddy; you knew me nine years ago, but lots has happened since then. Lots of water under the bridge, like they say, *Šveđani*. I'm a peaceful man now. I live here on Lidingö, you know, I've got a family, kids. I focus on my properties these days. Spend time with the neighbors, coach the kids' football team, that's it. If the train runs over a lady on the Lidingö line, that's the week's big news here." Kum turned to him.

"Have you ever thought about that, Teddy? We didn't have any Lidingö line where we grew up, no picturesque little tram taking us back and forth between the fancy houses. This is the only kind of place you get something like that, Lidingö, Saltsjöbaden, Djursholm, you know exactly what I'm talking about. You have your own tramline—you're a particular kind of person. Stuff like that doesn't exist to the south of Stockholm, or west of Bromma. True, they've got that train line there now, but it's not a cute little tramway, they'll never get that. A local tramline's a sign of whether a place has *it* or not. It's that simple. So listen to me now, Teddy, because you don't seem to get it. Everything's better out here, we're calmer, we spend time with tranquil people; everyone out here has Swedish values. Do you get it now? We're comfortable here. I'm not the same person I was. I'm not like you."

Kum took a sip of his drink. He was close to Teddy now. Short—shorter than Teddy remembered. But Mazern still seemed to loom over him like some kind of threatening tower. Teddy thought about what he'd said.

He asked: "What kind of car d'you drive these days, other than the X5?"

"Why do you want to know?"

"You're a man, aren't you? You like cars?"

"Of course."

"You don't have any other cars, then? Out here, you've surely gotta have at least two."

"Yeah, of course, my wife has a Golf. Then I keep my babies elsewhere. You can come for a spin sometime. I've got an old Porsche 911 from eighty-two, a Rolls-Royce Phantom, then I've got a 'rari."

"What model?"

"Ferrari California. From last year. It's my favorite. When you turn the key . . . you should hear the sound. It's like it wants to eat you up."

"That must mean you drive, then? You don't take the tram?"

"Of course I don't. Who do you think I am?"

Teddy replied: "I know exactly who you are."

Kum took another step toward him. As he did so, Teddy noticed that the gorilla behind the bar had moved.

"You don't want to believe in change, Teddy. You're just like the Swedish state. They're still hunting me, but I'm a new man now. Just because I paid no tax for years, like we all did. Now they want me to pay millions. It's not a dignified way to live, but I've got no choice. That's the reason the cars aren't in my name. All the crap the state keeps going on with; someone else has to front the businesses, this place is in my wife's name, you know what it's like. The state's like a terrier. Once it gets a hold, its jaws lock. Don't be like them, Teddy. Free your thoughts."

Teddy got up. He could see the signs of age on Mazern's face now—the gray flecks in his stubble. The furrows on his cheeks. The creases on his forehead. He'd been at the top, ordered Mats's kidnapping. And Sebbe Petrovic linked everything together somehow.

Teddy moved closer. Didn't back down. Two inches from Kum. "I hate to repeat myself . . ."

Pause for effect.

"But I'm going to crush you unless you tell me exactly what happened with Mats Emanuelsson. You'll regret not talking to me now. I want to know exactly who asked you and Ivan to order the kidnapping, and what the point of the whole fucking thing was."

He could smell the Slivovitz on Kum's breath.

"If I was still my old self, Teddy, I wouldn't just kill you for that. I'd take every single member of your family and crush them like insects."

28

Emelie and Teddy were at a table in Wienercaféet. Eating break-fast. Having a meeting. Almost two weeks had passed since the drive-by shooting. The mood was tense. It was the first time they'd met since.

Brass details, wooden interior, glass counters, marble tabletops. French-bistro style times a thousand, like so many other places in Stockholm right now. That was the weird thing about this town: everyone wanted to be individual, unique, but they all followed the exact same trends. Not that it mattered: the espresso and breakfast sandwiches were fantastic, and there was a back room where they could talk in relative peace.

Teddy was brief. He didn't feel like he'd made any progress. Dead ends no matter which way he turned.

Emelie went over what she'd found in the safe-deposit box. And recounted her conversation with the estate agent about who'd signed the contract for the house in Värmdö.

She told Teddy about the number and letter combination she'd found on the note in the bank: MTCNFE 30230403. After a little searching, she'd worked out that it stood for Money Transfer Control Number Forum Exchange. In other words, it was the number used when money was withdrawn from an account with Forum Exchange, a chain of the currency exchange. A so-called tracking number.

She'd gone to a branch on Götgatan. Shown the tracking number to the young woman behind the thick armored glass.

"Yep, that's right," she'd said brightly. "You can withdraw a cash transfer using this code. But I'll need to see your ID or passport."

Emelie handed over her driver's license.

The cashier had long brown hair and incredibly long nails.

"Sorry," she said. "I can't let you make the withdrawal. It has to be someone else, I'm afraid."

Then Emelie had an idea. She'd said: "Can I have it all in a blue plastic bag?"

The cashier looked like Emelie had just asked something inappropriate.

"Didn't I just say that with your ID, I can't do anything?"

Emelie had been about to leave, but then she'd had another idea. Behind the cashier, in the small space behind the glass, there were piles of envelopes and headed paper. She looked at the envelope and the note she'd found. The same logo, the same business: Forum Exchange. But they looked slightly different all the same.

"Can I ask you something completely different?"

"Of course."

Emelie held up the envelope. "Was this sent from you?"

The woman looked like she wanted to take out a magnifying glass to inspect it—there was nothing wrong with her willingness to help, anyway. She'd said: "Yes and no. That's what the envelopes and paper look like when they come from our head office on Vasagatan."

The businesspeople had started to leave the café, making room for old ladies in their seventies, with permed hair and dressed in camel-colored knitted sweaters.

Emelie and Teddy were trying to work out what linked it all. One thing was clearly of great interest to them: the man who'd acquired the house on Värmdö in the Spaniard's name was probably Sebbe Petrovic, the same man who'd been in business with Mats, his poker backer.

The old ladies around them peered at Teddy. He was strange, belonged to another world. He wasn't the kind of man you could go for a walk around town with, the kind you could introduce to your friends or potential clients. And that poor woman, Sara— what were his feelings for her?

He was different today. His eyes were dark, pushed her away.

"All I know is we're not getting anywhere, but Mazern knows more than he's letting on," he said. "Sebbe was one of his men."

"What do you want to do, then?"

"I'm not planning on giving up before Kum realizes he has to talk. Help me. This shit's going to blow up, but who cares. I swear, he'll give in. He won't be able to cope when I get going."

"Teddy, we're in this together. What are you going to do?"

He took out his wallet and put a hundred-krona bill on the table before he got to his feet. "You just don't get it."

She had to get back to the office. The SLA negotiations were done, but then she'd ended up in a due-diligence case. It was mostly supplier and customer contracts, employment agreements, stock option programs, and environmental and building permits. In truth, it was a small DD—most projects like that involved considerably more material—but they'd given her the project to handle alone. The business being sold was a refuse-collection company, so its most important assets were the agreements it had with the city and county authorities. The buyer had made a tentative offer of twenty million euros.

Still, Emelie didn't move from the café once Teddy left. She took out her laptop. She needed to gather her thoughts. Try to summarize what they did and didn't know.

First of all: they still had no idea who the dead man was. She'd tried to read up on it, and it seemed unusual for the prosecutor to keep a murder victim's identity a secret. There was rarely any real reason for it—it wasn't like the victim was at risk from any external pressures. But sometimes, they just couldn't determine who the victim was. Maybe that was what was going on here: whoever it was had been shot in the face, and unless they were in the fingerprint or DNA register, the prosecution only had dental records to go on. The problem in this particular case was that their teeth were probably damaged, so even that might be difficult.

Secondly, it wasn't just that someone had had their head blown off in the living room. Something had also happened in the hallway—there were flecks of blood there, too, and from someone who'd been on their feet. In the best of worlds, the police would've found the blood just like they had—but she couldn't be sure of that. Only time would tell what the police did or didn't have in their investigation.

Thirdly, the house on Värmdö didn't seem to be anyone's permanent residence, but it seemed like someone had wanted to spend time there, in privacy, every now and then. That was strange—there was an alarm system, furniture, and a certain level of decoration, but the place didn't really feel like it had been lived in.

And finally: she hoped Teddy would manage to hold it together. What she'd seen today had scared her: he was a different man. Someone a hairbreadth from snapping. Maybe this was what he'd been like nine years ago, before he went inside. Maybe it was his normal self.

The Forum Exchange on Vasagatan was bigger than the one she'd visited earlier. She tried the same procedure at the counter. Gave them the tracking number and asked for everything in a blue plastic bag.

This time, the cashier reacted differently. "Sure," was all she said, without even asking for ID. Twenty seconds later, she handed over a money bag as fat as a wallet. Emelie opened it and peered inside. Bills: it looked like thousands of euros and Swedish kronor.

There was a line behind her. The cashier wanted to move on to the next customer.

Emelie said: "Sorry, but I just need to ask, is it possible to see where the money's from?"

"Well, I mean, it's from here, like normal."

"What do you mean like normal?"

"Whenever you ask for the blue plastic bag like that, Stig Erhardsson's the one who arranged it. No?"

Emelie was speechless. She thanked the cashier. Googled Stig Erhardsson on her way out. She had a hit before she even stepped out onto the street.

Stig Erhardsson: not just anyone.

Stig Erhardsson was a bigwig.

She counted the money in the bag. More than a hundred thousand kronor.

29

In the car. Östermalm. Unmoving.

Teddy was waiting. Again.

Three days until midsummer. People were rushing around, moving like confused little birds.

In the exact same spot as last time. Banérgatan: Teddy remembered how he'd chased Fredric McLoud. How Magnus Hassel had grinned and said they would use the evidence of drug abuse to bring down the price by two hundred million. Emelie had told him the deal wasn't quite final yet. That was why Teddy wanted to find McLoud today.

A memory, pre-slammer. Him, his dad, Linda, and little Nikola, visiting Darko in Malmö. Nikola couldn't have been more than four. Teddy must've been nineteen, twenty—on the verge of the big jobs. Still, he'd gone down there with them; Darko had always been cool.

They'd taken Nikola to a beach, he didn't remember which. The sand stretched out into the distance, big grassy areas, a couple of jetties, a campsite up toward the parking lot, mini golf, and what they called the party center. All that Svensson crap. People absolutely everywhere—it had been a good summer that year.

Darko: the good son. Remembered to bring a blanket and a box full of stuff: Coca-Cola, Maryland cookies, tiny sausages for Dad. Bojan didn't even want to look at the Coke or the biscuits— restaurant man that he was. His brother had even brought collapsible chairs and mugs to drink from. Teddy hadn't felt so Swedish since high school. Nikola had run straight down to the water's edge. Despite the nine-to-five feeling, Teddy had enjoyed himself. Seeing Nikola shriek with joy as he ran into the water warmed his heart. They splashed about for more than an hour.

He went back up to the others. Linda was on the blanket, cutting up a melon. Darko and Dad were talking about NATO's bombing of Serbia.

Life was peaceful.

That was when Linda had looked up. "Where's Nikola?" she'd asked. They couldn't see him down by the water. They went to look. He wasn't in the water, either.

"He was here when you came up, wasn't he?"

He had been, Teddy was sure of it. Where could he have gone?

They walked back and forth. Looked everywhere. Kids in swimsuits. Hundreds of four-year-olds. Nicko's hair color, build, height: suddenly seemed to be Sweden's most common appearance. But none of them were Nikola.

Shit, shit, shit. Teddy had waded out into the water. It was green. He'd tried to see into the distance. Look for hands waving, legs kicking. Kids gasping for air.

Children were leaping from the jetty, letting their parents throw them up in the air, splashing about with their inflatable rings and armbands. But no Nikola.

Linda started to cry. Bojan started to yell at Teddy.

Darko was silent, pacing back and forth. Trying to spot something.

Teddy was about to flip out—the man who normally kept calm. He'd wanted to shout to all the other damn people on the beach to shut up and stop moving for a minute so he could find his nephew.

The minutes passed.

Bojan: "Run up to the party center and see if they can help."

Teddy sprinted off. They had a loudspeaker system there, and he got them to put out an announcement.

"We're looking for a four-year-old boy by the name of Nikola, red swimming trunks; his mom's looking for him."

The minutes passed. Teddy could see Linda on the grass in the distance, a crowd around her. She had her hands to her face. Sobbing.

Nothing bad could've happened. *Nothing* could've happened to Nikola.

Teddy felt sick. He walked in circles, around, around, around. He didn't know what to do.

Someone came up to him. "I think I've found your boy."

He was on one of the jetties, a stick in his hand. Nicko, he looked so peaceful.

Linda, crying, had run toward him.

"Shhh, Mama," he'd said. "You have to be quiet. I'm fishing."

Teddy had talked to Tagg about what the business looked like these days. They'd met in Axelsberg a few days earlier. El Bocado: a pint for only twenty-two kronor. Tagg lived nearby, and everyone there said hello to him like he was one of the staff. He looked like he always did: weight lifter's body with the stance of a mover, parted hair and stubble on his chin.

"What's he do these days, Mazern?"

"Shit, T, got no idea. Ask Dejan."

"I can't talk to him about stuff like that, he doesn't know which leg he's meant to stand on. And he never wants to talk about Kum."

"Aha, got it. Honestly though, I dunno. Five, six years ago, it was all blow, horse, whores, anything really. But now . . . sorry. Plus, I never did any of that, I'm in it for the game, the kicks. Me, I'm noble."

"You're not noble," said Teddy, though he knew what Tagg meant.

"You know how it is. I never had anything to do with the dirty stuff. I'm a heist man, honorable. You know what I did time for."

Teddy knew all too well. They'd shared a hallway for years. Aggravated robbery on a cash depot outside of Eskilstuna. Tagg

and a few other guys had planned it down to the very last detail.
They'd even test-driven the escape car along the different routes.
The haul: more than eighteen million in cash, a huge amount for
four guys from the hood. They were pros, laid low the first few
weeks, stayed home in their flats, watched every season of *The
Sopranos* and *Entourage*. Didn't go into town, held off on the champagne, didn't dance on any tables in the clubs around Stureplan,
and didn't blow thirty grand a night on women. But it all went to
shit anyway. One of the guys got stopped on a routine check, acted
super nervous, and for some reason the traffic police decided to
look in the long bag he'd shoved into his car: it was full of dummy
guns. The rest was history. The fake guns matched the weapons
the robbers had been using in the CCTV images, and they also
found Tagg's DNA on them. The cops started to wind him in: they
started doing house raids, found a computer, managed to recover
some deleted files, found a link to a landlord in Eskilstuna, got in
touch with him and showed him pictures of Tagg. "Have you seen
this man?" Sure, the landlord knew him, Tagg had rented an apartment in his building, right opposite the cash depot.

"Some of your guys might know though, no?" Teddy asked.

Tagg took a swig of his beer. "Maybe. I can give you some
names. You can ask them yourself."

His face suddenly lit up. "By the way, I heard from Loke you
ordered some stuff from his pharmacy."

"Yeah . . . but I can't talk about that."

"Honestly, man, you should try his boner pills. They're the shit.
My girl loves it when I pop those."

So: the past few days, Teddy had been talking to Tagg's friends.
Ali with the knife, Crazy Calle, the Snail Man, and the rest. Some
knew a little, passed him on. "It's not like when you were in the
game, man," they said. They remembered his name—trusted him.
They said the Swedish Slavs were practically extinct these days. Others had taken over: the Syrians, Kurds, Tigers, Taxi Aslan and his
haulers. *Summa summarum*: Mazern had switched to shadier activities. Played in the big leagues now—where Tagg's boys had no info.

Loke had promised to help Teddy by trying to hack into Swedish Premium Security's mail and getting at the countermail.com address. Two days ago, he'd called back: "Sorry man, they've got really fucking tough security at that company, worse than my own. I just can't get in. I'm sorry."

"And the address they got the job from?"

"Countermail's the most securely encrypted mailing system on earth. Hacking them is about as impossible as trying to assassinate Kim Jong-un with a water pistol."

Teddy hated dead ends.

Kum himself probably hadn't been behind the kidnapping. Someone else was interested in the computer—but either way, Mazern knew perfectly well who'd ordered it. He knew, but refused to talk. That was the point of their war. To make him talk, to guide Teddy onward. He had no other way forward right now: the predators themselves were too deep in the shadows. Cecilia and Swedish Premium Security could both have given him something, but they seemed more like dead ends.

Teddy was also starting to realize: there'd be a price to pay for his war. He might have to leave Sweden. At the very least, he'd need to send Bojan and Linda away.

That was when he'd gotten the idea: someone who might be able to help. Someone with plenty of dough.

It was taking a long time today. The brat didn't come out all morning.

Teddy tried to listen to an audiobook with the volume down low: *Wilful Disregard* by Lena Andersson.

His car didn't have a CD player, which annoyed him, but the guy at the rental place had given him a strange look when he asked. "What planet you been living on these past few years? CD players are from, like, the Bronze Age. With this car, you can stream straight from your phone."

Teddy knew exactly which planet he'd been on for the past eight years, but he had no desire to explain that to a twenty-year-old car rental employee who never would've given him the car if it wasn't for the fact that Leijon was footing the bill.

At one o'clock, he finally appeared. Fredric McLoud.

Better clothes this time: purple cotton pants, a white shirt, and a dark blue linen jacket. A small purple handkerchief flapping in his chest pocket. He set off toward Djurgårdsbron. After tailing him for weeks, Teddy knew the man's routines all too well. This was an unusual direction for McLoud.

Teddy followed him. Past the Porsche Panamas and mothers with strollers, power walking toward Djurgården island in their Nikes and compression leggings.

Fifteen minutes later, he understood. Liljevalchs, the art gallery—Teddy had never been there before. McLoud kissed a woman on the cheek, and they went inside.

He's been easy to follow again today: maybe he thought he had nothing to lose. Or maybe McLoud was just on honest business for once—spending some time with a friend.

Teddy climbed the stairs. *Liljevalchs Konsthall*, he read. Golden lettering against a red-painted wall. The building was huge: old-fashioned, but not too old. Different-colored stone, column feeling from the pillars. There was a banner across the entrance. *Right now: Market Art Fair—Scandinavia's leading contemporary art fair.*

This was far from Teddy's normal territory. But his tail was inside. His object.

He paid at the counter and moved inside.

High ceilings, light flooding in from the windows, huge rooms. Silent white people wandering around: peering at the artwork, staring at the paintings, drooling over the sculptures. Teddy took them all in: this wasn't a room of your average Svenssons, no—this was the cream of the crop. This was *society*: he saw Rolexes on wrists, loafers on the men's feet, the women's unnaturally even and well-made-up faces.

And the stuff on the walls: he spotted a list of items for sale. One hundred and fifty grand for a tiny canvas, completely white apart from two black streaks. Three hundred grand for a blurry photograph of a chimney.

I'm not the only one who's lost it, Teddy thought—the whole world's gone batshit crazy.

In the next room, Fredric McLoud was talking to his friend.

He seemed to have a cold: sniffling like a two-year-old in February. Or like a serious coke fiend who couldn't give it up, not even now that he'd been caught in the act.

The woman with him seemed to know everyone there. Kiss on the cheek, artificial laugh, hug. Kiss on the cheek, artificial laugh, hug. She didn't exactly mix things up.

Her pants looked like some kind of dance leggings, and her sweatshirt had a weird print on it: a bulldog baring its front teeth. She didn't really seem like Fredric's type. Maybe she was some kind of art dealer. After a couple of minutes, she was deep in conversation with someone from the gallery.

Teddy hesitated. If he went over, there was a risk his work for Leijon would be over for good. But still, he had to do this. There was no other way.

He moved up behind Fredric. Whispered in his ear: "Me again."

McLoud turned around and dropped the catalogue he'd been clutching. It hit the ground with a thud. The woman in the bulldog sweatshirt glanced over in their direction. Teddy smiled.

Fredric McLoud, wearing the expression of someone with a bad toothache and a powerful migraine.

"What the hell do you want?" he whispered.

Teddy answered in an ordinary, conversational tone. "I have a proposal for you."

30

Midsummer's eve. Pretty much the lightest night of the year. In that sense, Sweden was nice: the seasons actually meant something.

Nikola met Chamon outside his place. Someone had scrawled *Down with the Turks* in Arabic on the wall.

Everyone was partying today. Made no difference if you were some super-Swede, the grandkid of a Serb, or from Iraq and had only been in the country for ten years—midsummer was sweet. A hedonistic ritual: the ultra Swedish tradition everyone dug. Not that they all danced around the maypole singing stupid songs, *the fox runs over the ice*—no one really knew what that meant. Not that they all ate pickled fish—though Grandpa Bojan loved it— and drank cold schnapps from tiny glasses—Bojan loved that, too. And not that they all made flower crowns, got shit-faced and drove drunk, either. But everyone did something. And everyone needed to buy food.

Tonight, the safe in ICA Maxi would be bursting at the seams with dough. A record day. The fattest haul in recent history. It pretty much couldn't go wrong.

"Hey, man," Chamon said, pulling up his hood.

They were both dressed alike. Helmets under their arms.

"You ready?"

Nikola gave him a thumbs-up. "Hell yeah."

They took the bus instead of the train. That way, they could avoid the cameras on the platforms. Chamon told him a sick story.

"You remember Ashur? He got sent down for that blackmail shit. Those warehouse guys, y'know? Anyway, his dad died when he was locked up in Hall. So he asked to go to the funeral, and they started acting like absolute cunts. Had to get a lawyer to write a shit ton of complaints to the prison people, but eventually they agreed. So these three guards took him to the church. He was really fucking sad his dad had died, but he was happy he could go honor him one last time. And you know what happened when they got there?"

"No idea. I've been away from the world for a year."

"They said: 'We're not letting you out of the van unless you have hand and foot cuffs on.' Ashur told them he wouldn't go into the church, in front of all the mourners, in cuffs. But they wouldn't give in. Those pigs, you know, what the fuck'd they think he was gonna do? Run off from the church?"

"What happened?"

"He refused to get out. They just had to drive him back to the slammer. It's not cool, having to demean yourself like that in front of your mom, your grandpa and your brothers and sisters."

"Jesus, those dickheads."

"Exactly. And you know what happened then?"

"No."

"They created a crazy-ass *shurda*. The guy hates this country with all his heart now."

They'd parked the 125cc and the quad bike behind a nursery near the shop.

Freshly stolen: they took them yesterday. Nikola had opened the ignition lock with a fat screwdriver that had some kind of nut at the end of the shaft. He hit it with a hammer and then took a wrench and twisted. Pulled the bits of plastic out of the lock and followed the wires to the little plastic cube. A bit more work, then he just had to turn on the gas. They cut the wheel lock with a pair of bolt cutters.

They'd parked a moped behind the shop, too, in case they had any trouble with the other vehicles.

Now they were up among the trees above the parking lot,

looking down at the huge superstore. Seven, eight cars: still parked down there. Maybe they'd be there all night.

Chamon had a police radio in his backpack and thin gardening gloves with grips.

The building in front of them: an enormous Lego brick between the highway and the steel and glass high-rises. The high entrance with its automatic revolving doors was closed. Almost all the lights were out. But the place still looked like it was glowing: a glittering golden treasure chest waiting for them inside.

Midnight now. The only time it got even slightly dark this time of year. They started pushing the quad bike and the 125cc motorbike over toward the building. Nikola felt his pulse pick up. Maybe. A chance in a million. His big break. His claim to fame. His only way out.

They'd scouted out the place three days in a row. Walked around, counting the ways out. There was just one road into the parking lot, but then there were the loading bays out back, plus a path to what was probably the staff entrance. By the side of the parking lot, there was a bike path that disappeared away, up the hill. The smartest thing would be not to use a car. Too big a risk that someone would block the exit. The 125cc and the quad bike meant they could move more easily, more flexibly. They could cover more terrain.

They'd gone in and out of the shop. Ambled about with a cart, bought a few bags of chips and lukewarm juice. Navigated. Tried to work out which door they should use to break in, which was the quickest route through the shop. Always with sunglasses on and hoods up. They tried to glance up at the ceiling, find the surveillance cameras, the alarms. Afterward, they burned the clothes they'd had on.

Nikola pulled down his visor and started the motor. It was a beauty, the motorbike, a cross.

They drove the last seven hundred feet to the back of the building. There might be cameras, and they didn't want their faces on film. His backpack rustled. He'd shoved the tools, an Ikea bag, and the other stuff they needed into it.

The metal door was pretty weak, they knew that already. Less than two minutes with a crowbar, and it was wide open.

The alarm unit was to their immediate left: they entered the code they'd gotten from Saman. The bleeping sound reminded him of the coffee machine in Spillersboda.

Took a few steps back. Got back onto their bikes and drove up the hill again.

Police radio in Chamon's lap. They counted the minutes. Listened for any sign that the rent-a-cops had been alerted to the shop in front of them. The real police radio was blocked these days—they couldn't listen in on that. Nikola had a pair of binoculars around his neck. Every now and then, he lifted them up, stared down at the main road. Guard vehicle at the entrance? Maybe they'd set off a silent alarm, a siren no one could hear.

"Go?" Chamon asked after forty-five minutes had passed without incident.

Stomachache: Nikola immediately had a bad feeling about it.

"Shit, I dunno . . ."

"There's no alarm. They would've been here ages ago."

"Yeah, but still."

Chamon got up.

"Wait," said Nikola. He got onto the motorbike. Started the engine and drove over to the tunnel underneath Hågelbyvägen.

Chamon must've wondered what the hell he was doing—but Nikola needed to do this.

He took out his phone. It had been off—he turned it on. Called Teddy. He lived less than a mile away, but Nikola hadn't had time to visit him yet.

He answered after a while, but he didn't sound tired.

"Hey, Teddy, it's me."

"Hey, everything okay?"

"Yeah. Listen, can I come over in a bit? I might bring Chamon."

"Sure, yeah. But listen . . ."

"What?"

". . . I'm not home yet, I've had a stressful day."

"Ah shit. Another time, then?"

"No, no, come over in a bit. Whenever you want. Just ring the bell and keep knocking."

Chamon threw his chin in the air when Nikola came back.

"What was that about?"

"Had to make a call."

"The phones are supposed to be off, man."

"I know, but I remembered my uncle lives near. I asked if we could go over. Just so you know."

Stockholm County Police Authority

Interview with informant "Marina," 17 December 2010

Leader: Joakim Sundén

Location: Farsta Centrum

MEMORANDUM 4 (PART 3)

Transcript of dialogue (continuation)

M: In late spring 2006, Peder invited me to an event. He said: "A lot of people are interested in what you do, Mats," and gave me a rough idea of what would happen.

To start with, I got to see Sweden from above. Sörmland from the air. Hunting grounds, pale green trees, glittering lakes. Yup, we went in a helicopter. It was Peder's idea, he said we should make an "adventurous" entrance. "The boys are going to love it." I had no idea who the other guests were, but that was probably the point.

Anyway, the helicopter landed on a big lawn next to a barn. We got out. I didn't know what the place was called, or exactly where we were, but the house was huge, eighteenth-century style. It wasn't a castle. It had more of a country estate feeling to it. Yellow wood, red roof tiles, three chimneys.

Two men came out to meet us, and they took us toward the house through the wind from the rotor blades. I'd rented a tuxedo. Peder had dropped hints it'd be best if I did. The helicopter took off again, and I remember thinking that the taxi home would be expensive whenever I left. For a second, I regretted even going along. I wasn't exactly good at mingling. But there was something about Peder. Compared to Sebbe, Maxim, and the others I'd been working with lately, he felt like the only normal one.

And the evening was good to begin with. We had a drink in one of the big salons. I think there were about twenty others there. All men, but that didn't even strike me as being a bit weird. Peder introduced me to some of them. He laughed and called me Mr. Money Man. Then I ran through everything. Peder had assured me the others were "aware of the complexities of it all," as he put it. That I could trust them, in other words.

I think I talked for about thirty minutes. Explained everything in a way that didn't seem suspicious at all. More in the light-gray zone. I talked about the differences between the various banking paradises, about how the third money laundering directive was affecting regulations in Sweden. I didn't give them any concrete tips—that would've meant giving away Sebbe's, Michaela's, and my business ideas for free—but I think I implied enough for everyone to understand the basic premise: that there's a solution for everything.

After that, we ate a three-course meal. There was a mix of nineteenth-century portraits and modern photographs on the walls. People seemed happy, I was happy, the food and the wine—the whole thing was fantastically well thought out. But the whole time I was there, I had my own agenda. I knew who roughly half the people in the room were. Some had introduced themselves; some I just recognized. They were men from Sweden's industrial families, venture capitalists . . . some were partners in law firms. I listened, fished, tried to steer the conversation. They were all half-drunk, lowered their guards.

The man next to me was most promising. "There's definitely something under way, I'm completely certain," he said. "My man at Goldman Sachs said that Investor had turned to them for advice. And my friend at Bain and Company, he's been on a case they presented to EQT. *Then,* my lawyer happened to mention that he'd been working on a few agreements ahead of a due diligence in that company. We're talking about Gambro here. One hundred percent. It's overcapitalized, and it's got net cash of six point five billion. I just have no idea when. They'll try to buy her up like a little Thai whore."

The mood was good after dinner. There was some kind of show in one of the rooms, but I mostly talked to Peder, so I didn't see what it was.

He said: "Now that you're here, there's something I need you to look into. I've been getting a lot of questions from the Inland Revenue in the UK, and they want answers this week. It's about the companies in the Channel Islands."

I had all the time in the world. These men were a treasure trove.

Peder showed me into a side room—it looked like an office. There was a huge desk with an old inkwell, and it was covered in papers. A stuffed wild boar's head on the wall. The heavy green velvet curtains were closed.

They were asking about the payments to Estonia, said the invoices didn't add up. "Can you compare them, see if you can get it to make sense somehow? I really need your help with this as quickly as possible."

Peder sat down at the desk and took out a laptop; I hadn't even realized he had it with him. I was watching over his shoulder. He entered a password to unlock it. The strange thing was, I couldn't take my eyes from the keyboard. I've always had a head for numbers. I can just remember them better than most people.

He showed me some Excel spreadsheets. "Is it okay if I leave you with these for a while?" he asked me.

And so I started to check over the documents. Deposits and withdrawals. So-called *walking accounts*—strings of transfers between different accounts. All to make things more difficult for the authorities if they started sniffing about. But my eyes were drawn to something else. There was another laptop on the desk. I kept working on Peder's transactions and cash flows for a while, but I couldn't really concentrate. Something was bugging me.

I took my own laptop out of my bag, the one I'd been gathering information on. Since that's what I used it for, I had a few different cables with me. First, I linked it to Peder's computer. In under ten minutes, I'd managed to copy half his hard drive over to mine.

Then I reached for the other computer. Opened it. I tried the same username and password I'd seen Peder put into the first computer. It was a complete gamble. And now, with hindsight, I know it was the stupidest gamble I've ever made. Because it worked.

At first, all I could see were a load of files with nonsense names. But I looked a little deeper and found some more folders, ones with more suspect names. XXXDream. XXXBelow13. And for some reason, I had the same impulse I'd had with the first computer. I made a copy of everything I found.

An hour later, Peder came back. He said: "Mats, if you're done here, I think it's time for you to go home."

He followed me out. There was a black car already waiting on the gravel outside. "Thanks so much for coming. I know everyone found it incredibly beneficial." Peder winked and took hold of my arm.

When I got home, I turned on my own computer. I clicked on one of the files I'd copied over. It was a film.

I could see a dimly lit room and a double bed. Four men. A woman, though maybe woman is a bit of a stretch—it was a girl. I couldn't tell her exact age, but I don't think she could've been much older than thirteen, fourteen, I'm sure about that. She was on all fours on the bed. One of the men was having sex with her from behind. She was having oral sex with another. And I'm pretty sure she was crying.

I clicked on another video file. It was a different room, but I could see more bare walls, tile flooring, brighter lighting. This time, there was a girl tied up with what looked like rubber straps. She had something in her mouth, a ball. And there was something between her legs, a bottle maybe. Her body was covered with brown smears. It must've been shit. There was a man in the video too, urinating on her face.

I opened a third file and then a fourth, but I could only manage a few seconds of each. It's the sickest thing I've ever seen. . . .

JS: Do you know whose computer it was?

M: No, but the passwords were the same.

JS: But if it wasn't his, who would you guess owned that second computer?

M: I have no idea.

JS: What did you do then?

M: Nothing. And I regret that to this day.

JS: No, come on, it wasn't your responsibility.

M: That's not how I see it. I should've done something back then. It's every-one's responsibility.

31

When Emelie was small, they used to celebrate midsummer in Roslagen. Her aunt had lived there back then, in a small village: Berhagen. She and her husband had rented the place as a summerhouse at first, but then they'd bought it and moved in.

The yearly midsummer celebrations took place down by the village hall. Emelie and her cousin Molly used to go down there every day. They would buy ice cream, look at the old mill wheel, and talk about anything and everything. They weren't close, they barely saw one another for the rest of the year: but right then, for one week of summer every year, they could talk about everything. That kept Emelie going the rest of the year. No matter what else was going on in her life, no matter how she felt about school, her teachers, her friends, or her mom. And dad. She always had Molly: in a bubble, shielded from everything else.

The celebrations would start at twelve, with the dressing of the maypole. The year-round inhabitants, summer guests, and assorted other visitors went down there with birch twigs and flowers. After that, the majority of people went off to eat midsummer lunch. Pickled herring with sour cream, chives, and potatoes. Crisp bread and mature cheese. Västerbotten pie, egg and anchovy salad, strawberries with whipped cream. And, of course: the schnapps. At three, the real celebrations began. The pole had to be raised, it was more than thirty feet tall: a job for the men. Emelie was always terrified her father would hurt himself, or even worse: that he'd cause the pole to roll and hurt someone else. Because midsummer was one of his favorite holidays: one of the few days in the year it was socially acceptable to drink strong spirits and get "a little bit squiffy," as he liked to say.

She was probably about twelve when it finally happened. Emelie, Molly, her mom, aunt, and the others had been dancing around the maypole, following Olle Högström, who was leading the group. He'd been dressed in traditional clothing like usual; according to Aunt Ingrid, he'd done it for thirty years. *Ritsch ratsch filibombom-bom, filibombombom,* they sang. They did the movements, jumped around. If that had been the day aliens chose to make their way down to earth, to see what life was like on our little planet, they would've turned straight back around. Madmen like that couldn't possibly be part of an intelligent civilization.

There was no sign of Dad, but Emelie had been able to see the unease on her mother's face.

After a few more songs, people started to talk, some were laughing. Others had peeled away from the dancing and gone over to the little bridge over the stream. They stopped. What was going on? Her mom's face again: deep worry in her eyes.

Emelie and her mother had unlinked their hands. The dancing stopped. The music fell silent.

They went over to the bridge. Molly at their side. A few people turned around and looked at Emelie. Their mouths were smiling, but she'd seen something else in their eyes. She hadn't realized what it was at the time, but she felt like she knew by now: it was pity she'd seen.

Her father was sitting in the stream. Naked apart from the wet shirt clinging to his body. His knees were bleeding. He was half singing, half screaming some kind of poem: "The evening is festooned with golden clouds and the fairies dance in the meadow, the leaf-crowned Nacken plays his fiddle in the silvery brook."

Emelie never forgot that sight. Of all the times he'd put them to shame, been embarrassing and stupid, this was the time she remembered most clearly. It wasn't the first time, or even the worst. But something else had made it stand out. Maybe because he'd been practically naked. Or maybe because Molly had been there. Molly—who was supposed to be protected from Emelie's world. Molly—who was supposed to be untainted by the family secret.

They never celebrated midsummer in Berhagen again.

Today, she was the one drinking. Emelie and Josephine were at a party, at one of her guy friends' places.

A rooftop flat on Linnégatan, super-deluxe renovation. Jossan had told her beforehand: "He flew in these old wooden doors from a castle in Bordeaux and then turned them into a table. He designed his own TV unit, too, and got the carpenters at Svenskt Tenn to make it from walnut and gold leaf. You'll see. It's really something."

Terrace doors wide open: it was a nice evening. Emelie wondered whether Jossan wanted to sleep with the guy in question. He worked for SEB Equities, Enskilda before that, and was a definite up-and-coming star in the world of investment banking. Emelie had actually worked with him on a transaction a few years earlier, but she'd never really understood the appeal. He had an irritating habit of sniffing his hands all the time. Though maybe that was why Jossan saw a kindred spirit in him: she was pretty much a lotion and hand cream fetishist.

First, they ate dinner. Twelve of them. The others all talked about the same acquaintances, the same bars, cackled at the same jokes. Emelie wondered if they'd all known each other already—though she knew that wasn't the case.

They drank martinis before the food. Wine and beer with it. Then shots: Stolichnaya Elit and OP. She knew she shouldn't get drunk: the side effects of her pills might kick in if she drank too much. Emelie's thoughts went back to her father. She didn't understand why her mom didn't just leave him. Why he didn't stop drinking.

And now: her mom had called to ask if she and her father could come up to Stockholm for a vacation, maybe stay with her. Now that everything was better with him. Come on: stay with *her*—the idea was bizarre. But she hadn't had the heart to say no. She would just have to camp out in the office for a few days.

Their host was talking about a leveraged buyout he was working on. Jossan and the other girls clearly weren't interested. That was the strange thing about Josephine—she was an incredibly gifted lawyer: if you asked Emelie, the best of her generation in the office. She'd worked her ass off to climb the ladder; she was on the firm's entertainment committee, involved in the cultural club, the football tournament, and the pro-bono work they did. She had all the prerequisites for being a partner. But at the same time, she was completely uninterested in anything relating to business, and in the areas their clients actually made money. She just loved the law. Maybe that made her even more perfect—she was never jealous of the clients. Those guys who earned a hundred times what she did, worked half as much, and seemed brain-dead in comparison.

Emelie had tried to dress up tonight. She'd stood in front of the mirror for hours, trying on more or less her entire wardrobe in varying combinations. Eventually she'd settled on a pair of loose-fitting silk trousers from Zara and a thin black blouse from Marc by Marc Jacobs—probably the most expensive thing she'd ever bought.

Despite that, she still felt wrong somehow. Josephine and the other girls looked much cooler than she did. Jossan was wearing a diamond-encrusted watch and had a Cartier Love bracelet on one wrist. Another girl had a Collier de Chien bracelet, black leather and rose gold—Emelie wouldn't have even recognized it if Jossan didn't spend her time browsing those brands' home pages the moment she had a spare minute. Emelie asked her where she'd bought the bracelet. Outside her comfort zone: but that was what you were supposed to do when you made small talk—you discussed the gym, interior design, clothes, where you could buy things. She'd almost learned by this point—she was nearly thirty, after all.

Her thoughts drifted to the case. Teddy was different, tense. Emelie didn't even know what he was doing; his phone had been off for days now. She had to talk to him.

Jan had been in touch with more test results from the house: DNA. The news wasn't exactly encouraging. They'd found Benjamin's DNA in several places inside. Maybe he was guilty. Maybe he'd murdered the man in the house after all. She tried to bat back that thought. It wasn't her place to decide. She was a lawyer—her overriding duty was loyalty to her client. But emotionally: If he was a murderer—how could she work toward getting him acquitted? Fight for his release into society, back on the street, where he might do the same thing again?

She'd called Cecilia to ask if there were any doctor's notes about Mats. She'd given the envelope from the bank to Jan for analysis. She'd been to see Benjamin. He was still in bed, eyes tightly shut, but after she'd been there a while, trying to get him to acknowledge her presence, he uttered four words: "Has Teddy found anything?"

Emelie hadn't known what to say.

She'd gone back to the bank in Kungsholmen and asked who usually came to the safe-deposit box. They said they didn't know. Maybe they were lying, but in any case, it wasn't something they could really talk about. She should have known that.

Jossan and the other girls were talking about Instagram feeds— their own, but mostly others'. Emelie didn't have an account, she barely had Facebook, or at least she never checked her own page— she'd stopped getting any friend requests on there anyway.

Their talk moved on. A new lipstick that made your lips swell so they looked fuller. They toasted, ate dessert: strawberry trifle. The sponge cake in the bottom layer was soaked in some kind of liqueur, mixed with sliced strawberries, vanilla custard, and cream. Emelie loved the taste, though her mother would've laughed at the idea of having catered food for midsummer. The waitress poured sweet dessert wine. Emelie was starting to feel drunk.

They moved on to what they would be doing over the summer. Jossan was going to Biarritz, unless she ended up in an enormous transaction like she had last year; the banker boy was going to his family's place in Båstad. Two of the girls were headed to Torekov.

"You know, real Torekovers, the ones in the know, they go to Orskär from the sixteenth of July, once the shooting season's over. You go there before then, you don't know anything. You've got no business in Torekov," one of them said.

"No, no, real Torekovers, the old ones, the ones in the know, they take the boats to the left when they go to Kohallen, because the swimming's worse there. But the new ones, their boats are always on the right, because they think: there's no one there," another said.

The guy sitting opposite Emelie was named Eugene, a lawyer at one of Leijon's rival firms. He said: "Full of newbies. I even saw a nigger in Torekov last summer."

The boys laughed. Emelie stared at Eugene.

Jossan put down her wineglass on the table. Noisily. Everyone turned to her. Jossan in the center. "Say that word again, and I'm leaving," she said.

Bad vibes in the attic apartment.

Fifteen minutes later. Emelie's phone rang. Teddy's number. She pushed her chair back and breathed a sigh of relief at being able to leave the room.

"Hello?"

"It's me."

"I know."

"What're you up to?"

"Trying to celebrate midsummer with a bunch of idiots," she replied. "What are you doing?"

"Not much."

"Why didn't you call me back? I've been trying to reach you for days."

"Emelie, I don't have time to argue with you now. Listen: if you don't hear from me within an hour, call the police straightaway. Okay? I'm in Killinge, at the far end of Lidingö. And all I want is for you to call 112 if you haven't heard from me by twelve at the latest."

32

Midsummer's eve in the country.

Midsummer's eve with Emelie. She was beside him in the car. He definitely hadn't asked her to come. The opposite, actually: he'd protested. But she'd refused to give in. "Don't do anything stupid. I'm coming, I'll call a taxi. Stay there."

For some reason, he'd waited for her. Maybe: it felt good that she cared. Or maybe it was just a precaution, pure and simple: doing what he had planned, two was better than one.

Midsummer's eve outside a barn in Killinge. If this place had been out in the countryside: a refuge for cows or horses, for housing tractors and other machinery, for storing anything and everything—grain, tools, hay, potatoes. But not this barn. This barn contained something much more valuable. Its sliding doors were closed.

Teddy's pistol was tucked away in his pocket. Again: he gave thanks to his old treasure trove in the woods.

He hadn't told Emelie what he'd been up to the past few days. Fredric McLoud had given in fairly quickly back at Liljevalchs, followed him out. The brat hadn't wanted to cause a scene; it was understandable.

Peaceful Djurgården outside. A tram had rolled past, and Teddy's thoughts had turned to Kum's words. Djurgården might well be the most beautiful spot in the entire country. In the distance, he could see the entrance to the Skansen museum. The last time he'd been there must've been in school. No, that couldn't be right: he'd gone with Linda and Nikola once.

"It's simple," Teddy had said. "I want to do a deal with you."

Fredric McLoud's eyebrow twitched, and he'd started to fiddle uncontrollably with one hand. It looked like he was having spasms.

"There's something fucking wrong with you."

"Nope, I'm fine these days. I've been worse, believe me."

"You've ruined my life. My business. Everything."

They'd stopped opposite the entrance to Skansen. Families with small children were flooding toward the entrance.

Teddy said: "The deal isn't finalized yet. Nothing's closed. And without me, the other side has no evidence about anything beginning with 'c' and ending in 'ocaine'—you know, the thing you like so much. So here's my plan: I don't help them. You earn a hundred and ninety million kronor on that alone."

Fredric sniffed. Then he'd smiled. His odd behavior seemed to have vanished just like that.

"You serious?"

"Yup."

"You're a star. But it'll be two hundred million?"

"Nope. A hundred and ninety."

"Why?"

"I said we were doing a deal. I'm keeping ten. And I want a million of it by tomorrow."

The edge of Lidingö. Killinge. The bush. The middle of nowhere. The barn: surrounded by a fence. Teddy had gone there earlier to check the place out. He'd seen the dogs. Two Dobermans, plus security cameras. They probably had motion sensors, too.

They'd been sitting in the car for thirty minutes. Just waiting. Teddy wanted to be sure no one was there. The dark treetops looked like a black backdrop against the deep blue sky. The lightest night of the year. A dumb night to attempt something like this. But on the other hand: a good night. No need for a flashlight; no need to draw the cameras' attention.

"What're you planning, Teddy? Tell me now."

"You just stay here in the car. I'm going out for a while."

"That didn't even slightly answer my question."

"You're a lawyer."

"I am."

"It's best if you don't know everything."

"Why?"

"A lawyer's supposed to prevent injustice, isn't that the rule?"

"Yeah, but our primary duty is loyalty to our clients. That's also in the rule book. Benjamin's my client. And you're helping me support him. So, my question to you is as follows: Is whatever you're planning going to benefit Benjamin?"

"Depends how you look at it."

Silence in the car. The smell of leather seats and her perfume. Teddy wondered who she'd been at the party with.

The illuminated display read midnight.

It sounded as though Emelie groaned. She said: "Imagine if he's guilty."

"You have no idea whether he is."

Then he opened the door and stepped out into the night.

The fence was about six feet high. Plastic bag in his hand.

He stopped six feet from the fence: he would be difficult to see on camera from that distance—they were pointed at the area inside the fence, where they didn't want any intruders.

He smacked his lips. "Here, boy."

Nothing.

He whistled. Smacked his lips some more.

After a minute or two, the dogs appeared, glaring at him from inside the fence. Yellowish eyes.

They growled. He opened the bag and threw the pieces of meat he'd bought a few hours earlier over the fence. Entrecôte—fancy food. He'd cut the steaks in a few places and injected Propofol, the same crap he'd given to the man trailing him. Each steak: enough active substance to knock out a horse.

The two dogs were stock-still. Straight-legged, necks out. Nice animals—Teddy had nothing against them. They continued their glaring. Waited. Growled. The chunks of meat landed a few feet away from them. It seemed like they wanted to see what would happen. They continued to stand. Teddy took a few steps back, showed he wasn't interested in them. Above all: that he wasn't interested in getting in.

One of the dogs was bigger than the other. It seemed to be sniffing out the meat. Teddy could barely make them out. The smaller dog went over to one of the lumps of meat, sniffed at it, licked, but didn't take a bite. Maybe it was waiting to see what the bigger dog did. A minute or two passed. Both dogs were stooped over their steaks, examining the meat. Teddy thought: this has to work—it's a classic.

And right then, the bigger dog picked up the steak in its mouth. In under five seconds, it had vanished. The other dog followed its example. Now he just had to wait.

He thought about how he'd tried to help Nikola.

There was only one way, as Teddy saw it. According to his old ways.

Tagg had arranged a meeting with a black-market estate agent in a park by Liljeholmen—well-known: the rental market was run by guys Tagg knew from way back.

It was a weird place, all climbing frames and slides in the shape of pineapples, pears, and watermelons. A tropical explosion of color with plastic lawns that kept their chlorophyll green all year round.

"Sorry, I'm looking after the kid today. I thought the park might be a good place to meet."

The man who came toward Teddy with his hand outstretched hadn't looked at all like he'd imagined. His head was as smooth as a baby's bottom, and he had no eyebrows. Maybe he was sick, undergoing some kind of treatment—it looked that way anyway. And the fact was, he was dressed almost identically to Teddy.

The agent had gestured to a small child climbing up a slide shaped like a banana.

Teddy tried to catch his attention, but the man's gaze was constantly flitting back toward the slide.

"What exactly are you looking for?"

"It's for my nephew."

"Okay, so what does he want?"

"He just needs somewhere to live, not too far from Södertälje—his mom's there. It can be a studio."

"The suburbs okay, then? Between Stockholm and Södertälje?"

"Yeah—south of Södermalm, Flemingsberg, Tumba."

The agent had taken a step toward Teddy. His skin was unnaturally pale, and his neck was covered with small nicks, like he'd shaved badly. Maybe he wasn't ill after all, he just chose to shave his beard and his head.

"The process is pretty simple, really. I look after everything," he'd said. "We put him in the queue first, then assign him an apartment somewhere for a few weeks—Vällingby, for example, I've got good contacts with a few landlords there, and the housing wait list's relatively short. Everything looks good and proper in the register. It'll be his official, registered address, and since he's been in the queue for a while, no one's gonna wonder how he got it. Then after a few weeks, we switch to the apartment he's going to buy. That way, it's a completely clean swap. Whoever's selling the place just needs to be registered in the apartment his was exchanged for, his fictitious apartment, in other words—and that's for at least two months. Credibility's everything in this branch, as I'm sure you can understand."

"Okay. And how long does it take, in total?"

The agent showed his teeth.

"Hold your horses. If I'm even going to start the process, I want a hundred thou in an envelope."

"What?"

He continued to grin. "You heard me. If I'm gonna help you, I need a hundred thousand kronor. U.T.T. Under the table, you know?"

Darkness. The smaller dog was lying down with its paws out

in front of it. Its ears were still alert, but it didn't make a sound when it saw Teddy on the other side of the fence. He waited for a few more minutes. The dog closed its eyes. It lay its head on the grass—asleep.

There was no sign of the bigger dog. Teddy started to make his way around the fence. Skirted the rear of the building. Then he saw it. Right by the entrance: it was lying down, too, but when it saw Teddy it started to growl again.

He took a few steps back, wanted to avoid causing any kind of scene the cameras might react to. Not that he had to wait long: three minutes later, the Doberman was out like a light.

Teddy went back to the car, opened the trunk, and took out his things.

"Are you done now?" Emelie asked.

"Just five more minutes."

"What are you doing?"

He didn't answer.

Emelie got out of the car and stood in front of him. "You need to tell me what you're doing."

There wasn't much time. Teddy had to move fast. "No," he said, trying to edge around her. "I'm doing this my way now."

Back at the fence again. At the front. Bolt cutters.

He quickly clipped the fence—it was like cutting thread. He climbed through the hole—his eyes on the smaller dog the whole time. It was still lying there. Cute little doggy, that one.

Five minutes later, he was pulling the heavy sliding doors open.

He pulled out his flashlight. The beam of light hit metal.

He could see them in there. Ferrari California. Rolls-Royce Phantom. Vintage Porsches. Mercedes McLaren.

Kum's babies.

Teddy went inside.

33

Emelie tried to make a midsummer promise to herself: never to drink while she was on antidepressants again. Her head was pounding and she felt drowsy. She wanted to grab a fistful of painkillers, curl up on the backseat, and go to sleep. She also realized she'd been slurring when she spoke to Teddy—it wasn't the booze, she was sure of that. She hadn't drunk *that* much, even if she could feel the shots and the wine.

Her thoughts drifted to what Teddy was doing. Maybe she should've followed him. But at the same time, it felt good to be in the warmth and quiet of the car, safe somehow. It was a beautiful midsummer's night. Much more beautiful than the dinner at Josephine's friend's place.

She sent a few messages to Jossan.

You still at Calle's?

Yeah, what an idiot, that Eugene guy ☹

Seriously. Good job you said something.

Was that why you left?

Yeah, and work. I have to work.

Emelie, honestly: are you OK? ♥

Jossan cared. Under all the emojis, the jokes, and talk about new antiaging creams, she never stopped asking how Emelie was

really feeling. She wanted the best for her. But Emelie didn't know
what to say: it had been a long time since she'd had a close friend.

She'd contacted the ferry company to ask them for the date Mats
Emanuelsson had bought the ticket for the ferry he'd jumped from.
He hadn't just made the journey once, it turned out, but five times
in the space of a few weeks before he finally jumped overboard.
She wondered why.

She contacted the ferry company again. Asked about passenger
lists for each of the journeys, but they refused to give out that kind
of information. Instead, she began to match weather reports to the
different days he'd traveled. The weather had been bad each time.
It was understandable: he wanted to take his life—but then it made
no sense that he'd eventually opted for a day when the water was
as flat as a mirror.

The dashboard in the car suddenly looked orange. Flicker-
ing light. Something wasn't right. Emelie looked up, out the
windshield.

Shit: there was a fire outside. The flames were licking at the sky
as though someone had just dropped a firebomb on the barn. Like
it was made of paper. Like someone had poured petrol over it and
thrown on a match.

She opened the car door and screamed: "Teddy?"

If he was inside, she would never hear from him again.

Jesus. She ran toward the flames. Felt the heat, despite the distance. "Teddy!" she wailed again.

And then she saw him, walking slowly toward her. It was like
the ending of some Hollywood film: the hero avoiding the explo-
sions, tongues of fire lapping at the screen in the background.
What the hell was he dragging behind him?

Something bulky and dark in each hand.

And then she saw what it was: two huge dogs.

Teddy dropped them onto the ground and pulled open the
driver's-side door.

"Sorry that took a while," he said. "I just didn't want the dogs to fry."

He was driving too fast.

After a couple of miles, she found her voice again; she'd needed a few minutes to take it all in.

"What was that? Are you crazy?"

Teddy's face was calm. "Putting some pressure on him. He'll want to talk soon."

"I don't give a shit about that. Know why? Because setting buildings on fire is against the law. Because it's dangerous, too. And because this Kum guy's probably going to want to kill you now."

"I don't care about that, don't you get that? It's my honor on the line here. Kum had something to do with the network that wanted Mats kidnapped, and *they* had something to do with the murder in Värmdö and with Benjamin. So if it's legal or not, and if it makes Kum sweat, that doesn't matter anymore. I want to get those bastards—I owe that much to the Emanuelssons, everyone whose lives *they* destroyed, and to myself. Kum needs to start talking, it's that simple."

"You're insane."

"I didn't ask you to come out here."

"No, but what were you planning on doing now, huh? Don't you realize what you've just started?"

"Don't worry. I've got money. I'm going to send everyone I care about away until it's over."

"Where did you get the money from?"

Teddy told her how he'd handled McLoud.

Emelie said: "Jesus Christ, you're actually insane."

"You just don't get it. I won't be able to live with myself if I can't fix this."

Emelie grabbed the door handle. "Stop the car. I'll make my own way home."

34

Saman's code had worked. They'd waited. The place seemed calm as anything. No guards had turned up after they broke in.

Now: back down by the same door again.

A dark hallway ahead of them. Lights on. Cool strip lights on the ceiling.

They moved quickly. The next door was locked, too. They got it open in under forty seconds.

Darted through the enormous shop. The bread shelf had to be at least sixty feet long.

Still complete silence: no alarms, no sirens. They knew the route: past the hams, the sausages, the feta cheese. Turn by the deli counter.

Nikola followed Chamon. His helmet bounced up and down like some character from *Toy Story*.

It wasn't pitch-black inside: faint lighting from the ceiling. Maybe it was so the cameras could pick something like this up.

The cakes, jars of herring, bananas.

They rushed through the fruit and veg section, small clouds of vapor glittering like some kind of rain forest.

There: the door. By the apples. This one was heavier, they knew that already. But they had a solution for that, too: Saman had given them the code—his second biggest contribution to this little operation of theirs.

They entered the numbers, ripped it open. An office. Posters from different ad campaigns on the walls. Messy shelves. Huge computer screens on the desk. They hadn't been able to scope this place out. From now on, they were running on insider information.

An alarm started to blare.

Shit. Nikola looked over at Chamon. They couldn't see the other's eyes through their visors. He thought they'd turned off all the alarms.

Nikola yelled, though they'd agreed not to talk inside: "Y'think we should get out of here?"

Chamon shook his head. "Never."

Nikola grabbed a chair. Climbed up onto it and pulled out a can of black spray paint—neutralized the little all-seeing eye behind the ventilation grille. Saman's third tip.

They took off their helmets—they didn't need them in there anymore. They needed to do the trickier work now. He glanced at Chamon again: Were they really going to keep going? The alarm was about to burst his eardrums.

The safe was in one corner of the room.

Nikola took a screwdriver from his bag. Long, thin, stolen. Chamon was holding the crowbar.

Together: teamwork—Saman had told them roughly what the safe looked like.

After a few seconds, they'd managed to pull the handle off. Under it: a little hole. That was how it was meant to be. But seriously, that alarm, what a fucking racket: Nikola's vision was blurred.

Semtex. He'd gotten it from Gabbe as thanks for helping with the Internet. He and Chamon had rolled the red dough into four-inch-long sausages, which they'd put into plastic bags and then wrapped in Bubble Wrap. It wasn't dangerous as long as it wasn't exposed to any kind of explosion—that's what Chamon said, anyway. The guy claimed he'd done this twice before—maybe it was true: he'd been on a couple of big jobs with Yusuf.

Chamon pushed the first bit of explosive into the space where the handle had been. They'd practiced this, too—they were no amateurs. In the woods: a metal sheet they'd grabbed from a building site. Stuck the stuff onto it, damped it, and *kaboom*.

They added the detonator. Chamon had made it himself: gunpowder from cartridges and firecrackers that he'd shoved into a metal pipe.

He poked at it. Fixed it.

Then: backed up.

The first bang.

Boom.

The smell: smoke, burned paper, and metal.

They kept working: more explosives. The safe was about three feet high. They taped more of the stuff into the hole the first explosion had made. If they added too much putty, they'd blow the entire office to pieces: the money would go up in smoke—literally.

He saw the sweat on Chamon's forehead. "*Ajde*, gonna try a bigger load this time," he shouted above the alarm.

They pulled their helmets back on.

This time, Chamon connected the detonator to a socket on the wall.

They opened the door and went out.

Waited.

BOOM.

It was the loudest noise Nikola had ever heard. The jars of jam teetered on the shelves. The apples fell down from their trays, rolled across the floor like tennis balls. The alarm: like a gentle whisper in comparison.

Nikola couldn't hear a thing. Just a ringing in his ears. He didn't know if it was sirens or tinnitus.

They opened the door again.

Full of smoke, disgusting smell.

They couldn't see a thing.

They waited a few seconds.

The door of the safe was hanging from its hinges; it looked like the front of a crashed car.

They ran over. Started grabbing the plastic pouches full of money and shoving them into their Ikea bags.

Thirty seconds later. Nikola jumped onto his 125cc.

In and out like pros: it had only been nine minutes since they first went in.

He tore off. Hoped Chamon had done the same; he couldn't hear a thing. The ringing in his ears was getting louder and louder.

And then he saw it, the patrol car. G4S: security guards playing real cops. Motherfucker. He picked up speed. Realized the guards had spotted them.

Chamon was next to him now. His quad bike like some enormous wolf from the *Hobbit* films or something like that.

They saw the patrol car drive across the parking lot, toward the shop.

He didn't get how they'd had enough time to get there.

Not that it mattered. The useless idiots were too late: Nikola and Chamon turned off onto the smaller road by the Shurgard complex. Floored it: Lewis Hamilton in Monza—stick that up your asses.

He turned around: no sign of the car anymore. They must've lost them.

He was grinning like the Joker. Chamon's ride seemed quicker: he was in front of him. Hågelbyvägen up ahead. His ears were starting to work again.

He couldn't see Chamon anymore. He was too far ahead. He turned left, onto a cycle path. It was dark and narrow. Why did the fucking kids smash up the lights like that? Hooligans.

Then he heard another sound. Checked behind him. Son of a bitch. Sirens from a police car in the distance. It couldn't be.

He sped up even more. The bag on his shoulder was bouncing up and down—pretty unprofessional. He should've grabbed himself a quad bike, too.

But it was too late. Swaying even more. Too much. The motorbike started to wobble. He had to drop the fucking bag.

He was swaying even more now. Dropped the bag.

Everything tipped. The motorbike was fucked. He skidded on the gravel.

He flew through the air like a ball.

Now it's over, he thought.

It was like he saw himself from above: head hitting the ground. Cracking his back. Breaking a rib.

Shock. He landed softly in the tall grass by the side of the track. Rolled over. Got to his feet.

Dazed. Confused. Screwed. But unhurt.

He heard the sirens again.

At first, he thought about just squatting down in the grass: something told him to keep going along the track.

He needed to get rid of the helmet. If they caught him with that, he was screwed—direct link to the motorbike.

Balls. He'd lost the dough—the small plastic bags of bills were scattered across the cycle path behind him.

He ran down a little bank. Almost fell. Pebbles crunched beneath his feet. He heard the sirens. They were up there, the pigs.

He kept going. In the darkness. Trees all around him. He could see something glittering between the trunks. Water. A lake.

He took off his sweater. Filled his backpack and helmet with stones. Threw it all into the water.

He was practically crying: how much money had he just blown?

He ran on. A hill. Out through the trees. Tall grass. A meadow. He was tired now, wouldn't make it much farther.

It was dark, no houses or roads lit up anywhere around him. He was moving more slowly now—planned to walk away from the police.

Then he heard the barking. It couldn't be—they'd brought dogs.

Sniffer dogs.

He saw the silhouette of the Alsatian first, then the dog handler. He'd dropped the lead. What an idiot. The dog was barking like it wanted to eat him alive.

What the fuck should he do?

He crouched down in the grass. It was damp. A small ditch: he made himself as small as he could. Hoped the fucking dog's nose wasn't that good after all.

He could see Linda's disappointed face in front of him.

He hoped Chamon was long gone.

He thought about the girl, Paulina.

He could hear the dog yapping. Closer now.

Happy midsummer. Bitch.

PART III

JUNE–JULY

35

He wasn't living in his apartment. It was no secret anymore, not since midsummer's eve. Najdan "Teddy" Maksumic was at war with his old mentor.

Best Western Årsta, Hotell Ibis, the youth hostel in Hornstull. He planned to keep changing every night. There was no other way. Besides, he didn't know whether those Swedish Premium Security idiots were still in the mix: he wanted to avoid them at all costs, too.

The hotel rooms all looked the same. Vinyl flooring meant to look like genuine parquet. Ridiculously hard double beds. Bottles of shower gel screwed to the wall so the guests wouldn't get any ideas about swiping them. Low-energy lightbulbs linked to motion sensors; they went out after a while—the first time he was plunged into darkness, Teddy had been doing a number two. He'd thought there must've been a power cut. Eight years away from Sweden. Sometimes, he felt like a martian.

Teddy wandered around his new neighborhoods. Årsta, Järva, Södermalm. Tried to work out his next move. He could stay in nicer places, but it didn't feel right. He needed to live like this. Stay under Kum's radar. But keep pressing him at the same time.

He hadn't heard from Emelie since she'd freaked out in the car on the way back from Mazern's barn.

He'd sent Sara a message from a new phone—again: he didn't know what resources those Swedish Premium Security guys had:

Sara, hope you're feeling better. Thinking of you, just wanted to hear you're
OK. Teddy.

Linda had called on Midsummer Day. "They've arrested Nikola."
She'd been crying when she told him the little she knew.

Teddy hated it when his sister cried. He hated it even more
when his nephew was in the shit.

He thought back to the call Nikola had made to him the night
before, about coming up to say hi. He hadn't been on his best form
at the time: in the process of burning down a barn.

But he tried to comfort Linda. Then he said: "There was
another thing. You need to leave the country."

"What are you talking about?"

"My old life's caught up with me, and there's some stuff I need
to do to put things right."

"I don't understand what you mean. Stop talking in cliches."

Teddy did his best to explain.

Linda refused, but she agreed to stay in a hotel in any case, to
take a few days off work. Teddy promised to pay back every krona
she spent.

He phoned Emelie. No answer. He sent her a message. He
went to Leijon to look for her. Asked Magnus Hassel if he knew
where she was.

"No, Teddy, my man, I have no idea. You'll have to ask person-
nel. Are you two working together on something?"

He shook his head. Regretted even asking Hassel. On the way
to the lift, someone tapped him on the shoulder.

"Hi, you're Teddy, right?"

One of the lawyers, he didn't know her name, but he'd seen her
around. She was slim, dyed-blond hair, well-groomed nails. More
polished than Emelie, somehow.

"That's me," he answered.

"I'm Josephine. I share a room with Emelie."

He'd heard Emelie talk about her before, Jossan, they were
friends—it struck him that she might know where Emelie was.

"Are you looking for her?" she asked before he had time to speak.

"Yeah, I need to talk to her. But she seems to be ill or something."

Josephine gave him a searching look.

"Is she, Teddy? Is she ill? Or is it something else?"

Teddy didn't say a word. The elevator arrived and the doors opened.

"Listen, I've gotta go," he said. "But if you hear from her, will you tell her to give me a call?"

Jossan watched him as he stepped into the elevator.

On the way back to his hotel, he went to a 7-Eleven and bought a packet of chewing gum.

Textured paper on the walls. Mottled curtains he didn't bother opening. On the bedside table: a Bible. On the coffee table: a free magazine about the Stockholm archipelago—the Fjäderholm islands, wherever they were—pretty place to visit, apparently. Under the bed: the shotgun he'd dug up in the woods. He'd hidden the pistol in his apartment.

The only positive in all this crap: that ass from Swedish Premium Security had been noticeable in his absence since Teddy started living life on the move. Maybe it had been idiotic of him to go up to the Leijon offices, or to try to contact Sara. But on the other hand: he had to keep going. He'd known the path he'd chosen would involve some heat.

His old phone rang. Hidden number.

"Hey, Teddy, can we meet?"

It was Dejan—Teddy recognized his voice right away.

His old friend: a bad omen.

"Nah, now's not really a good time."

"But I want to see you. You need to talk to someone."

"It'll have to be later, when things calm down."

"What are you up to, man? You gone crazy? I want to talk to you 'cause you were my friend."

Were my friend. The last time they met—when Dejan had brought along his dog—he hadn't spoken in the imperfect.

Teddy said: "You can tell whoever told you to call me that there are no limits now. Understand that? No limits."

He hung up. *Heat*—that was a part of all this; he had to put pressure on Mazern.

He lay down on the bed. Closed his eyes.

Dejan and him, eighteen years old. Breaking into the conference center. The trip to Amsterdam after they'd carved up those ten kilos. The parties at Green Bar. The moments in the car: when they'd talked about their parents.

His phone rang again. Hidden number—what exactly didn't Dejan get?

"Hi, it's me."

This time, it wasn't Dejan. The voice was Sara's.

"Sara, how are you?"

"Better, but I'll probably be here a few more days."

"Where are you?"

"Karolinska, ward 57."

"I'm so sorry, Sara. Everything that happened, it's all my fault. I thought I'd shaken them off. And I'm sorry I sent you a message."

"No, none of this is your fault. I'm the one who started looking into everything when you were inside. I'm the one who asked you to come to my place. It was my choice, not yours. I want you to have everything I found out about Mats, Teddy."

He got up from the bed. "We can't meet now, it's too dangerous for you."

"But I really want to see you. I talked to my partner about it. I'm willing to take the risk."

Stockholm County Police Authority

Interview with informant "Marina," 19 December 2010

Leader: Joakim Sundén

Location: Flemingsberg Centrum

MEMORANDUM 5 (PART 1)

Transcript of dialogue

JS: Well, the plan is for us to finish up before Christmas, so if we don't manage today, we'll have to meet again tomorrow. Is that okay?

M: I guess it'll have to be.

JS: Good. Over to you, then.

M: Okay. So, it was time to put my plan into action. I was almost completely convinced there was going to be a takeover bid on Gambro. It was just a question of when. I remember I was checking the company's share price a couple of times a day. SEB funds had started buying shares, and they were linked to the Wallenberg group. I could see the pattern, understood the timings. Investors and other people would put in an offer for the majority of the shares within a few weeks, and that offer had to be sweetened—in other words, much higher than the actual share price. We're talking about a 15 to 30 percent increase in most cases. The alternative was to fill up on thousands of Gambro shares and then just wait—they were at ninety kronor each. But it'd cost a fortune, money I didn't have. And at best, it'd be a gain of maybe 30 percent, a hundred thousand kronor or so. Not exactly leverage.

The other option was to play the long game: in other words to buy purchase options and pay a premium for the right to buy two hundred thousand Gambro shares at eighty-five kronor each in September. For that, I'd only need one hundred thousand kronor. But the gains could be enormous.

I was sitting on information that maybe only fifty or sixty other people had access to. The others were bound by confidentiality agreements and anti-insider trading rules, but I was a free agent. I was a gambler.

There was just one catch. I didn't even have the amount of money I'd need for the purchase option route. But just like Sebbe had forced me to pay my debts by taking money from my clients at KPMG, I thought I could borrow a little from him now and make the bet of the century. All I wanted was to create a better future for my kids. Plus, it was a short-term loan. Just a couple of weeks. He'd have his money back soon enough.

And in practice, I bought the options through one of the companies I was looking after. No one would ever notice.

Summer 2006 passed pretty quietly. Even Sebbe seemed to realize I needed some time off. I took a holiday. Peder's customers had quieted down a bit, though I really didn't want anything to do with them anymore, not since I'd copied the contents of that computer.

We were at our place in the country. Lillan was learning to swim, and Benjamin was doing some waterskiing. I still couldn't forget what I'd seen at that party. Clearly, I'd managed to copy the movies—perfect blackmail—onto my computer, something any ordinary person would've taken straight to the police, but I didn't have the nerve to use it *or* do that. It'd risk revealing my entire double life, ruining everything.

Toward the end of summer, we went to Denmark and rented a little place in North Jutland. Every day, I cycled a few miles inland to get better a signal, and I'd scour the stock markets using my new phone. I was obsessed with the price of the Gambro shares.

Then one day in September, Michaela called me when I was at work—my ordinary job.

"What the hell have you done, you idiot?"

"What're you talking about?" I tried to sound surprised.

"You know exactly what I mean. Jesus Christ, Mats. You need to put it back right now."

The KPMG office wasn't exactly made for conversations like that. I looked at my colleagues—they were like meek little sheep. I tried to keep my voice calm.

"Okay, okay. Please, Michaela. I'll sort it all out, and more. It's a great investment."

"I don't know what the hell you're talking about. It's not your money. And look: some of us aren't planning to wait for you to pay it back. *Some of us* are completely fucking furious with you."

I took a taxi back home, ran straight up the stairs. I passed a man in the stairwell, a guy I didn't recognize, but it wasn't Sebbe or Maxim, which was something. All I could think about was keeping track of my laptop, the one I had all my evidence on, and about trying to convince Sebbe and Maxim that everything was okay. If they were planning to do something to me, I had enough dirt to sink them and half the people we worked with.

I wasn't normally home that time of day. I usually left early in the morning and went straight from KPMG to Clara's at some point in the afternoon. It was so quiet, weirdly quiet, and I remember thinking it smelled different, too. Like someone else had been in the apartment.

I opened the computer and started going through the different folders. There was one I hadn't named—the one with the photos and videos from the computer at the party.

But then I smelled something even weirder—a sharp, pungent, burning smell. I sat there for a while, thinking someone must be burning something, even though there weren't any open fires in our building, or not that I knew of, anyway. Maybe there was a fire outside somewhere.

I got up and went over to the window, opened it, looked out. It was like the air rushed into the flat, like it was being sucked in through the open window. I closed it again. The place really stank now.

I heard a sound in the kitchen, like the wind. I went over.

The room was covered in flames.

The walls were normally bright white, but now there were flames licking the ceiling, turning all the surfaces black. The heat nearly knocked me flat.

I started coughing. The smoke and the fumes caught in my throat. I realized our landline was in there, and I tried to remember whether there was any rhyme for what you were meant to do in a fire. *Alert, alarm, get out.* I wondered where I'd put my phone, but I couldn't remember. I was breathing really heavily by then; I knew I had to phone the fire department. I had to get hold of some water somehow, put it out. I had to save my computer.

The ceiling was thick with smoke. I was coughing like mad.

The whole apartment seemed to be full of smoke now, and I thought the air might be better closer to the floor.

I got onto my knees. The flames in the kitchen were touching the ceiling.

It felt like someone had shoved pine needles down my throat and gravel up my nose.

I crawled toward the bedroom on all fours.

But my face felt weird, like I was wet.

The floor lurched toward me.

They must've given me the wrong lenses in my glasses, I thought. I couldn't see anything. And then it was like my lungs were full of rubber.

I don't remember anything after that.

The midwife's calm voice when Benjamin was born. When Lillan and I went to the emergency room on her fifth birthday after I managed to crush her fingers in the basement door. Our wedding, how Cecilia's hair made her look like an angel.

I floated around. In a way, it was nice.

I don't know what kind of treatment they gave me, but they said I was out cold for days. I had first-degree burns, for the most part, blisters and sores, but I had some other injuries to my hands and arms, too. They told me I had inhalation injuries from the fumes and the smoke. They gave me painkillers through an intravenous drip and wrapped me up in clean, dry sheets. Damage to my lungs. Dehydration. I woke up with all kinds of tubes attached to me. They said my family were fine, that they were staying in a hotel. They told me to drink juice through a straw.

Then I could sense that someone was there. Sitting by my bed.

It was Cecilia. She held out a glass of juice, told me to drink.

We didn't speak—I couldn't, actually; the smoke had damaged my throat. But it wasn't just that. I couldn't explain it to her. Sebbe had burned down our apartment. It was his way of repeating what he'd once told me at the gym: "Don't ever fuck with me."

I fell asleep with Cecilia next to me. Sank back down into my world of dreams.

I woke up. She was sitting there again. I don't know if it was later that day, the next day, or even a week later.

There was a painting on the wall, a lake with trees around it. The sun was going down over the trees and the sky was reddish orange. I'm sure it was meant to make people feel calm, but the colors just reminded me of my kitchen.

"I saw your computer at home," said Cecilia.

I wondered what she was talking about.

"It was open, I saw the pictures on the screen. And the other ones saved on it."

It was like the ground opened up beneath me. Like I was tumbling help-lessly toward I don't know what, but I knew it'd knock me unconscious again. I turned away.

She'd seen the files on my computer. I hoped she meant the Excel spread-sheets and my parallel accounting, the lists of names and bank accounts. But something told me that wasn't what she meant. The videos from the laptop at the party. Maybe she realized what I'd been doing the past year. Maybe she realized I'd gotten myself caught up in an enormous shit storm. But the films . . . what could you say about those?

I only managed one sentence. "I think that's who set the apartment on fire."

Later that day, one of the nurses came in to see me. Cecilia had gone home.

"There's a man on the phone for you. Sebastian, he said. Do you think you can manage?"

The handset was hanging from the little cart next to the bed. I answered slowly. "Hello?"

"What'd I tell you, Mats?" Sebbe's voice sounded uncomfortably mild. For a moment, I wished I'd been able to record the conversation and report him to the police.

"You said I should never fuck with you, I know. But I just borrowed the money for a few weeks, that was all. Have you heard of Gambro?"

"I hope you get the way things work now, my friend."

There was something off with him. I knew Sebbe well enough by now to know that when he was mad, his voice didn't sound anywhere near as calm. And he didn't use words like "my friend."

He said: "Didn't you hear?"

"No, what?"

"Michaela explained it all to me. Some players with a company called Indap AB, it's owned by Investor and EQT, they made an offer on your little Gambro today. One hundred and fifteen kronor per share. Which means that thing you bought, the option or whatever it's called, it's worth six million. You're a fucking genius. It's *fantastično*."

I felt lighter than a cloud. Lighter than smoke, even.

Sebbe said: "I'll forget your little mistake if you keep your mouth shut about the fire. Deal?"

Cecilia was back the next day. But I started to realize exactly what she'd seen on the computer. She wanted to know how the photos and films had ended up there. She thought I needed help, that I was some kind of disgusting pedophile. It wasn't just crazy, it was really lonely.

She sat on the edge of my bed, talking at me in that subtle way of hers.

"When?" she would ask. Or sometimes just: "Mats?"

But I couldn't talk to her about it; it was impossible. The hours passed. Someone had the TV or radio on in the room next door.

A nurse came in to check on me. Once she left, Cecilia leaned down and whispered: "I'm going to hand that computer over to the police if you don't tell me what's going on."

I closed my eyes and tried to pretend I was sleeping. I'm sure she knew I was awake.

Memo continued on separate sheet.

36

The cell walls: the moment Nikola touched them, it felt like his body was going to shatter. The cell floor: even colder. He was curled up in the fetal position on the green vinyl-clad mattress. Icy feeling in his stomach. Sick feeling in his throat. The polar opposite of Hästens's fanciest model: the mattress from hell was only two inches thick.

Plastic: made it easier to rinse off the sick and blood spatters after each inmate moved on. But the state's generosity was limited: the blanket was thin, and he hadn't been given a pillow.

Graffiti-covered cement walls and a concrete floor that stank of piss. No toilet, no TV, no phone; nothing to read but the scrawls on the walls. No pen or paper. Not even anything to kill himself with. If he wanted to go to the toilet, he had to let them know at least half an hour in advance: none of the staff seemed overworked. And to those who thought it might look like one of the cells from a Swedish crime drama: a little bulb hanging from the ceiling, a microphone, too—forget it. The light was screwed in so high up that not even LeBron James would've been able to reach it with a thirty-foot run-up.

Nikola had been held in custody before, but never for this long. It was almost three days since the tracker dog had sunk its teeth into him in that meadow. They hadn't said a single sodding word so far. Nothing. All that'd happened was that two cops had interviewed him immediately after he got booked at the station.

"We'll do this without a lawyer so maybe you'll get out of here quicker."

Nikola hadn't had the energy to argue. His arm looked like finely ground mince. The Alsatian had bitten deep. They'd promised a doctor would look at it as soon as possible, but so far they'd just put some fucking liquid on it and taped a sterile dressing over the wound.

They hadn't found jack shit on him when they booked him, but they'd still made him sit for more than three hours on the trouble-makers' bench, as they called it, in nothing but his boxers. It was a worse display of power than Putin flying over Swedish airspace.

"You're being held on suspicion of aggravated theft . . ." He could barely bring himself to listen. It was all so boring somehow.

"No comment," was all he said. "I deny everything."

The cops looked like sad little puppies—disappointed. Like they'd expected him to lie down on his stomach, let them fuck him from behind. Both of them.

They came back a few hours later. "Come on, Nicko. Just admit it, and you can get out of here. You're not so old, this isn't the place for you. Just tell us, and you can go. You can talk to your mom. We'll give you a lift wherever you want."

All he answered: "Get me a doctor."

He hadn't been able to sleep. Or eat. He missed his smokes. Was desperate for a Coke. Despite the pills they'd given him, his arm hurt.

He didn't know how much they knew. He tried to go through all the different possibilities. All the different versions he could tell—what evidence they'd left. On door handles, on the safe, on the motorbike, on CCTV. He didn't even know how dog tracking worked. Where had the dog picked up *his* scent? Could it be wrong?

The cops still weren't telling him what they had. Just repeating the same old mantra: "Spill, and you'll get out of here sooner."

He cried as soon as they closed the door.

They should be interviewing him properly, he knew that much.

Knew they couldn't keep him here longer than four days without first trying to remand him in custody. That's what had happened to Chamon and a bunch of the guys from Spillersboda. He'd heard the talk: custodial prison was better than the police station cells—at least they had radiators in the cells there, proper beds and TVs. Not like here: cold storage, mini Guantánamo.

He needed a lawyer. But who should he choose? The problem was that Hans Svenberg, the dude he'd had last time, right before he ended up in Spillersboda, was half-senile. Plus he'd retired.

But anyway: there was talk in the hood. Chamon had a lawyer he always used, Erik Johansson—but Nikola couldn't ask for him. If they'd arrested Chamon, Erik J would already be busy. And if there was a God and they *hadn't* arrested him, he couldn't take Johansson anyway. There was still a risk they'd pick up his friend.

He thought back to other names he'd heard: Tobias Sandin, Clea Holmgren, Björn Fälth. The cream of the crop—the best of the best, according to everyone. But on the other side: Nikola had never met any of them. He didn't know them. And right now, he needed someone who felt familiar and safe. He wanted his mom.

There was a knock at the door. The hatch moved to one side.

"Visitor."

Nikola rubbed his face. "Who?"

The door opened. Light burned his eyes. The guard wrinkled his nose, maybe at the smell in the room.

"Police."

"Who?"

"Can't remember the name. He's waiting for you in the interview room."

Nikola got up. Shivered. Put on his slippers: the prison service's very own—no one was allowed their own shoes here. He shuffled out into the corridor, the guard behind him. Each door had a slot for an information card. Most were empty, but several contained information for the staff.

Diabetes.

No pork.

Suicidal.

Simon Murray got to his feet when Nikola entered the room.

"All right, Nikola. How're things?"

The guy tried to hug him. Nikola backed away. This man wasn't his friend.

They sat down.

"Look, Nikola, I just wanted to come over and talk a little. How're you doing?"

"Not so good. It's so fucking cold in that cell. They won't give me another blanket or jumper. Seriously, I'm gonna get pneumonia."

"I'll see if I can do anything. Want me to talk to the guard?"

"Yeah, if you want."

"Sure, no one wants you to freeze to death in here."

Simon riffled around in his bag. "Want one?" He held up a jar of snus and a cookie.

Nikola pushed a piece of snus under his lip.

"What've you been up to now, then? You've only been out a month." Simon Murray tried to smile.

Nikola was thinking: you've got a messed-up, false, cuntish smile.

"Nothing. This is all a fucking mistake. I didn't blow up any ICA shop, like they're saying I did. They haven't even interviewed me. And I haven't seen a lawyer."

"I can talk to them about that, too. Which lawyer have you asked for?"

"None yet. I was thinking about it."

"Well, that explains why you haven't seen one yet. How's your mom? Have you been able to speak to her?"

"Nope, haven't done that, either."

"I can probably work on all this stuff."

"That'd be great."

"But listen, I want to talk about something else."

Nikola focused.

"They've got Chamon, too," Simon said. "But they put him in

another hallway so you two couldn't do any knocking on the wall crap or talk through the hatches."

Nikola felt the chill return to his body.

Simon continued: "But that's not the important thing. You'll have to sort that out with the detectives on this case. It's out of my hands. What I want to know is if you'll talk about the trial. Isak's trial."

Too many thoughts at once. They had Chamon. Nikola tried to work out how they'd caught him. What he'd said.

"Hello, Nicko, anyone home?" Simon poked him in the arm.

"I'm here. I don't know what you're talking about."

"I know that you do. We've got another investigation under way, one with phone tapping. So we know you were involved. And we know you were talking about the war between the Tasdemir and Bar-Sawme families. They're tearing the whole of Södertälje apart. We need help stopping that crap. So just tell me what you know. That's all I want. You don't need to talk about Chamon or any of your friends—I'm not asking for that. Just that you tell me what happened."

"No idea."

"Come on, Nikola. I just told you, I know you and Chamon helped out at Isak's trial. Surely it's not so bad to confirm a few things? I'll figure out the blankets, a call to Linda; I'll bring some nice food tomorrow, some more snus."

"I told you already, I don't know anything."

Simon drummed his fingers on the table. "Okay, okay, I hear you. Look, I'm going to suggest something I've never done before. And it's just because I like you. You don't belong in this world. Your mom works hard, your uncle Teddy seems to have straightened himself out. And I can see it in you, Nikola, you don't want this, not really. So look, it's like this: I promise I'll help you get out of this mess. I'll fix things for you. Understand?"

"How?"

"I can't go into that, I'm afraid."

Brain ache. Breakdown. Whirring in his head.

Simon wanted him to inform.

Inform, inform, inform. The sin of all sins. Number one no-no in the code of thieves. A man's strongest principle: loyalty.

But all the same: if they convicted him now, he could look forward to at least two years inside, probably more. And this time, it'd be the real slammer. Plus, Simon wasn't even asking him to talk about his guys. Just those other idiots. And the Tasdemirs *had* tried to screw Isak over. They fucking deserved it.

Still: a memory.

Nikola: somewhere around seven, meaning Teddy must've been about twenty. He'd picked him up from nursery one day. It was raining. A birthday present: Teddy had promised they'd go to the football match. Assyriska had a good chance of making it into the Allsvenskan league. Game against Örgryte IS at home, at Bårsta IP. Everyone was talking about it—even the teachers at school.

His friends moved slowly around Teddy, waiting for Nikola to get his coat on. No one said anything, but everyone knew it, even back then: no messing around with Nicko's uncle.

They walked hand in hand toward the bus that would take them down to the stadium. Nikola's fist like a little mouse, calm and safe in its nest. Protected from the raindrops.

"How was school today?" Teddy had asked.

"Good."

"What lessons did you have?"

"The usual."

Sometimes, Teddy acted just like Mom and Grandpa. The same questions, the same nagging. Couldn't they talk about something exciting instead?

"Teddy, who's the world's strongest man? Have you met him?"

Teddy laughed. "It's me, didn't you know?"

"No, but really."

"I dunno, but there's a really strong guy called Magnus Samuelsson. Saw him on TV yesterday. He was pulling a train. But come on, tell me now. How was school today?"

"Good, but there was a fight during break."

"Why?"

"Nino and Marwan went out onto the big road and were doing some stuff, and then they were mad at me."

"I don't get it, why were they angry with you?"

"'Cause I went to the teacher and told her."

"You snitched?"

"Well, our teacher said it's really dangerous to go on the big road, that we had to say if anyone did it because you might die if you get run over and—"

"You snitched on your friends?"

"But it was dangerous. Shouldn't you tell?"

They continued toward the bus station. Teddy's hand felt tense somehow.

Later on, during the match: Nikola's favorite, Andreas Haddad, was playing like a god, like always. Everyone dressed in the red-and-white Assyriska kit. "We're AFF," people were singing. Nikola had heard Teddy mention the supporters to some other guy: "Even though I'm a Slav, I've gotta say, it's pretty sweet here: tons of girls and families." His friend had put an arm around him: "This is Södertälje. You're with us, we're with you. We're going up to the box now."

The rest of the match, Nikola and Teddy had shouted along with the fans: "We're Suryoye."

At halftime, they went to buy hot dogs. Teddy said: "Nicko, I've been thinking. What you said, about it being dangerous for your friends on the road. It was good that you said something. But it was also wrong."

"Why?"

"You did the right thing, talking to the teacher, because you were worried your friends would get hurt. But it was wrong, too."

"How can it be wrong and right?"

"I don't know, that's just how it is. It's a principle, you don't snitch. You know what a principle is?"

"No."

"A rule. Something you just don't do. You understand? Never snitch. Never, ever tattle."

Simon Murray's smile had vanished. The room stank of damp cement.

He wanted an answer.

True, the Tasdemirs were the enemy. They'd made sure the guys with the balaclavas got into the room, waved their fucking guns in the air, almost clipped Isak. Grabbed the money. Shot a guy in the leg.

But still.

"Nikola," said Simon. "I know it feels shady. But let me say this: they're already on the way out, I think. You might as well start something new, something honorable."

"What're you talking about?"

"The Syrians. Since that huge trial, so many of them are inside. You know that. And that means new guys are taking over. Isak isn't the only king anymore."

"What're you getting at?"

"It's simple. I'll help you—in every sense. I'm giving you a way out of something that's turning bad anyway. All I want is a tiny, tiny bit of information."

Nikola's thoughts turned to Teddy again. To what he did these days. All the crap that happened a year ago, before Spillersboda. That lawyer woman Teddy worked with.

He said: "Simon, maybe you should go home to your wife."

"What?"

"I think Isak's probably over there, fucking her right now."

"What the hell are you saying?"

"That I'm not gonna snitch. Never. Oh, and one more thing . . ."

He got up—their meeting was over.

"Tell the cops I want a lawyer. Her name's Emelie Jansson."

37

Emelie had called his assistants, secretaries, and subordinates first—there was no direct line to Stig Erhardsson himself. The MD of Forum Exchange. Clearly: a very busy man. His assistants told her a meeting might be possible sometime after summer, would the middle of October be okay? That was four months away—not a good joke.

Eventually she tried a dirty trick. She sent an email from her Leijon address and wrote that she represented a big player within money transfer and banking, a client who wanted to discuss the possibility of starting a conversation about FE's activities in Germany. Erhardsson replied a day later. "My office, tomorrow, 4 p.m."

Stig Erhardsson received her in a visitor's room. The head office was on the top floor of the same building as the branch she'd visited earlier. It had a great view, the church spires of Gamla stan rising up in the distance, but there was no comparison with the views from the Leijon offices.

When Emelie entered the room, she realized this might not be as simple as she'd assumed. Beside Stig Erhardsson was another man, who introduced himself as Forum Exchange's lawyer, from the Welanders law firm. Emelie knew of the company—it was the fifth or sixth biggest in Sweden. It was okay, definitely played in the big leagues, but it didn't come close to Leijon in terms of sophistication.

"Is it just you coming, or . . . ?" the lawyer wondered. "You aren't a partner, are you?" He'd done his homework, in any case.

"No, not yet. . . ." Emelie sat down. "I'll get straight to it," she said. "I haven't been entirely honest with you. I'm not here representing a bank. I'm not even here as a representative of Leijon. I'm here as the defense counsel for a man being held on suspicion of murder."

She paused for effect, waited for a reaction. The lawyer quickly straightened his tie. "This is remarkable. You made an appointment with Stig Erhardsson without stating what it was about?"

"It's important."

"That may be, but I think we're done here."

The lawyer got up. His cuff links glittered in the light from the window.

Emelie remained sitting. "My client's name is Benjamin Emanuelsson. Mats Emanuelsson's son."

Stig Erhardsson cleared his throat and turned to the lawyer. "You'll have to excuse me, but I think I'll take this meeting myself."

Erhardsson wasn't dressed like a managing director. Jeans and an unbuttoned shirt. Not even a jacket. No expression on his face.

Emelie said: "What's your connection to Mats Emanuelsson?"

Stig Erhardsson replied quietly: "Why do you ask?"

Emelie didn't know what kind of man was sitting in front of her. "It doesn't matter. All I'm interested in is what you know about Mats Emanuelsson's life, whether you knew him or not."

"And why should I talk to you about this?"

Emelie articulated every single syllable when she replied: "Because you put codes into a safe-deposit box his son has access to."

Stig leaned forward over the table. She couldn't work out how what she'd said had affected him.

"Mats is dead," he said.

"I know, but were you in touch? It would help his family if you talked to me."

Stig closed his mouth, maybe weighing what Emelie had said. She noticed his hands and nails were very well-groomed.

"I knew Mats. We did some business together. I liked him a lot. What's happened to Benjamin?"

"Did you read about the Värmdö murder in the papers?"

"Jesus, Benjamin's suspected of that?"

Emelie placed the codes she'd found in the safe-deposit box on the table, alongside the money she'd withdrawn from the currency exchange.

"Yes. And I managed to get hold of this through him. So, my question to you is: What's this all about?"

He studied her for a moment. It seemed like the dark patches of sweat beneath his arms had grown.

"I'm only going to say this once," he eventually said. "And I'll never testify or admit to anything. That money is for Benjamin and his sister. I've been trying to help the family financially. They've had enough problems."

"And Mats?"

"What do you mean?"

"How was he, when he was alive?"

Another long silence from Stig. The sweat patches under his arms were the size of dinner plates now.

"Like I said, Mats was a good business partner. But he's dead now, and that's all I have to say."

Stockholm district court. In half an hour, Benjamin's remand hearing would be under way. Emelie wanted to get there in good time. He would be taking part via video link, but she wanted to physically be in the courtroom this time, able to look the judge in the eye.

She'd told her secretary she had a meeting in town. Maybe this was her new life: criminal defense lawyer. Another request had come in yesterday. Teddy's nephew, Nikola.

It almost hadn't felt strange to say yes—even if, in a way, it was more idiotic than taking on Benjamin's case. Defending Nikola would be public, and it was hardly some premium case, as some people would put it. But all the same, she was starting to feel more and more at home in criminal law.

She still couldn't get over the fact that Teddy had set the barn on fire, or that he'd blackmailed McLoud for money. But she wouldn't let that affect his nephew, she knew that. She'd met the kid once before, maybe that was why she'd taken the case. Plus, the risk the papers would pick it up was minimal—it wasn't some kind of serious crime they were talking about. And if she was lucky, Leijon would never find out.

The tall oak doors into the courthouse were heavy.

Once inside, she got into the line for security. She wasn't sure whether she actually needed to wait—she was a lawyer, after all—but it would be too embarrassing to push her way to the front only to be turned back.

The entrance hall was impressive. High stone arches, marble floors, sculptures. An atmosphere of gravitas, history. Lady Justice's halls—the law had been administered here for a hundred years.

Emelie walked into the internal courtyard. Glassy new offices had been built in the old parts of the building, and fifty feet in the air, there was a huge glass ceiling that turned the courtyard into another giant room. She bought a cup of coffee and went over to the information screens.

The number of cases was overwhelming. She tried to work her way through them.

11:00: Prosecution Authority—Reza Ali, attempted murder, Room 12.

11:00: Prosecution Authority—Maria Kymminen, theft, etc., Room 3.

11:00: Prosecution Authority—Abdi Muhammad, assault and battery, etc., Room 28.

11:00: Prosecution Authority—Jon Svensson, rape, Room 27.

Nothing. She moved on to the next screen. Eventually she managed to find the room where Benjamin's remand hearing would be taking place.

She thought back to what Stig Erhardsson had told her—that

he'd been supporting the family financially. Maybe that was how they'd managed to keep going while Mats was alive: Stig's support had kept their heads above water.

She'd been to see Dr. Gunnarsson again yesterday.

"I'll prescribe it this time, but we really need to do a thorough check of your overall health." He'd looked serious.

"Yeah, okay, sure." Emelie had tried to look like she really agreed: big eyes, faint smile, quick little nods. But really: she couldn't do without the Stesolid now—she'd never cope. Inheritance from her father. Her genes.

She'd transferred the tablets into an empty Läkerol candy box. Swallowed one with a gulp of coffee. She was alone outside the courtroom. Rölén, the prosecutor, might come in through another entrance.

She felt a hand on her shoulder. Behind her was a middle-aged man. He had thin hair and round glasses. A beard and a taut mouth.

"Hi, are you the lawyer, Jansson?"

"Yes, who are you?"

"An old friend of Benjamin Emanuelsson. I'd like you to give him this letter." The man held out a brown envelope.

Emelie studied it for a few seconds. He didn't want to tell her his name. He wanted her to give something to Benjamin, though she had no idea what it was. It was impossible. She couldn't bring in letters, phones, or any other information without the prosecutor having approved it first.

"I'm sorry, but I can't. He's being held under restrictions. Do you know what that means?"

"Yes. But maybe you can make an exception?"

"I can't give him the letter without sending it to the prosecutor to read and approve."

The man put the envelope back into his bag.

"No," he said. "I'll have to leave it, then."

38

The taxi pulled up in the turning circle by the main entrance. There were people everywhere. One of Stockholm's biggest hospitals: pensioners, families with small children, tired, broken people—some of whom didn't really need to be there but had nowhere else to go. A cross-section of Sweden: a boiled-down version of the country. Almost.

"The upper classes have their own hospitals these days," Tagg said. "'Cause of the insurance, you know? But I don't bother. D'you?"

"Yeah, actually. Through the office." Teddy suddenly pointed. "There they are."

Another car had pulled up behind them. He'd thought they'd given up, partly because of what he'd done to Anthony Ewing, partly because he wasn't living at home. But the moment he stepped out of the hotel, he'd had that fishy feeling, the sense that someone was paying too much attention to him. Swedish Premium Security—he was sure of it, their methods were the same. One person shadowing him at a time. That was when he'd called Tagg, who'd come over to meet him. They took a taxi instead. Teddy had seen the same car behind them several times now. How the hell had they managed to find him again?

He didn't want them to know he'd come to see Sara, even less for them to know where she was. Maybe he should turn around.

He decided to go inside anyway. Tagg at his heels. Moving guy look: he swayed from side to side, shoulders and arms slightly forward. "We're not causin' any unnecessary problems, are we?"

"Honestly, man, it's not unnecessary today."

The automatic doors swung open and shut continuously. There was a line at the information desk. Strong institutional feeling from the chairs and tables in the café. The color schemes on the walls were about as easy to understand as Chinese.

The hallway smelled of food. Tagg drummed his fingers against his leg. Rocked his head like he was moving to some inaudible inner rhythm. *They* were somewhere behind them—Teddy had a tingling feeling at the back of his neck.

"You okay? You don't have to help me."

Tagg twiddled his thumbs. "Shit, man, I'm back in the Life. I like it, y'know?"

Teddy's thoughts drifted to something else: fucked-up irony. The shady estate agent had phoned him with some sweet news: "Got a great one-bedroom with a kitchenette in Tumba."

"Price?"

"It's top floor, great views. Otherwise, pretty crappy. Rent's three thousand five hundred. You can have it for two hundred."

Teddy: a pretty rich man. McLoud had sent him the first million; the rest would be following soon. His nephew could have a place of his own—but now the little idiot had gone and gotten himself locked up.

He opened the door to the oncology ward. As far from ward 57 as you could get in this place.

Tagg was going to wait outside. He sat down on a bench. "I'll let you know if I see anything." He grinned. "Just call me Jason Bourne."

Teddy went in. Huge devices on wheels. Clusters of doctors and nurses chatting away in Birkenstocks and green hospital scrubs. Patients sitting about, waiting for the most important conversation of their lives.

Teddy's phone beeped. *He's here. Same guy from the car on his way down the hallway.*

He replied, *Stay there. I'll sort it.*

A man, probably a doctor, was standing at a computer behind a pane of glass. Teddy knocked on the window.

The doctor pushed his glasses up his nose. "How can I help?"

"Could you show me where the fire escape is?"

"Ehh, why?"

"I'm here to repair something."

"No one told me anything about that." The guy had an irritating voice. He sounded like a teenager. Faroush Hooshmand, it said on his name badge.

"Well, it's true."

"Okay, just wait a second and I'll check the computer, see if you're registered."

Another text from Tagg. Teddy looked down at his phone. *He's outside now. On way in to you.*

There was no time. Teddy opened the door, went into the reception room where the doctor was working. Grabbed his neck—the man wasn't exactly a bodybuilder: Teddy could almost reach all the way around.

He squeezed.

"Just show me where the fire escape is, no bullshit. I don't have time."

Ten minutes later. Ward 57. Sara was sitting at the first table in the dining room. Hospital clothes, plasters covering injection points on her hands, slippers on her feet.

"Hi," she said. A dull tone to her voice.

Teddy sat down. The doctor had shown him the way to the fire escape without saying another word. He'd gone up one floor, knocked on the door, and been let in by a confused nurse. Ten seconds later, he got another message from Tagg: *He's inside the ward now.* Teddy didn't have time to reply—not that it made a difference.

He half ran to Sara's ward. The Swedish Premium Security guy could go to hell.

"You still don't have to see me if you don't want to," Teddy said.

"I do."

"How are you feeling?"

"I'm okay."

"How's Edward?"

"He's fine."

"Is he with his dad?"

"Yeah, they're staying in a hotel somewhere. The police are helping out."

"It was me they wanted. I'm just glad you're okay."

"I know." She sighed. "It's so long since we talked about Emanuelsson, but still . . ."

Teddy took her hand. Her skin was as white as milk. "Did you see the license plate, or anyone in the car? I was on my stomach on the floor when they got close."

Sara pulled her hand back. "Just fuzzy images. It wasn't very light. The police asked me that, too. I don't know the license plate number, but it was a man, Swedish-looking. One thing did stand out, there's one thing I remember. The bottom half of his face looked weird."

"Weird how?"

"I can't really put it any other way, just that his skin didn't look smooth somehow."

There was a box on the floor next to Sara. She nodded toward it.

"That's everything. I got my partner to go home and bring it up from the basement—that's the first and last time I'm going to involve him in this. I can't lift it myself, sorry."

Teddy bent down and picked up the box. "What's in here?"

"Everything. Division of property documents from Mats and Cecilia's divorce, death certificates, the film from the CCTV camera when he jumped, the preliminary inquiry report from when you were convicted of kidnapping him, the so-called slops from the police, the extra material from their investigation, plus a bunch of my own notes. Look after it—it's been hidden in a sleeping bag cover in my basement for more than four years now."

"There's one more thing I've been wondering, Sara." Teddy could hear the sorrow in his voice. "What exactly happened when you stopped coming to see me?"

She looked down at the table. "Does it really matter? The odds of things working out in the long run weren't all that great, if we're realistic about it."

"It matters to me."

Her voice sounded even flatter when she replied. "A man called me up and said if I kept dating you and asking around about Mats Emanuelsson, they'd rape me to death within a few hours, and that I should keep an eye on the time. They'd get to you, too, he said. I didn't know what to think, but the next day I got a parcel, and my watch was inside it. They'd been in my apartment while I was sleeping and taken it, so . . . the message was pretty clear."

"Okay, I understand."

"I didn't dare go on, Teddy. You need to be careful now. They don't mess around."

Teddy got up with the box under his arm. "I'm done being careful. I've got another strategy now."

He headed straight for Loke Odensson's office. A data security firm, right in the middle of town. Or like Loke always said: "You get to choose a side in life. I've gone over to the dark side now. Satan pays well, contributes to my pension, and I'm not gonna get my feet crushed because of my big mouth."

Loke stuck the USB into his computer and quickly brought up the contents on-screen: the film from the ferry to Finland. It probably would've taken Teddy an hour just to work out which hole to plug the memory stick into.

"Nice of you to come visit like this, sweetie pie," said Loke. "You want coffee? Red Bull? Or my new favorite—kombucha?"

"What the hell's kombucha?"

"Fermented tea, it's got shitloads of vitamins, healthy bacteria, antioxidants, stuff like that. Think it'd do you some good, too, man."

"Just help me with this. I don't have time for any healthy bacteria."

For CCTV footage, the image was sharp, even when Loke pulled it up onto one of his big screens.

The deck of a boat: green floor, white walls, and railings. Sky and sea in the background, you couldn't see where one stopped and the next one began, everything was just gray. Teddy recognized the man who came out on deck: Mats Emanuelsson. He was only wearing jeans and a sweater, though it looked cold. He stood for a moment, looking out to sea, then climbed up onto the railing, gathered himself, and jumped.

"What the hell is this?" Loke asked.

"Can you show me the whole thing again? In slow motion?"

Loke did something on the computer. "We can watch it frame by frame."

They rewound the clip. Teddy watched the sequence again. Mats was lightly dressed. Mats climbed up onto the railing. Mats gathered himself. Jumped. As far out as he could.

Again.

He really had jumped a long way.

And there was something about the jump. Teddy just couldn't say what.

Stockholm County Police Authority

Interview with informant "Marina," 19 December 2010

Leader: Joakim Sundén

Location: Flemingsberg Centrum

MEMORANDUM 5 (PART 2)

Transcript of dialogue (continuation)

M: They discharged me from the hospital. Cecilia wouldn't let me stay in the same room as her and the kids. Every time she looked at me, her eyes would narrow.

After a few weeks, I started back at KPMG, but only part-time. This was autumn 2006. The renovation—or decontamination, that's what we called it—of the apartment was moving slowly. I wanted to get back home as soon as possible. Hotels are like those ferries to Finland—we used to go on them a lot when I was a kid. Everything seems fun and exciting at first, but after a few hours it all seems uniform and depressing.

The fire itself didn't bother me all that much anymore. In a way, I understood Sebbe. I'd screwed him over, for the second time. In Sebbe's world, the world I'd been working in part-time, there aren't any insurance policies, you can't just report things to the police. All you can do is take things into your own hands. Manage your environment in a firm, clear way. I don't think he'd wanted to kill me or even hurt me, for that matter. How could he know I'd go running back to our place? He just wanted to send a message. And it had come through loud and clear.

He'd done it neatly, too. The fire investigators didn't find anything suggesting it was deliberate. They talked about appliances and bad installations. I just nodded along and added to their suspicions, told them: "We've had trouble with the dishwasher short-circuiting everything a few times before. I'm sure that must be what started it."

But with Cecilia, things were still terrible. She wouldn't let it go. She wanted to know, she said. She thought the pictures and films were mine. She wanted to *cure* me. And I knew I couldn't tell the truth. I couldn't turn around and say that the whole past year had been a lie. Above all, I couldn't tell her the truth because it might be dangerous for her and the kids.

She kept asking me, though, over and over again. Wanted to delve deep into my psyche. Now, in hindsight, I can see it was a bad move on my part not to answer any of her questions, that it just made her press even harder until I started doing things that led to the catastrophe. But back then, I just gave her weak nonanswers: "They must've gotten onto the computer when I was looking at something else."

I thought that would be it, but Cecilia wanted more—she wanted me to go to the police and report everything.

JS: What happened?

M: Eventually, she did it herself, called them up and reported what she'd seen on the computer. I had to go to the police station after that.

JS: They interviewed you?

M: Yeah, once.

JS: Strange, because I tried to find out when you were brought in, but I couldn't see any record of an interview.

M: Makes sense, but I'll get to that. What I told the police back then was closer to the truth than what I'd told Cecilia. I told them they weren't my films, that I'd copied them onto my computer by mistake. The policeman who interviewed me wanted to see the computer, of course, but I didn't have it. Cecilia had found it in the apartment after the fire, and she'd taken it away with her. I didn't know where it was. The policeman moaned, said I should try to hand it in, that it was the only way they could move things forward. I knew what he meant, and I thought maybe I could delete everything to do with Sebbe's business and let the police see the rest, those horrible films.

JS: Is that what you did, then?

M: It wasn't so simple. Cecilia wouldn't tell me where the damn thing was. She wanted me to go to more interviews, start having therapy and stuff like that. If she hadn't been so stubborn and narrow-minded, things would've turned out very differently.

But then something happened, and that made it all ten times worse.

I thought there might be a way out after all, hoped it was just a big mistake. So I called Peder.

He sounded like he was in a boat, or maybe it was the helicopter again.

"I need to ask you something," I said.

"Go ahead."

"It's a bit sensitive, but I saw some strange films on a computer out at that place in the country."

The engine, the rotor blades or whatever it was, I could hear it humming in the background.

"What is that crap?" I asked. "Because I've been to the police and told them what I saw."

After that, the noise was almost unbearable. It sounded like Peder said something, but I didn't hear what. The phone went dead after that.

A few days later, I got a text—I remember it word for word. It said: *We understand you have a computer containing some files you shouldn't. If you hand it over to the police, we'll rape your wife to death, and your kids will cease to exist.*

I just stared at the words, tried to work out how the hell things had ended up like this. I hadn't told Peder I had a copy. All I could think was that the police had leaked it somehow, because it couldn't have come from Cecilia.

JS: If you're right, that's the reason I can't find a record of that interview.

M: My thoughts exactly.

After that, I took the blame for everything with Cecilia. There was absolutely no way I could tell her the truth. It was like hooking a fish that's just too big. Cecilia pulled and pulled, and no matter how hard I tried to resist it, she managed to get even more out of me. I tried to explain that I'd been surfing porn sites: "Lots of men do it, millions, I was stressed at work, plus you and I . . . we're not so intimate anymore." And I tried to tell her it had gotten worse and worse, that I'd ended up on bad sites, that I just hadn't thought. That the whole thing was about stress and bad judgment.

It was a mess. I was describing myself as someone who couldn't stop himself from looking at sadomasochistic home movies. But the truth was, I was very aware that she could never suspect that those films and pictures had anything to do with anyone else. Then she'd start to look into who they were and probably hand in the computer herself. And they'd been very clear what would happen if she did that.

I tried to talk to her, get her to give me the computer instead, but then she just got more and more suspicious.

One morning, I was walking down to KPMG. Cool autumn air, and I was stressed, like usual. I walked over Barnhusbron. The whole area around the central station was changing back then. That whole area of town was being developed, hotels and offices everywhere. Cecilia and I were meeting in the apartment later that day. We had an appointment with a surveyor. He was going to take us through the decontamination. We'd been back to the apartment twice to choose new colors and paper for some of the walls. We'd talked about the kitchen and realized we didn't want anything like what we'd had before. Honestly, it was just nice that we could talk about something normally for once.

I was halfway across the bridge when a delivery van pulled up right next to me.

Two huge men got out. Instinctively, I knew something was wrong, but I didn't have time to react.

They picked me up from the pavement and more or less threw me into the back of the van. I was fighting back. Trying to get up. One of them was leaning over me. I saw he had a needle.

"What're you doing?"

I felt a sharp pain in my neck.

"Just stay calm and nothing's gonna happen."

And then it was like I couldn't control my arms and legs anymore, like they belonged to someone else. I remember thinking about the way the smoke had stuck in my throat. But this was different. Like a deep, peaceful sleep.

I opened my eyes. And . . . (inaudible) . . . I mean, this isn't easy to talk about, even though a few years have passed. . . . (clears throat)

JS: It's okay, take your time. Should we go for a walk instead?

M: . . . That might be best . . . (inaudible)

(Pause)

M: Nice to get out, anyway. Just so you know, I'm going to keep this brief. I've spent so much time talking to psychologists and therapists about what happened those few days, I feel like I'm talked out.

JS: Okay, that's fine, I understand.

M: So, okay. When I opened my eyes, it was pitch-black—like I'd been buried alive. In a way, I was in a grave of sorts. I tried to sit up, but I hit my head on something. I carefully felt all around me. Rough planks. It smelled like wood.

That's when I understood. It was like all the air left my body when it sank in, like all the energy and life just vanished. I was in a box. They'd put me in a fucking box.

I tried to keep calm. Think clearly. Breathe deeply, not hyperventilate. Then I started to shout. "Let me out! Help!"

Yeah, I was shouting like a madman. I shouted until there was no air left.

After maybe twenty minutes, a little hatch opened right by my face. The light was piercing. I squinted.

I could see a man looking down at me. I'll never forget his face.

"Take it easy, for fuck's sake," he said. "Are you hungry? Need a piss?"

"Please, just let me out."

"If you need a shit, I'll have to tie you up first."

"What do you want? Please, just tell me what you want."

"I'm not the one in charge of this. But listen: you pay up, this'll all be over soon enough."

It's hazy after that. I've made an effort *not* to remember, to repress those days I was shut up in a box with less room than the trunk of a Volvo. One thing I can tell you, though, that first man wasn't the one running the interrogations—I remember his shocked face a few days later when he opened the hatch and saw what they'd done to me.

Yeah, there were others. They took me out of the box. I don't know who they were. They always had masks on. At first, I was sure Sebbe'd sent them. That he hadn't forgiven me. That he wanted even more money because I'd tried to steal from him. The man who was guarding me in the house had said they'd let me go if I paid, anyway.

But after a while, I realized they were after something else. They wanted to know where the computer was, whether I'd let anyone else know what I'd seen. They weren't Sebbe's men. They weren't Kum's. They were working for someone else.

Someone much worse.

They pulled out seven of my fingernails. They stubbed out cigarettes on my face. They shoved things inside me. They . . . (inaudible) . . . I mean . . . I can't . . .

JS: It's okay, you don't have to. I've read your testimony. You said everything, then, right?

M: Most of it. But I never told them they wanted the computer. I never did that. I thought it was the only thing I could do to protect my family.

JS: I know, that's understandable.

M: Anyway, after five days and five hours, the police rescued me. Cecilia told me afterward that the kidnappers called her to say they had me, that they wanted the computer.

JS: Did she give it to them?

M: Yeah, she did. And at the same time, she told the police I'd been kidnapped. I don't know how they did it, but by handing over the computer, the police managed to work out where I was.

JS: And the computer, what happened to it?

M: I don't know, the kidnappers got it. It doesn't exist anymore.

JS: And only one person was ever arrested and convicted for what they did to you, right?

M: Only one person was convicted. The one who'd talked to me first. His name's Teddy Maksumic.

39

The remand hearing was over.

The prosecutor, Annika Rölén, had requested two more weeks. Cited the same reason she'd given the whole time. She'd also introduced a new element in support of their suspicions: something really shitty. They'd finally analyzed the clothes they'd found in the woods: a T-shirt and a pair of jeans. Benjamin's DNA had been found on the T-shirt, on the collar and one arm. The match confidence level was +4, the highest possible level. And the final blow: the T-shirt was more or less drenched in blood. The dead man's blood.

Emelie did her best. Asked whether traces of blood had been found anywhere other than the living room. If they'd found fingerprints, DNA, or any other objects. She asked whether any weapons had been found.

Annika Rölén refused to comment on most points. The only question she answered was about the murder weapon. "We haven't found it yet, but we believe the victim was shot in the head with some kind of hollow-point bullet that exploded on impact."

Forensics needed more time—it was a no-brainer: strong suspicions, compulsory grounds for detention. The court would never release a suspected murderer when they could give the National Forensic Centre a few more weeks. All the same: Benjamin was still more or less unconscious. The whole thing was highly unusual.

But Rölén had an answer to that, too: "Emanuelsson is doing

better. He can sit up. He can move around now. He responds to certain types of verbal communication. That means the risk of his tampering with evidence has increased."

After less than five minutes' deliberation, the judge had ruled that Benjamin would be remanded in custody.

Emelie went out onto the street. Hailed a taxi. As she did so, she Googled hollow-tipped bullets. Wikipedia delivered. The idea of that type of ammunition was that the bullet opened out when it hit its target, meaning that its diameter increased. It sounded brutal. Still, the Swedish police had been using Speer Gold Dot as their service ammunition since 2003.

"Wait."

She turned around. It was Teddy—half running toward her along Scheelegatan.

He was an idiot who set fire to barns and stole money.

An idiot who said: "I know what happened to Mats."

40

Mats Emanuelsson had taken the ferry to Finland five times, but he hadn't jumped when the weather was at its worst—when the chances of achieving his goal were greatest. Instead, he'd thrown himself into the sea during the trip with the best weather. Maybe he'd had trouble making up his mind.

Teddy stood in front of Emelie outside the courthouse and explained what he'd worked out. Emelie didn't move an inch. He was glad she was listening so intently.

There was something about the way Mats jumped. Teddy had watched the film over and over again on Loke's screen, and eventually, he'd worked it out: the natural way to jump would've been as close to the edge of the ship as possible—where the risk of being sucked under was greatest. But that wasn't what Mats had done: he'd gathered himself like he was aiming for the world record in the long jump.

Teddy had asked Loke to zoom in. Something else didn't look right. He'd tried to put his finger on exactly what. Mats had been slim, according to Boggan and Bosse—but in the video, he looked chunky, despite being lightly dressed.

Frame by frame. Rewind. Zoom. Rewind.

Then he saw it. Mats had something on under his sweatshirt. Something that stuck up at the neck. A collar. And it was thick.

Loke had zoomed in even further. There was some text on Mats's collar: *Ursuk BDS*.

Teddy had seen that somewhere else. Loke glanced at him: "Little mouse, you're thinking so hard, you keep forgetting to breathe. Sure you don't want some fermented tea? Some oxygen maybe?"

And then it had clicked.

Teddy had seen a dry suit with the same words on it. *Ursuk BDS*. And he knew where: in Cecilia, Benjamin, and Lillan's chaotic basement space.

He'd put the pieces together after that. Mats Emanuelsson had been wearing a diving suit under his normal clothes when he jumped from the ferry. He'd jumped as far from the boat as he could. The conclusion was clear. No one who wanted to kill themselves would dress like that. No one who wanted to drown jumped into the sea wearing a *Breathable Diving Suit*—an elite dry suit.

Emelie's mouth was half-open when he finished.

41

It took her half an hour just to get in, like usual.

Still in section six. Jeanette Nicorescu greeted her warmly in the hallway, like usual.

"We just had a remand hearing, but he was only present via video link. How's he doing?" Emelie asked.

"Seems okay. He even said hello to me when I went in to see him last."

Benjamin was sitting up in bed. His eyes were open. But he didn't seem to register she was there. Emelie could hear the faint noise of the guards out in the hallway.

"Hi, Benjamin."

He mumbled something in response.

"How are you?"

No answer.

"We shouldn't be too surprised they decided to keep you in remand," she said.

He whispered something; she could only make out the odd word: "I know . . ."

She said: "Benjamin, Teddy and I don't think your dad killed himself when he jumped from the ferry. We think he planned it so it looked like a suicide. Do you know anything about that?" She sat down by his bed and took his hand in hers.

Benjamin's skin was cool. She felt him squeeze her hand faintly.

"Is that a yes or a no?"

"Yes," he whispered, almost inaudibly.

"Is your dad alive?"

More mumbling. Still, Emelie thought she heard him say: "I . . . don't . . . know. In the house."

"What do you mean? Your dad was in the house with you?"

Another gentle squeeze: yes.

"Do you know who the dead person is?"

Benjamin shook his head. Quietly he whispered: "Maybe Dad."

"Mats was murdered?"

"Don't know."

"What were you doing in the house?"

His hand was tense. He really seemed to be struggling to find the right words. He said something, but Emelie couldn't make it out.

"Meet . . ."

She realized she needed to ask simpler questions. "You met someone in the house?"

He squeezed her hand: yes.

"You met Mats there?"

Another squeeze: yes.

"Does Cecilia know you met there?"

A moment of stillness, and then he shook his head.

"Does she know Mats didn't kill himself?"

"No."

"Does anyone else know?"

Silence. He was struggling to keep it together.

"Li . . ." He made it no further.

"Lillan?"

No answer. His eyes were closed.

"Please, Benjamin. Did Lillan know?"

The room was silent. Benjamin's hand had fallen down to the covers.

"Did he say anything?" Teddy asked. He'd been waiting for her outside.

"I don't really want to talk to you right now, actually."

"Okay. But did you manage to get anything out of him?"

"Yeah, he actually communicated with me today, a few words at least. He knows Mats didn't kill himself, but he also thinks it might've been him who got killed out in Värmdö."

"Oh shit," said Teddy. "Did he kill his own father?"

The thought hadn't even crossed Emelie's mind.

Teddy grimaced. "I don't care, he's gonna have to start talking to us now."

"He's getting better every day. I've got to go. I've got another court hearing today."

"What is it?"

Emelie didn't know if Teddy knew—confidentiality forbid her from saying who she was representing. Plus, she still had no desire to talk to him.

"It's another remand hearing," she said.

Teddy raised an eyebrow. "Aha, then I know. Linda told me. You're helping my nephew. Can I come?"

Emelie shook her head. "Enough now."

42

Almost four days in the cell now.

Two hours' time: his remand hearing. They would come to collect him, put on the cuffs, drive him to the courtroom in Söder-törn. His friends had talked about these hearings so many times, but Nikola was a virgin. Young offenders' was like day care compared to this.

He'd had the shivers. Diarrhea. His arm was still hurting like hell where the bastard dog had bitten him. He'd thought about using his belt to do something drastic, but they'd taken his belt away.

Simon Murray had been back. He looked like Matthew McConaughey—all taut mouth and intense eyes.

He said: "You're going to be remanded, you know that don't you?"

Nikola's feelings: I won't last a few more weeks in a cell.

Simon: "I think it'd be tough for you, spending months in isolation."

Nikola's mind was spinning: he hoped Chamon could handle the pressure; he'd always been the cooler one.

Simon: "You know Chamon's started talking, right? He says you were the one who needed the money."

Nikola shivered. Thought he needed to see someone who cares about him. Mom, Grandpa, Teddy, anyone.

Simon: "If you talk to me now, I'll fix it so Linda can visit you at the very least, and soon."

Nikola's thoughts drifted to Ashur. The guy Chamon had talked about, who'd refused to go to his dad's funeral in handcuffs.

He cleared his throat. "Simon, I might look a bit rough, but I'm not your whore. Get lost, and don't come back."

He was curled up in the fetal position on his mattress. A month out—that was all he'd managed. A big fat loser. A dude who wasn't good enough for the game.

His head: full of crappy thoughts. He tried to sleep. Tried to whack off. Sweated and froze at the same time. He had to bang on the door to go to the toilet once an hour.

He wondered what Chamon had said. The cells in the other hallway—he was here, too, somewhere. Unless he'd already had his hearing and been moved on.

Nikola couldn't even focus on what he was going to say at the hearing. Nikola: total ADHD behavior. Freak.

He considered asking the guard to call Simon Murray after all. Tell them he was ready to squeal.

Emelie had been to see him, too. She looked like he remembered. Long, dark blond hair; kind eyes. Black pants and jacket.

She got straight to the point: no bullshit from her. That was fine by him.

"What have they said to you?"

"I just had a short interview. They're saying I broke into an ICA Maxi."

"And what did you say?"

"I denied it. I was going to Teddy's. You know who he is. I was on the way there when their fucking dog attacked me and tore my arm to pieces. Look." He held up his arm and showed her the bandage. "I've got nothing to do with any robbery."

"Why do they suspect you, then?"

"I mean, I was nearby, like, in the woods, but I haven't been in that shop. I just got lost."

During the hour when Emelie was there, everything felt a bit better. They talked about the hearing and the process going forward. She seemed strong.

There was a knock at the door. The sound of a key in the lock.

It was the guards. They cuffed him and started to lead him down the hallway.

He tried to smile. "Which cell's Chamon in?"

One of them said: "We can't tell you that kind of thing, you know that."

They pushed him into a car: a V70 with mesh over the windows. It rolled up and out of the garage.

Outside, it was a bright summer's day. In the front seat, the guards were talking about what they were doing over the holidays. Nikola thought back to the first time he'd smoked weed: in a stretch of woodland on the hill behind the school in Ronna. The leaves on the trees had been pale green; he'd felt like nothing in the world could go wrong, like everything could start over.

The judge looked grumpy. Gray dress. Gray hair. Gray face.

The prosecutor was wearing a sweater, jeans, and a corduroy jacket. Nikola didn't see why they couldn't wear a tie, not even when they were planning to lock up an as-yet-innocent person for an indefinite amount of time.

Emelie walked slowly into the courtroom and sat down.

The other door opened, and a few people came in and sat down on the other side of the plexiglass. The reflection made it difficult to see who was there.

Nikola squinted. Tried to see. He could make out Linda. Teddy.

Then the door opened again. One more person came in. *Shit*—it was Chamon.

That snake Murray: he'd been lying the whole time. Chamon wasn't in a different cell in another hallway at all. Chamon: not even arrested. Chamon: free as a fucking bird. Murray had been trying to catch Nikola out. Put pressure on him. Give him even more stress, even more panic. But he hadn't counted on Chamon being ballsy enough to turn up to the remand hearing.

The prosecutor said: "I'd like to request closed doors."

Emelie shut her notebook. The request was entirely expected

when an additional, as-yet-unknown offender still hadn't been apprehended. "No objection," she said.

The judge spoke in an authoritative voice. "In that case, we'll proceed behind closed doors, which means the remainder of the hearing will not be public. Could I please ask the public to leave the room?"

Nikola turned his head. Chamon held up a thumb. Smiled a big smile.

A day later: remanded, of course.

The cell was a hundred times better than before. There was a bed, a little desk. A wooden stool. There was even a toilet. But above all: there was a TV. Still, he'd be there for weeks unless Emelie could work her magic.

He was at the top of the building—it must've been the eighth or ninth floor. Through the bars over the window, he could look out over Flemingsberg. See the commuter train station, the high school, the colorful Million Programme housing in the distance.

Nikola: grandchild of the Million Programme. Nikola: watched TV all day. He was climbing up the walls less than before. But still a hell of a lot. Wondered what the cops had on him. What Isak would say. What Murray had planned.

An hour a day in the exercise area on the roof. Mesh everywhere, but he could make out the sky through the metal railings. He bought Marlboro Reds from the cart and puffed his way through eight of them the first time they took him up there. The nicotine kick was just like a weed high. Everything started spinning. The bars shook. He swayed.

The second day up there on the roof, he took it easier with the cigs.

After a minute or two, he heard someone shout, "Yo, man, what's your name?"

He tried to see who it was: the bars were tightly packed. A guy on the other side, in another fenced-off area. Nikola replied with his name.

"What 'bout you?"

"Kerim Celalî. Where you from?"

"Södertälje. Ronna. You?"

"Axelsberg. But Västerås, really. What they wanna do you for?"

"Aggravated robbery. You?"

"Ehh . . . load of shit, man."

"C'mon . . ."

"They said I was sellin' blow from a warehouse by Axelsberg Square."

"How much?"

"Couple kilos."

"*Abbou.*"

"Yeah, y'know, but it's just what they're saying."

"Still . . . how old're you?"

"Twenty-eight. Fuck . . . lookin' at ten, maybe fourteen years if they want to do me for smuggling, too."

"Shit."

The guy on the other side laughed. "Eh, it'll be fine. Gotta believe it, anyway. Honestly, though, it's actually really fucking nice to be inside every now and then, y'know? Bit of peace and quiet. Don't gotta worry about undercover cops and Abdi's guys all the time. It's been such a fucking pain lately, you know?"

"I heard." Nikola had heard the talk. The Kurds controlled huge chunks of the coke trade along the red line of the metro, but lately, people from Västerort and Black Scorpions had started trying to take it back.

"Nice day today though," said Kerim. "Enjoy the sun, the blue sky. Could be worse. Coulda just as easily been where my cousin's at, in Kobane."

"Ko-where?"

"Doesn't matter, man. I just mean enjoy what you got here. All I'm missing's licorice, can't buy that from the cart. But the sun's shining, so I'm not gonna think about that."

Nikola was watching more TV than ever. *The Mentalist, Ex on the Beach, Lyxfällan, Paradise Hotel.* Hard to comprehend: how could they cram so much shit into so few hours?

He asked to borrow the PlayStation—there was one per hallway—and was surprised when it arrived so quickly. Until he saw it, that was—it was a PS2. They weren't allowed the newer consoles; they had built-in Wi-Fi. But a *PS2*, Christ—Nikola had been four or something when they came out—it was an antique, pre-flat-screen era. They should send some archaeologists over: this was what people did in the early 2000s. Put the thing in a museum, for God's sake.

He borrowed two books from the library cart instead. *Three Seconds* by Roslund & Hellström and one called *The Stranger* by some other dude. He didn't know why he'd picked it up, there was just something about the title. It suited him. That's what he was. Slav among Syrians. Swede among Serbs. The guy who was always on some kind of platform.

The next day, Kerim shouted over to him again.

"Yo, Nikola, that you?"

"Yeah, what's up?"

"Weather's not so good today, man, but y'know what?"

"Nah?"

"Doesn't matter. Can hardly see the fucking sky through these bars anyway."

"How long you been in for?"

"Thirteen months."

Nikola swallowed. The guy on the other side of the fence hadn't been convicted of anything—but they'd still taken over a year of his life.

Kerim continued. "Full restrictions, too. And guess what?"

"What?"

"You're the first person I've talked to the whole time, apart from my lawyer and the cops. They must've done something wrong, putting me in a cage next to you, forgotten they're meant to keep me away from all living beings."

"Shit, man. How the hell d'you manage?"

"Listen, it's like I said yesterday: could be worse."

Nikola thought. Could it, really?

Kerim said: "They got anything on you?"

"No idea, other than a dog that got my scent. I'm innocent."

"Everyone's innocent in here. But serious, if that's all they got, then you just gotta do one thing."

"What?"

"Shut your mouth, breathe through your nose. Keep shtum, y'know? They'll have to show their colors eventually—you'll get to see which cards they're keeping close. Stay cool, man. Think of Kobane."

43

Meeting with Magnus Hassel, the partner. Teddy was pretty surprised it had taken him so long to react.

The walls were covered with paintings, and the low bookshelves were full of more or less cryptic pieces of art: a human skull spattered with oil paint, cubes that looked like they were made from dried paint, a bird's skeleton, and a yellow tennis ball in a glass box. Magnus really did like contemporary art—which he always referred to in English. But he'd changed the big canvas behind his desk. From a distance, it looked completely black: an enormous expanse of darkness. But when Teddy moved closer, he could see small, dark tablets, pills and capsules embedded in the piece. Raining down, almost. He wondered what it meant.

Magnus could see him thinking. "Like my latest find? It's a Damien Hirst. *Cicutoxin*, that's its name, just three years old. I never thought it'd go on sale, but I got lucky a few weeks ago, good straw men."

Teddy sat down opposite Magnus. His desk looked messier today, but the man seemed calmer than last time they spoke.

"Let me get straight to the point, Teddy. What happened, it's not good."

Teddy knew what he meant: he'd called Magnus to let him know that someone had stolen all the evidence from the McLoud case. "I'm really sorry, but someone broke into the car. I had everything in there, the photographs, all my surveillance reports. My phone's gone, too. So that's all the pictures gone."

Magnus's face looked tense.

The canvas behind him was radiating darkness.

"Look," he said. "There won't be any more jobs for the firm unless you sort this out. Do you realize how much that information was worth to our client?"

"Yeah, you said. Two hundred million."

"Am I just supposed to tell them the evidence has vanished, or what? You need to sort this out, Teddy. It's that simple. Find the material. That's it."

Magnus got to his feet: a clear signal—as far as he was concerned, the meeting was over.

Screw you, asshole, Teddy thought—I'd counted on this. There won't be any evidence for your client—because I've given it all to McLoud.

All the same: this was the end of his first real job ever. What the hell was he going to do now? Who would he become?

Next day.

It was like everyone was moving back and forth inside the church. The huge icons above the altar. The candles. The red carpet on the floor. People kissing the icons' hands, Jesus's feet, lighting candles, crossing themselves over and over.

The last point: Bojan was a master—crossed himself twice, bowed twice, kissed the image of the saint in front of him. And then he did the same thing again—his dad was acting like his grandmother had. Teddy thought back to when he was ten and he'd visited her in Vinča, the village outside Belgrade. The priest's beard, purple robes, the thick smell of smoke.

But today: Dad.

Today: Saint Sava's. Sweden. Stockholm. Enskede gård. Just a few miles from the huge Globen arena.

Teddy's feet were tired. Another thing about this duty to God he remembered from his childhood. You were standing pretty much the whole time. He waited. Swayed along with the song. There was a small choir somewhere, singing a cappella.

Bojan glanced at him. Teddy tried to cross himself. Right hand. "Press—don't pull," his grandmother used to say. Thumb and index finger together. The others squeezed against his palm.

His father: "Aren't you going to honor the priest?" Teddy knew what he meant. He wanted him to go forward and kiss the edge of the priest's vestment.

"It's too crowded, Dad." It was true; the place was packed. But it was also a lie: he didn't want to kiss anything right now. But he did want to please his father. Show he cared. He had a bigger reason. A real purpose.

Sara had been discharged from the hospital and was being protected by the police. Linda was in a hotel, staying away from her job. Teddy had managed to get his father to go to a hotel, too, but it wasn't enough. They both needed to get away, leave the country. For a few weeks, at the very least. Until Teddy could make Kum understand. From that perspective: he was glad Nikola was locked up. At least they couldn't get to him.

He tried to relax. His dad would have to understand eventually—it wasn't like he had anything better to do, and Teddy could send him on an all-inclusive holiday anywhere he wanted with the money from McLoud.

He'd been trying to get in touch with Lillan the past few days, but she never answered her phone, and Cecilia said she didn't know where she was. But Lillan knew that Mats had faked his suicide, and with any luck, she was in better shape than her brother.

From the outside, the church didn't look like much. But inside, it was beautiful. Iconostasis in walnut, frescoes in bright colors and gold. "Our Byzantine tradition," Bojan explained.

Teddy stretched his neck. "I know, Dad. I know. I want you to say you'll go away now. Just for a few weeks. Linda's moved out."

Bojan turned around. "Why do you always have to cause trouble? I thought you'd finally changed."

Teddy froze. What had his father done to help out all these

years? During his childhood? What had he done when social services, teachers, counselors, and support workers had been on the
phone? When the cops knocked on the door that first time—Teddy
had been twelve—and told him he'd been arrested outside Teknik-
magasinet with seven airsoft guns in his bag.

He'd always wanted Teddy to be like Darko; he didn't understand a damn thing. And now—now that Teddy was *trying* to live
life on the right side of the law, now that he was working—he
started moaning. His dad had to realize—the past caught up with
you sometimes. Stupid old fool.

Outside the church, people loitered around, making small
talk for a while. His father wanted to introduce him to his friends.
Teddy wanted to leave.

Eventually Teddy and his father started walking toward the
metro station. The tunnel up to the ticket gates was covered in
scrawls: bad graffiti and shady words. *Ugly is beautiful. Animal Lib-
eration Front. Kill a citizen.*

Teddy said: "Have you made up your mind? I want you to leave
as soon as possible."

Bojan was moving slowly.

They reached the station.

High above them, on a metal bar stretching across the ceiling,
there was a silver-colored sculpture of a person, balancing.

Bojan pointed up at it. "Have you seen the new art SL brought
in? It's nice, I think."

"What about the question I just asked you?"

Bojan held his monthly pass against the ticket gate. The glass
barriers slid open. The new system still surprised Teddy every
time—it was part of the new Stockholm.

"I've got an idea. I'll get you tickets to Herceg Novi. I'll come
down in two weeks; Linda too. We can spend some time together
for a while," he continued.

His father looked up. "Herceg Novi. Montenegro? I always
used to go there as a boy."

Teddy tried to look kind. "I know," he said. "I know."

They separated at Slussen. Bojan changed to take the red line. Teddy knew where he was going now.

He went down, beneath the station: sub-Slussen—darkness, dirt, and noise from the buses. Someone was trying to sell bread and cinnamon buns from a little table under the information screens. Someone else was trying to sober up on a bench next to Pressbyrån. Up there, in the daylight: a bright summer's day. Down here, below the surface: a chill, a feeling of abandonment, and the stench of piss by the pillars.

The *new* Stockholm. The city that at least used to try. Now: sold out. Tired walls and graffitied stations. Those who could afford to used the app-based taxi companies. Even in the outer suburbs, house prices were going stratospheric—but in order to mortgage your life, you first had to be accepted by the bank—and the few tenancies still going were traded on the black market by criminal networks who wouldn't hesitate for a millisecond before fucking up anyone who talked back. EU migrants lined the streets, but no one talked about how people averted their eyes. Romanian and Nigerian whores sold their services in mini brothels—things that had always taken place on the street in the past had now moved behind the closed doors of the city's apartments and villas. Designer drugs ordered online were delivered faster than takeout from Lina's. And at the same time, certain people: those who carried society on their backs—they did what they wanted beneath the surface. Predators.

He got on a tram. Saltsjö line. Thought about Kum's words.

The new Stockholm: where the divisions were so clear, it was like someone had scratched them onto a map of the city with a needle.

And now he himself had more money than ever. Not that he wanted to use it for anything other than getting his father and sister out, helping Nikola.

Twenty minutes later, he walked up to Drevinge farm. Loke had helped him narrow down where Lillan might be.

The horses in the pastures looked happy. Kids everywhere:

exclusively girls, from small children to teenagers. In the distance, he could see more of them, sitting straight backed in the saddle.

He walked into the stalls. Same thing there. Horses, all different colors and sizes, standing in their boxes, or whatever those small stalls were called. Girls of all ages mucking them out, pulling on leather straps, carrying hay bales.

Lillan looked just like her brother. Like Mats. Teddy recognized her immediately. Sixteen years old.

She was busy with a horse in one of the boxes. She had a brush in one hand. Dressing it, maybe.

He went over. Tried to make eye contact.

Stockholm County Police Authority

Interview with informant "Marina," 20 December 2010

Leader: Joakim Sundén

Location: Högdalen Centrum

MEMORANDUM 6 (PART 1)

Transcript of dialogue

JS: Do you think we'll finish up today?

M: I've only gone through a year and a half so far, so there are about four years left—from 2007 on.

JS: Probably not, then?

M: I can try to just give more of a rough outline.

JS: Okay, good. How did it feel to talk about the kidnapping yesterday?

M: There are some things you never forget, no matter how much you want to.

JS: I know. Well, let's continue from where we left off. What happened after the kidnapping?

M: Everything went dark. They talked about PTSD—post-traumatic stress disorder. I kept having flashbacks from the torture. And not just when I was having nightmares—the smallest thing could set off a powerful reaction. If I saw a table that was the same color as the box, for example, I'd panic. If I smelled the chewing gum they'd chewed, I'd break down and have horrible cramps.

They talked about emotional isolation, a lack of interest in normal activities. I was even admitted to the hospital for four days. They gave me Zoloft. They said I was suicidal. After a few weeks, they decided I had post-traumatic depression.

And then on top of that, there were the police interviews and the trial, and I had to go through it all again. It was really awful.

JS: Were you working?

M: Not during the first four months. Then I went back to my old job. I started feeling better. It just took a while. I started phasing out the anti-anxiety pills, too. My nails grew back, though they were all uneven. The police had given me alarms and security routines, but I knew they wouldn't come back as long as I kept my mouth shut. They'd gotten what they wanted.

JS: What about Cecilia? What did she say?

M: Not a lot. I mean, she felt sorry for me, of course, but we never talked everything through properly. She probably just wanted to forget it, too.

JS: And Sebbe?

M: Yeah, Sebbe. He called me quite soon after I got back home, but I didn't want to talk to him. Then he just turned up at our house one day, a few weeks after the kidnapping. I was at home in bed, half-high on painkillers and anti-anxiety pills, when he rang the bell. Cecilia was at work, and the kids were at school and nursery. I crawled out of bed and pulled on a dressing gown.

"There's nothing for you here," I hissed through the door.

The police had sealed up the mail slot after everything that'd happened.

"Mats, listen to me. Let me in. I want to talk."

"I don't want to talk to you." My fingers were on the alarm button they'd installed.

"Okay, I get that, but listen: I'm not the one who ordered that shit. I swear on my mother's grave. I was pissed off with you 'cause you stole my money, and you know what happened then, not that we ever planned on you being home. But this thing . . . I swear . . . what they did was really shitty. . . . I just wanted to say that."

I think my voice cracked when I replied. Maybe he heard it through the door. But the thing was, I knew he was telling the truth. He had nothing to do with it. He hadn't kidnapped me.

"Get out of here, Sebbe," I said anyway. "And don't come back."

Eventually life started getting back to some kind of normal routine again, even though I wasn't working full-time. But things felt harder, everything seemed to take much longer. After I got the kids ready in the morning, I'd have to lie down in bed for a whole hour. Going shopping might give me a headache that lasted all afternoon. I wasn't performing at work, either. Niklas understood, he said, but I could see he was disappointed. I needed to get my strength back.

I went down to the club a few times. It was the only place I felt calm. Boggan, Bosse, and the others didn't ask me what happened. They just knew what they'd read in the papers. I hadn't told them about the computer. Neither had Cecilia. As far as the police and the courts were concerned, it was about money. The logic was simple. Someone thought I had loads of money because I played poker, and I'd been kidnapped because they wanted it.

The months passed, and that spring, I was going to the club at least two nights a week.

One night, something happened. Bosse and Boguslaw were there. Boggan had started with 'gammon, too, but he'd switched to poker over the past few years. He was pretty overweight, so he laughed every time he saw me: I looked like a stick, and I'd been thin even before the kidnapping. Then there was Bosse—or Bosse with the Boa, that's what he got called. The man with Stockholm's biggest . . . (inaudible) . . . if you see what I mean, he used to talk about it constantly.

"Shit, you on some new diet, or did you just catch a bit of HIV? I heard vitamin C's good, cures it all," he said when he saw me. They wanted me to liven up a bit, tried the same kind of talk as before.

We sat down at the table, and the cards were dealt.

Boggan was keeping his cards close and Bosse was going on like usual. The younger guys around the table didn't know whether to roll their eyes or laugh along with him.

"Honestly, though," Boggan said after a while. "How're you doing?"

"Head up, back on my feet," I said.

"You really don't look great, though. I know it must've been tough. You wanna talk about it?"

The younger guys' eyes flitted between us. They didn't know what Boggan was talking about.

"Nah, it's okay," I answered, and folded.

Bosse just grinned even wider. "It's not okay. You need cheering up, my man."

It was an odd discussion, but somewhere, deep down, I liked it. They were treating me like normal. Messing with me, trying to make me feel good. Eventually I said: "You're probably right."

"Okay, then," Bosse roared. "Once I've won this pot, I think we should move on to the strip club on Roslagsgatan."

"No, count me out."

"Yeah, you. Come on, you need to feel good tonight."

They kept going on about me tagging along. They just wanted the best for me. Once, about twenty years earlier, I'd gone to one of those places—this was before Cecilia was on the scene—but I'd found the whole thing embarrassing. The girls' glittering eyes, the way they moved so close to my body, their artificial laughs. It all felt so dishonest, not that I had any plans to do anything with those women, but still. It was the atmosphere, the hierarchy, the crass falseness of it all, that's what bothered me. But that night with Boggan and Bosse, I was exhausted. I was too tired to say no.

The sign above the door proclaimed that it was a gentleman's club with Stockholm's most glamorous ladies, but the entrance felt anything but luxurious. Black sheets of plywood and red fabric curtains framed the anteroom.

"One thing, boys: I don't normally go places like this. It's all for you, Mats. Girls like this get scared when they see me, if you know what I mean," Bosse boasted.

Boggan and I knew exactly what he was hinting at, but the huge bouncer in the doorway, a guy in a thick Canada Goose jacket with an ACAB tattoo on his neck, didn't seem to get it. He grunted. "The fuck you talking about? The girls are gonna be scared of you?"

Bosse acted like he always did. "Nothing for you to worry about, my friend."

"You wanna come in here or not?"

Behind the ACAB bouncer, another man had turned up. He was even bigger than the first one, if that's possible.

Bosse said: "I really, really want to come in. I was just joking about my one-eyed friend. The ladies get scared when I don't give them advance warning."

The other giant moved forward toward Bosse, grabbed his chin, and pushed him up against the wall.

"What're you doing?" Bosse tried to protest.

The giant snapped: "Take your friends and get out of here."

We should've just left then. Turned around and walked away. Those two men were full of aggression. It might've felt shameful and crappy, but we would've forgotten all about it by the next morning.

But for some reason, I stepped up to the giant. He still had ahold of Bosse. "Let him go."

"Who're you?"

"None of your fucking business. Just let him go."

Sometimes, it feels like certain moments in life play out in slow motion.

They must, otherwise it'd be impossible for so many thoughts to rush through your head in such a short space of time. A movement that takes no more than a second, but I'd had time to think about everything, from whether Bosse had been bluffing on that last hand to whether I was going to need stitches. I thought about how my life had turned out: there I was, arguing in the entrance to a strip club. That's not what I'd planned back when I learned how the doubling cube worked in backgammon, in that crappy little café in Södermalm.

The punch wasn't so hard. He hit me on the side of the head, but I fell over anyway. Probably because it was the first guy, the one with the tattoo on his neck, who'd hit me from behind.

Boggan launched himself at the ACAB guy, and Bosse started kicking the guy who was holding him.

I'd never been in a proper fight the whole of my adult life, despite all the stuff I'd been through, so when I was lying on the floor, trying to get up, I grabbed my phone. I was yelling like an idiot into it.

Then I looked up. The ACAB guy looked like he was about to kill Boggan. He'd pushed him against the counter and was slamming his head into it over and over again.

Bosse had managed to get away from the other giant, but he was going to start up again at any minute. I could see in his eyes how scared he was.

I rushed forward, started pounding the doorman's back. Somehow, I managed to push back the panic that was welling up in me. Images of the way they'd thrown me into the back of the van rushing through my head. The inside of the box. The glowing eye of the cigarettes they'd stubbed out on my cheek.

"Just leave him alone," I shouted.

Boggan's face was bloody. His head was lolling back and forth.

We had to get out of there, we were like field mice in comparison to those beasts.

I tried to pull Bosse away, and we opened the door. Felt the cold autumn air hit us. But then I remembered Boggan. He was still inside.

I turned around, went back in. "Let him go."

The ACAB guy snarled back at me: "You faggot. You're just embarrassing yourselves."

They knew no one called the police when they got abuse in a place like that.

So we stood there like that, fifteen feet between us, hissing back and forth for a few minutes. They refused to let Boggan go. We refused to leave him behind.

Eventually it all started up again. There was no stopping it. I ran inside to do what I could for my friend.

But those idiots weren't just big, they were quick, too.

The ACAB guy kicked me in the calf. My leg crumpled beneath me. I was on the floor again.

I tried to get up, onto all fours. Then I felt a kick to the chest. It was like someone had snapped a match, only the match was my body.

I collapsed.

Bosse yelled something in the background.

I felt another kick.

I curled up in the fetal position. Could see Boggan; he was on the floor, too.

I covered my face.

Tried to tense my body.

But there were no more kicks.

I wondered what had happened.

I unwrapped my arms just in time to see a baseball bat hit the ACAB guy on the back.

Two men, wearing balaclavas, were standing over us. The doormen were on the floor.

"You fucking bitches. Attack people your own size," the man with the baseball bat shouted.

He brought the bat down on the ACAB guy's thigh: *thud*—it sounded like when you kick a *really hard* penalty.

I scrabbled to my feet. We tried to pick Boguslaw up.

Thud, again. The bouncers were shouting in pain. Spitting out splintered teeth.

Thud.

I saw bodily fluids on the floor.

I saw a nose that looked more like a bloody lump.

Thud.

I saw a jaw that seemed to be hanging weirdly.

We dragged our friend out.

"Now you've got us to deal with, you motherfuckers. Sons of bitches," the guy with the baseball bat yelled.

Thud.

No one was shouting anymore.

The entrance was silent. The bouncers were motionless on the floor.

The man raised the baseball bat again, over the doorman's head.

To crack his skull. Bash his brains out.

"Wait!" I shouted. "Take it easy."

He paused. Pulled the balaclava up just enough so I could see his face.
"Shit, man, you called me, didn't you? You should be happy."

It was Sebbe. And I *had* called him—even though I'd been trying to push him away. There hadn't been any other way—I'd gone too far in a direction I couldn't control, and we would've been beaten to death without him.

I don't know if I was happy to see him. But I know I was relieved, and I knew right then that Sebbe was the most loyal person I'd ever met.

Memo continued on separate sheet.

44

In her room at work. Saturday evening. The holiday season had started—for the rest of Sweden, anyway. But in the office, things were going full steam ahead like always. Jossan wasn't there, but at least twenty-five of the others were working away in their rooms. Associates, partners, even some of the so-called administrative staff. The secretaries. The Leijon offices were like a communist state in that respect: even the partners worked their asses off, 365 days a year. But there was a huge difference: as a senior partner, you could expect a decent bonus of at least ten million kronor at the end of the year.

Emelie's office was on the seventh floor. She could see all the way to Södermalm from the window. The towers and spires of the Laurinska building, the old Mariahissen elevator, and the spire of the Katarina Church rose up in solitary union. Even farther in the distance, she could see the huge hulking mass of the Globe, the ball-shaped arena built twenty years earlier. There'd been a wave of arena-building in recent years—the Globe was a midget now, in comparison.

Her fingers returned to the keyboard.

Irritation. Too many things were bothering her.

It wasn't just the workload. She only had herself to blame for that. If you wanted to be a highly functioning business lawyer and play public and private defense on the side, you had to be prepared to work like a dog. But reality had caught up with her. It was payback time. She had things to finish before the holidays. In truth, the problem wasn't that the lawyers wanted their summers off—if a client said jump, the idea was that they asked "how high?" No, the problem was the clients themselves, *they* were the ones who wanted to take time off. They wanted to disappear. To Saint-Tropez. Båstad. The Hamptons. And they wanted to know that their deals were closed before they left.

Her mom and dad were bothering her, too. They'd arrived the night before. "It'll be nice, Emelie. We'll come up the first week of the holidays," her mother had said. They would be sleeping in the living room. Her mom on the sofa and her dad on an inflatable mattress on the floor. Why couldn't they just limit their holiday like normal people?

Not being able to train bothered her, too. She'd only been down to see Leo four times since all this crap with Benjamin began. She'd worked ridiculously hard each time—or maybe it was just that she got tired more quickly because she was in such bad shape. She shouldn't have let herself get caught up in all of this. But it was too late now.

She knew there had to be a connection she wasn't seeing. Had Benjamin killed his own father out on Värmdö? Maybe he'd seen an opportunity, given that his father was already officially dead. She needed to get away from those thoughts. It made no difference what had actually happened: she was his *defense* counsel. She had to take his plea and work with it, fight for it, as long as she followed the law and the codes of practice. And now that he could say more than the occasional word or two, it was clearer than ever that he denied the crime. Her job was to fight for that stance.

Then there was Teddy. He refused to get in touch. She wondered whether he was annoyed that she'd attacked him after everything that happened at the barn—but she'd seen him at the courthouse since then.

It bugged her. The fact that she wanted to talk to him. See him. It wasn't just about their work together.

She grabbed her bag. Fished out the Läkerol box. Shook out a pill. Stesolid—her friend. Her mom had already called five times, wondering when she'd be home. "It's Saturday, surely you're not going to be working all night?" Emelie had given evasive answers. She didn't have time for a lecture on how a firm like Leijon should treat its staff over the summer. "Your dad's put up the blackout curtains in the living room. Good, eh?" Emelie hummed in response.

"Hello, hello. Burning the midnight oil, are we?"

It was eleven thirty. Emelie spun around. Magnus Hassel was leaning against the doorframe. Her box of pills was still on the table.

Magnus had an orange pocket square in his jacket pocket.

"Tons to do this time of year."

"True, plus I've been off," said Emelie.

"Right, we talked about that. Everything okay? Are you feeling better now? Will we be seeing you back here full-time?"

"I hope so. I don't really know what was up with me. I feel a lot better now anyway."

Magnus took a step forward.

He was almost directly above the box now. Emelie glanced at it—it was wide open. If he looked down and studied the contents, he'd see it was filled with pale capsules rather than the usual green sweets.

He said: "And you've been hanging out in Kungsholmen, I hear?"

Emelie felt the color drain from her face. Kungsholmen—that was where the courtroom was. She didn't know how Magnus could've found out she'd been there for the remand hearing. Must be some lawyer she didn't know about who'd squealed to Leijon.

If Magnus found out what she was up to, that would be it.

"Nah, not really," she answered evasively.

Magnus unbuttoned his jacket and leaned back against her desk. He always did that: unbuttoned it before he sat down anywhere. The box of pills was just inches from his leg.

If he knew she'd taken on the case despite him expressly telling her not to, there'd be no way back.

He leaned forward. "No? Because I heard from Jossan you two had fun the other night. At her place."

And with that, Emelie understood: Josephine lived in Kungsholmen, just a few hundred yards from the courts. Magnus clearly knew she'd been there, to Jossan's place. He wasn't talking about her *other* trips to Kungsholmen. She felt her shoulders drop. Her fingers relax.

"Listen," he said. "I'm having a little summer party at my place in the country on Friday. It'd be great if you could come."

Emelie breathed out. "Sure," she said.

He picked up the Läkerol box and held it in his hand. Emelie froze. What was he going to do now? It was so dumb. If she got the boot for taking on the defense case, she only had herself to blame, but if they kicked her out because of the pills, that would be pure bad luck.

Magnus shuffled close, put the box down. He'd clearly just wanted to move it.

"You can come with Jossan and the others from the department. I'm going to book a water taxi from Stavsnäs."

45

Two weeks in custody now. The only okay part of each day: the hour on the roof. Kerim always had his turn outside then, always the same time. They passed each other cigs between the slats, they talked, sometimes they just walked around, like caged tigers at the zoo. Kerim right now: the only person he talked to. Nikola had never even seen the guy properly, just caught a glimpse of his silhouette through the gaps in the bars.

Today: another nice day. Strips of sunlight through the bars. Nikola wondered why they even needed bars above their heads— the walls were thirteen feet high: it wasn't like anyone could climb over them. And if someone did manage to pull a Spider-Man, they wouldn't have anywhere to go. Jumping a hundred feet to the ground was hardly an option. There was a reason they were on the roof.

Kerim said: "I'm buzzin' today, man."

"What about?"

"Everythin'. Honestly, everything. I get to see my kid today."

"Nice, supervised visit?"

"Something like that."

"Think I'm seeing my lawyer."

"Who you got?"

"Her name's Emelie Jansson."

"Never heard of her. She any good?"

Nikola didn't really know. "Hope so," he said.

Kerim moved inside his cage. He seemed to be walking around, thumping the bars. They rattled.

"I've had a bunch of them, but I've got Pehr Söder now. He's pretty sweet."

"Does what you want? Talks to the guys on the outside?"

"Nah, man, actually no. And I respect him for it, 'cause I know he's one of the best. He cracks the witnesses like eggs."

"When'd you have him last?"

"That whole Safe City thing, you hear about it?"

"Nope."

"I mean . . . ," Kerim began. He still seemed to be moving around his cage: his voice would occasionally disappear. "I did a few years, theft. But when I got out, I screwed things up right away. The more crap I got tangled up in, the better stuff the county and social services came up with. In the end, they fixed it so I was a group leader in their Safe City project. It was sweet. Free jackets, a place we could hang out at night when we weren't out patrolling. But the best was the actual patrolling—they fucking paid me for it, to go out there, recruiting brothers."

"That's insane."

"They've only got themselves to blame. Listen: my old man, he ran from the Turks, went to fucking university in Germany—he's insanely smart. But here, he's an unemployed nobody, he's applied to hundreds of things but all he can get's work as a cleaner on the metro. He sits around staring at TV from back home all day, eating börek and smoking Marlboros. Like all the other brothers' parents. 'Course I want the guys to work for me. Wasn't a hard decision."

A whirring noise.

Getting louder. It was coming from above. Suddenly it wasn't whirring anymore—it was thundering. Nikola looked up. A helicopter.

What the f— A heli-fucking-copter, right above their heads.

Kerim shouted something, but Nikola couldn't hear what he said. Hair blowing all over the place, like he was in a hurricane. His clothes flapped.

Nikola ran forward and tried to peer through the bars. It was the first time he'd seen Kerim properly. The guy: built like a brick shithouse—inked right up his neck. Even had a green tear beneath one eye.

Something was happening in there.

The helicopter was still hovering above them. Nikola saw something drop down: a rope, something hanging from the bottom of it.

Kerim moved in his cage: got into position—he grabbed whatever was hanging down from the helicopter. Nikola tried to see what it was.

Another sound mixed with the roar of the helicopter. Nikola could make it out now: Kerim was holding something. An electric saw. Fast: Kerim sawed into the bars on one side. Made a foothold for himself, so he could heave himself up.

Twenty seconds later: Kerim sawed through the bars over the roof of the cage. Nikola watched two of them fall to the ground with a clang.

The wind. The storm.

He heard a voice. Kerim. He was standing on the roof of Nikola's cage.

Shouting: "You coming, man? I'll get you out."

Linda's face when she found out.

Teddy's expression when he heard.

Bojan's sighs when one of them told him. Cutting.

Chamon's grin: thumbs-up. The guys in Spillersboda's laughter when they read about it.

Zoom forward. Isak's smile when he found out about something like that.

The thundering of the rotor blades was close now. Kerim shouted again: "C'mon, yes or no?"

Nikola shouted back: "No, man, I can't. Sorry."

A serious smile. A glint in his eye. A sulky voice.

Two days after Kerim's escape: Linda on her first visit. Supervised. They had all the reason in the world to allow it: Nikola had stayed in his cage when he'd had the chance to run. It wasn't even illegal to make a break for it in Sweden—there was nothing in the statute books that said you couldn't be rescued by helicopter.

The papers went wild. News reports sent sparks flying. *Spectacular escape from prison. Precision flight needed for escape. Drug lord still on the run—"Not many could manage to fly a helicopter like that."*

Nikola smiled. Hoped Kerim was somewhere warm, flip-flops on, a cold drink in his hand, a disgusting amount of licorice to eat.

"I'm glad you stayed," Linda said. "Though I do wonder whether your grandpa would've laughed if you'd gone with him."

The policeman sitting at the end of the table, supervising the visit, cleared his throat. "You can't talk about that."

Nikola saw the sadness in her eyes. She said: "Teddy's not doing too well."

"What, why?"

"I don't know what's up with him exactly, but he's stressed. Up to something shady, I think."

The policeman cleared his throat again. "You can't talk about that, either."

His mother pushed back her chair. "I can't talk to my son about his uncle?"

"No, sorry."

She said: "Grandpa's gone away, to Montenegro."

"Why?"

"I don't know, but I might go down there for a while, too. Come back for your trial. Is that okay?"

"Why?"

"I'll have to explain later. Teddy wants us to."

"Okay, I trust him."

"How did things end up like this, Nikola?"

"I haven't fucking done anything, I'm innocent. . . ."

The policeman interrupted them again. "Give it a rest now,

you can't talk about the case. You want me to bring this to an end or what?"

Linda's eyes flashed.

Nikola hissed: "You just have no idea."

Linda nodded. "You've got no idea what compassion is. You should be ashamed."

For the first time in years, they agreed.

46

The world did a series of emotional U-turns. Teddy: a walking firebomb. Teddy: a cunt hair from exploding. Teddy: unstable as a smack addict with a newly sharpened needle. But all the same: he had a plan. Squeeze Kum. Make it too risky for him not to tell the truth.

He was working day and night. He hated hotel rooms. He loved that Bojan and Linda had gone down to his dad's homeland. He liked the fact that Nikola was behind bars: protected. He saw in the papers that some guy had escaped from the same prison in a helicopter.

He bought five cheap prepaid phones, threw his old one down a drain. He wandered around, stopping at different ATMs, banks, and currency exchanges, withdrawing as much of McLoud's money as he could. He got Tagg and Loke dressed up to take out dough, too: he needed cash, didn't want to leave a digital trail.

He didn't bother calling Emelie. The truth was, he hadn't really had time to think about her lately.

Teddy took detours, made everything he did complicated, changed hotel rooms every other day, turned around at least once a minute. They wouldn't catch a scent of him again, not through Swedish Premium Security, Mazern's people, or the cops.

He continued his rounds of the gambling clubs: asked about Mats Emanuelsson and Sebbe. Most people just looked at him like he was an idiot, so he went back to Bosse and Boggan—pressed them as hard as he could. But they had no answers: "We already told you everything we know."

He went through the material Sara had collected over and over again. His eyes ached. He popped Cipramil and aspirin.

As far as he could tell, there was nothing strange about the divorce papers. He read the preliminary report. He went through the rest of the police documents line by line. Instructions from the prosecutor, interviews with neighbors living close to the cabin, incident reports, crime reports, exchanges with the phone company, trying to get the mast records. Flecks of light danced in his eyes, and he tried to take a twenty-minute nap to sharpen up his senses. Picked up the papers again. The desk in his room looked like it belonged to a nutty professor. There: he was in control again now. There was a crime scene report in the police files. He compared it with the report from the preliminary inquiry, the material that had been made public. Word for word. It was the same report: time, place, scope, photographs. The cottage where he and Dejan had been holed up. Where they'd kept Mats in the box. To which people had come when he wasn't there, and tortured Mats.

Then he saw it: something wasn't right. The crime scene technicians had found a cigarette butt on the stone steps outside the house. But that was missing from the preliminary inquiry report. Everything else was an exact copy—except for the cigarette. Someone had changed the report, made sure the prosecutor and court never found out about the damn cigarette butt. Someone had made sure it was never analyzed—there might've been DNA from whoever ordered the kidnapping on it.

Next day: he was waiting outside the Royal Tennis Hall, on the other side of the street. The shotgun in a bag on the ground by his feet.

Three Swedish flags fluttering by the entrance. A clock above the doors: ten o'clock. Mazern was inside.

Stable, steadfast Sweden. Kum played tennis with business leaders and start-up entrepreneurs. He could pretend to be fully integrated all he liked—but if he did that, he damn well shouldn't be hiding things from Teddy. And now: his morning game was almost over. His X5 parked next to the other SUVs and nine hundred thousand kronor rides.

They'd fired at Teddy, hurt others. Now it was Kum's turn to have a taste of his own medicine.

The building looked old-fashioned and modern at the same time. The yellow bricks—old-time feeling. The curved roof and huge windows—like it was space travel, not tennis, going on inside.

The doors opened. Out first: one of his gorillas. Or maybe it was just Kum's opponent for the day. The guy was broad shouldered, looked like a bouncer.

Then Mazern himself. Tennis racket in a bag on his back. Teddy took a step back, into the bushes.

Thirty feet away from his car.

The gorilla waddled forward.

Kum behind him.

Teddy would be able to shoot him soon, right in the stomach, nice spread of buckshot from his old Remington—but then whatever Mazern knew about all this Emanuelsson crap would go with him to the grave. That was no good.

Instead, he waited.

The gorilla's head snapped this way and that like some kind of secret service bodyguard. They knew Teddy was after Kum. They were on their guard.

Other people were coming out of the tennis courts now. The flags fluttered in the wind.

Now: Kum opened the car door. The gorilla climbed into the passenger seat.

Teddy stepped forward. Raised the shotgun.

Bam.

He took a shot, straight at the back of the car.

Could see clearly through the side windows: Kum and the gorilla were stooped down inside.

He walked around the vehicle. Stopped right in front of it. The SUV was high.

Bam.

A shot through the windshield.

It shattered into a thousand pieces. Mazern must've been covered in them.

A clear enough message.

Teddy ran. Made sure no one was following him on the other side of the bushes.

He'd called for a taxi to pick him up on Lidingövägen. It was waiting for him nicely.

He jumped in. Let them do a few loops until he was sure no one was following him.

He opened the door to get out and head for his own car. But first: he reached for the camera by the rearview mirror. Ripped it out. Just to be on the safe side.

Teddy kept up contact with his dad and Linda. They were enjoying themselves down there, even if Linda was worrying about Nikola. He visited the hospital Mats Emanuelsson had been taken to after the kidnapping, Saint Göran, and tried to talk to the doctors and other members of the staff. One after another, they gave him the cold shoulder. "Confidentiality, confidentiality, confidentiality"—he got it the first time. So he went back to Cecilia's. Wanted to understand. "He was only working part-time, so how did you manage? Do you know if he was doing anything on the side?" Cecilia cracked her neck. Maybe they'd just been living on his poker winnings.

"He jumped from the boat. Do you know why he did that?" he asked.

"No, but he was very depressed for years after the kidnapping."

"Tell me more about the computer."

"I've already told you."

It was all empty talk. Teddy couldn't take any more of it, and he took a step forward. Closer. He towered above her. Her breath at chest level. He took hold of her shoulders.

"What are you doing? Are you crazy?" Cecilia's eyes: wide, like she'd seen a ghost.

"Tell me about the computer."

Her eyes were even wider now. "Let go of me."

Teddy let go. Cecilia slumped down into a chair. He wondered what exactly he was doing.

After a few moments, she got up. Smoothed the creases on her blouse. Glared at him. "Get out."

"Not before you've answered one question. Did you make a copy of the contents of that computer?"

Her eyes narrowed. "How did you know that?"

That was what Lillan had told him.

Cecilia: "You should leave now. You're starting to get pushy."

The stables. The smell of the horses. She'd recognized him after a few seconds, it was only a few months since they talked in the park, after all. For a moment, he'd thought Lillan was about to run away, but she just kept grooming her horse.

"I'm not scared of you. Not if Benjamin's asked for your help."

"You don't need to be scared anyway," he said. He lowered his voice. There were girls and women everywhere. "Want to take a walk?"

Lillan sounded old for her age. "You don't ride?"

She'd been high up in the saddle. Teddy walking alongside in the mud. The horse was huge. Brown with a black mane. Lillan's helmet was black, and she'd been wearing a body protector over her sweater.

He went into more detail. That being held in custody was wearing Benjamin down. That her brother had asked Emelie to make Teddy "understand."

"And," he'd said, "he told us your dad didn't kill himself."

The horse was moving slowly. Lillan was holding the reins loosely in her hands. Still, he saw that she jerked.

Teddy said: "Why? Why did Mats want to go underground?"

Lillan had brought the horse to a stop. She climbed down. Squinted toward the sun.

She spoke quietly. "I don't know exactly, but he was scared. He'd gotten himself into a situation where no matter what he did, he'd always be threatened. And if he just disappeared, they'd come after us to force him out."

"Who?"

"I don't know. The police, maybe. Or you—whoever you were working for. Maybe others."

"And you've seen him since he vanished, just like Benjamin?"

"About once every three months for the past few years. Usually at the place in Värmdö. I love my dad."

Teddy had thought about her answer for a moment. She loved her father. He wondered how Benjamin felt about him.

One last question: "Have you seen or heard from him since Benjamin was arrested?"

The horse snorted in the background.

"No, that's why I'm worried. I've called him and emailed, but he changes his phone a lot. He's always worried he'll get found out. So either he's too scared to get in touch—probably to keep me safe—or he's dead." She turned away.

They started walking back.

"There's something else you should know, about the computer you wanted when he was kidnapped."

"Yeah?"

"Mom made a copy of it. Benjamin and I found it a few years ago."

Teddy had tried to gather his thoughts. He'd been such a fool; he'd known that the kidnapping was all about the computer and not about money—why hadn't he pressed Cecilia about it?

"What was on it?"

Lillan told him what she knew. It was the first time he'd spoken to anyone who'd actually seen the contents of the computer: awful videos, she hadn't been able to watch more than a couple of them. But Benjamin had watched more, just to make sure Mats wasn't one of the men. Information someone didn't want to see the light of day. A network of predators. Teddy felt himself grow hot. He'd dropped the whole computer business much too easily.

"Actually, there's another thing you should know, too," Lillan said as they approached the stable. "Another man came here look-ing for me. One of the other girls told me about it. That's why I've been laying low lately, staying with friends and stuff like that."

"Do you know who?"

"No, but she said he had a red mark on one cheek, like a scar. She said he was creepy."

The pattern: Sara's words in the hospital. The man who'd shot her had something "uneven" about his face, too.

Linda called Teddy from Herceg Novi. She told him that Isak had been in touch, that he wanted Teddy to call him—switching his phone and his number had worked just like Teddy wanted.

"Björne, is it true what I heard, you a lawyer these days?" was the first thing Isak asked when Teddy called him back.

They hadn't seen one another for more than nine years. Isak was the only one who called him Björne—somehow, it sounded nicer than Teddy. Teddy-*björn*. Teddy bear.

"Can we meet?"

"Is it about my nephew?"

"Yeah, kinda."

So: All Training MMA. Basement gym. Temple of violence. Fighting mecca with a capital "M."

The floor was soft. White-painted concrete walls. Punch bags and speed bags hanging from the ceiling. Gloves, MMA mitts, and jump ropes hanging by the entrance.

Kids in their early teens grabbing each other on the floor. A coach in sweatpants and a hoodie was darting around, giving them instructions. "Bend here. Grip there. Twist there." The principle was simple: use the laws of physics and the build of your body to deliver the maximum injury to your opponent.

"My nephew's fierce." Isak pointed to two boys in a heap on the mat. Teddy couldn't tell which of them he meant—the kids' arms and legs were an impossible tangle.

They left the training area. On the drainpipe, stickers advertis-ing some radio channel's Spotify playlists and propaganda posters for the Sweden Democrats.

Isak lit a cigarette. The gold chain around his wrist clinked like a handcuff. It had to weigh a ton.

"Been a long time, man. Real good to see you, *habibi*."

"You too."

They made small talk for a few minutes. Old memories from their childhood, teens. When they'd arranged to meet the Screwbacks at the gravel pit in Tuvängen, and walked the whole way there, alone. How they'd stood eye to eye with the Screwbacks' vice president, Sergeant at Arms, two ordinary members, and a group of prospects. How Teddy'd pulled out his piece right under the nose of the vice president and said it like it was: "You leave us alone or I'll shove this up your ass."

Isak laughed so hard, Teddy thought he'd forgotten to breathe. But then he turned to him. Blew a cloud of smoke in his face. The mood sank.

"Teddy, listen. I need to know where your nephew's at."

"What're you talking about?"

"They're always on our fucking case down here now, the cops. Infiltrating, looking for informants, putting pressure on people to snitch. And they've been on Nikola, I know it. They want him to squeal."

"What's that got to do with me? I'm out of the game. Ask his friends. Ask Chamon."

"I have, trust me. But you know how it is. Nicko's gonna pay more attention to you. And my fuse is about as short as a mosquito's dick—not kidding. You get me?"

Isak slowly ran his hand over his stubble.

Teddy said: "Even if I could help, you know Nicko's inside right now, full restrictions. I can't even see or call him."

Isak grinned. "You're fucking his lawyer, though, right? Emelie whatsherface? Do it through her."

Teddy: a nanometer from breaking his old friend's nose.

He could just see the blood on the pavement.

Hear Isak's yells.

His own death sentence—images in his mind.

No: he regained control of himself. For Nikola's sake.

Breathed.

Breathed deeply.

"I'll see what I can do," he said.

Isak grinned. "Sweet. Your heart's still on the right side, *habibi*. Oh yeah, one more thing."

"What?"

"The whole of Stockholm's talking about your beef with Mazern, Kum or whatever you used to call him. It's been years since I saw that old player, but you want to talk to him alone— one-on-one, y'know?"

"Already have."

"Really? Without any of his boys watching?"

"No, not like that."

"Exactly. I still got some contacts who know him."

"You can help?"

"If you help me."

"Okay, I'll try."

"Good. 'Cause it's like this: Mazern goes to see a whore after lunch every Saturday. He's the only john she sees at home. And I know the address. You in, Björne?"

Teddy smiled. "Isak, man, never been more in."

47

Magnus Hassel's place in the country was incredible. The manor building, as he called it, was enormous, at least three times the size of Emelie's parents' house. Turn of the century, probably built by some kind of merchant toward the end of the nineteenth century. And the views from the double-glass verandas were fantastic. Just a hundred or so yards down a grassy slope, the sea lay like a huge bluish-green yoga mat.

The lawns looked like they'd been cut with nail scissors. The boathouse was huge, too. Emelie could remember the regulations around public access to beaches from her student days—getting permission to build something like that was no mean feat these days. Either you had deep connections in the municipality, or else you managed it some other way. She could even see a pool and a pool house down toward the water.

Thirty people. All from the office, the vast majority from Emelie's department, M&A—Mergers and Acquisitions—mingling on the lawn. Magnus was giving a welcome speech: "We rally round on cases and create warmth in Leijon; we're the life and soul of the office. Its heart."

The waitstaff poured champagne and moved around with trays full of caviar canapés. Emelie knew everyone there, but still, she stuck to Jossan's side. It felt like her friend was her anchor for the evening.

She'd struggled with what to wear: the invitation was

ambiguous—smart summer. She couldn't decide between a pale purple dress from Greta and linen pants and a jacket. Her mother had tried to give advice. Emelie got annoyed. If she was honest, she wasn't in the mood for a party. But at the same time, taking part in social events was good for her—the firm looked favorably on things like that—and it might even cheer her up. Or that's what Jossan said, anyway. "It's the best way to make sure you're on track. Billable hours for every case, though most people here manage that easily enough. But it's social skills that matter in the end. Being liked. Being part of the gang in the office."

Dinner. Floral tablecloths, name cards, huge flower arrangements, a fleet of wineglasses—Emelie wasn't sure which order they were meant to use them in. Not that it mattered, she realized—the waiting staff only ever filled one up at a time.

Magnus himself was sitting next to her. He was busy telling their other neighbors about the place. He and his wife had seen it when they were on a boat trip with some friends twenty years earlier. "My wife fell in love with it. What wouldn't you do to keep the boss happy?" Everyone laughed.

Emelie: popped two Stesolid tablets in the restroom half an hour ago.

She hoped her pupils weren't giving away how she felt. The sweating, the dry mouth, the feeling of drowsiness. No, she thought, it's the opposite: I'm better on the pills.

They toasted. Magnus looked her in the eye. Held his glass with his little finger outstretched. Emelie sipped her wine: she couldn't drink more than five ounces *max*—not now that she'd doubled the dose of Stesolid. Still, she swallowed. It tasted good, fresh. Jossan winked at her from the other table. Magnus admired her dress. Asked what she was doing over the summer. How she liked living in Vasastan.

The truth was, she hadn't had time to make any summer plans. She'd requested a few days off on Monday, but hadn't heard back yet. As far as she was concerned, no response was as good as a yes. Her mother and father were "experiencing Stockholm" dur-

ing the day, as her mom put it, but Emelie suspected they really
wanted to experience *her*—that she was the reason they'd come up.
Because they didn't think she was doing too well. "Can we have
lunch together one day at the very least?" her mother nagged.

Emelie had been honest: "If you want to see me, you'll have to
come to Norrmalmstorg at twelve." She'd asked her secretary to
book a table at Prinsen. Dad was impressed, but skeptical. "You get
other people to do that for you?"

Magnus turned to her. He was talking more quietly now.

"Emelie, listen, I was thinking about the sick leave you took,
what we talked about in your development review. I just wanted to
say that I think you're back on track now—one hundred percent.
So cheers to that."

He raised his glass again: the bigger glass, full of red wine.
Emelie did the same. She swallowed.

Magnus leaned forward. "I heard you wanted to take some
vacation now, at the start of July?"

Emelie felt a wave of unease. She really needed some time off.
Time to work on Benjamin's and Nikola's cases in peace. To see her
parents. Maybe even get some rest.

Magnus continued: "Because the thing is, a spot opened up on a
summer course at Columbia University in New York. I think it'd be
a perfect fit for you. U.S. Private Equity for Experienced European
Lawyers. Six weeks in New York, we'd cover the costs. Plus you'd
be on full pay the whole time. How does that sound?"

His eyes glittered. He really did mean well—this was an opportunity to die for. Six free weeks in NYC over the summer, on a course
that probably wasn't too demanding, and above all: the company
was banking on her. They wanted to keep her—show they were
willing to step up, spend money, just to make her feel appreciated.

She raised her wineglass and took a huge gulp.

"It sounds fantastic," she eventually said. "I just need to check
my calendar."

"You've got it on your phone, haven't you? You can check now?

And don't worry about your cases, I'll make sure the others step in and take over those."

It felt like her tongue was pinned to the roof of her mouth.

Magnus didn't seem concerned. "Let's talk more later. Once you've had time to check."

After dinner, there was coffee with brandy in another room. Someone had turned on some music. There was a grand piano in one corner. The sun would be setting over the water soon. It was ten thirty.

Emelie sneaked away to call Teddy. He had to answer now. But his phone was still off. She went back to the party. Watched the people inside. They were making small talk, laughing. Still discussing their summer plans and the weather. Most had at least a few glasses of wine in them, so she could hear different topics of conversation, too. War stories from various transactions, rumors about colleagues. Gossip about other firms, even more gossip about the partners.

She talked to Jossan for a while. She talked to her secretary. She talked to Claes, Emma, and George. They were all legal associates and lawyers like she was. Everyone was drinking. Everyone was laughing kindly. Everyone was watching her glass. Studying her extra closely whenever she put her lips to the edge and drank. Though maybe it was all in her head.

She'd already drunk too much with dinner. She really should go and lie down. But the water taxi wasn't coming until two, and there was nowhere to sleep here.

She thought about Nikola. Wondered whether he was what Teddy had been like before he served his big sentence. He was always polite to her, but his position was rock solid: he *hadn't* committed any crime. He hadn't been to ICA Maxi. He didn't know anything about blowing any safe open. And he trusted the cops less than Magnus trusted his opponents in any big transaction.

The prosecution had promised the preliminary investigation would be done soon, and that meant the main hearing would take place within the next few weeks. She *couldn't* be in New York when that happened.

Magnus came over, two glasses of cognac in his hands.

"I know it's all a bit sudden, but we really need your answer by tomorrow at the latest."

He held out a glass to her. "Or would you prefer something else? Baileys? Gin and tonic?"

Emelie reached out and took the glass. She was an idiot.

"Want to go for a walk?" he asked.

They went out onto the lawn and walked down toward the pool. The lights beneath the water illuminated Magnus's face in an almost eerie way.

"Cheers." Their glasses clinked. Emelie took as small a sip as she could. Her head was spinning.

"You don't like cognac?"

"No, no, it's fine." She really couldn't drink any more now.

"If you keep working like you have been, you could have a place like this one day. You've got the ability. And I'm not the only one who thinks that. You're a rough diamond, Emelie—know what I mean by that?"

He took another sip, smacked his lips loudly.

Emelie swirled the amber liquid around her glass. She felt like she was about to throw up.

"Thanks." It was the only word she could manage.

Magnus bent down and dipped a finger in the pool. "The sea's still cold, but this is a nice temperature. Think anyone wants to swim?"

"Maybe."

He moved closer. "Is everything okay with you?"

Just one thought going through her mind: don't toast now. Not another drop to drink.

She closed her mouth.

Felt the nausea rising up.

"There you are." A familiar voice.

Magnus's face lit up. Emelie turned away.

"You two planning on taking a dip?" Jossan laughed.

"Maybe," Magnus said with a grin. "I'll go and ask if anyone wants to jump in. The sauna's already fired up."

Josephine put a hand on Emelie's shoulder. The air was cool now. "You're wasted."

"Yeah, but I haven't drunk much." She was slurring.

The pool felt like an enormous, pulsing wave that was about to swallow her up.

"You need to throw up?"

"I think so," Emelie answered, taking a couple of shaky steps forward.

Stesolid and alcohol: she knew the score.

She threw up, straight into the pool.

Starter, main course, dessert. Liqueur coffee.

Stockholm County Police Authority

Interview with informant "Marina," 20 December 2010

Leader: Joakim Sundén

Location: Högdalen Centrum

MEMORANDUM 6 (PART 2)

Transcript of dialogue (continuation)

M: On a personal level, I was out of the shit. Done with the therapy sessions and psychologists. I was working for Sebbe again, Michaela and I were back to doing what we always had. Maxim was in charge of the rest of it. This was mid-2007. A few months later, I handed in my notice at KPMG. Cecilia wanted to know why, they'd always been so good to me, supportive through those difficult times, but I just told her I needed to move on. She thought I'd switched to another normal, smaller accountancy firm, and I guess I had in a way. Emanuelsson, Petrovic & Co., Fraud Services—We move, launder, and reinvest.

The accountancy itself was demanding: good enough to be approved by an auditor, but also essentially nonsense. I looked after the tax returns and self-assessments, VAT returns. I registered new companies, gave them new names and addresses—I was finding new board members the whole time. I still didn't know where Maxim got his so-called goalkeepers from, but I knew there had

to be movement in the businesses, so the authorities couldn't keep up. I liqui-
dated companies and transferred real and invented activities to the new ones.
I created asset transfer and share purchase agreements. I faxed instructions to
banks across half the world.

Not much had happened while I'd been gone. Michaela had learned a bit
more, Sebbe had started to get a bit more aggressive with the whole arrange-
ment, and Maxim was looking after more smurfs and bringing in more goalkeepers than ever. But the work was the same. Aside from one thing: I refused
to do any more work for Peder.

Sebbe wanted to know why.

All I said was: "He's an asshole, a pig. Someone should put one bullet
between his legs and another one between his eyes."

He didn't dig any deeper. Maybe he understood. He was just happy to have
me back. Michaela had missed me, he said.

I told Sebbe I'd resigned from my normal job to be able to keep up with
everything he wanted. The very next day, there was a present waiting for me
when I got to Clara's: a gold watch, an Omega Seamaster Planet Ocean. I
picked it up, weighed it in my hand.

"Oh, so nice," Michaela said. "Looks like it'll fit?"

I reluctantly put it on—it was the perfect watch for someone like me. They
knew I liked windsurfing. Michaela looked at my wrist. It fit like a dream. I
said: "It's great, really."

She smiled. "You think? Cool. I picked it out for you."

There was an envelope under the box. In it, there was a stack of five-
hundred kronor bills, 120 of them, plus a handwritten note—written in a
terrible scrawl. *You're a good driver. Glad to see you back in action.* I could only
guess who'd written it.

The next day, I went to NK and bought a necklace for Cecilia—a one karat
diamond. I left the Omega watch in the office.

But sadly, things between me and Cecilia still weren't right. We moved
into a house in autumn 2007. It had been a year since the kidnapping, and I'd
hoped that having a project to work on would bring us back together. None
of us had really felt great in the apartment—but for me, it was a constant
reminder of the fire.

We started renovating the new place. I realized it was a great way to use
up some of the allowance Sebbe gave me. The carpenters wanted to be paid in
cash, after all. It was my expert area.

"Can't we do it legally, without your poker money?" Cecilia asked when I
tried to explain the benefits of my method.

"Just let me look after this," I said.

She took hold of my arm and just held me like that. Her fingers dug into my bicep. It wasn't nice, but I was glad she thought it was poker money.

"Mats," she said, "you've changed."

I didn't move. I knew she'd let me go eventually, or even better, pull me into a hug.

"You know what I've been through." I sighed. "It's not easy."

Her hand dropped to her side. We were facing one another, and it was like the air between us was thick, soupy.

"No," she said. "It started before all that."

We were having trouble with Benjamin around that time, too. He was being picked on at school. Some of the other kids had been getting to him for a while, but it got worse that winter. He was a teenager now, but maybe he was a bit childish for his age. Football and Lego Technic, that's what he was most interested in. But the bullies actually seemed to focus on the fact he did Thai boxing. They would push him up against the wall, show him he wasn't all that just because he did martial arts. He came home and told us how several of them had held him down, kicked him in the crotch. Then he started telling us they'd stolen his things. They ruined his coat with paint; he found his scarf covered in shit. But the worst thing was that they'd started doing the same thing to his classmates, punishing anyone who talked to him. They completely froze him out.

I called his class teacher. She just said: "Boys that age can be a bit tricky sometimes, and I know they have their play fights and things like that during break, but I haven't noticed anyone being singled out. It's a mutual game they have. Just boy stuff."

"But what about his scarf? It was covered in some kind of excrement."

"Yes, though I don't know anything about that. I took two of the boys to one side and asked them about it, but they didn't know anything, either. I don't think they were lying to me."

There wasn't much more to say. I tried to forget all about it by working even harder.

Sometimes, I think things happen automatically, that your body reacts before you have time to think. Like some kind of chain reaction. I was a bored teenager, so I started playing backgammon. Backgammon led to poker. Poker led to gambling debts. Gambling debts forced me to try to arrange things with Sebbe, who forced me to launder his money. The money got me to try to earn more through my financial derivatives instrument, which made Sebbe go crazy and led to Cecilia discovering the films on the computer, which led to me being kidnapped . . . which, in turn, affected me so that I did what I did.

I mean, sometimes I just think you can trace things back as far as you want. Nothing comes out of thin air. Nothing a person does is completely free from other people's actions, and whatever happens can, in theory, already be traced out at birth.

One Monday, I went to Benjamin's school. Before that, I'd gone to Järnia and bought a Stanley knife.

I went into the playground and waited. After awhile, I saw one of the boys who was bullying and harassing my son. I went over.

"Could you come with me a minute?"

The worthless little shit looked up at me like I was a stranger, though he must've known who I was. But he followed me anyway—kids are odd like that, even when they're thirteen. You say something with enough authority, they'll do whatever you want.

We went out onto the street, away from the playground.

I was pushing the boy in front of me, over to a parking lot, behind a van. His name was Joel, that kid. Benjamin had told me he was the leader. He was the one who'd started a chatroom online, just to stir up things against Benjamin, and he was the one who'd pissed in two of his classmates' shoes as punishment for talking to my son. He was the one who'd tied Benjamin to a tree behind the school. He'd been stuck there for five hours before he managed to get free, by almost pulling his shoulders out of joint.

What happened next isn't something I'm proud of, but I was fuming. I slapped the kid, hard. His cheek was as red as a stop sign. Then I pulled out the knife with one hand and grabbed his chin with the other.

I pressed the knife to his throat.

His eyes were full of tears.

I said: "You tell anyone about this and I'll kill you, just so you know."

He was sobbing. Kept his head perfectly still.

"From now on, this is how it's going to be. You don't touch Benjamin, you don't say a bad word about him. You're going to make sure everyone treats him with respect. You're responsible for him feeling good. Every single day."

The kid moaned, but I didn't know if it was because he was in pain or because he was ashamed.

I left.

When I got home, Cecilia was sitting in the kitchen. She looked so serious. I thought she must've heard about what I'd done to the bully.

"I want a divorce," she said instead.

I sat down. I didn't really understand, but it was also like I'd been expecting it. "Are you serious?"

"Yes."

"Come on, we need to talk first."

"We're past that, Mats. We can't live in parallel worlds."

I wondered whether she really knew how separate our lives had been these past few years. "We can fix this, Cecilia," I tried.

"No. You don't love me and I don't love you. I don't even think you love yourself."

Memo continued on separate sheet.

SNIFFER DOG REPORT

Dog Unit

Signed by Karl Järnnacke

Stockholm County

Date: 21 June

Service dog: Tassie, D1

Confiscation made: No

Material for analysis: No

Tracking after intruders from ICA Maxi in Botkyrka ran from escape vehicle on a dirt track off Hågelbyvägen, Botkyrka

TASK:

Colleague, Anna Petterson, had witnessed two suspects disappear from crime scene on a motorcycle and quad bike, respectively. Quad bike unfortunately lost. Suspect on motorcycle was, however, followed by RB 23-5849, down Hågelbyvägen and then onto a dirt track transverse to the road. Visual contact maintained throughout. Approximately six hundred feet down the track, the suspect left the motorcycle and disappeared into the wooded area to the north. The motorcycle was abandoned on the dirt track.

I, Stockholm dog handler K. Järnnacke, began the search for the suspect at the motorcycle. Service dog Tassie picked up the scent on the second attempt. The scent began by a ditch, roughly sixty feet to the south of the dirt track. The scent continued southward, along the ditch. The dog did not hesitate. After roughly three hundred feet, the scent veered in an eastward direction, toward the lake.

Approximately three hundred feet to the west of the lake, I came out into a meadow and made visual contact with a person moving in the same direction as the scent. It was still dark, but after roughly one minute, I determined that the person had also seen me. I shouted that I would release the dog unless he stopped. The person did not heed my warning, and I released the dog to apprehend him. When the dog reached the person, I was roughly one hundred feet away. As I came up to the person, I pushed him and he fell to the ground. I also administered some distraction hits with an open hand, to the head and the chest. I subsequently secured the suspect with handcuffs.

In service,
Karl Järnnacke

48

Teddy's one-man attack. Teddy's war against the gangster goliath. Teddy's lack of an alternative. He'd thought the man would crack sooner, but it still wasn't working. Teddy had called Mazern at least eight times to try to get him to talk. Kum just hung up the moment he realized who it was.

So today, Mazern would talk. It was that simple. Chaos notwithstanding. Regardless of the risk. Teddy was on the way to where Kum's woman on the side lived.

Surveillance society: tons of people complained about it. Most people didn't give a shit. But for Teddy, it was a problem. Outside the garage where he'd parked his car, above the entrance to Leijon, by the escalator down to the platform—small, round eyes everywhere. Plus: all these fucking smartphones—people didn't even read books on the metro or the bus anymore, they stared at their screens instead, and they could use them to take photos, make films, save audio clips. Keep a record. That was the last thing Teddy wanted today: to be on record.

For some reason, the rubber handrail was moving more quickly than the escalator steps. An out-of-sync movement. Out of step, like his life: he did things—still, he was out of sync with something else. Teddy—Emelie. Teddy—Linda and Bojan. Teddy—his new self.

His shotgun was in a bag by his side.

He'd spent the night in another crappy hotel. Hotel Star

Spånga. Five hundred a night, but the sheets had looked dirty and the carpet was covered in dark patches, which made him think of one thing and one thing only: blood.

He bought some baklava in the square, the sweetness and pistachio flavor reminding him of Bojan. He'd called him last night. Checked he and Linda were okay. His father had no complaints—he loved the heat, being able to speak his own language, and the swampy taste of the coffee. Linda wanted to come home—she was worried about Nicko.

Teddy, on the other hand, still hadn't been in touch with Emelie to pass on Isak's message to Nikola.

He went to the same woman every Saturday, according to Isak. Hjorthagen. A place on Artemisgatan. Nice and close to Lidingö—but the average income where she lived was probably about a quarter as high.

Tagg hadn't wanted to come along this time. Teddy understood—his friend had already gone above and beyond. It was okay.

Jalo, he read on the mailbox. No security door. Teddy rang the bell. Hoped Kum was still a horny bastard even though he knew Teddy was after him.

No one came to the door. He pressed the buzzer again.

He heard a shuffling sound inside. The lock clicked. The door opened slightly, the safety chain stretched out in front of him. A face through the crack: a woman in a pink dressing gown. Fake lips. High cheekbones and something naive in her eye.

Teddy could feel a vein pulsing in his forehead.

He threw himself at the door with all his weight. The safety chain gave way. The door flew open, and the woman was shouting: "What're you doing? *Cime se baviš?*"

Teddy raised the shotgun to her forehead. Closed the door behind him.

Shouted back. *"Gde je on?"*

He didn't have to look far. Her place was small: one kitchen, one room. Wooden bookshelves, empty apart from a few magazines and some withered potted plants. Condoms, lube, and pills on the bedside table. And on the bed: *him*. Naked. Pathetic.

A vision. His former godfather. Ten years back: a giant in Stockholm's underworld. A living gangster legend. Now: a wrinkled, scrawny old man with a limp dick.

Teddy pushed the woman to one side. She collapsed in a heap on the floor. Her hands to her face. Sobbing: *"Ne, ne."* There was a pile of clothes on a chair. Teddy spotted the monogram on something light blue: EMP. Emilijan Mazer-Pavić.

He pushed the barrel of the shotgun up against the naked idiot's temple.

"I'll blow you both away unless you start talking. You know what I want to know."

Kum slowly turned his head.

Teddy held the weapon steady: it was pointing at his forehead now. He wondered what bothered the old bastard the most: getting his head blown off, the whore on the floor getting hurt, or his wife finding out.

Their eyes locked.

"Was it really you who set fire to my stuff in Killinge?" Kum asked.

"Puši mi kurac." I'll set fire to this place, too, unless you start talking."

"And shot my car to shit outside tennis? You've gone mad, *mali* Teddy. You aren't thinking straight. I should've killed you."

Teddy lowered the gun. He saw Kum breathe out.

Teddy shot the bathroom door.

The noise was louder than he'd expected. Kum and the woman both yelled. The door was in splinters.

Barrel back to his head now. "Next one's between your eyes, *pičko."*

Mazern: in shock.

The woman on the floor: rocking back and forth, mumbling something in Serbian.

Mazern: dogged. "You going to tell my . . . wife?"

Teddy countered: "You've got bigger things to worry about right now. You talk, I'll leave her out of it."

He raised the shotgun again. Took aim. Saw something he'd never seen in Kum's eyes. He'd seen it plenty of times before, in others'. On Mats's face when they put him in the box. In the Screwbacks' president's eyes. On the faces of all those men he'd taken care of. Back in his old life.

Kum was afraid.

He tried to cover himself with the blanket. His voice was weak when he began. "You know me . . . I'm someone who'd keep doing what I was doing, either until I ended up in the morgue or in a villa with a pool out in Lidingö."

"The hell you talking about?"

"Wait . . . let me speak. I made it, didn't I?"

"What's that mean?"

"That I'm out. I swear on my *majkin grob*. I'm out these days. I stopped the coke, the speed. I'm done with the coat rooms, the cigs. I even stopped the invoice business. I don't want anything to do with my past. I've moved on.

"But then you turn up, asking questions about what happened nine years ago. About Mats Emanuelsson. I don't want anything to do with that shit. Is that really so hard to understand?"

"Except you *do* have something to do with it," Teddy replied bluntly. "So you don't have a choice."

His eyes, the whole time, his eyes—there was something about Mazern's eyes.

"What the hell's all this about?" Kum asked. "Tell me why you care, Teddy."

Teddy was holding the gun with both hands, didn't want to start shaking with tiredness. He explained as quickly as he could. That Mats Emanuelsson's son had been arrested on suspicion of murdering an unknown man, that things had happened when he visited Sara, that Mats had faked his own suicide.

He looked at Kum. There, again: his eyes. They weren't just full of fear. There was something else there.

It took Teddy a while to go through everything. He sat down in an armchair: the gun on the armrest, still pointing at the has-been on the bed. The woman on the floor was calmer now. Mazern wasn't moving. Silent.

"So, now you know," Teddy said once he was done. "And don't just blame Ivan. I know he's dead and can't explain it himself."

Kum pulled the covers higher, over himself. "I'll do a deal with you."

"You'll fuck me over."

"No, a real deal. You flashlighted my cars and shot at me, but I'll tell you what I know. But for that, you're going to fucking pay for what you did. The insurance company is refusing. They're saying it's fraud."

Teddy couldn't believe it: Mazern was talking about a deal. He'd assumed he would have to use McLoud's money to live abroad for the rest of his life, a price on his head. But now?

"I don't believe you. Why?"

Kum said: "Because I hate those bastards, too. I never knew what that kidnapping was about, either."

"How much do you want?" Teddy asked.

"Eight million, plus one more for scaring the shit out of my bodyguard by the tennis hall, plus compensation for the bathroom door you just shot to pieces." Kum smiled wryly. Maybe he was sure Teddy wouldn't be able to afford it.

Teddy smiled back. Held out his free hand.

"Expensive rides."

"You're fucking me over," said Kum.

"My word's my word."

Teddy took out his phone. Loke had shown him how to do this. He jabbed away at it with his thumb while he held the gun steady with the other hand. To avoid any suspicion, he'd spread the money between four different accounts. He held up screen after screen. Showed Mazern: he was serious.

"*Idi u kurac.* I'll be damned," his old godfather said, getting up from the bed. He'd wrapped the covers around him like a towel. "Then we've got a deal."

Kum got dressed. Sat down on the wooden chair by the little dining table. The woman was standing in the kitchen. She closed the door.

"Who ordered Mats's kidnapping?"

Kum twisted. "A man, a Swede. We only met once, outside. He used a runner to pay me in cash once the job was done. He emailed me a couple of times, but his main contact was Ivan."

"Name?"

"I don't know."

"What did he look like?"

"It was a long time ago. I can't remember the details. He was middle-aged. Glasses. Really white teeth."

"You still have the email address?"

"No, sorry. It was on an old computer I got rid of ages ago."

"And Sebbe Petrovic, what did he have to do with Mats?"

"You already know a lot, so I hear."

"Just answer the question."

Kum slowly scratched his cheek. "Sebbe was Mats's backer at first, poker, you know. Then Mats turned into *Mr. Gold*. The Magician, they called him. He helped them out, in other words—with everything, if you get what I mean. And with investments."

Teddy asked him to go on. Kum talked for a few more minutes. Mats had been the uncrowned king of fake invoices. An expert, a seriously good bookkeeper. He'd helped them for years.

"So why'd you go along with kidnapping someone who worked for you?" Teddy eventually asked.

"Because Mats was starting to become a burden. Sebbe overreacted and scared him, and then he went to the cops. He was a risk, simple as that. Mats became a risk."

"Then why did he jump from the ferry?"

Kum: "I don't actually know. Maybe he still felt like shit after what they did to him during the kidnapping."

Teddy glared at him.

Again. Those eyes. They surprised him. Bothered him. For a different reason now: he had the feeling Mazern was telling the truth. That he wasn't actually lying.

"You promised to tell me everything. We just agreed."

"I can't tell you anything else because that's all I know. But I did promise to help you, and there's one person who does know. In Palma."

"Who?"

"Go down there and see for yourself."

Teddy got up.

Kum: "One more thing, Teddy. Fuck those bastards up good from me. I regret ever helping them. And that you had to do eight years."

49

One of the guards, the one who always had shiny hair and smelled of garlic, led Nikola up to the cage on the roof. The handcuffs weren't tight. They thought he was great, not doing a runner with Kerim when he had the chance. They could go fuck themselves.

Today: a new guy in the cage next door. Nikola didn't care who. It was almost time for his main hearing. He'd be getting out of this shit hole anyway. Best-case scenario: he'd be a free man with a smile as wide as the E4 on his mug. Worst case: he'd be in the back of a transport van, on the way to prison. At least two years, probably more—and this time, there'd be no talk of being sent to young offenders'.

But he had a plan.

The preliminary report was 350 pages long. It had turned up yesterday. The guard with the shiny hair had knocked on the door and dumped the pile of papers on the floor before Nikola even had time to get up. He'd been watching a repeat of *Let's Dance*.

Nikola: followed Kerim's advice—hadn't said a word in any of the interviews, other than to complain about how disappointed he was with them. Instead, he'd listened to their questions—they had to ask them, to inform him of their suspicions—and tried to work out how much they knew. He hadn't even said much to Emelie. He'd told her the same thing he'd told the police: wrong place, wrong time.

But now: he could dig deeper into their evidence, see what they had on him. Counter their arguments. Details were his thing. He marked the pages, underlined the findings from the crime scene investigation, the reports from the National Forensics Centre, the dog handler's report. He read through their analysis of the motorbike, the surveillance camera images, and the residue from the explosives in the office. One thing was clear: they didn't have a clue about Chamon. He read on. Checked the interviews they'd conducted with him, with the guards who'd been first on the scene, with the cops who'd chased him. There was even a telephone interview with Teddy. Just a few short lines.

– Did you receive any calls on Midsummer's eve?

– I can't remember.

– Can we have a look at your phone?

– OK.

Note: p.i. leader checks witness Teddy Maksumic's telephone, and finds that on the relevant date, a call was received from 0733-577488 (suspect Nikola's cell phone number).

– Looks like your nephew called you, could that be right?

– Yeah, now you mention it. Nikola called me to ask if he could come over.

– Had he been to your apartment before?

– You mean that night?

– No, I mean had he ever been to your apartment.

– No, never. He only got out of the young offenders' institute recently.

That decided it. Nikola knew what his strategy would be in court. He couldn't congratulate himself enough for having made that call to Teddy. If Emelie did her job right, he might have a chance after all.

But regardless of the trial: he was fucked. This bastard spell in custody hadn't canceled out what he'd promised Isak—that he'd get the money and find out who derailed the agreement between Metim Tasdemir and the Bar-Sawme family. He had no idea what to do. The money from ICA had been on the ground when he crashed the 125cc. He hoped Isak would show some understanding.

All the same: slight hope. The old man, Gabbe, had told him he'd almost bought the same kind of weapon. From the same series of prototypes stolen from Finland. That couldn't be a coincidence. Abrohom Michel. One of Metim's guys. The weapons had to come from them. Nikola asked the guard to make a call.

He wasn't planning on letting Isak down.

Simon Murray turned up a few hours later. An empty holster on his belt. He'd probably handed his weapon in somewhere.

"I didn't think you wanted to talk to me anymore."

Nikola: "I don't. I wanna do a deal."

Simon sat down opposite him. He had stubble today. Somehow, he looked older than the last time they'd met—maybe because the hair on his chin was a completely different color from the hair on his head—it was bright white.

"I read the preliminary report. You tried to fuck me over with Chamon. You said they had him, but they never did."

Nikola had thought this through. Now: attack was the right approach. Murray: always trying to play good cop, but lying about Chamon had been a mistake. It gave Nikola the upper hand, a favor Murray would have to pay back.

Simon shifted in his chair. "Sorry about that. Made a mistake, I guess, I didn't actually know everything."

Nikola got straight to the point. "Like hell. You knew what you were doing. But I've got a question for you: want to be the cop who raids the biggest weapons stash in Södertälje?"

"Tell me more."

"Depends what you've got to offer."

A watershed moment. See whether Murray was willing to negotiate, play the game. Skirt the rules to get somewhere. Essentially: exactly who was Simon Murray?

"Tell me more," Simon repeated.

"If I give you the location of a weapon, and that place is linked to me, can you forget about it?"

"You said the biggest weapons stash in Södertälje, and now you're saying *one* weapon?"

"You can have the big fish if you're willing to let the little one go."

"Aha, so it's like that." Simon Murray fell silent. He didn't just have white hairs in his beard. The cop sitting opposite him had white strands of hair all over his head. Nikola almost felt sorry for him—a guy who'd gone gray prematurely, who'd never gotten to be part of the fun, who'd only ever taken crap from people like him. Who slaved away for the state without even being able to *dream* about a life of luxury.

"What d'you say?"

"I can't promise anything. But if you tell me, you have my word I won't report it so long as we keep it like this, between us."

Nikola took the step. Now: sink or swim. Out over the edge. It wasn't just a case of revealing something about himself. He was planning to talk about others. He wondered if it always counted as snitching.

He said: "There's an automatic weapon, an assault rifle—an Rk 62—in my basement. It's not mine, but that's where you'll find it. And if you do a raid on a certain person's house, you'll find a sweet load in *his* basement."

"How do you know?"

"Don't ask. I just do. And the thing in my basement—that's the little fish."

"Where's the stash?"

"Look me in the eye first, tell me whether we've got a deal or not."

50

The SAS plane would be taking off in thirty minutes. Palma de Mallorca. The Swedes' dream destination for more than fifty years: there were constant flights down there.

Beside her, in the café opposite gate thirteen, sat Teddy. The smoothie and coffee they'd just bought had cost ninety-four kronor. You could get a decent lunch in town for the same price, but airports were airports. If Emelie hadn't been in such a rush, with such a raging headache, she would've spent the time browsing the perfumes, alcohol, and Samsung bags; she would've bought something for herself. An unwritten rule: you were expected to shop mindlessly when you traveled.

She'd called Teddy two hours earlier. This time, she withheld her number so he wouldn't see it was her—he answered.

"We really need to talk," she'd said.

"Maybe, but I'm on the way to Arlanda right now. I'm flying to Mallorca in two hours."

"What're you doing there? You can't go on vacation now."

"Do you really think that's what I'm doing?"

"I'll come out to you, then."

She didn't really know why she'd done it. Maybe she was just exhausted from everything. And she was actually on leave from work, still hungover from Magnus's party last night. Either way. She really needed to see him.

She paid for her ticket at the airport. SAS Plus: business class remade—they called it something else but demanded just as hefty a price.

Teddy told her he'd met Lillan. And Kum.

"I hope you didn't do anything stupid to him," Emelie said.

"He's been through worse," he replied. "Actually, I gave him pretty much all of McLoud's money."

They tried to gather their thoughts in the short time before the plane took off and they'd be crammed in among curious ears.

The plane rolled out onto the tarmac. Outside, the rain was pouring down. The drops slammed against the asphalt like tiny little bombs. The sky was grayer than one of Magnus Hassel's cashmere suits. Emelie found herself thinking that the farmers back home in Jönköping would probably be over the moon.

They hadn't been given places next to one another. The seats next to Emelie were empty. She thought about asking Teddy to come and sit with her, but decided against it. Maybe he already thought she was pushy, following him all the way to Palma.

She sat back in her seat—tried to sleep. Her hangover, or whatever it was, still felt like someone had installed a bass drum in her head.

She'd called Magnus, too. A short call—much too short, maybe.

"Thanks for the party yesterday. It was great."

"Thanks. Feeling a bit heavy today, shall we say, he he. Was the boat home okay?"

"Yep, absolutely." She thought about how she'd thrown up in his pool—Jossan had used her own cardigan to swirl the water and catch the particles. "It was seventy percent off on Net-a-Porter, so it doesn't matter," she'd said.

"I thought about what you said, about New York," Emelie had said to Magnus.

"Yeah?"

"I can't go, I'm sorry. I have other summer plans."

"What plans?"

"I guess you could call it a kind of job. Mostly that."

"I see, well, I'm not going to pressure you. But I do think the course would've been perfect for you, and New York . . . I love NYC, don't you?"

Four and a half hours later. It was five thirty in the evening. The damp heat hit them like a wall when they stepped off the plane in Palma de Mallorca.

They didn't bother going to check in to their hotel; they had only hand luggage. And if things went to plan, they would be able to meet someone with more knowledge that evening, leaving again the next morning.

"I've called on you as a witness," Emelie said. "Since Nikola called you."

"Sounds sensible. But I'm just going to say what happened, nothing else."

"What did you expect?"

"You're a lawyer. You think justice is a game."

Emelie watched Palma through the wound-down window in the taxi. The coast road: dual nature. To the right: first, the cathedral—enormous. Then: the picturesque heart of the old town. Sun-drenched tourist traps in the distance. Sangria bars and ice cream cafés. Farther along the road: tired old buildings mixed with flashy hotels. And to the left: the boats. They got bigger the farther west they drove. Genuine fishing and motorboats with cabins replaced by big family boats that would've looked like scrap if they were docked in the Stockholm archipelago. And finally: the yachts—they were huge. Emelie had never seen anything like them. They looked more like the ferries to Finland than private vessels.

"Teddy," she said, "why've you been avoiding me lately?"

Now it was Teddy's turn to face the window. "Because you were so pissed off about the whole McLoud thing."

Emelie tried to think back, but then, almost without thinking, she said: "I was really mad at you. Maybe I still am. But do you know why, really?"

"No."

"Because I've been let down by irresponsible people who put

themselves first so many times now. So with you . . . I don't know, I guess I'd hoped you'd be able to stay away from your old life. Stick to the new you. Resist it, y'know?"

They climbed out of the taxi. Sensation on repeat: the warmth again.

Carrer del Bisbe Miralles. Number nineteen. Teddy knew where they were going. A white-painted wall. A yellowish villa behind it. An ornate pool along one side of the building. Emelie was sweating. It was pouring down her, everywhere—she hadn't gotten changed before she left Stockholm, just grabbed her passport, a couple of pairs of pants, a top and a toothbrush, and jumped into a taxi.

There was a doorbell by the gate, and a tiny video camera. Teddy held down the button.

They heard a voice: *"Buenas tardes. Cómo puedo ayudar?"*

Teddy answered in shaky English. "We would like to see the owner. About Mats Emanuelsson."

The man on the other side replied in broken English. "Sorry, not home. Tomorrow you can come back?"

"It's important," said Teddy. "And whoever lives here should already know I'm coming. Can you call, tell them I'm waiting?"

After ten minutes, they heard the voice again. "No, today no. Tomorrow. Ten. Come then."

Hotel Pere Antoni was at the other end of Palma, back where the boats were small. Emelie didn't know why Teddy had chosen a room there, of all places, but it turned out to be owned by a Swede: the muscular guy in reception talked to them with a strong Skåne accent. He was the yoga instructor, he told them. "If you're interested, there's a Mysore class at six thirty tomorrow morning."

Judging by the decor: a boutique hotel, but not *too* stylish—tasteful. Mediterranean feeling with a Scandinavian touch. Pale colors, cane furniture, cool stone floor, brass lamps on the ceiling.

"Breakfast is served at seven every morning," the tanned recep-tionist said as he handed over their key card. "And if you're inter-ested, we offer a CrossFit session afterward, at nine."

"Can I book a single room?" Emelie asked.

The receptionist looked surprised. "Oh, I thought you were together. I'm not sure we have any other rooms free, but I'll see what I can do."

They ate at a restaurant nearby. Calamari and shrimp in garlic. White bread in a basket on the table. A bottle of Rioja. She took off her shoes and let her feet brush the ground beneath the table. The paving stones were still warm.

They tried to make sense of what they knew. Bring structure to their theories. Get their facts straight.

Mats: money launderer for the Yugoslav mafia, a man who'd worked for or with Sebbe for years before faking his own death. Probably worked with Forum Exchange and Stig Erhardsson, too. Nine years ago, there had been a fire in the Emanuelssons' apartment—they still knew nothing about the cause of the fire. But a few weeks later, Mats had been kidnapped. And the motive behind that seemed to have been getting hold of a computer. They still didn't know whether Mats's business with Sebbe had anything to do with the kidnappers. Or why Mats had decided to go underground five years later, convincing everyone he was dead.

Mats was afraid, living on the run, though he hadn't been able to bear not seeing his kids. That was natural. The cottage in Värmdö was some kind of safe house, somewhere he could see Lillan and Benjamin. But someone had gone out there and tried to attack them. Maybe they'd managed. Maybe Mats was dead. For real this time.

It had to have something to do with that network; Emelie shared Teddy's conviction. Mazern wasn't in charge, he'd been as much an errand boy for whoever it was as Teddy. In a way, they hadn't really uncovered anything of value. Everything led straight back to square one.

There were three restaurants in the little square. The sound of water lapping at the shore, a warm breeze blowing in from the Mediterranean. They could see small pricks of light in the distance—probably from boats even bigger than those she'd seen today, anchored out there in the darkness.

She'd been here before, with her mom and dad, when she was eleven. Magaluf: it wasn't far from Palma. Her only clear memory from that trip was that her father had almost drowned in the hotel pool. A German tourist had jumped in to rescue him: hauled him up out of the water like a drowned rat. He'd stayed in their room for the rest of the holiday, playing patience and listening to the radio.

It was eleven o'clock. Teddy paid the bill. They went back to the hotel, and the receptionist told them that unfortunately, there were no free rooms.

"Maybe I should try to find somewhere in another hotel, then," said Emelie.

Teddy picked up her bag. "At this time of night? I'll ask for an extra bed instead, and you can sleep in my room."

The room was nice: fresh. Pale walls, a sober-gray bed, iPhone speakers in dark wood. A terrace facing out onto the hotel grounds, the outdoor bar and the pool below.

The small boats in the marina bobbed in the breeze. She stood there for a while, looking out to sea.

Teddy was busy making up the extra bed. He was wearing just a T-shirt and boxers, and in the warm light from the bedside lamps, he looked unbelievably powerful, like an animated superhero, tired from saving the world. Such calm, simple movements—a peace that spread through the room. He was as far from being her type as you could get—jailbird, former professional criminal, still half-crazy—but she realized that she'd never been afraid to be alone with him, no matter how dangerous he might be.

The darkness wasn't overbearing. It felt safe. Still, there was a certain tension in the room. She listened to Teddy's breathing, the way he twisted and turned in the spare bed—it creaked. Emelie couldn't sleep.

And she could hear it: he couldn't, either. He was lying awake, too.

She'd been so ballsy a few weeks earlier: "You don't want to stay over, do you?" She couldn't understand why she'd been so obvious about it.

She tried to push those thoughts from her mind. Go over Benjamin's case. Nikola's. The whole Mats story. She thought about the food from that evening, the garlic—maybe that's why she couldn't sleep. The room was warm, too: she should turn up the air-conditioning, but it was already humming loudly. She thought about who they'd be meeting in the morning. She saw images: the barn, ablaze.

Until she couldn't do it any longer. "Are you awake?"

"Yeah," he whispered back.

"Your bed is creaking. It might be better if you come over here."

She heard him get up, three soft steps over the carpeted floor. His warm body next to hers.

Her fingers brushed his cheek: his stubble like sandpaper against her fingertips.

The white-painted wall. The yellowish building behind it. Carrer del Bisbe Miralles, number nineteen again. The next morning. Ten o'clock sharp—just like the voice on the intercom had said.

The sun was already bearing down on Palma. Emelie was tired. They hadn't slept until about four. Clung onto one another like they never wanted to let go. Fucked like it was the last time they'd feel another person's touch.

The gates swung open. A short man with a mustache came out to meet them. *"Por favor, síganme."*

They entered the villa. From the outside, Emelie had thought there were two floors, but now she saw it: the grandeur on the inside was striking; the ceilings were at least sixteen feet high. Yellow stone walls, sculptures, and other objects on pedestals, small tables and display cabinets. What looked like antique mirrors and sconces on the walls. There was a small marble fountain in the hallway. Leopard- and tiger-print cushions on the sofa. Emelie had never seen anything like it: there was a feeling of luxury that not even Bosse's or Magnus's place came close to.

A woman came toward them. She looked roughly the same age as Emelie. She had short, dark hair, thin white linen clothes, and flip-flops on her feet. Sunglasses covering her eyes. Her breasts were straining beneath her shirt—they looked unnaturally large.

"Hello," she said in Swedish. "I thought you'd be coming alone, Teddy."

"Everything I know, Emelie Jansson here knows, too. I hope that's okay."

The woman looked Emelie up and down. Then she nodded.

51

They sat down beneath a pergola by the pool.

Teddy didn't say a word, just stared at the woman. There was something familiar about her, but he couldn't say what. Maybe she looked like someone else.

"Would you like anything to drink?" she said. Emelie asked for juice. Teddy for water. The man with the mustache served them.

Teddy was tired. Emelie had lowered her guard last night. It didn't feel like it had *just* been about the sex, but maybe he was fooling himself. He'd wanted something more for so long now, he realized. They hadn't talked much, but it felt okay. In their own way, they were in sync.

The woman took a sip of her gin and tonic. "I've been wondering what the hell you're up to."

Her Swedish didn't sound entirely natural—maybe she had been living abroad for so long, it had affected her pronunciation. But then he realized what it was: she had a Serbian accent. He didn't know how he could've missed it.

"What d'you mean?"

"Exactly what I said. You've set fire to a garage and been charging around Stockholm like an idiot. Attracting all kinds of crap and drawing attention to yourself. What're you up to?"

"Who are you to ask?"

The woman opposite was probably staring at him from behind her sunglasses. "You don't recognize me?"

Serbian accent. A woman who looked around thirty, a woman he definitely recognized. He should get it—but his mind was blank.

"You shoot at my dad and want to know about Mats Emanuelsson, but you don't know who I am?"

With that, it all fell into place in his head. She'd been much younger the last time he'd seen her, at a party at Clara's years ago. The woman sitting opposite him was Michaela Mazer-Pavić.

"You're Kum's daughter. Do you want to know why I've been doing what I'm doing, or do you just want to hear your own voice?"

Michaela lifted her sunglasses. Her eyes were red; she looked tired.

"Take it easy," she said. "Tell me what's going on."

Teddy briefly explained the same things he'd told Kum. That Benjamin Emanuelsson was being held on suspicion of murder, what they'd managed to find out themselves, what Kum had told them.

He said: "I knew your dad knew something, but he wouldn't talk at first, so I had no choice but to smoke him out. Then he tells me you know even more."

Michaela shouted for the man with the mustache. "Miguel, *puedo conseguir otro? Gracias!*" He was quick, her little butler. There was a fresh G&T on the table in less than a minute.

When Teddy was finished, she leaned back. "Well, everything my dad told you is true." Her glass looked frosty.

She started to talk. About how Mats had owed Sebbe because of his gambling debts. How he'd helped them with their money on the side of his normal job. How she'd been his assistant and his supervisor. It had been a crazy time: the system hadn't stood a chance against their methods—the EU, the U.S., and the Swedish authorities were like babies in comparison. And Mats was the driving force, the cog wheel, and the oil that made everything run smoothly.

"But then he tried to screw us over. Sebbe went crazy and wanted to scare him. He set their place on fire. The plan was never for Mats to be there, but for some reason he'd rushed home that day. Sebbe was the one who called the fire department, because our man had passed Mats in the stairwell. Something happened there, after the fire. Mats's wife, Cecilia, she saw something on a computer and forced him to go to the police. Then, a few weeks later, he got kidnapped. On my dad's orders. By you."

Teddy was still holding his glass in his hand, realized he hadn't drunk a single drop.

"I know about the computer. But how did the files get onto it? Where did Mats get it from?"

"We don't really know. Mats would never say. But we think he got it from someone linked to a guy we called Peder."

"Who's that?"

"Peder Hult was his name. We did business with him for a while. Mats was his contact. But Hult was so fucking secretive, we don't know much about him. I'm not even sure his surname was actually Hult. After the kidnapping, Mats refused to keep working with him."

"But how could anyone have known that Mats's wife was pressing him to go to the police?"

"We wondered that, too. But you know what the cops are like in Sweden. There must've been a leak. Someone on the inside selling information. Pay them more, I reckon, and they'll stop behaving like such greedy bastards."

Michaela paused, gave them time to take in what she'd said. Then she continued: "Mats came back, though. He worked with us for years after that. But then something happened, and it made him jump from that ferry."

Teddy leaned forward in his cane chair. "We know he didn't kill himself."

Michaela nodded. "Yeah, my dad told me you knew that."

"So what I want to know is why? Why did he need to fake his own death?"

Michaela took a sip of her drink. "I don't know."

"And who helped?"

"Both of us helped him."

"Both of you?"

Michaela looked downhearted. "Sebbe Petrovic and I. We did what we call a Stockholm Delete. Know what that means? Sometimes we needed people to disappear from a business, so we'd organized stuff like that before. But it was mostly Sebbe who helped out. He's the one who knew why it needed to be done. He kept me out of it. The less I knew, the better."

"So Sebbe helped Mats fake his own suicide?"

"Yeah."

"Where is he now?"

Michaela took a breath. "I don't know if he's even alive. I'm worried it might be him they clipped in Värmdö. These guys are clearly willing to do anything to stop this mess from getting out."

The dark rings beneath her eyes suddenly looked bottomless. "Or maybe it was Mats they killed. Maybe he got himself deleted for real this time. I haven't heard from either of them since."

Stockholm County Police Authority

Interview with informant "Marina," 20 December 2010

Leader: Joakim Sundén

Location: Högdalen Centrum

MEMORANDUM 6 (PART 3)

Transcript of dialogue (continuation)

M: Just like Sebbe said, that boss got in touch with me. This was 2008. It turned out to be Stig Erhardsson. I hadn't heard from him in almost three years. And he wasn't just a branch manager anymore, he'd moved on—he was CEO of something called Forum Exchange now, the second biggest chain of currency exchanges in Sweden. In fact, we were already doing some of our transfers and withdrawals through them.

We met at their head office on Vasagatan. They had their biggest branch on the ground floor, but farther up in the building, that's where they had their numbers guys—their equivalent of me, basically—plus the management.

Stig came down to meet me in reception. He was fatter than last time we'd met, and he had a thin beard. It suited him.

He showed me into his office. It was sparse, minimalistic. Nothing on the walls, nothing on the desk—not even a computer. The only thing indicating it was Stig's room was a framed photo on the windowsill. A little girl in a dress, with a ribbon in her hair. She was the spitting image of her dad. The photo made the room seem a tiny bit more personal, but I was sure he normally had his meetings in one of the conference rooms.

We went through all the usual niceties first.

Then Stig lowered his voice. "I understand you're involved in a number of transactions through us again."

I didn't know if it was a threat or a cautious promise. By then, Michaela and I weren't supposed to be visible anywhere in what we were doing.

"Maybe," I said.

"I think it's great you choose to use us as often as you do. And I'd like to see you using us even more. So, I have a proposition."

This Stig was a different man than the one I'd met before. I thought about how Sebbe and Michaela had laughed at his sweaty shirt. How they'd talked about wrecking his fancy Merc. Now, though, he was relaxed and confident, like a heavyweight boxer ahead in the first round.

"I can guarantee you a much smoother process than you're used to, no problems, no unnecessary questions. My little twinkles can sort everything out."

"Your little twinkles?"

"Yeah, the young girls in the office. They're so nice and simple to deal with."

"Sounds very interesting."

Stig scratched his beard. "But we'll need to come to some kind of mutually beneficial agreement, you and I."

"Of course. How will it all work, from a purely theoretical point of view?"

We discussed the practicalities for a few minutes. A timer-controlled awning started to lower down over the window.

Stig said: "Your people will have to use phrasing we've agreed to in advance. It'll be our key, let's put it like that."

"I'm all ears."

"The first time, your man should say he wants everything in an envelope in a blue plastic bag. We can vary it a little after that, but let's do it like this the first time. That's the only important thing, that he says that."

Things were pretty calm on the Cecilia front. I'd moved out of the house a few weeks after she told me she wanted a divorce. I quickly realized that she'd been thinking about it for a while. Or actually, that she'd made up her mind the year before and just kept putting it off. The kids were obviously upset. Lillan took it hardest—she couldn't understand why Mom and Dad couldn't just keep on living together. "You don't even fight," she said. "Not like Axel and Ebba's mom and dad—they're always shouting at each other."

But that was the problem, I thought, or that's how Cecilia saw things. We'd started out on a journey together, but for the past three years, we'd been traveling in such different directions, we couldn't see one another any longer.

I found a flat in Östermalm. There was no more talk of tiny amounts in an envelope from Sebbe anymore. Every month, I made sure I transferred at least fifty thousand euros to different accounts I controlled in Switzerland, the Isle of Man, Dubai.

I still saw Benjamin and Lillan every other week, Thursday to Sunday. We would have a cozy night in or go to the movies. Sometimes, we'd all go to Lillan's stables and help her with the horses. The only difficult part was Sunday evenings, when they went back to Cecilia. I hated being without them.

A while after that, it was time for the first of our new Forum Exchange transactions. I sat down at the desk in Clara's. It was ten in the morning, and the branch on Vasagatan had just opened for the day. That's when there were the fewest people there. Maxim had promised to keep me updated over the phone.

"I've told him what to do hundreds of times. Trust me," he'd said. "The little smurf's gonna go up to the counter and ask for a rigid plastic pouch. He's going in now. I'm two hundred yards away."

We all waited on the line. My heart was beating like mad.

"See anything?" I asked after a while.

"Not a damn thing. It's snowing."

The minutes passed. I thought about how good my life was, despite everything. My finances were good—even if it was all abroad. I'd just had a great weekend with the kids. Cecilia and I virtually never spoke, apart from when we needed to decide on times to drop the kids off. That was just how I wanted it.

Maxim said: "He's coming back now."

"How's he look?"

"Like normal. Sunken mouth, rotten teeth, bleary eyes."

"What?"

"Just kidding. Wait a sec."

Every second that passed felt like a minute.

I heard rustling and a fuzzy conversation between Maxim and someone else, I hoped it was the smurf.

Maxim came back on the line. "Yup, four million cash in eight envelopes, every one of them in a really *soft* plastic pouch. The code works. Uncreased five hundreds. And the smurf didn't even need to fill out any form about what the money's for. Congrats to us."

It was incredible. No questions, no forms to fill out, no waiting—no *know your client* crap. I felt electric. Endorphins. I felt the kick—it was like wiping the table in poker.

That's when we really got going.

After three months, I let one of our companies buy a Mercedes AMG GTS, and we rented it out—for zero kronor—to our friend Stig Erhardsson, as thanks for his help. It was twice as fancy as the Merc we'd smashed up for him the first time we met.

Over the next few years, I moved five hundred million kronor through the Vasagatan branch. Do you understand that? *Five hundred million.* Everyone we worked for pushed their money through there. There were hundreds of companies involved, mostly from the construction sector, but we even had restaurants, hotels, the cleaning sector, home-help firms, schools, security, gyms, and advertising firms. The process was simple, the client base was huge.

So say, for example, a contractor was building a housing complex in town. This contractor would employ a whole load of others—carpentry businesses, concrete guys, prefab firms, electricians, plumbers, and anyone else they might need. Those firms would be invoiced by companies we'd invented, most often they'd be recruitment companies on paper. The firms would pay their invoices and by doing so, they got deductible costs, plus the accompanying VAT. Our companies would then move the money on down various channels, mostly via banks and companies in the Baltics, but sometimes via Dubai—or Luxembourg, Lichtenstein, and the Channel Islands if we were dealing with bigger things. We'd then send back the money via various transactions, fake loans, payments for imaginary consultations, property purchases in the East. Or else we'd just transfer them without any explanation via the currency exchange on Vasagatan, where our smurfs would withdraw the money as cash and deliver nearly all of it back to the building firms, who'd then use the money to pay their guys' wages *without* any unnecessary tax.

Everyone involved gained from the system. Our man Erhardsson's company earned about twenty million in withdrawal fees from us. The contractors could employ cheaper people. The building firms could avoid paying employee fees and take people on for less. The guys themselves avoided paying tax and earned more. And we took 15 percent for our services.

But the real money came from the purchase option business. After the financial crisis in 2008, stock exchange prices fell, and lots of companies were suddenly hot property. I was meeting bankers, auditors, and lawyers all the time anyway, not least Stig Erhardsson, and let's just say I kept my ears open. I listened to all the rumors I could snap up. I steered conversations where I wanted them. Not many of the people I met really worked at the necessary levels, for the registered companies, but lots of them knew people who knew people. And again: in every single transaction, there were so many people involved, it was impossible to keep it quiet.

So I would invite the right people to dinner, I went to London and took auditors to Premier League matches, I booked weekend trips to the Monaco Grand Prix with a group of chief accountants. Have you ever heard the sound of an F1 car close up?

JS: Don't think so. Loud, I guess?

M: It sounds like it's built to hurt you. Anyway, I was in the race when K-Med got bought out. I knew about the rumors around the purchase of AstraZeneca—it never actually happened, but it still raised the prices. I was well prepared when Custia made an offer on JK Display last autumn. Stig Erhardsson came on several trips with us.

I had contacts in Luxembourg and Lichtenstein fronting businesses for me. The authorities back here were trying to stay on top of things—if they saw someone suddenly buy up huge amounts of options, they would react. Everything had to be done via proxy, be carefully weighed up and planned.

Benjamin was doing better at school. Lillan loved her horses. Sebbe made sure I had plenty of candy, as he called it. Pills that made me happy. Michaela helped me update my wardrobe every now and then. The guys were always wanting me to go out with them, but I only went when we were abroad. I preferred to stay anonymous in Sweden. To keep things short: they sometimes called me the King. The Magician. Mr. Gold. I was living the life.

I do sometimes ask myself what kind of life it was, though. Our apartment had been burned down, I'd been kidnapped and tortured. I was changing my phone once a week, looking after hundreds of different companies a year, popping Losec and MDMA just to be able to deal with my ulcer and my broken psyche.

I was doing it for the kids, no one else. So that Lillan and Benjamin would never end up in debt like I did. But still . . . I mean, shit . . . all the crap I went through, it spilled over onto them. I sometimes wonder how I could've let it get so far. I've been an idiot. And two months ago, the first cracks started to appear.

JS: What happened?

M: Maxim died.

JS: How?

M: I don't know. They don't tell me everything. But something went wrong, I think it was a car crash.

JS: Where?

M: On the E4. Sebbe was in the car, too. He made it, but he cracked some ribs and broke his arm.

JS: Okay.

M: Mmm . . . and he's still a complete mess, I'm sad about the whole thing, too. We'd worked together for years. Maxim made me laugh.

JS: You said cracks before. What else happened?

M: I got arrested and ended up here with you.

Memo continued on separate sheet.

52

The moment Emelie turned on her phone when the plane landed, it started beeping and buzzing. Tasks, calendar reminders. Missed-call alerts, message tones, the bleeping of 208 unread emails pouring in. It even buzzed with new Facebook alerts, despite the fact she never used it. She needed to turn that function off; it was insane.

Though it was five o'clock on a Sunday afternoon, she went straight to the office. She couldn't keep this up much longer. Trips to Mallorca, two criminal cases where she was about as clueless as a first-year law student. Plus: Mom and Dad back home in her apartment, desperate to take a trip to the Fjäderholm islands with her, visit the Royal Armory, go out for a meal at the very least. Most of the missed calls were from her mother.

She popped two Stesolid pills in the taxi. She was nowhere near done with the Investor Incubation PPL agreement. And she really should try to cut back on the pills. Though she hadn't been taking them for *so* long yet. A few more days couldn't be too bad.

She ate a microwave dinner with Jossan in the office. They didn't even bother going down to the dining room on the floor below. Emelie needed to start searching for Peder Hult, or at least mention his name to Benjamin, but she didn't have time. She had to get ready for Nikola's trial, too.

The food was unevenly warm. Emelie burned her tongue on one mouthful, but the next bite tasted like it had just come out of the fridge. She regretted not just running down to McDonald's.

Jossan hadn't even warmed anything up. Instead, she'd taken a huge plastic bottle from the fridge. "I'm on a new diet," she said, pouring the green contents into a glass. "Juicing."

"Meaning what?"

"Nothing but cold-pressed juice today, for breakfast, lunch, snack, and dinner. This one's kale, wheatgrass, spinach, apple, sunflower, cucumber, lettuce, and ginger. Super healthy. Want a taste?"

Emelie sipped the drink. It tasted sour, strongly of ginger. She pulled a face.

Jossan said: "It's better than the pills you're popping anyway, Pippa."

Emelie looked around. No one else was about. She hadn't realized Jossan knew.

She said: "I'm not doing so well, Josephine. There's so much you don't know."

She was longing for Teddy.

The next day, she'd promised to eat lunch with her parents. Her secretary booked a table for them at Lydmar; they had a nice terrace. But it was still raining—at least that should send her mom and dad back to Jönköping before long, if nothing else.

She was waiting for them now. An hour, max: she just didn't have time for longer. Last night, when she got back from the office, she'd started reading the preliminary inquiry report from Nikola's case. It wasn't especially thick, but it was all new to her. She underlined, made notes in the margins, transferred the same notes to a document on her computer. Her starting point was his plea. It made no difference what *she* thought had happened. Nikola denied any crime—he'd been on his way to Teddy's.

"Oh, what a lovely little place," her mother had shouted when she sat down. "Do you know what they asked us when we arrived? If we were the Janssons. They must've been able to see it on us. Isn't that wonderful?"

53

The last time Nikola was on trial: petty theft, handling stolen goods, assault. This time, it was aggravated burglary. Actually: he'd expected a flashier courtroom, grander somehow.

Södertörn district court: less than ten years old. Through the window, he could see the prison where he'd been locked up these past few weeks. He could even make out the cages on the roof. Kerim—*Shawshank Redemption*—had vanished without a trace, "like a fart in the wind."

The room: big. The bench: high. The seats were made from pale wood, with light-green leather upholstery. Modern atmosphere: no flourishes. Straight lines everywhere. Behind the judge and the lay judges, there was some kind of green fabric on the wall. Clear color scheme: light and green. Basically: make him feel like it was somewhere that'd be kind to him. Fib of the century.

The judge: a middle-aged woman with a face like she had a constant sore throat. The corners of her mouth never moving north of her lower lip. She reminded him of the creepy old woman in *The Woman in Black 2*. The lay judges looked like they'd been born in the nineteenth century: Nikola wondered which of them would start snoring first. The only one who didn't look like he'd made up his mind the moment he stepped into the room was the clerk, a young guy with a beard, constantly adjusting the knot in his tie.

"Good morning," Emelie said loudly as they entered the room. She had come down to meet him in the custody room, and followed him and the guards up to the court. He liked her strong, confident tone.

The prosecutor was already at her desk: busy setting up her computer. A thin-haired woman with steely vibes: total I'm-your-bureaucratic-executioner look fixed on him. A cunt in the most cuntish form.

Emelie pulled out Nikola's chair, put her bag down on the table, and started taking out piles of paper. She took her time: document after document—everyone was sitting but her. Nikola dug that, too—his lawyer wasn't going to rush for anyone.

"Yes, good morning," said the judge. "Let's begin today's hearing in case B 2132-15. We have here public prosecutor Karin Forsryd, correct?"

The prosecutor replied flatly: "Yes."

"And on the other side, Nikola Maksumic?"

Nikola bent down toward the delicate microphone. "Yes." He thought it sounded like his voice echoed through the room.

"And next to you, your public defense counsel, lawyer Emelie Jansson."

"That's correct." Again—Emelie spoke clearly.

The judge wrote something down, then said: "In that case, I wonder, is there any reason to adjourn today's hearing?"

The prosecutor and Emelie replied simultaneously: "No."

Nikola glanced to his left: the public seats were almost full. More people than he'd thought. Maybe they were just general visitors, some sad school class on a field trip. He could see Chamon and Yusuf, in any case: both winked at him. Paulina was there, too. He tried to read her expression. She looked serious. No smile—right? She was at least fifty feet away, so it was hard to see. But at least she was there. And then his mom—back from her shady trip.

The presiding judge kept talking: about the procedure for the hearing, who everyone was. Then the prosecutor began with her opening remarks. Emelie had already gone through the order of things with Nikola, and explained how the prosecutor would probably try to frame it. He'd been through this before, anyway. He tuned out—he wasn't *that* interested in trials.

They saw CCTV images from the shop and the area around it, two people, both in dark clothing and motorcycle helmets, breaking in and running between the shelves. They hadn't found a helmet, though, and when they tested Nikola's clothing for explosive particles, they hadn't found zip. No fingerprints or traces of DNA, not in the shop and not on the motorbike abandoned nearby. The explosives had been traced back to a building firm in Bålsta. It had been burgled two years earlier, but they didn't know any more than that. The technicians had taken casts of the damage done to the doors, but they hadn't found a crowbar, so there was nothing to compare it to. The police had taken his phone and emptied it: even there, they hadn't found anything detrimental to his case.

Nikola's first bit of luck: that he'd worn gloves the entire time, kept his helmet on, and sprayed over the CCTV camera in the office: his face had never been visible.

The second: that he'd thrown the sweater, helmet, and backpack into the lake.

It was a clean job.

His bad luck: that the pigs had managed to get a tracker dog on scene so fast.

After an hour, the prosecutor had finished making her opening remarks. The next point on the agenda was his interrogation. He leaned over to Emelie and whispered: "I can't do this."

"What?"

"I don't feel good."

She requested a break. Nikola ran to the toilet—felt like he was about to shit himself. But nothing happened. Eventually he got up, rinsed his face, and went out. The guards outside smiled—maybe they were used to people cracking under pressure.

He tried to keep it together. Stared straight ahead, clasped his hands under the table. Listened to the prosecutor's questions.

It felt like it lasted three days, but after about an hour, it was

over. He hadn't had much to say, just repeated the same thing over
and over again: "I was going to my uncle's. He can back me up. You
can see in my phone, I called him. I got lost, then the police dog
came running up and ripped me to pieces."

He wondered whether Emelie really believed he was innocent;
it kind of seemed that way.

The hearing dragged on. They stopped for lunch. The police
took him back to prison and gave him a bowl of pea soup and some
bread. He couldn't even manage a mouthful.

Back in the courtroom, it was time for the guards and the cops
to get up on the stand. One by one, they came forward. Answered
the prosecution's questions: "What did you see outside the shop?
What did the motorcycle look like? How was it being driven? How
long after this were you in your car? What did the person riding it
look like?"

They didn't seem to know much, but a few of them tried to say
that the biker was built like Nikola. That their trousers were like
those he'd had on when he was arrested. Emelie didn't ask a single
question. Nikola wondered what she was doing—she should be
laying into them. Cross-examining them all, making them admit
that they couldn't actually say anything about who was like who.

They took another break in the afternoon. Emelie came down
to the small holding cell with him. The first cell he'd been in was
like a huge Östermalm apartment in comparison. There was nothing but a seat in this new one—both he and Emelie chose to stand.

"Why're you letting them spout all that crap?" he asked the
moment the guards closed the door.

"They're not adding anything."

"But they're saying they recognized me."

"They can say what they like, but the person they saw was
wearing a helmet and dark clothing. It's impossible for them to
know if it was you or someone else. You didn't have a helmet with
you when you were arrested. And that means I shouldn't run the
risk of making them say something that could hurt you."

"But the judge looks like she wants to give me fifteen years."

"Just take it easy. All that really matters is the dog handler. That they say the dog picked up your scent. And we haven't had that testimony yet."

But now. The door at the very back of the courtroom opened. A uniformed policeman stepped into the room. His belt jingled: walkie talkie, keys, flashlights, and other police crap. Nikola recognized him: the guy's Alsatian had mistaken his arm for a bone.

"Karl Järnnacke?" the judge asked.

The policeman nodded and sat down in the witness box. He had thin, reddish sideburns and rough hands.

"You have been called here today as a witness in this case, on the request of the prosecutor. Have you given testimony in court before?"

"Many times."

"In that case, let's proceed with the witness oath: I, Karl Järnnacke . . ."

"I, Karl Järnnacke."

"Do solemnly swear . . ."

"Do solemnly swear."

"To tell the truth, the whole truth, and nothing but the truth . . ."

"To tell the truth, the whole truth, and nothing but the truth."

The judge glared at the dog handler in the same way she'd glared at all the earlier witnesses. "I would now like to remind you that anything you say is under oath."

Järnnacke started to talk. He followed his own memo word for word—he must've reread it just before he came in, what a nerd.

The prosecutor asked a few questions about the search. How hard the dog had pulled on the lead. How sure Järnnacke was that it had all gone as it should.

Nikola tried to sit upright in his chair: it was hard. This pig invited violence, like a disgusting bug you wanted to crush under your foot. His words were sinking Nikola: making the court believe the dog had picked up the right scent, that the evidence was clear. After a few minutes, the prosecutor said her thanks. It was all over:

Nikola was going to be sent down. He wondered how many years it would be this time.

But then the judge turned to Emelie. "Now to the defense for cross-examination."

"Thank you, Your Honor," said Emelie. Her voice was softer now. She looked up at Karl Järnnacke. "How long have you worked as a dog handler?"

"About four years."

"And you completed the police training course on dog handling prior to this, correct?"

"Correct."

"I assume there are certain rules and regulations you have to learn as part of this?"

"Yes, of course."

"And certain texts about using dogs on searches, correct?"

"Correct."

"So you must have read these, since you completed this training course?"

"Yes."

Nikola didn't know what she was doing. The cop was just answering yes to all her easy questions. She wasn't doing anything to fight him—it was insanely weak.

Emelie asked: "You produced the memorandum in this case, correct?"

"Yes, that's correct."

"And the content, this is all true and correct, yes?"

"Yes."

"And you haven't left out any vital information, correct?"

"No."

"Is that correct?"

"Yes, I haven't left anything out."

"Okay, let's work from that basis. I'm now going to read to you from the report, *The scent began by a ditch, roughly sixty feet to the south of the dirt track*—yes?"

"Yes."

"That's what happened?"

"Yes, that's what happened."

Emelie paused and started riffling through her bag. The room was dead silent. Nikola didn't understand a thing. She took out three books and a couple of booklets and put them on the table in front of her. Then, she said: "I've just taken out the following books: *Tracking Training* by Janne Salminen, *Search Dogs* by Frans Larsson, and the Swedish Working Dog Club's *Dog Tracking*. I assume you are familiar with these books?"

"Yes."

"I've also downloaded the National Police Board's guidelines and general advice on examining the dogs owned by the police, RPSFS 2000:5, FAP 214-2. You are aware of this, too, correct?"

"Yes, of course."

"Then my question is this: Is it written, in any of these books or in the Police Board's guidelines, that the dog tracking method is one hundred percent reliable when a scent begins as far as sixty feet away from the object?"

"I don't know, but it's possible."

"Does it say so in *Tracking Training* by Janne Salminen?"

"I don't know."

"Aha . . . My claim is that there is no such statement in that book."

"Okay . . ."

"Do you disagree? Do you believe Salminen comes to any other conclusions in his book?"

"I don't know, I just said—"

"No, of course. Does it say so in *Search Dogs* by Frans Larsson?"

"I mean, I have no idea, I don't remember."

"You don't remember what the book says?"

"I didn't mean that, but I don't remember whether *that* particular book says anything about *that* particular subject."

"You don't remember?"

"No."

"Okay. What about in *Dog Tracking*?"

"Oh, come on. I don't know, I've told you. What difference does it make? You set out with the dog different distances from the origin point, and eventually you get a hit. Sometimes, it might be that our colleagues have contaminated the scene."

"And by contaminated the scene, you mean that other police officers—who reached the motorcycle before you—might have left a scent that the dog then followed, correct?"

"Yes, roughly. But then the dog analyzes the ground and follows the right scent—though perhaps from farther away."

"Yet you didn't write anything about this in your report, did you?"

"No."

"So that implies that you left out information from your report?"

"You might say that, but it isn't essential information."

"It isn't essential information that other police officers might have contaminated the scene?"

"No. I knew what we were looking for. That's the important thing."

"So you left out that the scene might have been contaminated?"

"I've already answered the question."

Emelie raised her voice slightly. "No, you haven't. Just answer yes or no, please. Did you, in your report, leave out the fact that the scene may have been contaminated?"

"I don't know."

Emelie turned to the judge. "Thank you, Your Honor. No further questions."

Nikola melted. It was brilliant. It was beyond smart. The dog handler looked like an idiot with no idea what was in the books he'd read, and who'd either lied in his report or been sloppy. Plus, she'd stopped just in time. Hadn't actually gone on to ask whether the scene *was* contaminated. He thought about what Kerim said: Emelie had cracked the guy like an egg.

54

Peder Hult. Who the hell was he? In total, there were more than a thousand people with that name in Sweden. Four hundred of them between the ages of forty and seventy. Roughly a hundred of those living in the Stockholm area.

Michaela hadn't been able to describe him very well; she'd never met him in person, and it had been years since they'd last talked about him. Middle-aged businessman, that was pretty much all she knew. She had no idea where he lived, when he'd been born, or even which company he'd worked for. She didn't know how Sebbe and Mats had originally come into contact with him. "Our customers were often pretty secretive, for obvious reasons," was all she said when Teddy tried to fish for more.

Still: Teddy was searching like a madman. He'd asked Loke to use all the tricks in the book. He himself had gone back to Boggan and Bosse to find out if they knew anything, but they had no idea. He'd asked Lillan, Cecilia, and Kum. They just shook their heads. He got Emelie to ask Benjamin, but the kid, who was clearly doing better, had just looked blank. He even sent an anonymous email to Anthony Ewing and told him he'd have trouble unless he told them everything about Peder Hult. He never got a reply. Swedish Premium Security was the beginning and end of the chain.

He'd paid Kum. Nine million reasons to hate Mazern. But on the other hand: Teddy should be happy to have fixed things without being given a bullet between the eyes. Life was back to normal—he was no longer a millionaire, though he still had a few hundred thousand left over after he paid for Linda and Bojan's vacation and bought the apartment for Nikola. He should be able to manage without any more work for Leijon for a while.

Emelie seemed to have done a good job in Nikola's main hearing, even though Teddy hadn't been allowed to sit in the courtroom before he testified. The questioning itself had gone quickly: he simply repeated the same thing he'd already told the police. It felt strange to be questioned by Emelie, someone he'd slept with—he wondered whether that was really in line with the moral and ethical principles of her job.

He'd also asked Michaela why she thought Sebbe might be the dead man out in Värmdö.

"Because he lives here with me. He went away on business for a few weeks, but I haven't heard from him since the fourteenth of May."

"You know whether he's in the fingerprint or DNA register in Sweden?"

"I don't think he is, actually," she groaned.

"Does he still have the tiger tattoo on his arm?"

Michaela looked like she was about to start crying. "Yeah. That one and far too many other tats. I used to complain about them."

Teddy: "Could we get his DNA from anything here? Hair? Blood? Anything at all, so we can compare it with the victim's."

Stockholm County Police Authority

Interview with informant "Marina," 20 December 2010

Leader: Joakim Sundén

Location: Högdalen Centrum

MEMORANDUM 6 (PART 4)

Transcript of dialogue (continuation)

M: It was twelve days ago now, and it sounded really simple. Sebbe was going to pick something up from someone in Gamla stan. It was actually Maxim or one of the others who usually looked after that stuff, but you know, he's not with us anymore. It was a one-off. I was just meant to sit in the car and wait. When Sebbe came back, I'd drive him somewhere. I didn't ask any unnecessary questions. It wasn't my place.

JS: Why couldn't Sebbe drive himself?

M: He broke his arm, in the same car crash where Maxim died, I told you.

JS: Oh, right, yes.

M: Anyway, it was the middle of the day. I don't know why they chose that time and that place, but maybe it was a good idea choosing somewhere always full of people.

I parked the car in Kornhamnstorg. It was a rental. So yeah, the Range Rover you asked about a few days ago, it's not mine or Sebbe's.

Sebbe got out. I watched him walk away and stop under one of the bare trees. There was a café to the right. The lake was covered in thin ice—it'd come early this year. I waited. Sebbe just stood there, smoking. The time passed slowly—I didn't know why we'd been in such a rush. Nothing was happening.

I thought about Benjamin—he had just turned sixteen, and he borrowed my apartment to have a party with some friends the weekend before. When I got back at two in the morning, the place was oddly tidy. He was asleep on the sofa in the living room. I wondered how many of his friends had actually come.

Sebbe lit his fourth cigarette. He seemed calm. We'd been waiting for more than half an hour by that point.

For a while, I thought about just quietly starting the engine and driving off. Going back to Clara's and waiting for Sebbe to turn up and start yelling because I'd wimped out; it really wasn't something I was used to, sitting in a car out on the street. But that thought disappeared just as quickly. Of course I didn't have the nerve to do anything like that. And if I'm honest, I didn't want to. Sebbe's . . . well, he's who he is, and we'd all taken Maxim's death hard.

But something didn't feel right out there. An hour passed and nothing happened. Sebbe had sent me a message: *Must've got the time wrong. I'll wait a bit longer.* But I had a really bad feeling in my stomach. It wasn't that it was taking ages. It was two men. One of them was wearing some kind of scarf. He was sitting in the café across the road; I could see him through the window. He seemed to be talking into a hands-free headset. The other was wearing a camouflage jacket and standing under a tree, about thirty feet away from Sebbe. He was on the phone, too. Two men who'd been in the exact same positions for more than an hour without taking their headphones out once. Two men who kept looking at Sebbe. Who occasionally seemed to exchange glances.

After fifteen minutes, I sent a message back to Sebbe. *Think we should go. This feels wrong. Got a bad feeling about two guys looking at you constantly.*

I didn't get a reply. Sebbe was standing about 150 feet away from me. I watched him light his eighth cig and look across to Slussen in the distance.

A few minutes later, something happened. Sebbe turned around. There was a man coming toward him—he was wearing an old-fashioned hat, it was at a kind of nonchalant angle, and he was carrying a shoulder bag. Sebbe greeted him. I thought he must be one of our smurfs, the ones Maxim used to look after. I watched them exchange a few words and then start walking down Lilla Nygatan. Straightaway, I saw the man in the scarf get up and leave the café, and the man in the camouflage jacket move from under his tree. They were following Sebbe and his friend. There was no doubt now.

I called Sebbe. No answer. I sent a message: *They're tailing you.*

No reply. I thought about when he'd come down to the strip club and saved me and my poker friends. I got out of the car.

Gamla stan: the historical heart of Stockholm, its midpoint. I don't have any relationship to that part of town, other than vague memories of a guided tour there sometime in high school, when the guide told us about Stockholm's bloodbath. Christian II—Christian the tyrant, you know?—he'd chopped the heads off a load of Swedes there. That was five hundred years ago. The same thing still happens in other parts of the world.

Sweden's changed, and changed again. It's a safe country now. It's for the people, that's what they say anyway—a welfare state without parallel. And maybe that's true. All I know is that it's too fucking easy to make dirty money clean in this country. And that if you're high enough up in the hierarchy, you can do whatever you want to other people.

I followed Sebbe.

He and the guy in the old-fashioned hat were chatting. They were walking slowly up one of the narrower streets. The two other men kept a distance of fifty, one hundred feet. I couldn't believe Sebbe hadn't noticed them. I thought he was experienced, always on his guard, like Maxim. I tried ringing him again.

After a few more feet, they stopped. The guy in the hat took off his bag and gave it to Sebbe. Farther down the same street, the man with the scarf held something up. I moved closer and saw what it was. A camera. I worked out what was going on. They wanted proof of the handover. Some kind of evidence against Sebbe. They moved forward.

That's when I understood their next move. They wanted to secure more evidence, they wanted to arrest them. The man in the scarf and the other one, in the camouflage jacket, they were moving toward Sebbe and his friend, and behind me two more men were moving quickly in the same direction.

They hadn't seen me, though. I could still warn Sebbe, shout to him, get him to see.

Our burning kitchen. Sebbe in the fight at the strip club. His screwed-up face when he told us what'd happened to Maxim. The darkness in the box, the man who'd been in charge.

I yelled as loud as I could: "Run, Sebbe—police."

He turned to me. I think he understood right then. They were about fifty feet away. He could make it. He ran.

I'm pretty sure it wasn't drugs in that bag. Sebbe doesn't do that kind of thing.

Five seconds later, I was facedown on the ground with a knee on my back. They handcuffed me, drove me to the station. And you already know the rest.

JS: Yeah.

M: Sebbe's still free, right? You haven't arrested him?

JS: We haven't, no. Can you help us?

M: I've told you a lot, but I'll never do that. Sorry.

JS: We might come back to that later. I wanted to thank you anyway. You've given us lots of valuable information. And as far as our agreement is concerned, you'll be kept out of all of this. You'll be my anonymous source, Marina.

55

Her secretary phoned: "There's a delivery for you down here."

"A delivery?"

"Viveca says it's a bouquet. Should I bring it up?"

"No, I'll come and get it."

Emelie wondered who would send her flowers. She could only think of one person. She didn't take the elevator, half ran down the stairs instead.

The floor in reception was made of huge slabs of Gotland limestone, and the walls were clad in wooden panels. Not old, British-inspired panels, but a smooth, matte wall of birch. The reception desk itself was made from a piece of dark gray granite. The idea was that it symbolized ancient Sweden: stability and tradition.

The room was Leijon's pride and joy. The message: we're playing at the same level as the exclusive London firms like Slaughter and May, Parabis, and Stewarts Law—in other words, those with the highest PEP, or Profit per Equity Partner, where partnership after four or five years meant, in principle, economic independence for years to come. No one could mistake Leijon for some provincial Swedish law firm anyway, full of local, general lawyers, but nor did the reception give the same echoing sense of emptiness you often had in the big firms. When their clients stepped through the seemingly nondescript oak doors on the seventh floor, they would feel, in all respects, like they had just entered one of Europe's fore-most legal firms.

Emelie was panting when she made it down. She was clearly in worse shape than she'd thought.

Viveca handed over the bouquet.

Emelie tore open the paper in the stairwell on the way back up. Huge pink roses and peonies—it must've cost a fortune. There was a card taped to one of the stalks.

Thanks for your help! / Nicko

Emelie thought back to the ruling from the day before.

"Nikola Maksumic maintains that he was in the area because he planned to visit his uncle. An outgoing call was, indeed, made from his telephone to his uncle just before the time at which the crime occurred. It does not, however, seem particularly credible that he would choose to visit his uncle so late at night, nor that he would get lost to such a degree that he would find himself in the location where he was intercepted by the dog handler.

"In Sweden, we abide by the principle that, in order for pros-ecution to take place, the deed attributed to the individual in ques-tion must be proved beyond all reasonable doubt. In other words, all other sequences of events must be ruled out.

"The district court concludes that tracking did not proceed directly from the motorcycle in question. Additionally, it has not been established whether the area around the motorcycle was con-taminated, nor how many additional scents may have led from this area. We cannot with confidence say whose scent the dog picked up at a distance of sixty feet. It can therefore not be ruled out that the dog picked up Nikola Maksumic's scent some distance into this area, and followed this instead of the true suspect's scent. It is thus difficult, in the eyes of the court, to draw any conclusions relating to Nikola Maksumic's connection to the motorcycle or the crime scene, on the basis of dog tracking alone."

The case had been dropped. The court had followed the prin-ciple of benefit of doubt.

Benjamin was getting better and better. He could get out of bed and take a few steps; he was eating simple meals by himself and could express certain things. According to Jeanette from section six, he had reached somewhere around fourteen on the Glasgow Coma Scale. He was heading in the right direction—he should be back to normal within a few weeks.

But all the same, he didn't know any more than what Emelie had already gotten out of him. He knew he'd been in the house with his dad, and he was sure he hadn't killed anyone. But he couldn't remember anything else. He didn't, for example, know who the dead man was. That didn't bode well.

The prosecutor had indicated that the preliminary inquiry would be ready very soon. That meant she would be able to look through the evidence the police had actually managed to gather. Finally. But it also meant that the charges would be brought against him shortly afterward. And then: the main trial. She shuddered to think how Benjamin would make it through that, feeling the way he did. But she was almost more worried about how she herself would cope. She was still a complete newbie. Even if Nikola's case had gone fantastically well.

She was snowed under with work at Leijon. It was like Magnus was giving her twice as much to do as normal. He hadn't said anything directly, but when she was in his room, reporting on something, he'd interrupted her midsentence: "Anders Henriksson is starting the restructuring of Kungsborgen tomorrow. They've already had some preliminary meetings with their chief counsel. I recommended you to head up the DD team."

It was clear what that meant: good-bye summer. He was probably in a huff because she'd turned down his New York offer. This was her punishment. The only plus was that Jossan had also been put on sunshine duty, as she called having to work over the summer. "I'm actually not that bothered," she said. "My plans were pretty boring anyway, if I'm honest. All my friends have boyfriends, some of them've got kids now, and I hadn't even dared hope you'd

be free. You're in your own little world. By the way, are you sleeping with anyone these days?"

Emelie couldn't help but smile.

"Yeah, a bit," she answered.

"A bit? How do you sleep with someone *a bit*?"

"You have sex, but you don't know if it's with the right guy."

"Aha, in that case, I've never slept with anyone *a lot*."

Emelie laughed.

Jossan: "It's not a lawyer from the office anyway, I'm sure of
that."

"How do you know?"

"Going with my gut."

"Your gut's not good enough for you to guess who, though."

For some reason, she *wanted* to talk about Teddy, but at the
same time, she would've died if Jossan worked out who she was
actually sleeping with.

"Maybe not," Josephine said, "but if I know you, it's someone
who lets you stop pretending. Someone who makes you relax, be
yourself, and forget all about being a sensible career woman. That's
what you need. But—and this is your problem, Pippa—he might
not be what you expected. He might not be someone you'd choose
on paper."

"Who do I want on paper, then?"

"Idiots."

"And who makes me be myself?"

"You might not even know that yourself. But your muscles
down there, they worked it out a long time ago. So you should
listen to them, stop fighting it."

Her phone rang. Direct from reception this time.

"Delivery for you down here."

"Can you see what it is, Viveca?" Emelie didn't think it could be
more flowers from Nikola.

"Yeah, it's from the prosecution authority. Folders and documents, a case of some kind. I guess it must be a mistake?"

"Yeah, guess so. Keep it there, I'll come down and have a look."
The preliminary report. Rölén must've sent it to the wrong place: Emelie had never given Leijon's address. Still: she felt her pulse pick up, wanted to grab the files and start reading right away. Did they know who the dead man was? Could they tell Mats had been in the house?

56

A shady gathering. He hadn't seen these guys for years. Teddy: the elephant in the room. Or maybe that should be: the elephant on deck. Anyway—to the others, he was like a fish in water, one of the gang.

A different kind of party: Dejan's thirty-fifth birthday. Flag raised. His friend had rented a boat: a fucking yacht. Not quite as big as those beasts Teddy and Emelie had seen in Palma, but big enough to look like a huge white spaceship, screaming *new money* from where it was docked on Nybrokajen.

Black Pearl, it read in huge letters at the back. After more than a week of heavy rain, the sun had finally come out. Dejan welcomed them onto the quarterdeck: grinning like a man who'd just won a boat in some kind of bet. Though he hadn't—the boat was a rental, Teddy realized that much.

"It's so fucking sweet. Hydraulic swimming platform at the back, three Jet Skis. Shit, man, today's gonna be fun."

Dejan showed them around: Teddy and a few of the others took in the luxury. Dejan blabbing away: *high gloss black American walnut* on the floors, a Gaggenau grill in the bar, and its own sauna, with an entrance from the swimming platform at the stern. "Sunseeker Manhattan 84, eight years old. Sweet, right? Top speed over thirty knots, they said. Gonna cost twenty grand for the juice alone."

Teddy guessed that the rental for his friend's huge toy was at

least four times that. But to Dejan: blowing that much dough was
part of the charm.

The inside was posh. Ice buckets and bottles of champagne
everywhere. Star-patterned cushions and a real Yankee feeling
from the leather sofas. They went up to the bridge. The guys who
recognized him said hello. Champagne glasses in hand. Hawaiian
shirts and T-shirts. Sunglasses *en masse*. Alex, Safia, Birra, Denko,
guys from before. New faces, too. Younger guys in short sleeves
and Bermuda shorts, fresh-looking tats and pumped-up guns.

Teddy wasn't rocking shorts today: the usual chinos instead.
Under them: cold steel—a combat knife, carbon fiber. Just in case.
He was still lying as low as he could, moving from crappy hotel to
crappy hotel and only making calls from secure numbers—and he
wanted to make sure he could defend himself if he needed to.

The dark green treetops in Berzelii Park were like a calm backdrop beyond the dock. The Raoul Wallenberg monument under
the trees: like great cool lumps of lava. Teddy thought about his
father. In his world, Raoul Wallenberg was the greatest Swede
ever to have lived. "One of the few times a Swede did something
other than stand to one side, moaning at the rest of the world,"
Bojan said.

Teddy was actually surprised he'd even been invited. He
wondered whether it was such a good idea, leaving town for a
whole day. He had things to do. But all the same: someone might
know what happened to Mats. Someone might know Sebbe. Or
Peder Hult.

The engine hummed. The gangway was pulled in. Dejan
shouted: "We're off. All those fuckers with sails better watch out."

The skipper pulled down on the handle: the boat picked up
speed. Teddy pushed a piece of snus beneath his lip and chewed a
stick of gum.

In the distance, he could see the turrets and towers of the Nordic Museum—like something out of a Disney film. He'd thought it
before: the city was divided into sections as clearly as the countries
in a game of Risk.

Two hours later. It was four in the afternoon. The sun was almost too warm. Dejan's dog, the Mauler, looked like it had passed out. They were floating off Vaxholm. "Heading for open water." Dejan laughed. "Time to drop the anchor and get the Jet Skis out soon, eh man? Then it's party time."

Teddy had kept mostly to the bridge. Let people come and talk to him, not the other way around.

A guy came up the narrow staircase. Moved slowly toward Teddy, like he was posing for a camera. Some people were like that: their entire lives played out like they were in an action film. The dude had a wide nose, flat forehead—his whole face looked like he'd run straight into a wall as a kid. He grinned. "Hey, man, been a fucking while."

It was Matteo—he and Teddy had done two years together in Hall. The guy'd earned himself five years for aiding and abetting in an aggravated robbery. He looked exactly the same as he had when they were inside, other than the fact that his T-shirt was straining tightly against his stomach. They embraced like men: wide hug, back thumps—always careful not to be too intimate.

"What're you up to these days?"

Teddy could see Alex and Safia out of the corner of his eye: their ears like satellites—of course they were interested in what Najdan "Teddy" "Björne" Maksumic was doing. None of them had spent anywhere near as long inside as he had.

"Not a lot."

"I heard you were, like, a lawyer or something." A gold tooth glittered in Matteo's mouth. "But that can't be true, right?"

"Nah, it's not. What're you doing?"

"Small invoices, man."

Teddy understood. The past few years: that kind of fraud had spread quicker than a new fashion fad in Stockholm. Identity theft, benefits being paid to made-up people with fake disabilities and other stuff like that. Fake invoices for a few thousand kronor, companies would pay them without thinking. The last of these: Matteo's thing.

His friend from the slammer picked up a handful of cheese puffs. "Send out a hundred invoices a day. It's enough if five people pay, y'know, then I've made twenty-five. You get the math? It's like a cookie jar. You just gotta help yourself."

Teddy looked out across the water and tried to seem interested: his old world—the constant pull of what you might be able to bring in from various crimes.

There were lots of sailing boats out today. He'd never been on one, and immediately, it felt like that fact belonged to the life Matteo still lived. Never having been sailing: what, exactly, did that say about Teddy's childhood?

"You remember the equation we used to do?" Matteo asked.

Teddy did. Back before he met Sara. When everything he did was about turning coins into bills. Easy money, gliding through life like a lubed-up dick. Teddy and Matteo: worked out what they could earn on different crimes, and what kind of time they were risking if they got caught.

Pieces of cheese puff sprayed from Matteo's mouth when he spoke. "Kronor per year inside. You remember what had the highest kron-p-y-i?"

Teddy tried to be polite. "No, not really. Whores?"

"No, Christ. They punish love harder here than they do anywhere else. Even if you're handicapped to the max, you can't pay for a happy ending."

"Charlie?"

"Nah, nah, nah—you lost it? Coke gets you ages."

"Fraud?"

"Exactly, my man, but against businesses. No normal people getting hurt. No violence. I swear, you can turn over five mil a year, easy, and there's hardly any risk of doing time. Kron-p-y-i record."

Matteo jabbered on. Talked about how he'd asked his lawyer to shut down his Facebook page the last time he was on trial. Not because he was afraid of what the cops would find. "No, I just wanted to make sure the missus wouldn't see all the messages I was getting from the girls I had on the side."

They talked on. Alex and Safia moved over, kept up. Teddy with his own agenda: asked about Sebbe a few times, about Michaela. He carefully tried to squeeze it out of them: How'd you launder money before? Anyone help out?

But it was a mistake: normal guys didn't talk about stuff like that—simple principle: keep things to yourself, live longer. Matteo was the only one who seemed to want to impress Teddy, like a two-year-old—but on the other hand, he'd also never been part of the inner circle.

Dejan interrupted them, shouted: "Meat's ready! Come down here."

Eight hours later. Dark now. A whole day at sea. Warmth on their skin. Happy lines on their faces.

They'd driven the Jet Skis like they were F1 cars. Done a bit of clay pigeon shooting from the deck, strung a rubber ring from the back of the boat, lapped up the sun, popped champagne corks across the whole fucking archipelago. At fiveish, an RIB had pulled up to the *Black Pearl*. Eight girls tottered on board: twenty-year-olds with dyed-blond hair and floral bikinis.

Matteo, Alex, Safia, and the others almost fell overboard with happiness. They turned up the stereo: cheesy old hits at full volume. Dejan was glowing like the sun. The Mauler swayed along with the music. *Wolf of Wall Street* vibes, but on twenty-degree water—the guys partied so hard even a teetotaler would've had a hangover.

Teddy felt a little light-headed—in more than one sense. Kum was cool with him—and in a twisted way, it was actually nice to have lost the McLoud money: it had been burning a hole in his pocket, shitty as it was. His dad and sister were home now. His nephew was out—he'd definitely been involved in the robbery on that shop, but unless the prosecutor could prove it, all they could do was let him go. Still: Swedish Premium Security, the predator, dishonest cops—people were still out after him.

A few hours later, the boat swayed as it thudded gently against the dock. The guys were making noise in the background.

Teddy and Matteo headed off toward the taxis. The rest of the gang were going out in town with Dejan. They'd booked a table. Arranged some escorts.

He and Matteo would be sharing a taxi; his pal lived in Hallunda, not far from Alby. After five minutes, Matteo was asleep on Teddy's shoulder. What a player—drooling like a dog.

Teddy leaned his head back. Maybe he should just dump Matteo outside his door and head back into town, stop by Emelie's place. She should be home by now—Emelie, the dependable, conscientious working woman. But no—he was too drunk for that.

He paid the driver and staggered out of the car. Matteo was crawling along the pavement.

"The ground's soft," he slurred.

"Come on," said Teddy.

"Nah, I'm going, it's not far."

The taxi disappeared. The high-rises around them looked like exact copies of one another, or maybe he was just seeing double, triple even. It was dark. Not a person in sight. Matteo was trying to get up, but Teddy still doubted he'd be able to make it home on his own.

Both of them were swaying—like masts in a storm.

A dark Volvo V70 pulled up. All antennae and dark windows.

Two men got out.

Teddy had a bad feeling.

One of them came over to him. Light hair, black bomber jacket.

He punched Teddy in the stomach as hard as he could.

Teddy bent over double. Lost his breath. Still: old habit, he raised his arms to protect his head.

Lucky. The man swung something at him. A searing pain shot up his arm.

He backed up. Tried to find his balance. Jabbed: it was like punching a tree—the guy must've been wearing a protective vest under his jacket or something.

He heard them shouting: "Police, get on the ground."

He groped for his knife.

A noise. He didn't see what happened, but Matteo ended up on the ground. His friend roared.

Teddy grabbed the handle of his knife.

Blows hitting his chest.

Hitting his face.

He felt something break.

Then, from behind: the other man appeared. Held him tight. He tried to protect himself.

Shouted in pain. He fell to the ground. Felt his blood mix with the dirt.

The man held up something plastic: a Taser.

One last effort: Teddy hauled himself up, still in the arms of one of the attackers, swung his head back. The man yelled.

As he did so, the pale-haired man jabbed with the Taser: Teddy saw his face. From his ear to his mouth: a red mark.

The jolt went through his legs, his stomach, his chest—like someone had run steel cables down his spine and was pulling them back and forth.

Everything went black. His eyes.

Dark outside.

PART IV

JULY

57

LARGE WEAPONS SEIZURE IN SÖDERTÄLJE

Four were arrested and detained in Södertälje yesterday, on suspicion of possession of firearms.

Within the framework of Operation Secure in Södertälje, the Police Authority has, under the leadership of the International Public Prosecution Office, carried out an investigation into the smuggling of weapons from other Nordic countries. This preliminary investigation was carried out in the Stockholm area, with support from the reconnaissance unit from the so-called Special Gangs Operation.

During a raid on a basement on Oxbacksgatan in Södertälje this week, a large cache of weapons was found. Technical investigations are still under way, but the results so far indicate five automatic weapons of the Kalashnikov variety, and similar foreign assault rifles. Eleven pistols, and a huge amount of ammunition were also found. In the basement and the apartment to which the basement belongs, four men between the ages of twenty-six and thirty-seven were apprehended. All are being held in police custody.

The Police Authority believe that the weapons found were intended for use in the criminal gang environment.

58

Nikola: happy as a guy who'd just dodged a life sentence and scored his own pad to boot. Maybe not so weird: he'd been released. And Teddy had fixed a place for him. It was *sweet* for real. Genuine payback: stroke of good luck to balance out all the bad he'd had these past few years. Nikola vs. the State: 2–1. Maybe there was a god after all.

But still: things to do. Unfinished business. Metim's insane raid. His mistake. Isak's orders—you chickened out, now you fix it.

He did nothing the first few days. Just chilled to the max. Rolled joints but didn't even smoke them. Stayed home and played with his new iPhone—another gift from his uncle. He had hardly any furniture in his new place, but Teddy had set up a bed, a table, and two chairs. Chamon lent him a TV. That was enough for Nikola. Linda brought him sheets, cutlery, and two bowls. Nikola still just ordered pizza and kebabs with all the extras—ate them straight from the box.

His mom was really happy. Giggling like a fourteen-year-old. "Your lawyer was fantastic."

But Nikola was cool. "Why'd you run off when I was locked up?"

"It was Teddy, he wanted us to, he didn't tell you?"

Nikola was hard as stone—not. He softened after five minutes. "Yeah, I know. It's so good to be out, Mom. I'm gonna pull myself together now, I swear. You know where Teddy is, by the way?"

She didn't know; she'd been wondering the same thing. They'd both been trying to call him all day, but hadn't heard a thing.

Tonight: Nikola was going to Chamon's. He really wanted to show him his new place—but he guessed his friend wanted to celebrate him being out. Release party number two, in the space of nine weeks: might be a fucking world record.

Murray had kept his end of the deal. The assault rifle in Nikola's basement had vanished by the time he got out, but there hadn't been any raid. He spotted it in one of the pictures the cops released, though. Three assault rifles in a row: Rk 62, 95 TP, with a collapsible butt. All with the safety on the left-hand side—but only one of them had black masking tape on the grip. Murray: that sly fox. He'd added the huge gun to their haul. Couldn't be better. In Nikola's head: a wicked smart plan.

Plus, a different feeling. He didn't start sweating when he thought about what he had to do. No stomach cramps. No headaches. Actually: he was sleeping well. Something must've happened during his time in solitary, during his talks with Kerim in the cage on the roof. What would happen would happen: anything was better than being locked up in isolation.

He rang Chamon's bell. Silence.

He rang again. Heard whispering.

The door flew open. Chamon, Yusuf, Bello, and a few of the other guys in the hallway. "You're a winner, man!" they roared.

They carried him in on their raised arms. Chamon's little apartment: total party vibe. Chips, popcorn, sunflower seeds. Bottles of Red Bull and Coca-Cola in ice buckets all over the place. Vodka and cans of beer in a line on the coffee table. Colorful fucking balloons on the ceiling. Plus: a nice line. Big fat pile of coke on a metal tray, and a silver tube to snort it through. Chamon must've blown most of what he grabbed from the raid on this. Like a kid's birthday party crossed with some kind of *Scarface* homage.

There were only six of them, but they partied like half of Stureplan. The balloons were gone after ten minutes. His pals looked

like they'd dipped their faces in vanilla sugar. Half-full glasses
of vodka and Red Bull on every surface. Music from Chamon's
iPhone booming from the speakers: Rihanna, Kanye West. Zara
Larsson.

They crammed onto the leather sofa and played *GTA* for hours.
Xbox One—newly lifted and shiny. The neighbor rang the bell,
asked them to keep it down. Chamon yanked down his pants and
showed his poor Iraqi neighbor his ass. They rolled up five-hundred-
kronor bills: snorted more. Took selfies. Tried on Chamon's caps.
He had more than fifty of them—all swiped from the same Stadium shop in town. They climbed onto the sofas and swayed with
the music. The neighbor banged on the door again: this time
with his sons-in-law behind him. It turned into a fight in the stairwell. Everyone falling all over the place. Chamon laughed that Hill-
ary Clinton would be turning up with a peace settlement, and then
everyone would have to suck his dick.

Nikola downed five bottles of beer in under an hour. Chamon
kept going on about calling Darina to come over, the whore he'd
met last time they'd partied. Nikola was holding the Xbox controller upside down, made no difference to his game. He pissed
from the balcony. Did a bit of pretend MMA with Yusuf in the
middle of all the spat-out seed cases on the floor: they managed
to knock Chamon's only picture from the wall—a load of weird
symbols on a bit of parchment. "The fuck you doing, those are
real hieroglyphs!" Chamon yelled, trying to grab Nikola and Yusuf
at the same time. They were laughing so hard, they almost pissed
themselves.

The hours passed. The sound system broke when Chamon
spilled vodka on it. Some of the guys started heading home. Nikola
hugged them all—"You're the best, guys. Real. If you were Slavs
like me, I'd have jumped you in the shower."

Another hour passed. Chamon, Yusuf, and Nikola started to
come down. Nikola was drinking water. The others had all gone.
Suddenly the doorbell rang. Nikola found a baseball bat. They

looked at one another—that fucking neighbor again? Or was it the pigs this time?

Chamon peered through the peephole. He opened the door.

Outside, alone: Isak.

He talked slowly: "Can I come in?"

Chamon was staring. Nikola wondered what he was doing there, what he wanted.

Yusuf didn't seem surprised—maybe he'd called Mr. One over.

Chamon swept the Xbox controllers and the bottles from the sofa. Brushed seed casings and unpopped popcorn to one side. Isak sat down. Rubbed the back of his hand against his stubble. The flat looked like a town that'd been plundered by ISIS.

"Been having a party, I see."

Chamon and Nikola were still on their feet. "Yeah, we were celebrating Nikola," Chamon said.

"Good, boys, good." Isak turned to Yusuf. "You open the window? Smells like a whorehouse in here."

Chamon held out a bottle of beer. "Want one?"

Isak, stone-faced: "I drove the A8 here."

It was dark outside now. The TV was off. The area silent.

Isak said: "I just wanted to come and congratulate you, Nikola. Must've been a hell of a lawyer you had. How'd you find her?"

"Emelie Jansson," Nikola said. "You met her. She's the one who worked with my uncle."

"Ah shit, her. She was fiery, that one. And sharp, seems like."

Isak scratched his crotch.

"Yusuf told me about the raid on Abrohom Michel's place. That you made sure it happened by . . . talking to the . . . authorities."

Nikola felt his face burn. He'd talked to Murray, told Chamon about it. Worked with a cop—against all rules. Deadly sin in their eyes.

Isak continued: "Don't worry. You did the right thing. There are always exceptions, to everything. They attacked me, crashed my trial, shat all over my honor. Now we know who they are, and they've got no weapons left. They're under pressure. The cops did the job for us. But you still haven't taken care of the guilty one, Nikola."

Isak got up. The floor crunched beneath his feet as he left.

Half an hour later. One in the morning.

Nikola and Chamon sitting in Chamon's ride. Shit, the after-effects of the coke were still playing Lil Wayne in his head.

"Seriously, Chamon, I dunno what to do. They're fucking organized."

Chamon's head bobbed up and down. "Not as organized as they want you to think. Plus, four of his guys are inside. We'll fix this, bro . . . somehow."

Nikola tried to get in touch with Teddy again, for maybe the two hundredth time that day: his phone was still off. What the hell?

Chamon pulled up in front of the house. Word was, Metim Tasdemir lived here.

Chamon tried to fish something from his pocket. "Y'want any?" He held up a bag of powder.

"Nah, no more for me."

Chamon bent down, took a snort straight from the bag. "Nicko, man, *now*'s the time."

They got out of the car. Nikola slowed down. He'd thought he was past this—but he could feel it clearly: the lump of fear in his stomach again. Enough, he had to switch off now.

Chamon was a few feet ahead of him. They smashed the window next to the kitchen door. There were plastic toys and an inflatable pool in the garden. Chamon stuck his arm through the hole and opened the window. His thumb was bleeding.

They helped each other in. Each with a baseball bat in hand. Nikola wanted to be steady, but still: he was shaking like a fucking electric toothbrush.

Then they heard a kid crying. Chamon went first, his baseball bat raised above him like a samurai sword.

Darkness. They flipped the lights on. Striped wallpaper. A fake open fire. LED lights under the furniture—they gave everything a bluish tinge. Huge candles on the floor.

More crying. They went into a room: pink everywhere. Teddy bears and *Frozen* characters. By one wall: Metim fucking Tasdemir changing his daughter's diaper. He mustn't have heard them smash the window. The guy's eyebrows when he saw them: almost up to his hairline.

A nanosecond: pictures flashing through his mind. The cell. The cage on the roof. Where Nikola would end up again if all this went to shit. He was about to break down. He just wanted to drop the bat and run.

Still: he held the wooden bat to Metim's forehead: "You son of a bitch."

Drops of sweat on the guy's forehead. "Take it easy now, boys." Faint voice. Weak vibes. "My kid's here, for fuck's sake. Gentle, gentle. We can fix this."

The baby was crying. Metim held her tightly.

Nikola didn't know what to do. He felt paralyzed. A baby. He couldn't hurt a baby.

Chamon: "We'll take it easy when you stop trying to fuck us over. Sit."

Metim sank down onto a footstool in one corner of the room. There was a kid's stroller next to him.

Metim Tasdemir—probably the only man who could compete with Isak in this city—was starting to whine. "Don't hurt her, please."

"We're not going to," said Nikola.

Metim put his daughter down on a play mat covered in pictures of flying elephants. The girl seemed calmer now.

Nikola hit Metim straight in the face. Felt his fist meet his nose: Metim stifled a shout.

Chamon put his bat against the guy's temple.

"We saw the cops' pictures. We're not idiots—those were yours. And they're the same Finnish guns you used when you fucked over Isak's trial."

"The hell you talking about?" Metim used his T-shirt to wipe the blood streaming from his nose. What a pathetic little dick he was.

"Oxbacksgatan, that's where Abrohom lives; he's your guy. He's in fucking prison. So cut the crap."

Metim groaned. "You assholes, I thought there was one too many in that picture, the one with the tape. You snitched somehow, you rats."

Nikola gave him another punch. The blood spattered onto the baby's pajamas. Metim bared his teeth, but he kept quiet.

The girl started to cry again.

Chamon held up his phone. "I just recorded what you said. Isak wants five hundred big to cover the wound. How d'you want to do this?"

Nikola put a hand on the baby girl, gently stroked her back. Her pajamas were pink, and he felt her tiny backbone through the soft material. She was the smallest person he'd ever touched.

She calmed down.

Maybe he should call Simon Murray instead? Hand Metim over to the police. Let this end properly, not start another clan conflict that'd escalate and go on for years. Lead to more people getting hurt. More people dead, probably. And pretty much guarantee more stomachaches and nightmares.

But Metim just nodded. He looked relieved somehow.

Afterward: Chamon and Nikola, in O'Learys. Laughing, taking it easy. What a fucking night. They couldn't even manage any alcohol. Instead, they both ordered a Coke Zero with extra ice and three straws. The place was closing anytime now. The whole thing almost seemed too easy. Metim had handed over a plastic bag full of cash in under ten minutes. The baby had gone to sleep like Sleeping Beauty after Nikola's soothing pats.

"Seriously, though, we shoulda squeezed him for more. He must've had at least a mil stashed back there," Chamon mused.

The bag of banknotes hung beneath the bar. Nikola touched it. *Biodegradable*, he read. He wondered how long it would take for the money to turn to mush if he buried the whole lot in the woods.

They called Isak. He laughed for at least five minutes when Nikola told him what had happened. "He was changing a diaper, you said?"

"Yeah."

"Number one or number two?"

Nikola: "I think it was a shit."

It sounded like Isak was about to choke, he was laughing so hard. He cackled for so long, Chamon's battery almost ran out.

He calmed down by the end of the call. "You're a real man, Nikola, not like Metim—busy doing woman's work, changing diapers and crap like that. You and Chamon can keep a hundred and fifty each. Have fun tonight. Make sure you get a lay. You deserve it, my friend."

Nikola took his boss's words seriously. He jumped down from the stool.

It was time.

Paulina opened the door. He'd never thought she would let him come over at half past two in the morning—but she'd replied to his message right away.

Paulina: sweatpants and a baggy knitted top. Comfy clothes. No makeup. Hair in a bun. He could smell her perfume all the way down the hallway and into her room. She was glowing.

Her parents were asleep upstairs.

She led him into a small room. A narrow bed, an armchair. A bookcase filled with books and a TV. It was on. Some American show.

"What're you watching?" he asked.

"*Homeland*," she said. "I'm totally hooked, watch it all night."

"Ah shit, it's that good?"

Paulina sat down on her bed. She turned off the TV.

Nikola felt completely sober and clearheaded now. But he could still see a fuzzy image in his mind: Metim's baby girl.

Paulina said: "I was so happy when you got out, you know."

She took his hand. Still: the girl's tiny body on his mind. He wanted to say something to Paulina about her. Tell her that though he might've done a bad thing, it was over now. That everything would be okay.

He sat down next to her on the edge of the bed.

She put her hand on his thigh.

A rush pulsed through him.

He was free. He'd gotten Isak's money and done what he needed to. The baby girl hadn't been hurt. And now, he was in a quiet room, alone, with the girl he was totally into.

It might be the best moment of his life.

He leaned forward and kissed Paulina on the lips.

EXPRESSEN, 21 JULY
21-YEAR-OLD CHARGED WITH MURDER OF UNIDENTIFIED VICTIM

The 21-year-old accused of the murder of an unidentified man on Värmdö appeared in court today.

On an evening in mid-May, a guard was called to a villa close to Ängsvik, on Värmdö. Upon arrival, he made a macabre discovery. Inside the house, he found a brutally murdered man. The 21-year-old man was subsequently found in a car in the vicinity of the house. He was taken into custody the next morning.

Today, charges were read against the 21-year-old, said to have taken the man's life by shooting him in the face. The victim's identity is, however, as yet unknown. The preliminary investigation, also made public today, claims that tests on the dead man's DNA have been performed, and attempts have been made to match him to dental records. Despite this, it has not been possible to confirm his identity.

Public prosecutor Annika Rölén will invoke a number of witnesses in the trial, including testimony from guards, coroners and, not least, the crime scene technicians.

According to Rölén: "No one else can have done it. The 21-year-old was the only person nearby, and has refused to give any explanations as to what he was doing there."

No comment has been made by the 21-year-old male's lawyer, Emelie Jansson.

59

Flash meeting with Magnus Hassel and Anders Henriksson—
Emelie could guess what it would be about. They weren't meeting
in either of the partners' offices but in one of the conference rooms
on the top floor—the more formal spaces usually reserved for clients, the ones with the fantastic views. Again: that in itself was a
clear sign of what they wanted.

Jossan had already seen the article on expressen.se. It had been
published some time the day before. The first thing she'd said when
she came through the door was: "I thought you were smart."

Emelie had spun around in her desk chair. "Me too. Looks like
I was wrong. Any advice on what I should say? You're a lawyer,
aren't you?"

"No idea. Is this something to do with Teddy?"

"Indirectly. Think I'm on the way out now?"

"Probably," Jossan replied, without sounding especially sad
about it. "Why, Emelie? Why?"

Emelie took a deep breath. "I'll tell you later. If I have any good
answers by then."

She thought about how she'd never *really* known why she'd chosen law and about how she'd gradually homed in on business law.
She'd nailed the tests, chosen the right specialist courses, applied
for jobs at the best firms in Stockholm—she'd been selected by all
of them. Leijon had been her first choice.

Josephine almost snorted. "They're going to kick you out head-first, no matter what you tell them. But you're brave, I'll admit that. Send me a message when you're making your final statements in court. I want to come and listen. And if you win, I'll take you to dinner at Matbordet. You heard of it? It's got two stars—Mathias Dahlgren's new place; you sit at the table where he actually makes the food."

Emelie was alone in the meeting room. There was a tray on the table, four coffee cups, a silver-colored thermos, and a small bowl of pralines. She didn't sit down. Instead, she walked over to the panoramic windows and tried to massage her shoulder. The number one complaint of lawyers: back problems from all the stress and too much sitting down.

Her mom and dad had finally gone home, and not a day too early. She assumed they were disappointed she hadn't spent much time with them, but they shouldn't complain. She wasn't the one who'd suggested they come up, plus they'd been able to stay with her for free. One positive was that she had the feeling her dad had been sober the whole time—like he'd been waiting for an opportunity to show her he could.

She did wonder where Teddy had disappeared to, though. She'd thought their relationship had seemed more relaxed after the Palma trip, though they'd barely had time to meet because she'd been so busy. But now his phone seemed to be off. She wondered whether he was still mad at her, and if so, why.

They needed to talk: Benjamin's preliminary investigation had arrived. She hadn't had time to go through it in detail yet, but one thing was clear: the dead man wasn't Mats. Despite his unstable condition, Benjamin had been clear about that: the dead man in the medical examiner's photos wasn't his father.

He couldn't say whether it was Sebastian Petrovic, though. None of the photos showed a tiger tattoo, and the face wasn't really a face. Still, Emelie sent a scan of them to Michaela so she could check. She hadn't heard back yet.

The door opened. Magnus Hassel and Anders Henriksson came

in, followed by Alice Strömberg, head of HR. It was like they were moving in a row, a little procession en route to a holy ceremony: for the first time in the history of the firm, a lawyer was about to be given the boot. Maybe.

She waited until they sat down. They were all smiling, making small talk about the changing weather: first sun and dry spells, then a downpour, then the heat again. "The weather's become much more extreme over the past few years. It must be the greenhouse effect," Anders Henriksson said in his squeaky voice. He reminded her of Mickey Mouse today.

Magnus Hassel scratched his head. "Yeah, I was thinking about when we helped Forsfall sell those coal-powered plants and avoid the fines from the Energy Agency. They wanted to force them to make the business greener."

Alice Strömberg poured each of them a cup of coffee. Magnus Hassel took a praline.

"So," he said. "It's not so long since we talked, during your development meeting in June. And back then, we said everything was going okay for you, but that you'd been off sick for a few days. Then I offered you six weeks in New York, paid for by the office. But this morning, we read in the paper that you're representing a man on trial for murder. We'd like an explanation. Is it even true?"

Emelie took a deep breath. "Yes, it's true, unfortunately."

Magnus's eyebrow twitched. An involuntary tic. "Why didn't you let us know?"

"I called you and tried to get your approval, do you remember?"

"No."

"Early one morning in May. You sounded like you'd just woken up. I think I probably woke you."

"I don't remember that. I have no idea what you're talking about."

Emelie said: "It probably makes no difference. You said no anyway."

"Exactly." Anders Henriksson entered the discussion. Maybe his voice sounded more like a eunuch's than Mickey's, practically falsetto. "Unfortunately, we can't accept this type of case, and we really can't accept someone going behind our backs. So, we have a suggestion. Alice, would you?" He gestured to the HR manager.

"Emelie, what you did is very serious." Alice's expression was like she was looking at a cute little kitten when she tilted her head theatrically. "It risks damaging the firm's reputation. Our clients might start to wonder why one of our staff is defending a murderer. . . ."

"He hasn't been convicted yet."

"Yes, but our clients will still find it strange. We don't work in that field of law, as you well know. Additionally, we have a rule that all cases go through our partners; taking on anything on your own initiative is unacceptable. You know this, too."

"I know everything you're saying," Emelie said. "And I want to apologize for not informing the firm that I'd taken this case. But as I see it, I've been doing it in my free time. I've managed to do everything I've been asked here—other than being forced to take two days off sick after an upsetting event. I've made sure not to link Leijon to this at all, I haven't provided the firm's address in any correspondence or anything like that, and the firm isn't named in any articles. I'm a lawyer, and according to Bar rules, all responsibility is on my shoulders. Not on Leijon."

Alice was looking at her. Magnus, too. Anders Henriksson was glaring.

Alice clasped her hands. "We're prepared to overlook what you've done to a certain extent, because we can see that you've done good work in the past. So, our proposal is as follows: you resign from the case you've taken on as private defense counsel. Your client will have to find another lawyer. You'll also be let go, with six months' full pay. We will arrange for a new job for you, however, as a business lawyer with one of our client firms."

Emelie had to force herself to stay clam. "I definitely can't give up the case. The charges were brought a few days ago, so the main trial is going to start soon. It would be incredibly unethical of me to leave my client at this stage in the proceedings."

Alice's face didn't change. "The other option is that you will be dismissed. No paid period, no new job for you. You'd have to pack up your things and leave right after this meeting."

Emelie was on the verge of tears now, for real. "I can't just give up the case, not at this late stage. It would be wrong. Disloyal to my client. I know I should have told the firm, but I felt like I had no choice but to take on this case. You know I was practically made for this place. There has to be some way out of this. If there were questions from the press, we could release a statement saying I'd done it on my own."

Alice pursed her lips. "Please, Emelie . . ."

Anders Henriksson's face had taken on a reddish tone. Magnus, on the other hand, slowly leaned forward in his chair. It creaked.

"Emelie, I'm going to be totally honest with you. You're one of my favorites." He paused slightly, let his words sink in. "And I'm no less impressed to hear that in parallel with all of the work you've been doing here, you're handling a murder case, on top of being off sick for two days. I'm willing to give you a second chance."

Anders Henriksson's face was no longer reddish. It was scarlet—like a stop sign. "Hang on, Magnus, what's this?"

Magnus didn't turn around. He simply continued: "Emelie might be the best lawyer I've ever met."

Even if Anders Henriksson was highly regarded at Leijon, and had been a partner for several years now, Magnus Hassel was his senior. Magnus was one of the country's real heavyweights. He brought in at least five times as many cases as Anders, and turned over ten times as much in revenue; he was Leijon's poster boy, the man who played golf with the Wallenbergs, went hunting with the management of the SCA group, and went swimming in Torekov with the rest of the elite of the Swedish business world. If Magnus Hassel wanted to keep someone on staff, that's what would happen.

He continued: "All I ask of you, Emelie, is that you withdraw from the case. You can't continue with that. I'm sorry. I believe in you, and you know that."

Emelie stared at him. She could stay with the firm; she had one final chance. But there was a price to pay. What the hell had she been thinking? That the suspicions against Benjamin would die down on their own, just because she'd taken on the role of his lawyer? That the press would ignore a murder charge just because she was working as *private* defense counsel? That Leijon would accept one of their lawyers spending more than 30 percent of their waking hours on a criminal case? She'd been naive, she'd been so shortsighted.

Emelie set off toward Rörstrandsgatan. She had more work to do once she got home. Preparations. The place stunk of rotten trash.

Jossan had hugged her after the meeting. "Let me know if you want to go for a drink in town later."

When she got back, she sat down on the bed. Hugged her legs tight. She needed to get to work, but her mind was blank.

She called Teddy. Sent him a message. Even phoned Nikola.

When she hung up after leaving a message on Nikola's phone, she realized someone had been trying to call her. She had a voice mail.

"Hey, this is Matteo, I'm an old friend of Teddy's—I think you know him. Dejan said I should get in touch with you. Can you call me as soon as you can? It's important."

It was three o'clock in the afternoon. A particularly dreary afternoon in late July.

OFFICIAL NOTES

Stockholm County Police Authority

Signed: Joakim Sundén

Date: 12 January 2011

Regarding the handling of informant "Marina"

The undersigned has, over the past few weeks, worked with and handled an informant by the code name of Marina. A large amount of information has been given, much of which is deemed to be highly reliable (in accordance with current judgment methods). The undersigned has attempted to check and further investigate the details. The undersigned has also reported to detective superintendent Anders Mieler on a regular basis.

Marina has been guaranteed anonymity by the undersigned in order to ensure that the informant can provide information as freely as possible and, in doing so, contribute to fighting organized criminality both at a county and international level. The undersigned wishes to reinforce that no documented interviews with Marina have taken place, nor have any recordings or notes been made.

It has recently come to the attention of the undersigned that Ivar Löv-berg, deputy chief public prosecutor, has requested the real name and contact details of Marina. Lövberg has informed the undersigned that he requires for-mal interviews with Marina to commence immediately, in order to guarantee that the information is documented and that the examination of the witness can occur in a court of law.

The undersigned is opposed to releasing such details. The undersigned is of the opinion that Marina must remain anonymous going forward; this is the agreement the undersigned has with the informant.

In service,
Joakim Sundén

60

A cell.

It couldn't be. A fucking cell.

No. No. No.

Yes.

He was back, locked up. More than a day and a half now. The cold floor. The bare bulb hanging from the ceiling. Cold everywhere. In custody.

No.

When he first woke, he'd tried to get up. Cried out loudly in pain, searing through his foot. Something must be broken or fractured. The pain in his ribs—one or more of them must be busted. There wasn't a mirror, but when he touched his nose, he practically passed out.

He eventually managed to get to his feet. He looked for the call button but couldn't find one. This seemed to be one of the older places, somewhere you just had to pound on the door.

He hit it as hard as he could. Shouted. He was *never* supposed to end up somewhere like this again, he'd promised himself. Behind a locked metal door. Thick, worn-looking bars covering the window. Heading toward a prison sentence.

He tried to see out, look over the wall. The grass down below looked wild. He had to be in Österåker or maybe Salberga. He wondered why they'd taken him so far from Stockholm.

No one opened the door. He couldn't even hear the jingle of keys out in the hallway.

He pounded against it again. Louder. Harder.

Nothing happened.

He lay on his back on the floor and tried to kick the door as hard as he could with his good foot. It echoed through the cell.

Eventually the hatch opened a fraction. A tiny chink. He saw an eye and half a nose on the other side. "What d'you want?" A gruff voice.

Teddy started to get to his feet. "I want to know what the hell's going on. Why've I been arrested?"

"Sorry, not my place to get into that. You'll find out soon enough."

"I need to see a doctor. I'm smashed up. Foot's a mess. Broken ribs."

"Yeah, maybe."

"Can you at least turn off the light in here?"

"Yup."

The hatch closed again with a clang. The light on the ceiling went out—the circuit breaker must be outside, too. Teddy crawled over the floor to the mattress. Tried to gather his thoughts: what exactly had happened? He couldn't remember much other than having fun on Dejan's boat all day. Half-drunk with a wasted Matteo in the taxi. Then: the men who'd attacked them and shouted that they were cops. Fragments: they'd floored him, torn off in the car, him inside and Matteo still on the street. The rest was blank. He remembered one thing clear enough, though: one of the bastards'd had a red scar on his cheek. From his ear to his mouth.

He tried to relax. It didn't exactly work.

The cell walls seemed to be closing in, pressing down on him. The air was hard to breathe. He couldn't start hyperventilating, no panic attacks. He'd been in this situation before. He'd managed eight years without falling to pieces.

His first few hours in the cell back then, when they arrested him for kidnapping Mats Emanuelsson: the special ops cops had shot him in the stomach, he'd just been operated on. He'd lain on the mattress, just like he was now, half-high on Citodon and Ipren, and thought about the very same thing: his mother. The cozy kids' area in the library, all sofas and cushions, curled up in her lap. *The Brothers Lionheart* in her hands. *"But there are things you have to do, otherwise you're not a human being, just a piece of dirt."* His mother's voice. "My golden boy," she'd said. "Do you know what that means?" He'd shaken his head. Six or seven years old. "What things do you have to do, Mama?" She kissed him on the cheek, though he didn't like it when she did it in front of others. "You have to be kind, Teddy. Sometimes you have to be kind, even if it's hard."

He tried to get up. He hadn't always been kind over the years. This was the result, the cosmic balance: that he'd be locked up because of his countless sins.

He looked out of the window again. The grass wasn't just tall and dry out there. The walls looked tired, too. He couldn't see much other than a few treetops beyond them. But he spotted an old Ping-Pong table and two overturned goalposts. This couldn't be Salberga—the remand cells there were connected to the bigger prison complex, and it had been renovated quite recently. It couldn't be Österåker, either; he would recognize the surroundings there, even if the remand wing was in another building. Maybe they were holding him somewhere else—even farther from Stockholm.

Something wasn't right, he was sure of that—he just couldn't put his finger on exactly *what*.

61

Nikola felt fresh. Despite the hard-core partying last night and the serious nerves he'd had before what they did to Metim. Above all: despite being with Paulina until long into the morning. He hadn't looked at the clock. Turned off his phone. Just enjoyed life. Enjoyed Paulina.

But now he'd turned on his phone. Seven missed calls from a number he didn't recognize. Four missed calls from his mom.

It was afternoon, and he was heading home. Normally Linda was used to his phone being off—but he'd promised to sharpen up. He didn't have the energy to call her back. Right now, he just wanted to enjoy the sweet vibes a bit longer. No distractions. Hang on to the happiness bubbling away inside him for a few more hours.

They'd slept until lunch, he and Paulina. When they finally got up, her parents weren't home. Nikola wasn't sure they even knew he'd been there.

"Doesn't matter," Paulina said. "They're Poles, not Saudis."

Breakfast: orange juice and toast with ham. Paulina ate a grapefruit. Local newspaper on the table. He could see an article about police successes in the war against the so-called criminal gangs on the front cover. The same picture of the guns from the press release.

After breakfast, they went back to Paulina's room. Watched TV. Talked about school, Nikola's trial. They kissed. Hugged. Slept together.

They took a walk around the neighborhood. Nikola with an arm around her. They sat down on a park bench by Brunnsängs-skolan and made out like teenagers. After a while, they went back to Paulina's place, watched half an episode of *Homeland*. Nikola liked the guy with the glasses and the beard. Same coolness he felt right now. They made smoothies. Talked about friends they had in common. Slept together again.

Nikola slowly climbed the stairs. One more floor. To his own flat. He had no plans for the rest of the day, just wanted to take a shower and change his clothes. Maybe he'd call Chamon. Or Teddy—if he answered this time. Or maybe just hang out with Paulina, if she wanted to.

Then: Spider-Man senses tingling. Like someone was watching him. He took a few more steps. In the hallway outside his place, a woman was leaning against the wall. He couldn't see who it was before she turned around. Emelie *fucking* Jansson—his super lawyer.

"Why don't you answer your phone when your lawyer calls you?" she asked with a smile, and he hugged her.

"Was a bit busy last night."

Emelie was still smiling. "Aha, like that. But it's actually four thirty in the afternoon, you know, and I've tried calling you about a hundred times. Something's happened."

Her smile vanished. They went inside—he didn't bother explaining that Teddy had gotten the apartment for him. He just wanted to hear why Emelie had made the effort to come over like this.

She explained. Someone named Matteo had called her an hour or two earlier.

"He and Teddy were at a thirty-fifth birthday party yesterday. They shared a taxi back to Alby last night. Both of them were really drunk, apparently. But when they got out of the car, they were attacked by two . . . cops, he said. They took Teddy."

Nikola almost yelled, "No way."

"They turned up in a car. Matteo thought it was an unmarked

police car, and they shouted that they were police, but their behavior seemed a bit . . . off, he thought. They more or less knocked Teddy out. Threw Matteo against the hood of the car and put him in cuffs, even though he could hardly stand up. Then they left him on the ground, still cuffed, and drove off—with Teddy. Normal policemen hardly behave like that."

"Did Matteo call the police?"

"No, I don't really think he's the kind of guy who'd call the police as a first resort, if you know what I mean."

Nikola studied the floor.

"Plus, I told him not to," she continued. "Teddy and I have been working on something for a couple of months now, and it's starting to look like it's linked to dirty policemen. Someone changed a preliminary report, and now we've got what Matteo is telling us. We can't contact them. We need to fix this ourselves."

"Fix it how?"

"We need to find your uncle. And you're going to help me."

They started by going to Teddy's place. Taxi—felt weird, but Emelie didn't seem to have a car of her own, even though she was the sickest lawyer in town.

The door was unlocked. Teddy's place looked like Chamon's flat after the party. Worse, actually. The bedding had been torn up, cutlery, underwear, and books everywhere. Nikola recognized a few titles Teddy was always talking about: *Slaughterhouse-Five*, *Mystic River*. His potted plants were smashed on the little rug by the sofa. The garbage can had been tipped out onto the floor. Pretty clear: someone had gotten there before them. Someone who wanted to find something.

Emelie started talking quickly—she seemed stressed. Nikola had a bad feeling in his stomach.

Emelie called someone she called Jan. "Can you come over to Alby and take a look at a crime scene? Break-in. Thanks."

Nikola just stared. Teddy had made the place nice, but it was all wrecked now. Chairs—overturned. Duvet—scrunched up on the floor. Wardrobe doors—wide open.

Then he remembered something. He went into the little bathroom. It wasn't as messy in there, probably because there wasn't as much to mess up. The cabinet was open. Teddy was a man of simple tastes: some deodorant, a razor, a can of shaving foam, toothpaste, a toothbrush, and a pot of plastic toothpicks. It didn't even seem like his uncle had any aftershave.

Nikola went over to the toilet. He lifted the lid from the cistern, peered in. It was dark, but he spotted what he was looking for—whoever had been here hadn't found it, at the very least. He reached into the water. Remembered what Isak had said: Björne—"who never backed down, always had a piece hidden in the toilet, just in case."

The water was cold. He pulled the bag out and opened it. A Zastava. Teddy's old gun: Nikola had heard him talk about it before. It was loaded.

Emelie was talking nonstop on the phone. To the guy named Jan. To others, Nikola had no idea who. It was a beautiful afternoon, the sky still that shade of blue it was during the summer. They got into a taxi. After a while, she put down the phone.

"I was just talking to Teddy's friend. Loke Odensson. You know who he is?"

"No, but I've heard Teddy talk about him."

"He's a computer nerd. He's going to help us."

"How?"

"Matteo didn't see the license plate on the undercover car. But I was thinking: he said that the car smashed into a lamppost when it drove off. Matteo's sure—there has to be a dent on the front wing. Loke was just looking up all the body shops that repair that kind of damage on Volvos in Stockholm. There were quite a few if you include the unauthorized ones. But that's where we'll have to start looking. There's a chance the car's been dropped off at a garage somewhere. Loke's going to send a list of the addresses."

"Should we split up?"

"Probably best, yeah. Do you have a car?"

"No, but I can borrow one."

Fifteen minutes later, Nikola jumped out of the taxi outside Chamon's place. Emelie gave him a stern look.

"Call me the minute you get into the car?"

"Yeah, no worries."

The furrow on her brow suddenly looked even deeper. "When's all this crap going to end?"

Nikola shrugged.

62

She read the preliminary report from ten in the evening until five in the morning. The main hearing would begin in three days, and she could hardly spend her nights searching for dented Volvos. The prosecution's evidence was strong. The question was whether it was strong enough. So far, Emelie had searched in vain for anything that came to Benjamin's defense. She was still clinging to hope: they had to prove he was guilty beyond all reasonable doubt. If she could create even the smallest of doubts, he would have to be released.

His DNA and fingerprints had been found in the house—that was expected. He'd been found in a car nearby and hadn't even been able to say anything of substance in his most recent interview—she noted that he hadn't even told the interview leader, Kullman, who he'd been with; he'd just mentioned an "acquaintance." That wasn't enough for him to be sent down.

But they had found worse things: gunpowder residue on Benjamin's hands. The National Forensic Centre's weapons experts had analyzed it. The residue was a match for similar particles on the expanding bullets that had penetrated the back of the victim's head and made his face explode. And above all: the T-shirt and jeans from the woods, covered in Benjamin's DNA and the victim's blood.

Since seven that morning, Emelie and Nikola had been visiting car garages. She'd started at one end of town, Nikola at the other. Checking off places in order.

Bilia was her first choice. They were Volvo-authorized work-
shops, and there were fourteen of them in the county. Tumba,
Tyresö, and so on. She tried to work out the best possible route.
In a few places, she asked them to call ahead to the next garage
and ask whether any dark blue Volvo V70s with a dent in the front
fender had been dropped off for repair. She double-checked everywhere anyway—went to all of them herself. Trusted no one.

The taxi bill would've been enough to break an oligarch, the
way Emelie was planning on driving around. So she'd borrowed
Josephine's car instead, a "quick little X1," as Jossan herself had
put it.

Plus, she'd forced herself to flush the Stesolid pills down the toilet. Something had made her make up her mind: she needed to be
able to do this without them—no more benzo for her. Stesolid: a
quick fix, but not quite as quick to come off them. Maybe she'd flip
out, maybe she'd just fall to pieces. Still: she was taking that risk.
She needed to cut them out. She had to be 100 percent herself now.

Instead: she smoked with the window down. Hoped Jossan
wouldn't be able to smell it. She stopped in Skärholmen Centrum—
wolfed down a Big Mac and fries in under five minutes. She drank
some tea with an odd name to calm down. Hoped everything
would work out.

She talked to Jan. He hadn't found anything worthwhile in Teddy's flat. She was constantly checking up with Nikola. She spoke to
Loke: wondered if there was any other way to track an unmarked
police car. If he could find a policeman with a scar on his face.

She called Matteo again, asked if he could remember anything
else about the car, but the combination of his drunken state and
the attack had plunged everything into a haze. She even called
Teddy's old friend Dejan—she got the number from Matteo—and
he replied politely, sounded hungover, seemed to be worried about
Teddy. But he had no idea, he said.

Thirty-six hours without sleep now. Like the homestretch in a
huge transaction. But worse, obviously—this time, someone was
really in danger.

She began the same way everywhere she tried: drove up to the garage and walked around, studying the cars parked outside. Then, once she'd checked every single one, she asked to talk to someone instead. "My husband brought our car in, but I don't know the registration number," and so on—they saw her as harmlessness personified: young, white, well-behaved woman. And it worked everywhere she tried: they let her in—usually, there weren't more than ten, twenty cars inside.

In a few places, she spotted dark blue Volvos, the right model. She called Loke—he was on standby the whole time, and she read the license plates out to him. He checked. All of them were registered to private individuals, no connection to the police. Or not as far as Loke could see, at least. Teddy wasn't just in her hands now—she had to rely on Nikola, on Loke. And Matteo, whoever he was.

It was a long shot, no matter which way she looked at it: that the car had even been brought in. But according to Matteo, it had been a real bump. "That kind of dent isn't something you can just drive around with. 'Specially if it's a copper's car. They always fix 'em up straightaway. Anal like that, the bastards."

It was even more of a long shot that they would be able to connect any car they found to whoever was behind Teddy's disappearance, but she had to try. She couldn't give up now.

Bilia, Nacka branch. She turned off, past the gas station. Its angular logo shone in huge letters above the bright orange entrance. Huge windows in this branch: this wasn't somewhere they just fixed cars—they sold them here, too. You could tell they wanted to show them off. Volvo and Renault. Ads everywhere: *One Stop Shop—from servicing and repairs to retouching and chips. Free service for three years. Win a rental car!*

She climbed out of the car. Started walking across the huge parking lot. She tried to light a cig—her twenty-first of the day. It was windy, her hair was blowing all over the place, so she moved between two parked cars and squeezed up against the wall of the building. The flame took; she breathed in. She turned her head. She was staring straight at a dark blue Volvo V70 with a huge dent on the right-hand bumper, above the front wheel. She moved around it. Three antennae at the back, dark windows. If anything looked like an undercover car, it was this.

She called her last-dialed number: Loke O.

PERSONAL RECORDING

15 January 2011

JS: Thanks for coming at such short notice. Something happened.

M: What?

JS: Your name's out.

M: What the hell? You promised me—

JS: I know, I know. But one of the fucking prosecutors got involved, and wants you to testify—

M: That's completely ridiculous. What the hell am I supposed to do?

JS: Look, listen: I refused to give your name to the prosecutor. But then they requested my phone records from the network, and they can see who I've been calling these past few weeks. You're one of them. This is the dumbest fucking thing I've ever been involved in. The prosecutor looked you up, and they've got your name.

M: I'm not going to testify against Sebastian and the others. I'm not doing it. Tell the prosecutor. That was never the plan.

JS: Believe me, I've tried. My detective inspector spoke to the prosecutor. But the prosecutor's saying it's their duty to get to the bottom of the information I got from you. They say they can't leave things as they are, unverified, you know? And that means you have to testify publicly. They're bastards, the lot of them.

M: Shit, shit shit . . . I can't.

JS: They'll catch up with you sooner or later, and then you'll have no choice but to testify.

M: So tell the prosecutor I'll testify, but only against that man from the place in the country. . . . And there's one thing I never told you about the computer Cecilia handed over to the kidnappers.

JS: What?

M: There's a copy, on a hard drive. I'm willing to do a deal with the prosecutor. Tell them that.

JS: Christ, Mats, it's the Slavs they want.

M: I don't give a damn. I'm not going to talk about Sebbe. I'm just not. But that bastard Peder, or whoever's computer it was . . . whoever had me kidnapped . . . maybe.

JS: Yeah, that information's also really valuable in terms of negotiating, considering what they were willing to do to you . . . if you know what I mean. Someone's clearly extremely keen on stopping that information from coming out.

M: Am I in a position to negotiate?

JS: I don't know. Maybe not you.

63

He woke to the sound of keys. The door of his cell swung open. A man in a dark blue prison guard's uniform was standing in the hallway outside. He wasn't wearing a name badge.

"Interview time."

The man was holding a pair of handcuffs.

Teddy held out his hands and let the guard put them on. No point kicking up a fuss.

He limped a few feet—his foot hurt like hell—before the guard opened another door and pushed him in. The interview room smelled shut-in. At least the chairs weren't screwed to the floor like they were in most other prisons.

"Wait here," the guard said, and closed the door. Teddy heard the lock turn.

There were no windows, no phone. There was usually a phone, a secure line, so those in custody could make supervised calls to their relatives.

He wondered what they thought he'd done. The only criminal things he'd done the past few months were getting at Anthony Ewing, blackmailing Fredric McLoud, and setting fire to a few of Kum's cars. But there was no way on earth any of them would've gone to the cops. They each had their own reasons for keeping quiet.

Teddy had eaten the sandwich they'd thrown into his cell,

wrapped up in foil. He'd shat in the bucket in the corner. There was something off about this place. But still: the room they'd been keeping him in must've been a prison cell at some point in time— that was 100 percent. That was the only thing he knew to be true in the whole building. People had been locked up there before him. Everything else was off.

The door opened.

A cop came into the interview room. Sturdy boots, sweatshirt, normal jeans, an empty holster on his belt. He rolled a TV cart into the room. Someone closed the door from outside. Teddy studied the man's face. It was the guy who'd attacked him when he got out of the taxi, who'd arrested him. The pig with the scar on his face.

"Najdan Maksumic," he said. "Or would you rather I called you Teddy?" He had an odd way of talking, like he suffered from chronic hoarseness.

Teddy met his gaze: his eyes looked watery somehow.

"I want a lawyer."

The policeman slowly pulled out the chair opposite him and sat down. "No, I don't think that's necessary."

"What am I accused of?"

"I'll get into that. Serious drug offenses, for one."

"In that case, I want a lawyer."

"Yes, Teddy, you'll be needing one, but we're going to have a special little interview first. It's not going to be the kind of interview you're used to."

Teddy asked: "What's your name?"

"We'll get to that later."

That's when he realized: he wasn't being held in police custody at all; he wasn't in prison. It was all fake. The long grass, the over-turned goalposts, the guard without the name badge, the lack of a phone. He didn't know where he was, where they'd taken him, but he was certain: this wasn't an aboveboard operation. This was part of the *other stuff* somehow. Plus: this man was a real police offi-cer, that much was clear. But he was completely unfazed by being found out—Christ, maybe the plan was that Teddy wouldn't have the chance to talk about it afterward.

"If we keep things calm, this'll be quick," he said, turning on the TV screen.

Teddy's hands were still bound. He wondered what the hell they were doing. The man went out.

It took a few seconds for the picture to appear. It was split. On each side of the screen, he could see a woman in what looked to be the same situation he was in. Handcuffed, in an empty room. One of them seemed to have wires of some kind attached to her arm. Teddy recognized them.

The woman on one side was Cecilia. The other was Lillan. He took a closer look: Cecilia had what looked like a white clip attached to her finger, and that linked up to a machine on the table. It looked like an old-fashioned tape recorder. He watched the man with the scar enter the room where Cecilia was sitting. He turned to the camera.

"That's a lie detector on the table. As you can see, it's attached to Cecilia. I learned to use them in special courses in Langley. This country doesn't allow me to use them, unfortunately, but they're actually more reliable than many people in Sweden think."

The man moved over to Cecilia and held something against her neck—it might've been the Taser they'd used on Teddy.

"I want you to realize how serious these interviews are. If you lie, I won't just see it on the detector. I'll punish you for it, too."

He put the Taser to Cecilia's neck.

She shook.

Cried out.

Through the TV screen, her bared teeth looked almost like a wolf's.

"Everyone understand?" The policeman turned to the camera again. His scar looked like it had been daubed on with oil paint.

Teddy stared at the screen. Cecilia was crying. Lillan was breathing heavily. He didn't know if they could see or hear him.

The policeman pulled out a chair and sat down opposite Cecilia.

"So, Cecilia, let's get going. Just a few calibration questions first. Answer yes or no."

"Please, let me go."

"No, no, I'm going to ask you some questions now. Is your name Cecilia Emanuelsson?"

Cecilia was rocking slowly.

"Answer the question, please. Is your name Cecilia Emanuelsson?"

"Yes."

"Good. Do you live on Brännkyrkagatan?"

"Yes."

"Were you married to Mats Emanuelsson?"

A slight pause before she answered: "Yes."

"This is going well." The man turned some dials on the machine.

"Were you ever unfaithful to Mats Emanuelsson while you were married?"

Cecilia's rocking stopped with a jolt. Teddy had seen her move like that before.

"No, never. Why?"

"Just curious." The man turned the dials on the machine again. "Okay. Now, I'd like to know the following. Did Mats Emanuelsson take his life by jumping from a ferry in January 2011?"

Cecilia started rocking again, like everything but her arms was in a rocking chair.

"Answer the question, please."

Her face was pale. "Yes, he did."

"Do you have any idea why he jumped?"

"No, not really, but he'd been kidnapped a few years earlier. I don't think he was well. . . ."

The man got up. "Just answer yes or no."

Cecilia closed her mouth.

He raised the Taser. "Do you know why he jumped?"

"No."

"Did you talk to him in the weeks before he jumped?"

"No, not that I remember."

Teddy could hear the blood pounding in his head. He wanted to kick out, tear the door open, and floor that bastard with the scar. But he knew: he had no chance. Not with handcuffs, locked doors, and a pretend cop with a weapon somewhere outside.

The man asked: "Have you seen Mats over the past three months?"

"What do you mean? He's dead."

"I'll repeat the question. Have you seen Mats over the past three months?"

"No, I haven't."

The policeman studied the lie detector for a few seconds. It felt like Teddy was in the room with Cecilia; he could even hear her breathing.

"There was a fire in your apartment about nine years ago, wasn't there?"

"Yes."

"You saw something when you went into the apartment afterward, didn't you?"

"Yes. There was a computer."

"Exactly. And later, Mats was kidnapped. Do you remember that?"

"Do I remember? I'll never forget."

"And you handed the computer over to someone?"

"Yes, I put it in a locker in Central Station like they told me to."

"Right. Now we're starting to get to the main point. I'd like to know if you or Mats made a copy of the information on that computer before you handed it over?"

More silence. Cecilia's jerky movements were back, her upper body moving back and forth.

The man with the scar was motionless.

Teddy thought about the aluminium foil the sandwich had been wrapped up in. He'd kept it. He had a plan, but no idea whether it would work.

Cecilia sounded like she was crying. "Ohh, what did we do to deserve this . . . Jesus."

"Just answer the question now, please. Did you or Mats make a copy?"

Teddy got up. He went over to the door. It was locked. He pounded on it as hard as he could.

On the TV screen, he saw the man with the scar turn his head. After a few seconds, the door opened and the guard was back.

"What do you want?"

"I've got a confession to make."

"What?"

"Tell your colleague, or whoever the fuck he is, I can tell him about the copy, the hard drive."

Teddy noticed the man's reaction to the last words. The hard drive.

Five minutes later, the man with the scar was in Teddy's interview room. Cecilia's lie detector test had been put on hold. Instead, they were busy linking Teddy to the machine.

The chair creaked as the man sat down.

"So, a confession, you said?"

He turned on the lie detector. "Time to give a few questions."

Teddy grinned, though it felt like his stomach wanted to eat itself. "It's *ask* questions, actually."

"You're in that kind of mood, are you? Should we give Cecilia another go?"

"No, just get on with it."

The policeman began with similar calibration questions to those he'd asked Cecilia. Then he moved on. He asked whether Teddy knew if Mats had really killed himself, if Teddy had met him. Whether Emelie had told him about Benjamin saying anything about what happened in the house in Värmdö. Teddy answered him honestly.

Eventually the man said: "So what is it you wanted to confess?"

He was Teddy "Björne" Maksumic. The guy who never

snitched. The gangster. The living legend. He'd been through a lot of police interviews in his time, so many he'd lost count even before he turned eighteen. And when he was even younger: welfare officers, social services bitches, juvenile investigators. Teddy: a pro at this game. The experts' expert. If there was one thing he knew, it was how to handle people trying to interview him. How to keep quiet about the truth. To lie. In other words: this bastard with the scar could take his lie detector and shove it right up his ass. Teddy was planning to trick the shit out of him—like he'd always done with cops.

He said: "I've got a copy of the contents from that computer."

The policeman's eyes were lifeless—still, Teddy saw something in there. Maybe: a glint of surprise. Then he looked down and studied his machine.

"What did you say? You've got a copy of the contents of the computer Mats Emanuelsson had nine years ago, when you kidnapped him?"

Teddy tried to wind down. Relax. Breathe Prozac. Pretend he was nineteen again, sitting in a cell for GBH, drugs, or some crap like that. Pretend he was back to where he was most used to being—in a fix with the law.

He didn't know if he'd be able to pull it off. He had no idea how lie detectors worked. But he gave it a shot anyway. "I kidnapped Mats on the orders of a guy called Ivan; he's dead now. I know they wanted the computer in exchange for releasing Mats. And when Ivan got hold of it, he made a copy on a hard drive. I've had that copy since he died."

The policeman turned the dials on his lie detector again. "Just answer yes or no to my questions."

"You didn't ask that kind of question, you idiot."

"Do you think you're in a position to talk to me like that? Want one of the women to have another taste of the Taser?"

Teddy smiled tensely—even wider this time. He brushed aside all his worries, pushed back the fear. Owned the room. He'd gone back in time. A hundred fucking percent now.

"If you so much as *breathe* on Lillan or Cecilia, or carry on with your fucking lie detector tests, I swear on my mother's grave my copy'll be sent to the *real* police. I saved it in the cloud, so you can never get at it. Just so you know . . ."

Pause for effect.

"You *son of a bitch*."

64

Nikola had never met this player before, just heard Teddy going on about him. But you could see it from a mile away: he was a genuine super nerd. Beard and a huge Thor's hammer hanging around his neck, dark pants, big black boots, and a leather jacket that went all the way down to the ground—even though the weather was great. Ordinarily, Nikola would've thought the guy was just an old, hibernating lump, especially with the name he had. But he was one of Teddy's closest friends—that was enough to convince him of anything.

The three of them met at the Bilia garage in Nacka—Emelie, Loke, and Nikola—but not right next to the car, there was no need for that. Instead, they were sitting in Emelie's car. It was sweet, an X1. Nikola wondered where she'd managed to conjure it from.

Loke said: "They brought the Volvo in the day after Teddy got taken. It's registered to the Stockholm Police Authority. I sent a picture of it to Matteo, too, and he confirmed the color and appearance looked familiar. I'd say the probability is good. I think it's the right car."

"Can we tell who was driving it?" Nikola asked.

"Unfortunately not. I even hacked into Bilia's client database to see who dropped it off, but they've just put "Police Authority" and a reference number. I guess the undercover cops don't want to give their names. They're shy, y'know? But I had another idea."

Loke held up a black plastic cube, about as big as a matchbox. "GPS tracker. I thought I could stick it under the car. Then we can see where it goes when they pick it up."

Emelie twisted in the front seat. "But it might be ages before they come to get the car—days, weeks maybe. It hasn't even been fixed yet."

No one said anything for a few minutes.

The mood: shitty.

Nikola tried to think of something smart. Outside, cars were moving around the premises: he didn't know how there was room for them all in the already-full parking lot.

Maybe, he thought. Maybe he had an idea.

Now: five hours later. Seven in the evening. They'd gone with Nikola's idea.

Emelie had buttered up one of the guys inside the garage, offered him ten thousand in cash if he started working on the dark blue Volvo right away. "And I mean right away, like *now*. Actually, it'd be great if it was done yesterday."

Then they took a chance. Nikola called 11414.

"Hi, I'm calling from Bilia Nacka. It's about one of your cars, license plate number NGF 239. It was brought in for bodywork the other day."

"Aha." The operator seemed to have limited interest.

"The person who brought it in, they left a reference number. Could you give me their name?"

"Sorry, no, but I can pass on a message."

"You can't just connect me to the right person?"

"No, I'm sorry, not without anything but a reference number."

"Aha, Okay. Well, the car's fixed. We did a premium assessment, so it was pretty quick. But it can't stay here for long, because we're starting work on remodeling the parking lot tomorrow morning. All the cars need to be gone before that, and if it's still here we'll have to tow it. I'm sorry it's such a rush."

"Yes, I have to say, it is. If we don't have time to pick it up, where will you take it?"

"I don't actually know, I'm afraid. But we've got a warehouse north of Uppsala. We're just hoping people will be able to come and pick them up in time."

"Hmm. Well, I'll just have to try to find the right person."

"If you could, thanks. As soon as possible."

65

The next day. A man had picked up the Volvo early that morning. They hadn't been able to see much of his face, he'd been wearing a cap and sunglasses, but it probably made no difference: they had something to go on now. Someone to follow.

The car drove into town first, to Kungsholmen. It pulled up outside the police station on Polhemsgatan. Emelie stayed in Jossan's car. Waited. Nikola got out to check.

She felt hounded. The main trial in Benjamin's case was starting in two days, and even though she'd spent last night going through the preliminary report, her power was starting to run out. She needed to find something—inaccuracies, or anything that went in Benjamin's favor.

She missed the Stesolid. But the pills were down the drain now. She would have to make it through this without them; she'd made up her mind, even if she couldn't quite remember why.

Nikola called a few hours later. He was in Kronobergspark, using binoculars to keep track of the car. "The same guy's getting back into the car," he said. "I'll come down, and we can keep following it."

They watched the Volvo drive along Drottningsholmsvägen, down toward Thorildsplan, and then up onto Essingeleden. A blinking blue dot on their GPS screen. They kept a distance of between a thousand and five thousand feet. Loke's idea with the tracker: so easy to follow.

The highway, southwest. Past all the suburbs. Past Alby, Teddy's apartment, and a robbed ICA Maxi. And then, a few miles before Södertälje, the car turned off and continued dead south.

Emelie wondered what they were heading toward. Maybe she should've asked Jan for help. But no—he was her consultant, not her soldier. Or maybe she should've called the police; they had to have some kind of special department for stuff like this. But that was risky, too: there were policemen involved, albeit on the wrong side, and they clearly had resources.

A country road, no. 225. South of Södertälje. Nikola was sitting with the GPS in his lap next to her, like some kind of rally navigator.

They saw the Volvo stop.

Håga, they read on a sign. It was one o'clock, the middle of the day. Deep green nature all around them. Summer would soon be entering its final phase.

Emelie and Nikola parked by a cluster of trees one thousand feet away from the Volvo. They were in the sticks now. Fields and farms all around them. Cornfields and cows lining the road. She looked at Nikola. He seemed much calmer than she felt.

"What d'you think?"

"Google it?"

Emelie took out her phone and searched the name of the place. The first hit was Wikipedia:

In 1943, the Prison and Probation Service opened a hospital for criminals in Håga. In 1970, the operation was wound down and reopened as a correctional facility. The prison closed in early 2015.

Nikola read over her shoulder. "What the hell? They're keeping him locked up in an abandoned prison?"

"I hope they're keeping him prisoner," Emelie said quietly. "I hope he's still alive."

Nikola snorted. "This is completely messed up."

Emelie felt like Jossan when she replied—someone who could make anyone laugh, no matter how tough the situation was; who managed to see the funny side of a situation, no matter how bad things were looking.

She said: "I'm your super lawyer. Just trust me."

66

It was sick. Fucked-up in a completely batshit way.

All the same, Nikola loved it: he worked like crazy all afternoon. Barely had time to breathe. Rushed about like some manic nine-till-fiver with three jobs. The thing: for the first time in his life, he was fighting for a *good cause* somehow. He was going to save his uncle. Thousand percent.

Emelie bossed him about worse than Sandra in Spillersboda. She sent Loke out into the surroundings—but he didn't even get out of his car. He just sat there with a laptop on his knee, working away. Nikola didn't know what on. Emelie herself went back to Stockholm, to the City Planning Office, whatever that was. While she was gone, he trudged around the woods with his binoculars like a total forager.

There was a wall around the place, and outside that, a fence. Electrified, judging by the warning signs. He tried to see whether it was intact. It looked that way, unfortunately, and he could hear the low hum of the current flowing through the metal. Plus: someone had put up small cameras in a number of places on the fence. When he was done, he went back to Loke and told him what he'd seen.

Emelie came back two hours later, with sketches of the old Håga prison. "City Planning just lifted confidentiality on these drawings, because the place isn't high security anymore."

They could see it all: every old cell, the common areas, the stairwells and—above all—the entrances to the main building.

"You were on trial for blowing up an ICA, and I know you denied it—and got let off—but if, by any chance, you know how to get hold of some explosives . . . we need to go in here."

Emelie pointed to a spot on the drawing.

Nikola went into Södertälje. It took less than fifteen minutes. It was four in the afternoon, and he was in luck: Gabbe was home. This time, Nikola paid for the explosives.

The old man said: "I've got myself Wi-Fi. You know what that is?"

Nikola thought on his feet. He replied: "Nah, sorry. Been in young offenders' for ages."

"Shame, you could've helped me set it up otherwise."

Nikola promised to come back another day. He went straight to Chamon's. "Hey, man, you here to drop off my ride?" his friend asked when he saw him in the doorway. "You know it's not mine for real, but one day . . . *walla.*"

"Nah, *habibi.*" Nikola lowered his voice. "I want you to help me blow open a five-hundred-pound metal door."

They spent a few hours working with the explosives. Chamon made a seven-foot-high, three-foot-wide frame, and they attached the plastic explosives and the detonator to it. Carefully, bit by bit, cautious. They listened to "King Kunta" on repeat, pushed snus under their lips, drank water.

"You can't drink Coke or coffee or Monster or anything like that when you're working on this stuff, man, makes your hands too shaky," Chamon said. "And that's not what you want. By the way, you need help with this later?"

Of course they needed help, but Nikola replied: "Nah, it's cool." Chamon had already done enough for him. Nikola was just happy his friend hadn't asked what it was all about.

As the sun started to set, Nikola went out to a construction site he'd spotted in Norsborg. Block of apartments, huge cranes, foundations. Enormous stop signs: *No unauthorized entry.* Nikola pulled the feeble fence to one side and stepped in. After fifteen minutes, he left with what he needed: long cables.

Night now. They were all standing outside Loke's car. The weather was still sweet. The stars glowing like planes up in the sky. The only other light was from Loke's computer, whenever he sat down on a rock and started jabbing away at the keyboard like some hyper kid on speed.

Emelie held up a pack of cigarettes. "Want one?"

Nikola lit hers first, then his own.

"Have you thought," he said, "he might not even be in there?"

Emelie blew out smoke. She was standing up straight, and the dark T-shirt she was wearing was tight against her upper-arm muscles. But he could see lines around her eyes that he hadn't noticed when she was his lawyer.

"No, you're right," she said. "But they've got something they don't want anyone to get to in there. Just think about the cameras they've put up, the electric fence."

Nikola thought about her answer. He didn't know if it made him feel much better.

"Was your office happy you got me off?" he asked.

Loke looked up from his computer.

Emelie took a long drag. "I don't know."

It was time. Emelie and Nikola went toward the fence on the north side. The narrow end of the building jutted out there, and according to the plans they had, that was where the cells were—the risk that someone would be gazing out into the darkness at that end of the building was small.

Nikola had changed his clothes: dark Adidas pants and a black hoodie, hood up. He felt at home—the same dress code as when he'd robbed ICA.

They fixed two cables to the fence. It shook slightly, but not loudly enough that anyone in the building would hear it.

They laid them down on the ground: each was fifteen feet long.

Then they went to get Emelie's car. Nikola drove silently over toward the cables. Headlights on the lowest setting, taped over. They got out. Fixed the cables to the X1.

Emelie called Loke. "You can turn off their cameras now."

All according to plan. They weren't using the old prison cameras anymore—those were gone. Someone, as Nikola had discovered, had replaced them with their own digital surveillance cameras instead. They were controlled wirelessly, according to Loke. A wireless network he was now going to switch off, using his own jamming equipment.

After a few seconds, Emelie held up her thumb.

"Okay, let's go," she said.

Nikola put his foot on the accelerator. He looked back, into the darkness. The cables were taut. He pressed his foot down harder. Felt the pull, how the car was fighting. A strange feeling: his foot was almost on the floor, but the car still wasn't moving forward.

Their initial plan had been to cut the fence with bolt cutters—but the electric current was problematic. Plus they might've linked it to some kind of alarm in case someone tried to breach it, and if that was the case, it would take them too long to cut through—a little hole would be no good.

Nikola pressed his foot down further, gently, tried to hold it steady.

Suddenly: the car jerked forward; he heard the rattle, and then a louder thud.

The fence had fallen. Nikola kissed the gold cross hanging around his neck.

Emelie had taped her Bluetooth earpiece to her ear to stop it falling out. She'd bought backpacks and dark sports clothing at XXL in town. She'd also bought three walkie-talkies and given one to each of the others in case they managed to lose their phones. Everything else had been bought from Järnia. She'd spent at least two hours studying the sketches and satellite images from Google

Maps. By this point, she knew the area like she knew her own apartment. Still, she felt like the most inexperienced commando soldier ever.

They kept Loke on the line.

"Any activity over there?"

"Nope, not that I can see or hear."

He'd set up his own parabolic microphones and night vision cameras around the prison. He was also using an ordinary police radio to pick up any broadcasts they might make.

"It's dead," he repeated. "But I can see a faint light in two of the windows."

Emelie and Nikola were each carrying a ladder. She'd bought those earlier that day, too: they'd barely fit in Jossan's little car, but she'd tied them in tightly and driven with the trunk open. They unfolded one of them and set it against the wall. Everything seemed easier than she'd thought it would be, even though Nikola was dragging a wooden frame behind him. Together, they managed to get the other ladder over the wall—she'd had an idea in her mind that a prison wall should be a difficult obstacle, but this was more like going over a climbing frame and down again.

The two of them were now inside the perimeter.

A few seconds' pause—Emelie wanted to check in with Loke.

"Still as quiet as Nifelheim in there," he whispered.

"Nifelheim?" Emelie hissed back.

"Opposite of Valhalla, kingdom of death for the bastards, I guess. The goddess Hel, Loke's daughter—"

"Thanks, that's enough. How sensitive's your equipment?"

"Insanely sensitive. It picks up all sounds within an eight-hundred-foot radius, though not through thick walls."

"In other words?"

"I can definitely hear if someone's outside somewhere in that area. But assuming they're talking at a normal level indoors, and not sitting close to a window, there's no guarantee I'll hear it. But let's say this: I can hear you two fussing in the grass over there."

They passed the main building from the west. Nikola with the wooden frame on his shoulders—he looked like some kind of kite surfer carrying his equipment on his back. Though not quite: the way he'd pulled his hood up reminded her more of someone who wanted to protect their hair on a rainy day.

They turned the southern corner. The darkness wasn't a problem. Emelie could see the yellow wall sixteen feet to her right the entire time. That was enough—the grass wasn't too long here, and there didn't seem to be anything to trip over.

She paused again. Waited for Loke.

She was cold. She should have called the police, after all—this was madness. They didn't really have a plan: just to get in and hope there was no one but Teddy inside the old prison building. What would she and Nikola do if there were others in there? If there was someone waiting for them? Insanity. She should say something to Nikola; they should turn back right now. Call it off. They were playing cops. Amateur spies. Clown rescue team on a mission. Without any idea what they would have to deal with.

"Come on," Nikola whispered.

"I don't know . . . ," she mumbled as quietly as she could. "Maybe we should wait a minute, go back."

She could see Nikola's dark eyes in the gloom. "I dunno what you're talking about," he said. "But even if you chicken out, I'll go in myself."

He carefully put down the frame and took something from his pocket. She couldn't see what it was at first, just an outline. Then she realized: a weapon, he was holding a gun.

She felt her head grow hot. "Where'd you get that from? Are you crazy?"

"I found it in a toilet. And I'm gonna save my uncle with it."

They were standing in front of the entrance she'd picked out. Not the main entrance, since that would mean getting past a pair of locked doors. Instead, they'd chosen the goods entrance at the side of the building. According to the documents used as a basis for closing down the prison, the locking mechanisms inside the building itself shouldn't be functioning. In other words: if they managed to get in that way, they should be able to get to floor 2, corridor A. Where they'd seen the lights.

Nikola wiggled out of the wooden frame, carefully. Then he took off his backpack. The place had never been a high-security prison, it hadn't been built with a perimeter that would stand up to attack, just one that would make it more difficult for the inmates than in a completely open prison.

He started taking things from his bag: a drill, a head flashlight. This was probably the most crucial moment—in terms of noise, anyway.

But this was also when Loke would play his second role. Emelie sent him a message. "Okay, we're in place now, the explosive frame's ready. You can start your little *spiel*."

Five seconds later, they heard the sound of Loke's engine and saw his headlights light up the building. She knew what he was doing: he'd driven his car up to the gates by the main entrance.

Then he started blowing the horn. The silence meant the noise was incredible—even though he was more than a hundred yards away.

At the same moment, Nikola turned on his headlamp. Lifted up the drill and started working on the metal door in front of him. Loke's noise continued.

After a minute, Nikola was done. The honking was still going on.

Emelie helped Nikola hold the explosive frame while he screwed it into the holes he'd just drilled. It fit like a glove. She thanked the City Planning Office again: the drawings were precise.

She could hear Loke's voice over the honking. "Someone's coming. I can see a man in the headlights. He's heading for the gates, came out of the central guard room. I'll back up a bit if he gets too close."

67

The claustrophobia wasn't getting any better. He was an animal in a cage. If they didn't let him out soon, into the yard, or even one of the outdoor cells, he'd go crazy.

It was dark. They'd turned off the light earlier that evening. Teddy was happy about that, very happy—it was all part of his plan.

He could hear a horn outside, probably from a car. He heard the honking faintly through the window. It sounded like an animal, howling in time with some inaudible rhythm. He wondered whether this place was close to a residential area, like Salberga—maybe it was just a car alarm that had gone off when someone tried to steal it.

He didn't care about the darkness now, even if it had stressed him out a few hours earlier, as the sun slowly set. He'd had plenty of time today. Aluminium foil from eight sandwiches: lunch, dinner, lunch, dinner. His meals these past few days. Each piece of foil carefully laid on the floor, the creases smoothed out, the metal thoroughly flattened. He'd torn off strip after strip, holding the foil as straight as he could, slowly pulled at the fragile material. Five strips per sandwich. Each strip roughly eight inches long. He'd thrown away one strip per sandwich—he had to hand over some trash. With the rest, he twisted the ends together. The final product: a strip of aluminium more than six feet in length. In other words: a six-foot-long electrical conductor. Or so he hoped.

He'd unscrewed the lightbulb on the ceiling. Teddy. A tall man.

If he turned the shit bucket upside down and stretched, he could do it. It had been enough—the strip of foil looped like a glimmering spiderweb from the light fixture to the door handle. Metal on metal. When someone switched on the light, turned the handle . . . *zzzzap*. He could only hope it had the desired effect. He'd carved birdhouses and park benches in prison before—never worked with conductors.

The plastic mattress was sticky. His head was pounding. He'd told them he'd saved a copy of that fucking computer in the cloud—Loke was the one who'd taught him that word. And it had done the trick, that much was clear. Teddy had saved Cecilia for now. He'd seen the fear in that scarred bastard's eyes. What he didn't know was how long his lie would hold. He didn't know what their lie detectors could show. He didn't know anything, for Christ's sake.

How had things ended up like this? A chain of events leading to him lying awake in a cell again. His karma so dirty from once kidnapping another person that he was now being held captive by the same powers. He wondered when it had all started. Him and Dejan. Him and Isak. Him and all the others they'd grown up with.

Teddy, maybe fourteen years old, playing billiards at the youth center in Geneta. Dejan too. Talking the rules of eight ball, the nerds from the parallel class they used to beat up, and Henke Larsson's goals in the Allsvenskan league. In a few weeks, it'd be summer—they were both ending the school year with crappy grades: not even passing half their subjects. Still, they knew it'd be the best summer ever. The wildest.

One of the older kids came into the room. He walked over to their table. His gold chain looked like it weighed at least half a kilo. Turned to Teddy: "You're Serbs, yeah? Can I give it a whirl?"

You didn't say no to a guy like that. He took Teddy's cue, bent down, struck the ball hard—missed the hole: the ball bounced from the table. Thudded onto the floor.

Teddy and Dejan pressed against the wall. The guy: unknown in the hood, already been inside for a year even though he wasn't much older than nineteen. "Shit, this cue's a piece of crap, not chalked well, either. You guys in tonight, by the way?"

"In what?" Teddy had asked hopefully. This could be his break.

"We're doin' a thing, need people on the lookout so the po-po don't turn up. Pay you five hundred each."

Teddy and Dejan: they would've done it for free any day of the week. Didn't care about the money. It was the cred that counted. Being someone. But: it was also about keeping your style. Teddy took the cue back: didn't say anything. Bent forward. Took aim. Sank the four in the right-hand pocket—like a stone-cold snooker king.

Dejan stomped nervously in the background: wanted Teddy to answer.

When he did, he spoke slowly: "We'll come. For a grand each."

The guy moved closer. "You got attitude, little man. Maybe you'll have a career with us one day." He held out his hand. "I'm Ivan."

The honking continued outside. Teddy wasn't planning on staying put here. He needed to see his nephew—they'd spent too much time apart. Then he thought: I need to see Emelie, too—I'm lonely without her.

The thin aluminium strip dangled in the darkness.

And then he heard a crash outside. He went over to the window. His whole body still hurt.

It was pitch-black out there.

He couldn't see a thing.

68

His ears were ringing. Light from his headlamp shining through the dust. An empty room. Old shelves or something like that along the walls.

The door had popped like it was made of Legos. Nikola and Emelie had been waiting around the corner, fifty feet away—he didn't see it happen. Still: the noise was almost worse than when he and Chamon blew the ICA place.

They were inside now. A hallway. No lights, just his headlamp. Darkness and concrete.

Emelie was talking. Nikola could hardly hear what she was saying. "Loke . . . get out . . . the man . . . ."

She squatted down first, showed him the way.

Nikola raised Teddy's pistol: held it in front of him with both hands, like that Beck idiot in those unrealistic Swedish films.

Stairs up. Echoing. His headlamp casting white circles onto the gray walls.

In the best of worlds: just one player keeping Teddy prisoner. The cameras were still down. The idiot had gone out into the night to chase Loke away.

But in the shittiest: they were up against paramilitary cops. Lots of them. Armed. Perfectly ready to massacre them all in any rescue attempt.

Nikola was starting to feel short of breath. Side by side with Emelie. Wide steps. Real prison feeling. He could just see the guards rushing up here during a disturbance. Plexiglass shields like a wall in front of them: the guys called them the black force.

"Here." Emelie's breathing: quick too. Her forehead was dirty. They'd moved through swirling concrete particles back there.

Nikola went over to the door. An abandoned fucking ghost prison. Four doors so far—none of them had been locked, other than the first one, just like they'd thought. He grabbed the handle. The door was heavy.

A hallway. Even more of a classic prison feeling now: a row of doors with small hatches along one wall. The lights were on in here. A corner at the other end; he couldn't see where it led.

He saw three people ahead of him, toward the end of the corridor. One man, two women.

Emelie shouted: "Let them go."

Nikola didn't understand a thing: what was going on? Who were these women? One of them looked older than his own mother. The other one was young, younger than him. And the man? What the hell was he up to?

Instinctively, he wanted to stop, but he couldn't; he had to fix this now. He kept running. The gun in his hand like a baton in a relay race. "Where's Teddy?" he roared.

Nikola was approaching the people at the other end of the hallway. The girl was crying.

Then he saw it: the man had a pistol to her head. Nikola was getting major cop vibes from him. But at the same time: something was clearly fucked-up here.

69

This wasn't what she'd imagined. They would just have to break down one door, go in—open up and let Teddy out. But now: hostage drama, à la Hollywood. The policeman with the scar was holding a pistol against the younger woman's head. Emelie paused.

She recognized the older of the two: it was Cecilia. The younger woman looked like her, like Benjamin. It had to be Lillan.

"Stay back," the man snarled.

Nikola was standing in front of her—his gun pointed at the policeman. Quietly Emelie said: "Take it easy, Nikola, don't do anything we might regret."

She could feel the sweat on her back. Her ears were still ringing. She wondered where Teddy was. She could hear Loke's voice clearly in her earpiece now. "The guy's out here, but he's on his way back inside. I'll see if I can bring him out again."

"There's one here, too," she almost whispered back.

They had to act. The other man would be inside soon, and he would probably be armed. She had no idea what to do. Pistol versus pistol. It was deadlock.

The man pushed the women in front of him. "We're leaving," he said. He spoke almost as if he was reminding himself. "And we're taking your little protector with us, too."

Both Lillan and Cecilia were crying now. Emelie almost started to sob; it was all so unfair, so wrong.

The man stopped farther down the hallway, almost at the corner. In front of the last door. He took out a key and unlocked it. Still with his gun pointed at Lillan's head. Then he grabbed the handle to open it.

He fell to the ground with a shout.

It looked like he was shaking.

70

The strip of foil was in pieces on the floor. It had stretched as the door opened, then torn apart. Teddy flung himself out—the door couldn't be conductive anymore. He heard a voice that didn't belong there; he heard Nikola shout.

He leaped.

Landed on his feet.

His ribs and his right foot hurt like hell, like something in him had broken again. He collapsed.

The hallway was bright. There was a man on the floor. He saw who it was: the cop with the scar—and he was trying to get back to his feet again. Lillan and Cecilia were standing behind him. They were hysterical, clutching one another.

Teddy turned his head. Farther along the hallway, he could see two more people: Nikola and Emelie. Nikola ran toward him.

Teddy tried to get up, but his foot bent beneath him, like he was trying to balance his weight on a straw. The cop was back on his feet now, on his way. Lillan screamed. And Teddy saw what he was moving toward. A pistol, a few feet away on the floor—right where the hallway turned the corner. The man must've dropped it when he got the shock. A Sig Sauer, he saw. A police weapon.

Nikola roared: he'd made it to Teddy now. "Stop."

But the man didn't listen. He was three feet away from his gun now.

Teddy attempted to get up again, but the fracture in his foot must've gotten worse when he flung himself at the door.

Lillan and Cecilia leaped at the man. He realized they were trying to grab the weapon.

Everything happened too quickly. Still, it was like it was slow motion. Each movement like something Loke had replayed to him, frame by frame.

Nikola raised his arm. Took aim.

The man with the scar grabbed his pistol at the very same moment.

Nikola again: "Drop the gun."

The man raised his weapon.

The crack of a gun echoed like a bomb had gone off in there.

Teddy turned around. Nikola was on the floor. The man disappeared around the corner.

Emelie bent down, crying: "He's hit."

But she didn't bend down over Nikola; she just picked up the pistol he'd dropped and rushed off down the hallway.

"Take care of him, he'll be okay," she shouted as she ran past Teddy. "I'll stop that bastard."

Teddy steadied himself against the wall, limped on one leg, toward Nikola.

He'd recognized the weapon Emelie had been clutching. It was his Zastava. The pistol Nikola'd had with him for some reason.

71

Ninety-degree angle. The hallway soon came to an end. And she couldn't see the man with the scar anywhere.

Emelie could hear Cecilia's and Lillan's breathing behind her; she could hear Nikola's cries. She hadn't been lying to Teddy: the shot had grazed the edge of his shoulder. He would make it, that was clear.

The door in front of her was unlocked. The handle looked dusty, but she could see someone had grabbed it.

She heard quick steps in the stairwell on the other side.

She was alone now. An even wider staircase this time. Downward. Teddy and Nikola: still upstairs. Lillan and Cecilia somewhere behind her.

She had the gun raised in front of her, but it was almost impossible to run like that. It was much heavier than she'd expected—the first time she'd held a weapon. She didn't even know if it was loaded, or how you took it off safety.

Five steps at a time. She was breathing heavily.

She lowered the gun: that made it easier to move.

Floor after floor.

She heard a door slam somewhere below her. The man had gone out; it should be the main door.

She reached the bottom. Tore the door open, it was unlocked, too.

Double doors. Bars. Concrete walls.

She ran on. Saw doors slam shut in front of her. Saw the man with the scar from behind. Saw bright spots.

Out in the yard. He was fifty feet ahead of her. It was dark. She'd dropped her headlamp, but she could see a light bobbing up and down—it had to be him. The gravel seemed to be a beige color, like it had rusted.

"Stop," she shouted.

But he didn't listen. Instead, he ran to the main guard room. She heard the sound of the doors opening. Saw the light disappear.

She was close.

Inside the building. More doors. Reinforced glass. Gloominess that would've been pitch darkness without the man's flashlight beam. The smell of dust and dirty metal. Old surveillance cameras. A waiting room. The sound of footsteps up ahead.

She made it out onto the other side. In front of the prison.

Suddenly: blinded by a bright light. It took her a second to understand. He was shining a light straight in her eyes. She squinted, tried to see past the glare of the flashlight.

It was the man with the scar. Ten feet away. And his weapon was pointed straight at her.

Behind him, the Volvo was parked.

He lowered the flashlight slightly. She could clearly make out the evil eye of the gun.

The man sounded hoarse, but not out of breath. "I'm leaving now. You take another step, and I'll blow your brains out."

He moved backward, toward the car. Emelie heard the driver's door open. She clutched the barrel of her gun.

A heartbeat: she should try to shoot him.

She raised her arm. Aimed the pistol at him. Pulled the trigger.

Then: a bang. A shot. Just like up in the hallway, but the sound was lower. Fainter.

The bastard had made it first. He'd shot her. She was hit.

She would drop to the ground, take her last breath alone in the darkness.

It was all over.

So many things had happened these past few days, but she'd still neglected so much. She hadn't told her father she loved him, despite all the crap. She'd forgotten to thank Jossan for all her support. And Teddy—there was something she should have said to him. Something important.

But she didn't feel any pain. No palpitations, no panic.

A jingling sound. A flashlight fell to the ground over by the car. Its beam of light shone straight up into the sky, toward the heavens. She could still see almost nothing. But she realized: she hadn't been hit.

She heard a gurgling sound.

"Hello?"

A hissing noise.

"Hello?" she tried again.

The sound of footsteps disappearing over the gravel.

She slowly moved toward the car.

Picked up the flashlight. Shone.

The policeman was on the ground. His eyes had rolled upward. At first, she didn't understand. He was completely motionless.

Then she saw: his chest.

A dark patch on his sweater. Blood pouring out.

The sound of crunching steps was farther away now.

The man with the scar had been shot. Someone else had gotten in there before either of them had time to shoot.

Someone on their way into the darkness.

PART V

AUGUST

72

She took out the bottle of nail polish remover and soaked a cotton ball. A simple procedure: nail by nail. She cleaned. Liberated. She was in no hurry.

Once all the old dirt and grease was gone, she took out the file. She brought it to the edge of each nail in a sweeping motion. In one direction only, never pulling it back and forth. Finger after finger. After that, she polished the surface of her nails with a buffer, that's what Jossan had told her it was called. Slowly, carefully. This wasn't Emelie's area of expertise. Still, she kept going until they shone. She thought maybe she could skip the nail polish entirely; her nails looked good as they were. But she took the bottles from the bathroom cabinet anyway. Transparent base layer first. Then the nail polish, bright red, nothing strange, nothing extravagant today. It wasn't a party she was going to. First coat. Second coat—there was a noticeable difference once it was done. Finally, she applied the top coat—Jossan had taught her about that, too—and her nails were suddenly strong and shiny, like she'd paid six hundred kronor for a professional manicure.

Today was the day the main hearing in the murder case would begin—there was no more serious crime in the eyes of the law. It was also her second-ever trial. She really should have called it all off. Like Magnus Hassel and the office had expected. Plus, so much other crap had happened these past few days. The chaos out in Håga. The interviews afterward.

The police had wanted to know everything, down to the very last detail. She complied as best she could—told them how they'd worked out which car had been used to take Teddy, how she and Nikola had torn the fence down, blown the entrance open. She told them everything that had happened in the hallway, other than that Nikola had been armed, and that she'd used the gun, too. She left that out. She told them how the man with the scar had threatened the women. How he'd dropped his weapon but managed to grab it again, shot at Nikola. How she'd chased him down the stairs, out into the yard, through the central guard area, and then seen him attacked by some unknown person in the darkness outside.

"But why were they even keeping Teddy prisoner there?"

"I don't know."

"And Cecilia and Lillan Emanuelsson?"

"We didn't even know they were there."

"But you're the private defense counsel for Cecilia's son, Lillan's brother. How does this all fit together?"

"I don't know for certain. Maybe they took them to try to influence the trial against Benjamin, influence what he's going to say, something like that."

She and the others had agreed that they wouldn't mention anything about the real background to it all. The man Loke had lured out of the building with the horn was gone, vanished. And they didn't know what he would do if they started talking about a secret network desperate to get hold of a hard drive. They didn't even know if he was a policeman.

"I've got a question for you," Emelie said. "Who was he, the man with the scar on his face? The one who got shot by the car right in front of me?"

The man leading the interview looked down at his notes. "I can't go into that right now, I'm afraid."

She could have cited some sort of obstacle. Given up the case. But no: this was who she was. This was what she wanted to do.

She was ready now. She'd read the preliminary report forward and back, made her notes, refined them, refined them again. She'd prepared her cross-examinations, thought through all possible angles and evidence. She'd been out to the crime scene, would refer to her own findings there. She was as ready as she would ever be.

It was seven in the morning.

The shadow of the law courts fell over the café on the other side of the street. Emelie was sitting at one of the tables outside. She had a double espresso in front of her, the sugar she'd added resting in a little mound on the foam on the top. Good quality, she thought, when the sugar didn't immediately sink. She hadn't been hungry this morning—but she needed coffee, that much she knew.

When the clock struck eight thirty, she went over to the court building and into reception. She could do this. Ten minutes later, she was sitting in the Pit, one of the remand cells beneath the court, with Benjamin.

She thought back to the first time she met him. His hair had grown since then, his stubble had become a full beard—and his eyes were open.

They'd met the day before to go through everything one last time. Jeanette Nicorescu had explained that Benjamin was almost completely back to normal now. He would need to rest more than he usually did, and he might become disoriented when he got stressed, but on the whole, he should be able to manage a trial.

Emelie had tried to explain what happened in Håga.

The main trial began on time at nine o'clock.

The courtroom was grand. Much bigger and more old-fashioned than the one she'd defended Nikola in, over in Södertörn. The clerk and the members of the court were already in place up on the bench: but it was no ordinary presiding judge today. It was a senior judge, Sverker Järnblad—probably because of the gravity of the charges. He was wearing a black suit and tie: serious mood, even in his choice of clothes. The three lay judges looked sullen— maybe their way of marking how serious the case was. The clerk was young. She'd probably gone straight from high school to her legal studies, and then to working for the court here; it was the most sought-after placement in the country for law graduates.

Emelie walked over to her seat at the right, below the bench. She had a proper desk chair with an adjustable back support and seat, but Benjamin's chair was much simpler. He followed her in, two guards at his side. Cecilia had brought him a striped shirt a few days earlier. His handcuffs rattled.

The prosecutor, Annika Rölén, was wearing a dark blue dress. During Benjamin's remand hearings, she'd almost looked scruffy. Not today.

Rölén heaped some papers onto the table in front of her. Emelie did the same. She glanced over to the public seats: Teddy, Cecilia, and Lillan. Teddy had a crutch leaning against his seat. There were two more men and three women at the back of the room. Maybe they were journalists. Maybe just curious members of the public. Maybe they were something else. Emelie saw one of the women, who seemed much too well-dressed to be a journalist, take out a small notepad every now and then. She seemed to be calmly making notes.

The judge started to introduce the different parties. And then the door opened at the back of the room. Another member of the public came in and sat down. Suit, colorful tie. Slicked-back hair.

It was Magnus Hassel.

Emelie's heart wanted to leap from her chest.

The prosecutor read the charges. The hearing was scheduled to last three days. The morning was devoted to Rölén's opening statements, and Benjamin's interrogation would begin after lunch.

The clerk tapped away at her computer. The lay judges were listening carefully—much more focused than those who'd been in court during Nikola's trial. Once they had heard the prosecutor's statement of the criminal act, the judge turned to Emelie.

"And how does the defendant plead?"

Emelie cleared her throat. Bent down toward the microphone so that it was right in front of her mouth.

"Not guilty."

73

Court 5, Stockholm County Court. Teddy had seen many court-rooms in his time: this was definitely the grandest. Tall wooden panels on the walls and an impressively high wooden ceiling: it was a grid, a symmetrical pattern that fit in with its surroundings in more ways than one. Stronghold of squareness.

The judge and the lay judges, Benjamin and Emelie, the pros-ecutor: they were all sitting far away from him—the room was big and long. If it hadn't been for the microphones and the speakers, the public wouldn't have had a chance to hear what was being said.

Magnus Hassel was sitting five seats away from him, listening. Teddy didn't know if that was good or bad for Emelie. Maybe she'd told him about the case by now. Maybe he just wanted to see how she did.

The clerk lowered two white sheets down the walls, one to her right and one to her left. The prosecutor had begun her statement of facts. She was showing PowerPoint images as she talked.

The yard outside the house in Värmdö. The hole cut into the window. Dirt on the floor. A man's body: his head a broken mess. Nothing new. The prosecutor's statement of the criminal act was simple, but her account and presentation of the evidence was long-winded. Still, her claims were plain and clear. Benjamin had gone to the house in a car, broken in by cutting a hole in the window, and then shot a man in the living room, using expanding bullets.

He'd had gunpowder residue on his hands and the victim's blood on his clothes, that was why he'd taken off his bloody T-shirt and jeans and thrown them into the woods. There was no doubt in her mind: Benjamin was guilty.

She went through the findings from the National Forensics Centre. Each point had a log number, date, inspection of process, legal opinion scales, etc. Analysis of the empty casings, the bullet used. The results of the search for DNA and fingerprints. The traces of gunpowder found on Benjamin. The tire tracks that showed his car had driven away from the house. The bloody T-shirt in the woods. The longer she continued, the more convincing the evidence became.

"We also found DNA and fingerprints from someone other than Benjamin and the deceased," Rölén said. "The house has probably been inhabited by others, though we haven't managed to identify who."

The lunch break was depressing. Benjamin was taken back to his cell through the so-called Walk of Sighs. He would eat his lunch alone there. Teddy followed Emelie, Cecilia and Lillan to a restaurant over the road. He ordered a steak with fries, but he had no appetite. He glanced at the others: no one was touching their food.

Emelie said: "It is what it is. I'll do my best. But you heard what the prosecutor was saying: it's not looking good."

Teddy wanted to talk to her once they were done, but she just waved an arm. "I don't have time. Not right now. It's all too much as it is."

He watched her stop to light a cigarette at the corner of the courthouse on Scheelegatan. Alone. He pushed more snus into his mouth, chewed more gum.

He'd spent several hours in police interviews over the past few days, too. They wanted to know why he and the women had been kept prisoner in the abandoned prison, of course. What it was all about. Teddy told them as much as he could, without revealing any link to Mats Emanuelsson or a copy of a hard drive.

All he wanted to know was who the man with the scar was—

the man someone had shot under the cover of darkness, right in front of Emelie.

It was time for Benjamin to take the stand.

It started like normal—the judge asked him to go over everything in his own words. "And if you need to take a break, just speak up. I'm aware you've been bed bound."

Benjamin had his hands clasped in his lap, under the table. Despite that, it was obvious how tense he was, his eyes fixed on some invisible spot on the opposite wall. Emelie had told Teddy he was on strong tranquillizers, which was maybe just as well.

"Okay, well . . ." Teddy wondered whether he would manage. "I don't remember much from before the crash. It's mostly black."

The judge said: "Just tell us what you remember."

"I went to the house to meet an acquaintance—I can't say who," Benjamin said in a monotone voice. He looked up at the senior judge. "And another acquaintance was there, too. His name is Sebastian, but he gets called Sebbe. Then something happened, and I'm sorry, but I can't remember anything after that. I can just see two things, like time stopped at two different moments. One is Sebbe lying on the floor with his face covered in blood, and I know he wasn't breathing. The other is that I tried to turn on the road, but the car skidded and crashed. I've really tried to work out why I can't remember what happened before and in between, but it's a total blank. The doctors said I had a bad concussion and that it can affect your memory. All I know is I didn't kill anyone. I didn't murder Sebbe. That's all I can say."

Although his account was meager, Teddy practically felt his jaw drop—from what Emelie had said, Benjamin had never been able to tell them this much before. Sebbe was dead. The dark circles under Michaela's eyes would get even darker. Maybe even Kum would be sad.

Teddy could also understand why Benjamin didn't want to mention having been in the house with his dad. He didn't want to tell them that Mats was alive.

The judge said: "Thank you. I'll now hand over to the prosecutor."

This was where it started.

Rölén straightened the papers she had in front of her.

"With whom were you in the house?"

Benjamin looked sad. "Sebbe and one more person I can't talk about."

"Why can't you talk about them?"

"I just can't."

The prosecutor continued.

"How did you get to the house?"

"When did you get to the house?"

"Did you have any possessions in the house?"

Benjamin couldn't answer many of her questions; he couldn't remember. On a few occasions, he replied that he didn't *want* to answer. The minutes passed. The prosecutor continued along the same lines; she went through his brief statement again, in much more detail this time.

"What were you wearing?"

"What did you do with your clothes before you got in the car?"

"Who is Sebbe?"

Benjamin shook his head occasionally, mumbled, answered as it was: that he simply didn't know or didn't want to answer.

The prosecutor persisted.

"Did you sleep in the house?"

"What did you do the day before?"

"Why was your DNA on the bloody clothes we found in the woods?"

Benjamin had no answers.

The minutes turned into hours. The judge called for a recess. Teddy saw Emelie go outside, to the same corner as before. She smoked her cigarette slowly. He wondered what she was thinking.

After the break, the prosecutor continued in the same vein. "Why did you change your clothes?"

Benjamin sighed. "I don't remember changing clothes."

Emelie raised her voice: "Leading question."

Rölén pretended she hadn't heard Emelie's objection or Benjamin's answer. "How close were you standing to Sebbe when you shot him?"

"Another leading question," Emelie interrupted.

The prosecutor snorted but dropped the subject. Instead, she started asking questions about the house, who owned it, and so on.

Eventually she came back to her killer question. "Why don't you want to say who you were with?"

"I just can't."

"You're on trial for murder."

"I know."

"And there's someone who could testify on your behalf, no?"

"I guess so, yeah."

"But you don't want to say who? That sounds very, very strange to me."

Benjamin took a deep breath. Teddy saw him glance over toward Lillan.

He said: "I'm sorry, but I can't say."

The prosecutor turned to the judge. "Thank you. In that case, I have no further questions, Your Honor."

The room was dead silent.

Teddy had been watching the lay judges. Their expressions gave them away much more easily than the judge's—they all must think Benjamin was guilty as hell.

The judge was making notes. It was probably time to break for the day. Then, suddenly, the door at the back of the room opened.

A man came in. Thin hair, round glasses. Chinos and a white shirt. He walked up to the witness stand.

Everyone's eyes followed him. The judge looked up.

The man said: "I'd like to stand as a witness."

The prosecutor practically leaped from her seat. "Who are you? You have no right to speak."

The judge turned to the man. "The prosecutor is right. But it may be that you have important information. Who are you?"

Again: you could've cut the tension with a knife. Everyone in the room, the public, the lay judges, even the clerk had their eyes fixed on the man who had just come in. Teddy thought there was something familiar about him.

Everyone was waiting for his reply.

When he spoke, he did so in a clear voice. "I'm Mats Emanuelsson, Benjamin's father. I was in the house with him."

Teddy realized why he hadn't recognized him immediately; he'd done a good job of changing his appearance.

74

Magnus Hassel didn't love his job, but it was okay. And they paid him pretty damn well. Last year, he'd taken home fifteen million kronor in dividends, paid record low tax, and brought in another million euros from a couple of ad hoc transactions organized by the firm's St. Petersburg office. Entirely tax free. The tax laws were there to be used, after all.

Still, he'd always dreamed of being a different kind of lawyer. The courtroom represented drama, excitement on a level he never came close to, no matter how many hardball negotiations with German business lawyers or public actions he worked through.

When he first found out that Emelie Jansson had completely rejected their proposal that she resign from the case, he hadn't known what to do. He'd called in Anders Henriksson and Alice Strömberg, and before they'd even closed the door, he'd been shouting so loudly, they could probably hear it down in reception. "Can either of you tell me what the hell's going on here?"

Two cups of tea and a few beta-blockers later, he was a little calmer. But his rage was still bubbling.

Alice Strömberg had tried to talk softly. "I don't think she was ever fully on board here. I never really had the feeling she had all that much to offer. But the trial she's involved in hasn't been postponed, in any case, and the court says she's still serving as private defense."

Magnus had asked them to leave the room. He wasn't used to

people acting like Emelie had. He needed to see it with his own eyes. He went down to the courthouse.

It was the first time he'd been in a law court since the placement he'd done early on in his career. It was strange, really—he was one of the country's foremost business lawyers, but he almost never set foot in court. He'd had to take part in divorce proceedings on a few occasions, but that was completely different. Informal, somehow. The courts, on the other hand, were a world of their own: the confused visitors, turning their heads in an attempt to work out how they'd ended up there; the clerks clutching documents and law books; the lay judges, talking quietly while they waited for their trials to start. And then the main parties themselves: tragic figures who were something like the pieces in these legal chess matches. It was all very exciting.

The only thing bothering him was that he was losing about seven thousand kronor an hour just by being there. And that Emelie had tricked him.

He sat down in one of the rearmost seats in the public area. His secretary had already ordered the summons application and certain sections of the preliminary report. There was no doubt, it was a tough case Emelie Jansson had ahead of her. He hoped she would lose.

And soon enough, it was pretty clear that the hearing wasn't going Emelie's way. The prosecutor was flawless, proceeded calmly and soberly through the evidence without leaving anything out. When Emelie's turn came around, all she had to offer were a few weak assertions about the uncertainty surrounding the blood found in the hallway—claims that wouldn't lead anywhere.

At lunch, Magnus crept off before Emelie had time to leave the courtroom. He didn't want to confront her now. He wanted to see how the case panned out first.

But then, during the afternoon, the thing that only ever happened in criminal cases happened—the complete surprise. Magnus had never heard of anything like it. A man walked into the room and claimed to be Benjamin Emanuelsson's father. He wanted to testify. It was incredible.

The prosecutor protested, of course. Emelie Jansson's huge, sweet eyes glared at the man who'd just made such an unexpected entrance. Still, Magnus wondered whether she hadn't planned this, whether she wasn't an accomplished actress on top of everything else. Though it did actually seem like she was just as surprised as everyone else.

After a few minutes' back-and-forth, Emelie requested a break in proceedings. Magnus watched her take the man claiming to be Mats Emanuelsson into a side room.

After an hour, they came back out. Emelie knocked on the door to the courtroom, and everyone was let back in.

"The defense calls Mats Emanuelsson as a witness," she announced.

The prosecutor was just about to protest when the judge interrupted her. "What is the evidence and purpose of questioning?"

Emelie seemed ready for the question. She read from a notepad.

"He will be questioned about his observations in and around the house on Värmdö over the course of the fifteenth and sixteenth of May, in support of the assertion that Benjamin Emanuelsson did not take Sebastian Petrovic's life."

The prosecutor went mad. Practically spitting teeth. "Your Honor, this is completely unacceptable. This is a classic surprise attack, not permitted under the code of judicial procedure, not at all. Any statements from this person, whoever he is, should be denied."

"Your Honor, I can assure you that I was unaware that Mats Emanuelsson was willing to testify, nor that he was even alive. Had I known, I would, of course, have requested his testimony earlier," Emelie replied.

The presiding judge seemed perplexed. He squirmed. The prosecutor continued her protests. She talked about statement periods, irresponsible litigation, and how inexperienced Emelie Jansson must truly be.

Emelie, on the other hand, kept calm. "The defendant is accused of murder. As his defense counsel, we request one single witness in support of his plea. Such a request simply cannot be denied. It would be a serious procedural error."

The judge groaned. "The court will take a break to deliberate."

After two hours, they reentered the courtroom. It was eight in the evening. Magnus was annoyed, but he'd stayed behind anyway.

The judge's voice was more confident now. "The court determines that the witness examination should be permitted," he said. "But first, the witness must be interviewed by the police."

It was an anticlimax. The trial would have to be put on hold for a few days to give the police and the prosecutor time to interview the man claiming to be Benjamin's father, and to prepare themselves based on what he had to say.

Magnus Hassel still couldn't help but wonder whether it really was Mats Emanuelsson. A man who had been dead for more than four years.

But more than that, he wondered how the hell Emelie Jansson was planning on explaining why she'd spent the day playing defense lawyer here.

EIGHT DAYS LATER

75

"First of all, I'd just like to say that I'm incredibly nervous about all of this. My son is facing a life sentence for something he didn't do. He got mixed up in this because he's been loyal to me and refused to say anything that might compromise me. That's why he didn't want to give my name. Everyone thinks I'm dead. According to all of your registers and records, I'm not alive. But here I am.

"I've been trying to get in touch with Benjamin without giving myself away since he was first arrested. I even spoke to Emelie Jansson here at one point. I asked her to pass on a letter to Benjamin, but she refused. I guess that was in line with her rules and regulations. Maybe I should've gone to the police and come forward as a witness. But believe me, I've had bad experiences with the police force. Twice in my life, I've tried to cooperate with the police. Both times, it led to catastrophe for me and my family.

"But I've realized now, there's no other way forward than what I'm doing today. Stepping up and talking about what happened out on Värmdö.

"I'm going to keep things short. The background to all of this is a serious threat I was subject to a number of years ago. That's why I decided to make it look like I'd died.

"The problem was, I couldn't live without my children, and I didn't want them to have to live without me. So even though I've been living in different places all over the world, I've always tried to see them on a regular basis. For the most part, we met at the house

I got hold of on Värmdö. My friend Sebastian Petrovic helped me buy it under the name Juan Arravena Huerta. It was a simple procedure, really; we did everything through a proxy. I know how to do that kind of thing.

"I've been living with a new identity for more than four years now. All so I wouldn't be forced to do anything that might hurt me, so everyone would think I was gone. So no one would go after my kids or my ex-wife.

"I came back to Sweden two and a half months ago, I'm not going to say how, and I think someone must've recognized me. That's the feeling I had, even at Passport Control.

"I came back to see the kids and do some business with Sebastian Petrovic, Sebbe. Benjamin and I spent the day down by the water next to the house, just fishing and talking. Sebbe came over later. The three of us ate dinner. Sebbe was going to give me a lift to the airport the next morning. Benjamin would drive home in his own car.

"Sometime in the middle of the night, I woke up. I'd heard a loud noise. I went into Benjamin's room. We were both sleeping upstairs, Sebbe downstairs, but his bed was empty. The noise was coming from downstairs. It sounded like shouting. I went down.

"It was dark, but I could see Benjamin fighting someone in the hallway; I didn't recognize the man, but he had a weapon in his hand. His cheek was bleeding. I think Benjamin must've hit him with a bottle—there were bits of glass all over the floor.

"Benjamin was shouting. And then I recognized the man he was trying to get out of the house. His name was Joakim Sundén— he's the dirtiest policeman I've ever met.

"Anyway, I tried to help my son, to get rid of Sundén. We were fighting with him, trying to hold him down, but it just got worse. We moved into the living room.

"That's when I saw him. It's probably what woke me up. It was awful. Sebbe was on the floor. He'd been shot. Joakim Sundén must've come in on the ground floor, but he hadn't been expecting to see anyone down there. It was the end of Sebastian.

"We ran out of the house, Sundén behind us. He was shooting at us.

"I told Benjamin to get out of there, and I ran into the woods.

"That's all I know. That's what happened. I was there. Benjamin was there. Sebastian Petrovic was murdered by a policeman who'd wanted me as an informant in my previous life. Sebbe saved us. He was my best friend for nine years."

76

Prosecutor Rölén couldn't sit still. She twisted and turned in her chair as Mats Emanuelsson talked. She pulled faces, sighed loudly. Emelie could understand her, in a way—Mats's story sounded like something from a film, one big fabrication made up to protect his son.

But there were two facts Rölén couldn't ignore. Firstly, Mats had given DNA samples, and these had proved—to +4, the highest-level match—that he was related to Benjamin. The samples were a match for something else, too: the DNA found in the house. Mats was Benjamin's father, and he'd been in the house on Värmdö. Not even Rölén could dispute that.

Secondly, Mats had provided identity documents, Spanish doctors' notes and photographs showing a smiling, suntanned man with tattoos on his arms. They corresponded to the victim's. There was no longer any doubt that the man killed in the house was Sebastian Petrovic.

Despite this, Rölén tried to undermine his testimony. She continued to question who he was, why he'd turned up so late. She seized on the fact that he didn't want to talk about his past. She tried to get him to say he couldn't be sure Benjamin *hadn't* killed Sebastian Petrovic. That he couldn't explain the bloody clothes in the woods or the gunpowder traces on Benjamin's hands.

Above all, she tried to make a point of the fact that the dead man was Sebastian Petrovic, of all people.

"You were kidnapped nine years ago, were you not?"

"That's correct," Mats replied.

"By people involved in the so-called Yugoslav mafia, correct?"

"I can't answer that."

"My assertion is that Sebastian Petrovic was known to the police, and that he had links to those circles. I believe Benjamin's motive in taking his life was revenge for what happened to you nine years ago. For them kidnapping you."

Mats replied calmly and steadily. "All I can say about that is it isn't true. Sebbe had nothing to do with the kidnapping. And as far as the gunpowder particles are concerned, Benjamin and Sundén were fighting, and those particles can be transferred, end up on someone else. I've got no idea about the clothes in the woods. Benjamin had a change of clothes with him, I know that much. My guess is that Sundén took them and made sure they were covered in blood. He planted evidence, simple as that."

On the whole, Mats didn't budge from his story. He consistently maintained the same thing. Sundén had broken into the house. He'd probably arrived by boat and then approached the house through the woods. The alarm hadn't sounded at the response center because the power had been cut. Maybe Benjamin had heard an alarm and woken up, or maybe it was the shot, and then he'd gone downstairs. Mats had seen Sundén trying to neutralize his son, and he'd seen him take out his gun and shoot at them. It was terrible no matter which way you looked at it.

Once the cross-examination was over, the judge turned to Emelie. "Does the defense have anything to add?"

She knew what needed to be done. Her head was crystal clear today. She said: "First of all, I'd like to request that the National Forensic Centre compares the expanding bullet found in the wall behind the victim with Joakim Sundén's service weapon. I suggest that Sebastian Petrovic was shot with Sundén's Sig Sauer P226.

"Secondly, I insist that the detention of Benjamin Emanuelsson cease at once, that he be released. There is no longer even probable cause for the crime. The prosecution has not managed to reduce the value of Mats Emanuelsson's testimony given here today. Mats was present at the scene, and everything he claims has been backed up by forensic evidence. The prosecution is responsible for demonstrating Benjamin's guilt; there is no requirement for Benjamin to prove his innocence. But today, through Mats's testimony, the defense has demonstrated in good measure that Benjamin Emanuelsson *did not* kill Sebastian Petrovic. I will show that he was shot using a weapon in the possession of Joakim Sundén at the time of his death outside the Håga prison complex recently."

The judge seemed less confused today. "The court shall take a recess," he said, "and deliberate on the question of detention."

The minutes ticked by outside the courtroom. Benjamin was back in his cell in the Pit—Emelie tried to imagine what was going through his head.

Cecilia, Lillan, and Mats were standing together not far from her. Teddy had gone down to the cafeteria. Maybe he didn't want to risk Mats seeing him up close. Magnus Hassel had disappeared, too—the two of them still hadn't talked. Emelie didn't even know if she *wanted* to talk to him—she would be getting the boot, she knew that, so what else was there to add?

A memory. She must've been fourteen, fifteen. She and her dad had been sitting in the kitchen, he was helping her study for an English test, and her mom was cleaning like usual. Word after word. She was good, she knew the words forward and back. But there was one term she couldn't quite grasp: *liability*. Her dad had tried to explain: "It means responsibility, but more economic, you know? Responsibility in the sense that I'm responsible for you as your father, but with money, you can owe someone money. Do you understand?" Responsibility, she'd thought—*you* don't know what the word means. You'll never know.

She looked up. Magnus Hassel was coming toward her. His hair seemed even glossier than usual.

"Do you think he'll be let out now?"

Emelie wondered what he really wanted.

"I hope so," she said. "If he does, it suggests they're planning on dropping the case."

"And what do you think will happen to your job with us then?"

"I guess I'll have to leave."

Magnus nodded. "You will. But you know I would've liked you to stay."

Emelie shifted her weight from one leg to the other.

Magnus said: "There's just one thing I want to know. Why, Emelie? Why did you take the case when you knew how the firm would view it?"

They could hear the faint murmur of people talking in the background, and farther down the hallway. Emelie breathed in. "I took it on because I believe in something."

Magnus waited for her to go on.

She did so. "I think our most important function, as lawyers, is to defend a society that protects the interests of individuals. I didn't become a lawyer just to work with business money. I'm tired of helping stinking-rich venture capitalists get even richer. I want to work with people; I want to feel responsibility for people who really need me. I want to contribute to a system that's there for everyone, even when the prosecution and police claim they've done something wrong. Someone who helps others find a voice, to look into what they're being accused of. A system that's fair. One that takes care of the weak and the isolated. People who have only one other person on their side. Their lawyer. Me."

Magnus's face was pale. It looked like he needed a moment to gather himself. Eventually he said: "But you could've given up the case. You could've kept your job with Leijon."

"Never."

"Why?"

"I'm a lawyer."

"I know that."

"And a lawyer never abandons their client."

77

Teddy saw Emelie and Magnus Hassel in the distance. He didn't know what they were talking about, but it was the first time during the whole trial that he'd seen them anywhere near one another. He tried to read their faces. Magnus's mouth was a straight line, his lips pressed tightly together. He looked pale. Emelie's eyes were shining.

She'd requested an analysis of the barrel of Joakim Sundén's service weapon to be able to compare it with the bullets that killed Sebbe. Emelie and Teddy had, of course, known what Mats Emanuelsson would say in court, but he hadn't known she would put in that request. He was fairly certain it would be a match.

She was strange, Emelie. Teddy still didn't know where he stood with her. But one thing was clear. She was impressive. Her strength, after all she must have carried on her shoulders these past few weeks, but she still acted like a master in the courtroom.

Joakim Sundén: the name of a murderer. The name of a man Benjamin had slashed in the face with a bottle. That would've been enough to leave a real cut. One that, after a few weeks, would've turned into a scar.

Dejan had called him a few days earlier.

"He wants to see you."

"Who?"

"Kum."

"Why?"

"He'll tell you that himself."

Teddy had thought they were in agreement now—what could this be about?

They'd met at Mazern's house. He looked normal, but the sense of threat was gone. Or maybe it was just that once you'd seen a man naked, like Teddy had, it was difficult to feel any real fear of them again.

After he kissed his hand, Kum said: "I've got some good stuff, if you want it."

"Sure."

"Ardbeg, from the eighties. Single malt. I bought it at an auction in London, three thousand pounds a bottle, but it's worth it. Luxury has a price."

Kum nodded to someone. Teddy realized there was another man in the room, just like last time he'd been there. This time, he was standing by the huge potted plants.

Teddy took a sip from his glass. The whiskey was so smooth, he could hardly feel it fill his mouth.

Kum said: "We were at his place yesterday, in his apartment."

"Whose?"

"That bastard's."

"Who d'you mean?"

"The pig."

"Joakim Sundén?"

"He was a pig, in every possible sense."

"I'm not gonna argue with that."

"We got in before the police arrived. I thought you might want to hear what we found."

"I do."

Kum took a sip. "First of all, he had two and a half million in cash stashed away. Half in a double floor under the sink, half in a big safe."

"Ah shit. That's more than five years' pay for a cop. He must've been really dirty."

"Exactly. He had a load of other crap in that safe, too. Old reports, evidence bags full of material, snitch notes, interview records. The pig seems to've been a hoarder."

Teddy gave a start when Kum went through the objects—interview records. Sundén had interviewed Mats, after all—Mats had told them that during the trial.

Kum clicked his fingers. The man who'd poured the whiskey came back with a folder.

"Gift for you," Kum said. "Between old friends."

Teddy opened it. After a few minutes' reading, he realized what he was looking at. Printouts of interviews and conversations Joakim Sundén had held with Mats Emanuelsson more than four years earlier. Code name Marina. He wanted to read it all now, but Kum seemed to want to keep talking.

"That pig would do anything for money. Had a load of small, private conversations with Mats Emanuelsson, pretended none of it was being recorded. But I've got my sources, even in the authorities. Joakim Sundén sold information. Those conversations with Mats definitely weren't aboveboard, so he could earn money on whatever came out. He was selling Mats to *them*, whoever they are. But then a prosecutor caught wind of it and demanded information about Mats, wanted him to testify like any normal witness, and that's when everything started to backfire in that pig's brain. I don't know exactly what happened, but I've spoken to Michaela, too. Mats was well aware of how bad things could get if he tried to reveal *them*, those filthy bastards, as I like to call them. So when he had a choice between testifying publicly or disappearing, he chose the latter. Because if *they* thought he was alive, they would've gone after his family. And then, just three months ago, they realized he'd screwed them over, that he'd never killed himself. That's when they sent Sundén to the house on Värmdö. Maybe it was just to threaten Mats, maybe they didn't plan to kill anyone, but that's what happened. My daughter's fiancé."

"Sebbe."

"Yeah, Sebastian Petrovic. One of the most loyal over the years, you included." Kum scratched his head. "We found some more stuff at Sundén's place, by the way. He wasn't just working as a cop these past few years. He'd been doing extra shifts for something called Swedish Premium Security. And he did everything you could think of for them."

Mazern paused again, sipped his whiskey.

Teddy thought he was starting to understand.

"I've done a lot of stupid stuff in my time," Kum continued. "You have, too, Teddy. Only difference between us is I've never been inside. No one took a third of my life from me. But that's just what you've got to put up with, no?"

Teddy didn't know how to reply. His thoughts were swirling. Sundén had been paid by someone, probably the firm calling itself Swedish Premium Security, the money Kum had found spoke for itself. Paid to protect *their* interests. The predators'd had their own men in the police. A cop who'd started to leak for money at first, but then moved on to working for anyone who'd pay. It probably wasn't as uncommon as it sounded: once a man of the law had crossed the line, that in itself was a hold over them. They could be forced to do more.

But killing Sebbe, hurting Sara, kidnapping Teddy, Cecilia, and Lillan—that was worse than anything he'd ever heard of. And there was definitely at least one more person involved, the man who'd been helping Sundén out in Håga, the man who'd disappeared after Loke managed to lure him out of the building. Maybe he was part of the police force, too.

Loke had been looking into Swedish Premium Security over the past few days—it had closed down, on paper at least, and their offices on Sankt Eriksgatan seemed to be empty. But one thing was clear: Joakim Sundén had been a foot soldier, a hired hunter, a protector of *their* secrets. The one who took the risks. But there were people above him.

Peder Hult, or whatever the hell his real name was, Teddy thought, they still needed to look into his role in all this. He paused, midthought: did they, really? Maybe it was time to put all this behind them. For good.

Kum had tapped him on the shoulder: "Hello, *moj drug*. You listening? You have to assume it's not all going to go to plan, no?"

Teddy dropped the thought. Tried to understand what Mazern meant. "I guess you're right."

Kum said: "But you don't have to accept people lying. Right?"

"No, maybe not."

"And you shouldn't accept anyone helping those who hurt women and children."

"No."

"Or murdering your nephew."

"What d'you mean?"

"I hope you don't mind that I clipped Sundén."

Teddy swirled the expensive whiskey around his glass. He'd heard the shot outside of Håga, but Emelie was the only one who'd seen anything.

"I thought you'd stopped," he said.

Kum got to his feet.

They shook hands. Teddy could see gray hairs in Mazern's eyebrows. "I'm older," he said, "but I'm still Kum. My reputation's all I have."

"The verdict will be read out in court five," the clerk's gentle voice said over the speakers.

It was crucial. If the court released Benjamin now, it meant they didn't think the evidence was convincing enough. It meant the charges would be dropped, that they would set him free.

Annika Rölén was first into the courtroom. Then Cecilia, Lillan, Mats. Emelie went in after them. The room was silent, funereal. Benjamin was led up from the cells.

Teddy couldn't see Magnus Hassel anymore.

He himself entered the room last. He didn't want to frighten Mats, didn't know what memories seeing him might bring up.

An air of gravity hung heavily over the room. The lay judges studied everyone as they entered. The clerk typed more quietly than before.

The judge cleared his throat. Teddy saw Emelie's tense neck and shoulders. Benjamin was looking down at the desk.

The judge said: "The detention of Benjamin Emanuelsson is hereby revoked. He will be released immediately."

Benjamin looked up, like he hadn't understood what the presiding judge had just said.

The Emanuelsson family, outside the courtroom, hugging. Benjamin looked like a living human being again. His eyes were glistening; his posture more upright. Cecilia and Lillan were crying. Teddy thought he could even see tears in Emelie's eyes, but maybe he was wrong—he was standing some distance away from them.

Watching them. Taking part in his own way.

Then he saw Mats turn around, meet his eye.

He held his head high, proud. Benjamin's father had done the right thing. But Teddy could see something else in his eyes, a glimmer of something. Maybe it was fear. Because it was all too clear to Teddy, too. Joakim Sundén was dead, and the threat Mats faced had lessened, but it hadn't vanished completely. What awaited him now? The witness protection program, a trial? Both? And the hard drive—where was it?

Though again: maybe it was time to drop all this.

Mats nodded at Teddy. Clearly, that was what he needed.

He had atoned for his crime.

Completely.

Half an hour later: the café on Bergsgatan. Emelie had sent him a message and asked him to meet her there.

"Congratulations," Teddy said.

"Congratulations to the both of us, we did it together," she replied. "Though really . . ."

Teddy filled in: "Congratulations to the Emanuelssons. If Mats hadn't turned up . . ."

They both knew what he meant—without Mats, Benjamin would almost certainly have been sent down.

Neither of them spoke. A car horn sounded at the crossing behind them.

"Have you paid Jan?" Teddy asked after a moment.

Emelie nodded. "Thanks for the money. It went to some good use after all."

"What are the Emanuelssons doing tonight? Celebrating?"

"Just dinner, I think. I guess Mats has quite a lot of explaining to do, to Cecilia above all."

Silence again. A cyclist rang their bell at another on the cycle path next to them.

Teddy said: "Maybe you and I should celebrate somehow? Talk things through. I'm thinking: *just* you and I."

EPILOGUE

SEVEN DAYS LATER

78

Nikola was going to Teddy's place later today, but there was something he had to do first. He was standing on the hill behind Flemingsberg prison, where he'd been locked up. A joke. A little practical joke. Kerim was inside again, and the tabloids were loving it: *Flying gang leader back on firm ground. Helicopter escapee back behind bars.* It was lousy luck.

The middle of August. Nikola was starting work in a week: George Samuel had changed his mind—offered him a real probation period. Installing electrics, apprentice work, early mornings. Linda was over the moon, and honestly: maybe it wasn't so bad. George was a good guy, and Nikola needed dough.

Teddy had phoned him to see if he wanted to go out to eat. The final verdict had been delivered in Benjamin Emanuelsson's case—though they'd all known how things would play out when they released him from remand prison. The case had been dropped. Weapons analysis had shown that Sebbe Petrovic was shot using Sundén's Sig Sauer.

Nikola opened his bag. The drone was about the size of a carton of milk. He'd borrowed it from Yusuf. It had four little rotor blades and a GoPro camera on the bottom. He'd been practicing for two days now. He knew it better than he knew his own dick.

He'd taken the bandage off his shoulder yesterday. Sundén's bullet had ripped through him, but no more than that. He was fine now.

He switched it on. Heard a whirring sound. He'd cut his finger the first time he used it: the little blades were surprisingly powerful.

The drone rose straight into the air and then disappeared over the treetops like a bird. High up. Higher. Above the prison, the cages on the roof.

He'd been here before, yesterday. He'd seen on the camera that they'd strengthened the bars above the cages, probably to prevent any more Kerim incidents. But there was one thing they hadn't protected themselves against—licorice. He'd hung a roll of the disgusting stuff that Kerim loved so much from a string on the bottom of the drone.

Nikola was holding the controller with both hands, gently directing the gadget with his thumbs. He lowered it. He made it wobble. He'd tested this, too. It should work.

He let it bob back and forth. Eventually the lump of licorice fell down. Through the bars. Into the cage where, at some point today, Kerim would be taken for his daily break outside. He'd find his favorite sweets there, the kind you couldn't buy from the kiosk.

Nikola had taped a little note to the licorice. *Thinking about you, man / N.*

Up the stairs.

Sudden knot of worry in his stomach. He thought back a few weeks, to when he'd been on the way up to his own apartment and Emelie had been waiting for him outside. Same feeling today: *Spidey senses* tingling. Like someone was watching him. Or waiting for him.

He didn't even know if Teddy was home, but it made no difference. He had keys. He could just go in and wait for his uncle to turn up.

He thought about Bojan: they were all going to a football match tomorrow. Him, his grandpa, Teddy, and Paulina. Watch Syrianska trash Varberg in the Superetta. It was the first time Paulina would meet any of his family.

He rang Teddy's bell. Silence.

Nikola took out his key ring and tried to find the right key. He turned the top lock first. It was stiff.

Then: a huge explosion. He was thrown back, flung into the opposite wall.

He couldn't hear a thing.

He heard everything. The atoms smashing into him. The dust scratching his skin as he slumped against the other wall.

He thought of Teddy. He thought of Paulina.

The place was burning. Smoke was pouring from the doorway.

He looked down at his body. His clothes were torn to shreds. Wet with blood.

An explosion. The irony. The last thing he had time to think: he was going to die because of a fucking bomb.

LIFE DELUXE

Translated by Astri von Arbin Ahlander

The final chapter in the electrifying Stockholm Noir trilogy: here is the no-holds-barred, rapid-fire tale of a supreme struggle for the legacy of the Swedish underworld, as the power, honor, and respect commanded by Stockholm's largest criminal organization are passed from father to daughter. Jorge was making a living as a drug dealer until he was caught and thrown into prison. Recently released and warned to keep out of trouble, he's already bored with his new existence: selling lattes and cappuccinos at a café. Who wouldn't be? But Jorge has a plan, and big money looms on the horizon if he can pull off one final audacious heist and flee the country before the police close in. Meanwhile, Deputy Inspector Martin Hägerström—entrusted with a secret mission, code name Operation Tide—has gone deep undercover as a disgraced cop turned corrections officer. He's slowly earning the trust of Stockholm's imprisoned expert money launderer, Johan Westlund. A career criminal with a taste for the jet-setting lifestyle, JW is a dangerous man to befriend, one who may demand more loyalty than Hägerström had planned on offering. Natalie is the twenty-two-year-old daughter of Radovan Kranjic, the Serbian crime boss who rules Sweden's underworld. When an assassin threatens Radovan's life, Natalie is hurled into a chaotic struggle for control of her father's empire—and the competition is fierce. Who will rise to power in the voracious hunt for money, prestige, and luxury to become Stockholm's new king—or queen—of crime?

Thriller

VINTAGE CRIME/BLACK LIZARD
Available wherever books are sold.
www.blacklizardcrime.com